SUICIDE MISSION

As the car continued to accelerate away, the Italian sentry guessed immediately what was happening. Adrenaline and terror rushed through his body. He pulled his pistol and began firing at the speeding automobile. Two bullets shattered the rear window, one of which hit the driver at the base of the neck, shattering his spine and sending the terrorist into Allah's arms at the same moment the car hit the edge of the pier.

The car hit the port stern line, flipping the car upside down just as it slammed into the USS *La Salle*. The impact crushed the front of the car as one thousand pounds of semtex plastic explosive packed into the back seat, the trunk, and the panels of the car exploded.

Within minutes, the warship and the sailors who manned her were sitting on the bottom of the harbor. . . .

THE SIXTH FLEET

DAVID E. MEADOWS

This is a work of fiction. Names, characters, places, and incidents are either the product of the author's imagination or are used fictitiously, and any resemblance to actual persons, living or dead, business establishments, events, or locales is entirely coincidental.

THE SIXTH FLEET

A Berkley Book / published by arrangement with the author

PRINTING HISTORY
Berkley edition / June 2001

For information address: The Berkley Publishing Group, a division of Penguin Putnam Inc., 375 Hudson Street, New York, New York 10014.

The Penguin Putnam Inc. World Wide Web site address is http://www.penguinputnam.com

ISBN: 0-425-18009-3

BERKLEY®
Berkley Books are published by The Berkley Publishing Group, a division of Penguin Putnam Inc., 375 Hudson Street, New York, New York 10014.
BERKLEY and the "B" design are trademarks belonging to Penguin Putnam Inc.

PRINTED IN THE UNITED STATES OF AMERICA

10 9 8 7 6 5 4

Dedicated to
the United States Navy Sixth Fleet

ACKNOWLEDGMENTS

A special thanks to Mr. Tom Colgan of Penguin Putnam Berkley Publishing Group who came up with the idea of this military thriller series and provided much-needed encouragement and editorial advice during the process. Of course, every writer needs a strong advocate and coach, and that is what I had in my agent, Ms. Nancy Coffey. Her continuum of enthusiasm was a much-appreciated tonic.

I would like to express my gratitude for the gracious technical advice received from CDR Roger Herbert, U.S. Navy SEAL, and Maj. Andy Gillan, U.S. Marine Corps, while writing *The Sixth Fleet*. And, a special thanks to Capt. (ret.) Frank Reifsnyder, former commanding officer of the nuclear attack submarine USS *Baltimore,* who read the manuscripts for the first two books of the *Sixth Fleet* series. His in-depth technical advice and encouragement were very much appreciated. While these three provided their recommendations, any technical errors in this novel are strictly those of the author, for there were times when technical advice was overridden by literary considerations.

THE SIXTH FLEET

ONE

THE AMERICAN DESTROYER WAS FIFTY MILES NORTH of the Libyan coast when the signal entered the telecommunications system at the Red Sea harbor city of Port Sudan over a thousand miles away.

The intense concentration of the portly crewmember caused the Oriental features of his face to scrunch up as if he had taken a bite from a particularly sour lemon. Satisfied, he hit the transmit button. The package was gone, disguised within a facsimile transmission. From outside the hidden compartment directly behind the captain's stateroom, the sounds of the afternoon, arguing between the Sudanese tradesmen and the visiting merchant sailors, distracted him slightly, but the innate desire for a long life kept him from fouling his directions.

The signal hit the coaxial line that ran from the loading pier to the main telephone center in this summer hot and dusty African city. At the telephone center the signal was automatically shunted among millions of others to a landline that carried it to Khartoum. There, it joined the main East African trunk and began a near light-speed journey along the busy line to Cairo.

At Cairo, the signal manipulated the local telecommunications system's attempts to transmit it via microwave until the "protect" programs successfully queued it to an alternate coaxial landline to Alexandria.

At the breezy Mediterranean seaport the system automatically amplified the signal to restore attenuation lost during its brief trip. Microseconds later the Egyptian telecommunications complex transmitted the signal along an undersea trans-Mediterranean line that connected the North African coast to Europe, routing it via Athens, Greece.

The signal hopped from one relay to another in Athens as it avoided multiple attempts by the Greek telephone system to transmit it via satellite. Hundreds of thousands of firewalls, connections, and internal loops later, the program tripped the proper series of switches to divert the signal to another trans-Mediterranean cable. The transmission headed to Malta, jumbled amid millions of communications packets, ranging from voice to computer to data to facsimile.

The Maltese relay redirected the signal to its intended destination, Tripoli, but registered the signal as destined to a telephone number for a florist on Via Veneto in the heart of Rome. When the signal left Malta, evidence of its real destination was electronically erased.

At Tripoli, the modern telephone system shunted the signal through a series of routers as it moved from relay to relay until the correct sequence occurred.

An autoswitching function sent the program and its host signal through a firewall that restricted access to a military coaxial land cable, running from Tripoli Telephone south, under the desert floor, to a hidden Libyan military command post one hundred miles from the capital. Since the early years of the new twenty-first century, Libya hid much of its military infrastructure underground in a series of bunkers and tunnels that made the London Underground look simple and small.

The signal arrived and bore straight for the active and waiting IBM PC. The beeper from the internal speakers alerted Major Walid. Over the PC hung a handwritten sign in bright red Arabic script that read, JIHAD WAHID—Arabic for "Holy War One."

The beeping brought the nearby Libyan colonel, a taller man, to the console in long fast strides. Ashes from a cigarette dangling from his lips dropped on Major Walid, who sat quietly in front of the screen. Walid's attention was so riveted on the computer that he failed to notice the snow of ashes falling on his crisp gray army uniform. The colonel leaned over Walid's shoulder and pushed the "wait" command, trapping the signal.

"It's here, Walid," Colonel Alqahiray said, his deep bass voice carrying throughout the room. "The package is here, on time. They've kept the first part of the agreement." He took a deep drag on the cigarette, letting the smoke filter out of his nose like some medieval dragon.

The entire trip from Port Sudan to the operations room in the command post had taken less than thirty seconds. Alqahiray pushed a few strands of hair back that had fallen across his forehead. They had met their responsibility to ensure the package arrived undetected. The responsibility rested with him for the next transmission of the "information attack" program. This last portion would be through the air; through the electromagnetic spectrum where Western satellites waited to detect anything of interest or unusual.

Colonel Alqahiray looked at the sensors that lined the walls around the operations room. Patience, he thought. He took a couple of deep breaths, each polluted with a deep drag from the strong cigarette. Calm and patient. This was a great moment for Libya! His leadership must instill the necessary confidence for Jihad Wahid to take Libya to its righteous height of power and drive the devil Americans from the Mediterranean Sea.

Colonel Alqahiray's dark eyes narrowed. He took the cigarette from his lips, for only a moment, and then quickly brought it up for another deep drag. The yellow stains on the index and second fingers wrapped nearly completely around the two and, even on sun-darkened skin, was eye-catching in normal light. He surveyed the operations room, noticing how the blue fluorescent light cast dark shadows around the two rows of active, scrolling computer screens. The soft green CRTs reflected off the intense faces of the operators.

Impatience could ruin this plan. A plan he'd personally developed, written, and orchestrated. Alqahiray thought of himself as a great conductor, bringing together varied and diverse instruments to complement each other. Jihad Wahid was the symphony he would deliver. He smiled at the comparison. Something as simple as impatience could, in the blink of an eye, send months of planning spiraling into failure. Patience was a virtue he hated, but recognized. He twisted his bushy mustache, discovering a drop of tea hidden in one end. He twisted the end together until the moisture disappeared and then wiped his fingers on his starched gray uniform.

He reached over, tapped Walid on the shoulder, and was rewarded with a mousy jump from his nervous underling. He enjoyed the fact that people feared him and rule by fear meant his tasks were accomplished quickly. Respect could be earned many ways, Alqahiray rationalized.

"Major Walid, well done. I know this is your position, but for the start of Jihad Wahid, it is only appropriate that I press the transmit button."

Walid glanced up at Colonel Alqahiray, whose eyes met his for a second before focusing on the CRT—at least, he thought Alqahiray's eyes focused on him. His stomach contracted like a fist as he mumbled an acknowledgment. He looked away quickly, pretending to study the console with Alqahiray. As calmly as possible Walid wiped his clammy palms on his trousers and fought the urge to shiver. Alqahiray's unattractive but powerful face shocked even those who had faithfully served years with him. Bright daylight sometimes softened the man's abnormal features, but in the dark, blue-lighted confines of this room, for a split second, Walid saw a death head vision staring at him.

The Libyan colonel's forced smile of yellow-stained teeth set against a heavy smoker's map of wrinkles pulled an expressionless face leathery tight. Sun damage spots sprinkled a forehead exposed too much to the desert sun. The low light in the room shielded from view the charismatic leader's dark eyes—eyes obscured in shadows from abnormally deep recesses and overarching, heavy eyebrows.

"Gather everyone together," Colonel Alqahiray said.

"Yes, sir, Colonel." Walid nodded respectfully. He stood, clapped his narrow, almost feminine hands twice, and motioned everyone toward him. The small crowd rose. Soft conversation broke out among them. They walked in twos and threes toward the end of the operations room, past the steel double doors, their eyes on the floor. Not out of respect, but because most had tripped or fallen at least once on the bubbles of the cheap rubber antistatic mats that covered the raised metal floor.

"Come closer!" Colonel Alqahiray commanded when the group seemed to falter as they neared him. He raised his hands and waited for them to face him. "Today marks the return of Arab greatness. You are the modern warriors on today's weapons that will take us there. No more will we be unheard. Together we shall follow Allah's will and restore Barbary to its greatness," he said, using the nineteenth-century term for this region of North Africa. "Yes, to its greatness!"

From the crowd came a lone chant, drawn out as if in song, of *"Allah Alakbar"*—"God is great"—joined quickly by others until it rose to a crescendo of respect, bathing Colonel Alqahiray, who spread his arms, basking in the recognition he so richly deserved. After a couple of minutes he lowered his arms and allowed the chanting to fade.

"Go! Prepare your hearts and minds for the battle in the days to come, until Jihad Wahid purges the sea of the Great Satan and we cast them from our shores. For only then will we have returned Islam to its rightful place. Pray to Allah for his love and guidance. Pray to him to give us the wisdom we need to lead his people to greatness. *Allah Alakbar!"*

With fists pumping the air and praises to Allah echoing through the room, the soldiers surged back to their positions. Several spread their tattered prayer rugs on the bubbled mat and, facing east, solemnly offered their prayers to a God equally worshipped by the Jews, the Christians, and the Moslems.

Colonel Alqahiray reached into his shirt pocket and grabbed his pack of Old Navy cigarettes. He lit the unfiltered Greek fag, knowing the strong tobacco may one day kill him—that is, if he truly believed everything the Western press printed. As long as Allah smiled upon him he was invincible. He ran his tongue against the gap between his two front teeth—best money he ever spent. Already some were interpreting the gap as a sign of the Prophet.

After a deep inhale on the cigarette, the colonel returned his attention to the console where the package waited. He hit the print button on the keyboard and waited impatiently for the laser printer to spit out the facsimile mask of the complex, and very expensive, "information attack" program. He pulled the paper from the printer and nodded absentmindedly as he read it. He took a couple of steps to a second console nearby. Seated, Colonel Alqahiray pulled up a formatted message to acknowledge receipt of the merchandise. Walid, his thin frame nearly invisible in the overpowering presence of Alqahiray, stood quietly to one side. His nervousness gone, Walid waited for him to reveal what he needed to know.

With one finger Alqahiray typed the coded preamble from the sheet, keyed in the appropriate routing instructions, and with a "save and send" transmitted the receipt. Internal "information protect" registers misdirected and misled any database management or sniffer programs in the various telecommunications systems to hide the passage as the receipt sped back to Port Sudan.

AT PORT SUDAN THE RECEIPT ARRIVED AT THE PERSONAL computer that had transmitted the program, aboard a salt-rusted freighter that rocked softly against the pier. The name *Iran Bandar Abbas,* painted in large black letters across the stern, could be easily read from the nearby public road that encircled the harbor.

The same portly Oriental operator hurriedly poked in the shirttails of his white short-sleeve cotton shirt. He snatched the Libyan acknowledgment before the printer fully coughed it into the tray, ripping the bottom edge off. Then dashing out the door, he ran up three decks, tripping only once, to the bridge, where the captain jerked it from his hand. The captain smiled, revealing several teeth missing on the left side of his mouth, the result of a harbor bar brawl in Hong Kong many years ago. He read the receipt before grunting and nodding curtly to the messenger. Success was good in his line of work. Failure, though, could be a life-stopping event.

Mission accomplished. The ship's holds were full. Everyone was on board. He could leave. The sooner out of Port Sudan, the better. He picked up the bridge-to-bridge.

"Port Sudan Harbor Control, this is merchant vessel *Iran Bandar Abbas.* We will be departing on time. We would like to take in all lines within the hour so as to be past the outer marker before sunset," he said in an Oriental accent.

"*Iran Bandar Abbas,* this is Harbor Control. Permission granted. Please ensure that you have completed departure paperwork, settled accounts, and have customs approval. You may single up all lines, but contact Harbor Control before casting off."

"Roger, Harbor Control; this is *Iran Bandar Abbas* standing by on channel sixteen."

The captain ordered the purser ashore to settle accounts with good Iranian currency, reminding him to pick up the customs forms and shipping manifest. Other members of the crew hustled to disconnect the phone and utility lines between the ship and shore. Within the hour the ship had all crew back on board, a customs stamp on the manifest, and an approved underway time. By 1700 hours the rusted stern of the freighter, with an oversized Iranian flag flying from the mast, caught the attention of the evening crowd as it eased past the narrow harbor entrance.

A day later the same freighter was detected by a French Air Force Atlantique aircraft flying an afternoon reconnaissance mission over the Gulf of Aden. The freshly painted bright red hull caught the attention of the Atlantique's pilot, causing him to divert the plane ten kilometers north, where the large-bodied jet circled the freighter twice before returning to normal track. The aircrew returned the waves of the Chinese sailors. The French operator recorded the course and speed in the visual sighting log for the merchant vessel *Shanghai* along with a notation that it was flying a normal maritime Peoples Republic of China flag.

COLONEL ALQAHIRAY STOOD LOOKING AT THE OPERAtions room. Here, Jihad Wahid would unfold. The entire complex had been built for this. If he snapped his fingers—*just like this*—he could man every console and keep it manned forever. This was a snapshot in history that he wanted etched into his memory, for Alqahiray was going to be the catalyst and mover who changed the world. He, an orphan, who had fought his way to the top. He smiled as his eyes narrowed, the bushy eyebrows arching to form a sharp V. This day would start the revenge on the cowardly attacks of the American devils in 1986. His lips curled in disgust. Events begun today, he knew, would send the United Nations Security Council scrambling into their useless and pitiful never-ending discussions and debates. Events meticulously dovetailed and calculated were poised now, like a tight row of dominoes, waiting for the first one to tilt into the second until, too fast to stop, they would knock each other down—one after the other. Today, Jihad Wahid—Holy War One—would be unleashed upon the world, starting with the Americans.

He had never forgotten 1986: the raining carnage from F-111 fighter-bombers roaring by overhead, dropping canisters of death on the city. A loving mother dedicated to him and a hard-working father, more dedicated to the revolution, both died that night. His relatives never let him forget who killed his parents. When he reached seventeen he joined the Libyan Army—family prestige obtaining him a commission as an officer. Since then, over thirty-five years ago, all his plans and schemes had been to avenge the dishonor done to his country. And that dishonor would be avenged in the next few days.

Installed at equal intervals where the top of the white-washed walls met the fake ceiling tiles of the operations room were six-inch-wide glowing green lights. The colonel looked at each, mentally counting until he reached the total of seventeen.

He leaned back in the raised chair at the center of the room and rested his feet on the metal stanchion that ran around the platform. He flicked the cigarette butt away. It was time to start.

Colonel Alqahiray rose and walked to where Major Walid waited. The major reminded the colonel of a weasel, with the too narrow eyes, crooked teeth, and explosive, nervous energy that burst forth at the most unexpected moments. Walid's short, badly cropped hair did little to dispel the weasel image that Alqahiray had developed of Walid. Look how scared the man had been earlier.

"Walid, I know it's your duty to transmit the package, but to mark the beginning of this historical moment I will assume responsibility for initiating Jihad Wahid. One day our sons and daughters will celebrate this moment in Arab history." Without waiting for a reply, Colonel Alqahiray turned and shouted, "Assume stations, everyone!"

Twenty-four pairs of eyes stared intently at the green lights. Seldom were the seventeen lights green at the same time and even less were they all red. Once every three weeks for nineteen seconds they glowed red at the same time and that time was nearly here again. If they missed this window of opportunity, it would be three weeks before it would happen again. A lot could happen in three weeks. Secrets never stayed secrets long and a secret like

Jihad Wahid was like water in a sieve. It was today or never.

He lit another cigarette. Taking a deep puff, he shoved himself off the chair and strode to the computer that held the package. Walid nodded as the colonel passed. A humorous thought flickered through Alqahiray's mind as he walked by Walid that if he jumped at the weasel, the man would spring off like a pinball, bouncing off the walls. Alqahiray found this amusing.

The Libyan colonel stopped at the console to watch attentively, along with everyone else, the green lights. His attention alternated between the clock and the lights. The screen saver blanked out the CRT. Three minutes later the first green light turned red. He butt-lit another cigarette. His face, enshrouded in a cloud of bluish smoke, looked as if it were surrounded by a halo.

"Satellite one below horizon," announced the sergeant monitoring the lights. He then continued for the next fifteen minutes until all the lights glowed red.

"Satellite seventeen below horizon!" shouted the sergeant. "All lights red, Colonel!"

The decisive nineteen seconds were here. Nineteen seconds to transmit the package to the weapons site before three of the lights would turn green at the same instant. Nineteen seconds when no Western electronic surveillance satellites monitored Libya. He casually reached down, smiling, and pressed the transmit button.

The CRT flashed an alert indicating an erroneous code word. The computer requested password reentry. The colonel's wry smile vanished beneath the heavy graying mustache. His dark eyes flashed from their caverns with an intensity that caused Major Walid to step back.

"Colonel," said Walid, his voice an octave higher than normal. "It needs your password! The system requires a password reentry if idle for more than fifteen minutes, sir." Sweat on Walid's forehead glistened in the overhead blue light. His stomach churned again. "A security caution," Walid mumbled, the words tapering off.

The array of electronic systems crammed into the operations room maintained a steady hum in the background.

The colonel threw his cigarette on the floor. Walid stomped it out. Colonel Alqahiray flopped down in the seat and hurriedly typed his password into the computer. He missed a letter, causing the computer to beep ominously as another stupid Microsoft message flashed on the screen. He glanced at the clock. Seven seconds. He rubbed his fingers against his wet palms and concentrated on the keys. The computer beeped acceptance and loaded the last page. He hurriedly pressed the transmit button. This time, without a covering mask, raw traffic headed toward the airways.

The compressed program raced for the microwave relay site where for the first time in its journey it entered the atmosphere and became detectable by threat sensors. It hit the first tower, where it was bent to the curvature of the earth before being sent reeling toward the second. Each of the twelve towers amplified the program and slightly changed its direction to focus its journey toward the next tower in the chain. At each tower it went through the same telecommunications cycle until it arrived at its destination—a specially built Jihad Wahid site deep within one of the numerous mountains that decorated the southern Libyan portion of the Sahara Desert.

Similar to the operations room at the main command post a suite of stand-alone portable computers awaited its arrival where the program downloaded into their system. With four seconds remaining, the uncompressed program projected duplicates of itself along six lasers that immediately fired their beams upward. For a fraction of a second the Libyan weapons illuminated the six global positional satellites that guarded Mediterranean navigation.

The twenty-four satellites, known as GPS, circled the earth in stationary orbits. Each satellite constantly transmitted a unique radio signature and an accurate timing signal so that anyone receiving the transmissions from four or more satellites had position and speed calculated to within seventy-five feet and one knot accuracy. GPS had replaced the old LORAN system of terrestrial-based radio data transmissions and, in many ships, manual navigational calculations had long ago ceased; such was the dependence on GPS.

The laser transported the "information attack" program to the GPS satellites. A preamble code triggered dormant viral software within the GPS program. The viral software initiated several security check programs against the laser-delivered trigger to ensure its validity. Satisfied, the viral software downloaded. The evolution completed, it initiated a correction to the GPS math coprocessor that caused the position read-out of GPS receivers to be off by five minutes of latitude. Ships now depending on GPS would discover, if they compared the readings to radar reckoning, or did a moving fix against land markers, that they were five nautical miles farther south than GPS showed. This was no problem if they were far enough north in the Mediterranean. When the virus completed the programmed function, it began to eat itself. Twenty-eight seconds later, it was as if the virus never existed.

"Event zero zero one implemented and functioning," said the soldier technician monitoring a GPS receiver. An intelligence screen above the double steel doors reflected a red event notation changed to green.

Colonel Alqahiray stood rigid at an attention posture,

his feet at a forty-five–degree angle, heels touching. "It begins!" he yelled, throwing his arms out wide.

A single clap was soon followed by a thunderous ovation. His lower lip jutted out—his Mussolini look, he called it. He raised his head and put his hands on his hips in what he thought of as his Patton pose. Soldiers stood and continued cheering and when the applause began to die Alqahiray began to clap, bringing renewed vigor to another round of self-congratulatory ovation. Alqahiray enjoyed the adulation. Jihad Wahid had been launched and only those in this room knew the exact time that war with America had begun.

The computer, where the program resided, beeped, drawing the colonel's attention from the festive spirits. A series of indecipherable script, numbers, and signs rushed across the screen, scrolling upward. The operating software was self-destructing from a daeman virus delivered with the package.

"Damn them!" Alqahiray shouted.

Walid jumped, throwing his hands up to ward off a nonexistent slap.

Colonel Alqahiray dove for the interrupt switch to save the program, desperate to keep the surreptitiously made bootleg copy.

Realizing what was happening, Walid leaped forward and jerked the plug from the wall.

"What do you think?" the colonel asked, stepping back.

"I don't know, sir. We'll turn it back on and see if we can recover the data." Walid wiped his brow. What if the colonel blamed him for this?

"Good, Walid. But I think you'll be unsuccessful. Obviously our friends had little trust and no intent of leaving us with anything that someday may be used on them. Seems our one-time buy was for a one-time use."

Alqahiray placed his hands behind his back and strolled across the room to the command chair, reconciled to the loss. "Play with it, Walid, but don't feel bad if you're unable to do anything. If they're capable of making what we bought, then they are easily capable of protecting their programs."

Walid saluted. He plugged the computer back in and began the mentally intensive job of recovering the software and reconfiguring the system.

The colonel sat down. The few standing followed suit, quickly turning their attention to individual tasks. A pensive look crossed his face as he watched the soldiers for a while before his gaze moved upward. Screens, the size of those in small movie theaters, mounted on the walls high above the electronic systems on the floor and below the satellite warning lights, showed various intelligence data and situational projections. From here Colonel Alqahiray would watch Jihad Wahid. He pulled a cigarette from his pocket and lit it. From behind, a young soldier in a white coat and gray slacks handed him a cup of strong tea.

All things come to those who wait, says the Koran, and the colonel had waited and planned for years. The next few days would be enjoyable. He laughed. This far underground, even if the Americans discovered the location, there was little they could do; and when he finished, the Mediterranean Sea would be an Islamic one and Europe would be a pawn forced to bend to his influence.

Ah, the tea was just right. Hot, steaming aroma, tickling the nose. Sweet, strong tea with a touch of cream to titillate the tongue. He savored the taste a couple of seconds before taking the first swallow.

He motioned to Major Samir, the intelligence officer. "Where is the American destroyer?"

"Colonel, the warship is approximately forty nautical miles northwest of Benghazi on a southeasterly heading."

"Like dogs attracted to poisoned meat they come, Major Samir. So, tell me the disposition of the American Navy. Aircraft carrier? Any change?"

"No, sir, Colonel. The American aircraft carrier *Roosevelt* is the nearest and it is in the Persian Gulf. It will not be allowed to return. That leaves only the American amphibious task force in the Mediterranean. The USS *Nassau* is the lead ship. She is an amphibious assault ship—called an LHA by the Americans—one of the older Tarawa-class units. The *Nassau* has a minimum of eight AV-8 Harriers on board. She also has at least six CH-53 Super Stallion helicopters. There may be more helicopters belowdecks. Our agent counted them when the task force visited Livorno recently. If she is fully manned by the United States Marines then she will have approximately one thousand seven hundred troops on board. We do not know what type of landing craft she has embarked."

"I am not concerned about the Marines at this time, Major Samir," Colonel Alqahiray snapped. "What will the *Nassau* do during the destroyer's mission?"

"Sir, they have already started supporting the destroyer USS *Gearing*. Two Harriers from the *Nassau* are orbiting about one hundred miles northeast of Tripoli. We expect them to continue a combat air patrol for the duration of the destroyer's mission along our coast."

"Do they really think Harriers can stand up against a high-performance fighter such as our MiG-25 or MiG-23? They are stupid if they do."

"What counts, Colonel, is that they are United States Marines and, regardless of the odds, we know they will fight. They won't run."

The colonel gave his intelligence officer a look of disgust. "Then they will die."

"Yes, sir. They will die, but they will fight."

Major Samir bent his head to break eye contact before he continued, changing the subject back to safer ground. "The amphibious task force has been redesignated a battle group by their Sixth Fleet commander because of the departure of the carrier two weeks ago. The nearest real fighter aircraft are United States Air Force F-16s stationed far to the north at Aviano, Italy. We have agents observing the base who will tell us if they move south."

"Tell me again the other ships with the USS *Nassau,*" the colonel directed, waving his cigarette at the major, the smoke weaving an erratic pattern between them.

"Along with the *Nassau* are two old Austin-class amphibious transport docks, the USS *Nashville* and USS *Trenton.*" Major Samir flipped hurriedly through the papers in his hands before he found what he was looking for. "The *Nashville* has four Sea Cobras on board along with a minimum of six CH-46 Sea Knight helicopters. The *Trenton* has a mix of two additional Sea Cobras along with two CH-53 helicopters."

"That is their air power in the Mediterranean?" the colonel asked, displaying a broad smile.

"Yes, my colonel."

He clapped his hands. "Why do I always feel so good when I hear this information, Major Samir? Is it because I know that Allah has ordained our victory even before we begin?"

Major Samir pushed a wisp of sweat-matted black hair back across the top of his head. "Colonel, along with the *Nassau* battle group are the Aegis-class cruiser USS *Yorktown—*"

"She is an old ship. Not much to fear there, Major."

"Yes, sir. She is old, but she, like the *Hayler* and the *Spruance,* has the vertical launch system in her bow loaded with Tomahawk and Harpoon missiles. The Tomahawks can reach Libya from where they are operating now, southeast of the Italian island of Lampedusa near the Strait of Sicily. They can launch them without warning."

"Quit worrying. They can, but they won't. The Americans will, as usual, beat their chests and chase their allies to get a consensus before they react and by then Jihad Wahid will be completed. Old Saddam taught us the secret of jerking the American tiger. No, we will have changed history by the time they can respond."

Major Samir nodded. He doubted Alqahiray knew what he was talking about, but he also knew the folly of disputing the colonel's views. So he continued, "Yes, sir. The destroyer USS *Gearing,* which is conducting this navigational freedom mission, is a new DD-21 destroyer. She is only one of two warships in the American battle group commissioned within the last ten years. Her combat capabilities are still being assessed. She was designed for minimum crew and ultimate computer-controlled war fighting."

The colonel chuckled. "Then, I guess we will find out how these capabilities stack up. And we know about computers, don't we?"

"Yes, sir." Major Samir licked his lips nervously.

The colonel smiled as he dismissed the intelligence officer with a curt nod. "Keep me informed of any changes to the disposition of American forces."

Major Samir, and the two junior intelligence officers with him, saluted and hastily departed through a side door. They never say anything, those two, thought Alqahiray, as he watched them leave.

I will be the most powerful man in the Arab world, Colonel Alqahiray said to himself. And even more worshipped than old Saddam, who still manages to hold on to power at his age. He propped his feet up on the metal stanchion in front of him and for the thousandth time began to go through the hundreds of things that could go wrong.

Minutes later he shook his head. "Steward, bring me another cup of tea."

Two hours later, a young captain standing near the primary operations console reported to Alqahiray that a supertanker had run aground off Morocco in the Strait of Gibraltar. The erroneous data broadcast from the GPS satellites was confirmed. Alqahiray watched expressionless as they monitored the joint Spanish and British maritime control on Gibraltar shifting transit shipping to the northern channels and closing the southern lanes. Jihad Wahid had claimed its first casualty, even if it was Panamanian registered.

"DAMN IT!" CAPTAIN DUNCAN JAMES, UNITED STATES Navy, grumbled. He wadded up the letter and tossed it. It bounced off the hallway wall to land beside a similarly discarded letter that had arrived from the Navy yesterday reminding him that he had to retire in August.

"It'll be a cold day in hell before I give you money to live with that boy toy, Cathy," he said.

Duncan James thought of himself as a strong, no-nonsense naval officer, but beneath that granite veneer was . . . *a sensitive man?* "Yes, a sensitive, goddamn twenty-first–century male who is going to ring that son of a bitch's neck when I get my hands on him."

He stared at the face in the hallway mirror as he straightened his tie. Duncan lightly stroked his chin. No double chin, he noted, thinking to himself that most men would have two by the time they were forty-eight.

He squinted at the image in the mirror and leaned forward for a closer look. With two fingers on his right hand he pulled his lower eyelids down. "Shit," he said, looking at the bloodshot eyes. He released his eyelids and his gaze drifted downward to his uniform. He leaned back.

"Damn, where did that come from?" He scratched at a stain on the dark tie, feeling a small crusty patch. "It's either last Friday's or this morning's eggs. Duncan, watch where your food falls," he said aloud. A slight echo came from the other end of the hall.

He brushed the tie straight and figured no one would notice unless they looked close. He turned sideways, continuing his appraisal. Flexing the muscles of his left arm, he was rewarded with the reflection of a firm bicep. He ran his hand across his head, rubbing the short stubble, noticing—really noticing for the first time—that gray strands far outnumbered the black and wondered how long his hair had been gray instead of black. He leaned closer and lightly traced a receding hairline that was in an impossible race against a bald spot for possession of the top of his head. His finger touched a faint three-inch shrapnel scar on the left cheek near the jawbone, courtesy of an Iraqi grenade during Desert Storm. His hand moved to his stomach.

"Maybe an inch too much around the waistline, but I still have everything I had when I was in my twenties; it's just further south now."

He squared himself toward the mirror and took a step back. "I'm six foot two, one hundred seventy pounds, and all muscle . . . well, nearly all muscle. Everything a Navy SEAL with twenty-eight years of service should be."

The shock of the past ten days hit again. He couldn't believe that his wife of twenty years had thrown him over for a stock boy at Safeway. Why, Cathy? The son of a bitch is nothing more than an anemic stock boy who can't be more than thirty! He's at least thirteen years younger than you are! I love you. But, he thought, maybe love was too strong a word. Maybe their marriage, like thousands of others, had become more one of convenience than love; acceptable friends rather than close lovers; roommates over husband and wife. He rubbed his hand over his head again. He didn't know. Maybe if they had been able to have children things would have been different.

Between the letters the two loves of his life had disappointed and left him.

Why did Admiral Hodges want to see him, he wondered for the hundredth time since the yeoman's call at 0600 hours this morning. There was no love lost between the two. Until he'd talked with Beau, thirty minutes ago, he'd believed the Navy letter was the reason for the unexpected phone call. To rub in the fact that Duncan was going home and William Tecumseh Hodges wasn't. It would be just like his former classmate. Of course, it wasn't as if Duncan had done anything to prepare for August. Well, he did buy a tube of sunscreen. Regardless, this being Admiral Hodges, then there was a snowball's chance in hell it was good news for Duncan James.

This week was starting as shitty as last week.

Last night Duncan had stumbled home from the club to find the dog dead on the front lawn, the victim of a hit-and-run driver. He had stuffed the animal in a plastic bag and put it in a trunk in the garage before staggering upstairs to pass out on the bed. He planned to bury it properly after work the next day.

But the next day was here and he woke to another whammy when he found a letter from his wife's lawyer on the rug beneath the letter drop of the front door. Divorce? Maintenance payments? She hasn't been gone two weeks and she's already hired a shyster talking divorce? If that weren't enough, his old banger of a car refused to start this morning. Probably would have helped if he'd remembered to turn off the headlights last night.

He tilted his head back as he put in eyedrops. Duncan rubbed his head, shut his eyes, and hoped the headache would go away. Two quick cups of coffee and several glasses of water had failed to chase the effects of last night's binge. He was lucky the Virginia State Police hadn't stopped him. The Reston judge was not known for his liberal views of drunk driving.

He kicked the two letters with the toe of his black dress shoe. Wife leaves him and the Navy's Selected Early Retirement Board, SERB, reminds him to retire—go home—by August; less than forty-five days away. He stared in the mirror, eyeball to eyeball—the eyewash had done little to stop them from looking like red-lined road maps of New Jersey—and unconsciously began to compare himself with Beau.

Whereas Duncan was forty-eight, Beau was thirty-nine. Whereas he was married, Beau was a confirmed bachelor. Considering how life was going, a confirmed bachelor lifestyle appeared the better alternative. Duncan had a scarred, middle-aged, wrinkled face, with too broad a nose between brown eyes. Beau, on the other hand—*the asshole*—had a smooth, almost Nordic, face accented with neon blue eyes and topped by waves of flowing brown hair—hair that turned blond when exposed to the sun for any length of time. The lieutenant commander's mischievous ways and his unnaturally boyish good looks drew women like moths to a flame. Duncan rubbed his chin.

Maybe if he worried as much about his looks as Beau did, things would have been different.

This was their third tour together. The two spent six years with SEAL Teams Four and Six and were on their third year at the Tactics Development Command at Quantico. Beau had also received a phone call telling him to be at the Pentagon by 0800 hours. Why would the admiral want Beau there to discuss Duncan's impending SERB from the Navy? The answer was, he wouldn't; ergo, the admiral had another reason—some asshole idea up his sleeve, no doubt. Whatever the admiral's reason, knowing the two-star's twisted thinking, it would be something Duncan was not going to like.

But it bugged the shit out of him not knowing why Hodges was bothering him in this twilight of his career. What could the admiral come up with worse than telling him to retire? He's been sleeping with Cathy, too? No, couldn't be that; Cathy hated the political asshole.

The beeps of Beau's car horn caught his attention. There's the Adonis now. Duncan grabbed his hat. He'd suffer through today; bury the damn dog; and then decide what to do about his wife. Maybe if he kept putting off trying to make a decision about the marriage, she'd come back. He stepped over the discarded running clothes in the middle of the floor and turned off the lights. He'd tidy the house when he came home. When he opened the front door, he found Beau standing beside his car.

"Hey, come on, Duncan, or we're going to be late."

"Fuck you, asshole."

"Well, I love you, too."

Duncan slammed the door behind him.

"Beau, where can you bury a dog around here?"

"In your mood? You can bury the damn thing anywhere you want. I doubt anyone would argue." Beau put his arm on Duncan's shoulder. "You can tell me, shipmate. Piles?"

FORTY-FIVE MINUTES LATER THE TWO NAVY SEALS SAT in the outer office of Rear Admiral Upper Half William Tecumseh Hodges. Duncan rubbed his chin, feeling the stubble from a bad shave.

Three hours later, they still sat waiting. Duncan looked at the clock for about the hundredth time. He knew they'd probably be here for a couple more hours for what would most likely be a ten-minute meeting. He shut his eyes and laid his head back against the top of the chair.

Duncan and Bill Hodges had been Naval Academy classmates, with Duncan graduating in the upper twenty-five percent of the class while Hodges brought up the rear. Just showed that success during Desert Storm, a Purple Heart and a couple of Bronze Stars with *V*s, and five rows of medals meant little against being able to balance a finance sheet, do a good "stand and smile" at receptions, and play Washington politics when it came to promotions. Hodges only had four rows in his fruit salad.

No, he wasn't bitter. Pissed off maybe, but not bitter. Twenty-eight years of solid "doing the Navy's work" was for naught when it came to downsizing the military.

Beau reached over and shook Duncan. "Duncan, how much longer is the old man going to keep us waiting?" Beau whispered. He crossed his legs and began to nonchalantly run a finger around the edges of a fingernail. "Not as if we don't have a lot to do today." He glanced up and caught the yeoman looking at him. He winked and smiled, causing her to blush and look away quickly.

"I don't know, Beau. We were to be here at eight. It's after eleven now." Duncan ran his finger around the tight collar of his white shirt. The air conditioning did little to stop beads of sweat trickling down his neck. Give him khakis anyday. Ties choked a man. He loosened the tie slightly, pulled a handkerchief out, and wiped his forehead.

If his whites had been ironed he could have worn them, as Beau had, instead of these heavy service dress blues. He thought that he may have seen his whites on the floor near the washer.

"If you wouldn't lift weights you'd have a neck and that shirt wouldn't bother you so much." Beau laughed. "On second thought, keep lifting and running. I hear that at fifty everything travels south faster." He held his hand out to admire the self-manicure.

"Forty."

"Forty what?"

"Everything moves toward the waistline when you reach forty if you don't work out. Besides, I keep telling you: I'm not fifty."

"Right! You're saying that because next month I turn forty," said Beau with a smirk that disappeared slowly as he tried to determine whether Duncan was serious or not.

The phone beeped on the yeoman's desk. "Yes, Admiral, they're still here." She looked at Duncan. "The admiral says to go right in, Captain."

Pettigrew was the first up. "Let's find out what we screwed up this time."

"I'm sorry, sir," the yeoman said tactfully, raising her hand. "The admiral would like a word with Captain James, by himself. Sorry, Commander."

Beau flopped back onto the settee. "I forgot. You're old friends. Tell him Rod said hi."

As Duncan moved toward the door Beau spoke up again. "Forty? Are you sure?"

Duncan ignored the question as he opened the door and entered the admiral's office. Strolling toward him in starched whites, hand extended, was Rear Admiral Upper Half Hodges. Pasted on the ruddy face of this dedicated jogger was his notorious "delightful to see you" grin. A "shit-eating grin," Beau called it. The tall, slender profile of the admiral highlighted a waist that looked as if it would snap in two in a big wind. Duncan thought of his own growing waistline as he wondered if the admiral dyed his hair to keep it that rusty color. Even a few gray hairs would have given Duncan some satisfaction. The rumors must be true—he must dye it.

"Duncan, old friend. God, it's good to see you. I'm sorry about keeping you waiting." He guided Duncan toward a group of chairs near the window. "You know how the Pentagon is. Everything's an emergency and everyone needs the answers to today's questions yesterday. But enough of my problems. How's everything?" he asked and, before Duncan could reply, he continued in a serious tone. "Duncan, I'm really sorry about the SERB. I know it's a tough way to go. We all want to choose our own time, not have a bunch of nondescript officers decide our fate over . . . God knows what!"

"Thanks, Admiral," he replied. So, he was here so the admiral could gloat.

Admiral Hodges motioned Duncan to a seat. Duncan chose the new leather wing-back near the window so the cool air from the wall units blew directly on him. With the shades partially closed to keep out the rays of the hot sun the cooling air felt wonderful. The air conditioning seemed more forceful in the admiral's office than in the reception area.

"Coffee, Duncan?" Admiral Hodges asked as he moved to the percolator on a nearby table.

"No, thanks, Admiral. I'm about coffee'd out. Your yeoman kept our cups full the three and a half hours we've been waiting."

"Sorry about the wait, Duncan. As I said, Pentagon work is never routine," Admiral Hodges replied as he poured a cup before sitting down opposite him. "One of the things about the Pentagon, Duncan, is that everywhere you go they have a pot of coffee. It never fails that the heads are down the passageways and never easy to reach when you need to take that inevitable leak. It seems to me the more you have to pee the more people there are who want just a few words with you on the way."

"Yes, sir," acknowledged Duncan. He relaxed the muscles in his face in an effort to keep his expression neutral.

"Not like the field," said the admiral, looking up as if he were reminiscing. "Now there's where they separate the men from the boys. There's where we get down to the business that our nation and our Navy designed the SEALs to do. Yeah, I miss that a lot being in the Pentagon." He took a sip and then pensively continued. "Sometimes I ask myself why we have a Pentagon admiral's billet in Naval Special Warfare, but someone has to fight for the few dollars they throw our way. Less and less dollars every year to do the training and exercises we need to maintain our readiness, but, by God, we've got plenty of funds for humanitarian efforts. Sometimes I think we should have a big Red Cross above our metals instead of the SEAL emblem." Hodges paused and shook his head. "But I didn't ask you here to talk about Washington money problems."

"Yes, sir, Admiral. I figured it was something important," Duncan replied, not believing it in the least.

"It is, Duncan. Something that only you can do."

That didn't sound good. Why, all of a sudden, did he have this bad feeling? He nearly lifted his left arm to save his watch from the bullshit he expected to follow.

Admiral Hodges stood and put his cup down on the edge of his walnut desk and strolled over to the window that overlooked the Pentagon's south parking lot. He twisted the bar to widen the shades. The sun hit Duncan squarely in the face and immediately offset the cooling effects of the air conditioning. Sweat beaded out again and quickly trickled down on his already soaked collar. Hodges turned and grinned. "It's great to have an office with windows."

Duncan looked away. They wouldn't allow him to retire if he knocked the twinkle out of an admiral's eye.

"Duncan," Admiral Hodges said, shifting into his command voice. Hodges moved out of the sunlight to the shade surrounding his desk and sat down before continuing. "I need you to do something for me, for the Navy, and for the SEALs." He picked up a pencil and began tapping it on the Plexiglas that covered the desktop.

The tapping sounded like a bass drum beating against the inside of Duncan's brain.

"Yes, sir?" Duncan asked, mentally willing the pencil to break or fly out of Hodges's hand—anything to stop the annoying noise.

As if hearing his wish, Hodges's tapping increased in tempo for a few seconds before the admiral laid the pencil down and clasped his hands together on top of the desk. "The Spanish have asked us to participate in an exercise next week at the Buffalero Training Site and Assault Village in Gibraltar. The British may also be there—"

"Admiral," Duncan interrupted, leaning forward. "Sir, I hope you're not going to ask me to go. May I remind you that I have been told by the Navy to retire and go home by the end of August? It's the middle of June now."

"I know, Duncan. That's why the Navy gave you seven months to prepare for retirement. Besides, August is over sixty days away. I know we wouldn't usually send a captain for this, but you speak Spanish and we need to improve—improve? Hell, we need to repair our relationship with the Spanish and it's my understanding that they're sending an officer of comparative rank."

"About forty-five."

"Forty-five?"

"Yes, sir. About forty-five days before I'm forced to retire. Not sixty," Duncan said curtly, raising his hand and making a chopping motion for emphasis. "Forty-five days."

The admiral dismissed the comment with a wave. "Sixty if we push it, Duncan, and I'll push it for you. Besides, I may even be able to do something about the SERB."

Duncan felt a flicker of hope before he quickly dismissed it as merely talk. Admiral Hodges was good at talk. That was to be expected of a peacetime admiral. Politicians, the bunch of them! And Hodges was a damn good politician and, like every politician, had hidden agendas. Duncan wondered what the admiral's were. He looked out the window at the noon joggers who dotted the sidewalks surrounding the Pentagon, wishing he were there. Wishing he were anywhere but here. Most ran toward the Woodrow Wilson Bridge and the monuments on the other side. Five point two miles from Arlington Cemetery to the Lincoln Memorial. He used to run it daily, years ago, when he was at the Bureau of Naval Personnel above Arlington Cemetery.

Hodges knew Duncan had to be angry. He would be if the Navy told him to retire. An angry person can be a vindictive son of a bitch and that's what Hodges wanted. Typical Duncan—hiding his emotions—staring out the window rather than show Hodges the anger he felt. He needed Duncan, but not for the exercise. The true reason would remain forever hidden between him and a select few subordinates.

"Here, Duncan." The admiral pulled out his lower right-hand drawer and took out a bottle of Ponche Caballero—the Spanish silver bullet of brandy, so called for the silver bottle in which Luis Caballero of Puerto de Santa Maria, Spain, bottled it.

"Admiral, I need to get my affairs in order these last forty-five days. I'm not sure if you are aware, but I also have a very personal problem I need to resolve," Duncan said, forcing his voice to stay level and calm.

Admiral Hodges stood and poured them both a shot of the strong brandy. He handed the fullest one to Duncan.

"You mean your wife leaving you? Shit, Duncan, you're not the first man to lose a wife. Fact is you're probably one of the few career officers in the military who's had only one wife. I remember when my first one left me. I was devastated, but you get over it, and after a couple of marriages you eventually meet the right one, like I did. Believe me, Duncan, this deployment is the right thing to take your mind off her and prepare for retirement. Cheers."

Christ! Are there no secrets in the Navy? Duncan took a sip of the fiery liquid. How did the admiral know about Cathy? His stomach rumbled in rebellion as the brandy landed. The headache pinged painfully against the sides of his head, screaming to Duncan that his brain wanted out. So much for today being a no-drink day.

"I love this stuff," said the admiral as he involuntarily wrinkled his nose, smelling the "night-after" ammonia sweats of alcohol whiffing from Duncan. He nearly curled his lips in disgust. The sooner this man was out of the Navy, the better. But, first, he was going to resolve a problem the SEALs were encountering.

Hodges cleared his throat. "It never ceases to amaze me how hard it is to find Ponche brandy in the United States. It's the finest in the world and the least well known. Look at the label—twenty-eight percent alcohol. Melts the wax in your ears when it goes down. Great during Washington winters, Duncan. I'm sure you've tried it before."

Duncan's stomach rumbled louder. The admiral swished the brandy around his mouth, savoring the taste and surreptitiously watching Duncan. Duncan James was a drunk; why hadn't he discovered this earlier? If Hodges needed anything to salve his decision last fall on the SERB, this did it.

Last night, it seemed to Duncan that one drink fed another until he was sad drunk, swimming in sorrow. Unusual, as Duncan was not one to drown in self-pity. It had been many years since he had drunk so much, and he had no intention of doing it again—at least, not in the near future.

Watching the admiral swish the brandy around his mouth, Duncan seized the opportunity to steer the subject back to his situation. "Admiral, there's legal complications also. I received a letter from her lawyer yesterday—"

Admiral Hodges held up his hand. "Enough, Duncan," he said, as he recapped the bottle and slid it under some papers in his lower desk drawer. "I know all about those lawyers and their letters. Don't worry about them. They've got a computer program that spits that stuff out and, besides, you'll be protected under the Soldiers and Sailors Civil Relief Act while you're overseas. They can't touch you until you return to the States. I don't mind telling you that that Relief Act helped me a couple of times." The admiral took another sip and slammed his desk drawer shut.

"By the way," the admiral continued smoothly, "the Spanish arrived on board the *Nassau* yesterday."

So, his destination was the USS *Nassau*. Talk about one of the older ships in the Navy. But, of course, most of the ships of today's Navy were old; and tomorrow, they'd be even older. Maybe Colonel Harry Summers was right. In an op-ed he wrote a year before he died, he said that we were witnessing the decline of American influence and military might. That America was following the footsteps of prior world powers, leaving the stage to others such as France, India, and Brazil.

Admiral Hodges motioned Duncan to hide his drink before pressing the intercom on his desk.

The door opened and the young yeoman entered. "Yes, sir?"

"Petty Officer Gonzales, will you bring in Captain James and Commander Pettigrew's orders, please."

"Yes, sir," she replied. Doing a smart about-face, the young sailor left the room and quickly returned with a brown envelope, which she handed to the admiral. She went over and opened the windows slightly. The hot air hit Duncan, sending another flood of perspiration down his neck. Right below his pecs he felt the T-shirt stick to his chest. Turning to the two officers she smiled and in a polite, but almost scolding voice said, "Can't have the admiral's office smelling like a distillery, now can we?"

They watched the attractive young sailor leave the room and shut the door gently behind her.

"I call her my Moneypenny, Duncan. Can't pull anything over on her generation. Here are your papers. You'll find your orders and your plane tickets. At Sigonella, Sicily, a helicopter will be waiting to fly you out to the *Nassau*. A detachment from SEAL Team Two is on board under the command of Lieutenant Mike Sunney. He's expecting you."

Duncan opened the envelope and withdrew the papers. His eyes widened.

"Admiral, these tickets are for this evening," he said, standing abruptly.

"Sit down, Duncan. I'm really sorry about the short notice, but this is a very important exercise. Ever since we closed Rota Naval Base, our last military site in Spain, our influence with the Spanish has hovered between zero and nil. Seems every time we need a favor they run to the Germans or the French to see if it's all right. We need to repair some bridges and you are the engineer to do it."

Duncan leaned forward and in an angry voice said, "Admiral, I have always done what the Navy has asked. Twenty-eight years I've been doing what the Navy asked. The Navy has now asked—no! it's ordered me—to go home. It's told me it doesn't want me in the Navy any longer!"

The admiral raised his hand. "Captain, this isn't open for discussion. I know you've always done what we've asked and if there were another officer in whom I had the confidence to do this mission, as I do with you, I would have tasked him. But this exercise has Duncan James written all over it. It's an opposed beach reconnaissance followed by a nighttime urban assault rescue. You cannot have a double operation combination like that without us SEALs thinking Duncan James. You wrote the book!"

"Sir, my SERB?" Duncan asked, resigning himself to the fact that he was heading overseas to the Mediterranean. He chugged the remainder of his Ponche brandy and thought he detected the wax in his ears melting.

"Duncan, don't worry about the SERB," Admiral Hodges said with exaggerated reassurance. "I'll take care of it. Just go and do this and quit worrying about retirement. Maybe I can change the Navy's mind. I'll talk to the chief of Naval Personnel, Vice Admiral Speck, and explain to him the circumstances. The more I think about it, Duncan, the more convinced I am that we can delay or rescind your retirement. Speck's a personal friend, a great guy who understands things like this, and a horrible golfer. I'll lose a couple of games to him and he'll be so hepped up about bagging a SEAL admiral that he'll feel obligated to grant me one wish. Okay?"

"Personal friend and a great guy?" Duncan asked, failing to keep the sarcasm out of his question. "Sorry, Admiral. You know how much confidence I have in you, but I can't go."

The admiral involuntarily stepped back. He knew what Duncan thought of him. Did Captain James think that friends didn't pass along scuttlebutt on who was loyal and who wasn't? "Captain James, I'm sorry, but it's a direct order. You're going and that's it. I'll work the retirement issue and have someone keep tabs on your house and your personal affairs while you're gone. At the most you'll be back in thirty days. It's an easy mission, so relax and enjoy the trip. Think of it as a vacation."

Admiral Hodges maneuvered Duncan toward the door. "I know you're angry. But what are classmates for if they don't help each other in times of adversity? And you need to quit worrying about that wife of yours. Good riddance, I always said when they left. Good riddance. And there's no better way to forget them than a good assault against hard rocks and friendly forces. Rids the soul of anger. Besides, when you return, you can tell me how the combined Spanish-British governing of Gibraltar is working."

The two entered the reception area. Beau, seeing the admiral, stood to attention. The admiral walked briskly over to the blond lieutenant commander.

"Rod, how the hell are you?" asked the admiral, smiling as they shook hands. "It's good to see you."

Turning to Duncan before Beau could reply, the admiral said, "You two wait a couple of minutes. I won't keep you much longer because I know you've got seabags to pack, passports to grab. And, Duncan, don't hesitate to call me if you have any problems."

"Aye, aye, sir," said Duncan, ignoring Beau's questioning look.

" 'Rod'?" asked Duncan in a soft voice. "I thought you were kidding."

"Seabags and passports?" responded Beau petulantly, cocking his head toward Duncan.

"Tell me Rod first and then I'll tell you seabags and passports."

"Okay, deal. When the admiral was at Naval Special Warfare Group Two at Little Creek, Virginia, I was at Surface Forces Atlantic. For some reason, he thought my first name was Rod so whenever we talked he'd call me Rod."

"You should have told him."

"Why would I do that? Whenever he called I always knew who was on the other end. It made him feel important. Besides, I need to be thinking about next year's Commanders Board so it's too late to tell him now. Hodges is a screamer, with a memory like an elephant. I hope you don't think he's forgotten how you made a fool of him in Alaska years ago. Don't bet on it. Plus, he can do things like send me out of town. Hint?"

"We leave tonight on United Airlines for Rome for further transfer to Sigonella, where a helicopter will fly us out to the USS *Nassau.* There, we join a party of Spanish Special Forces for an exercise against the combined defenses of Buffalero beach."

"Damn, I can't go, Duncan." Beau shook his head.

The door from the inner sanctum opened and Admiral Hodges stuck his head out. "Captain James, Rod, you can go, I won't need you like I thought I would. Duncan, by the way, I forgot to tell you that a Lieutenant H. J. McDaniels is going with you. It'll be the lieutenant's first exercise. The lieutenant is a new accession to the SEAL community, so run interference with the Spanish so they don't become upset about us sending a new officer along for this bilateral exercise. It's a great opportunity for a new

SEAL to have some hard, near real-life training. I want a positive endorsement on the lieutenant's performance. You hear? A positive endorsement is what I want, Duncan," Admiral Hodges emphasized. "We need people with the lieutenant's capabilities and skills. It's good for the SEALs and it's good for the Navy." Hodges knew ordering Duncan to produce a positive endorsement would have just the opposite effect.

"A lieutenant? Kind of late in a career to be switching over to the SEALs," Duncan observed.

"Yes, it is, but like I said, the lieutenant brings along special skills and meets our high standards." He looked at his watch. "Duncan, look, I hate to hold you up, but why don't you and Rod wait a few minutes more. The lieutenant has a twelve thirty appointment with me. Let me see if I can locate . . . Wait here. Sit back down. I'll contact Lieutenant McDaniels." He stepped back into his office. He wanted to see Duncan's face when he met Lieutenant McDaniels.

Petty Officer Gonzales stood and shut the door again for the admiral. Smiling at the two officers, she sat back down and returned her attention to her computer.

"We're never going to get out of here," Beau whispered. "At this rate, we'll miss lunch, too."

"Read a magazine."

"Already have. The ones I haven't read don't have pictures. How come they don't have *Smithsonian* or *National Geographic* or *Rolling Stone*? Look here, we've got *Surface Warfare, Navy Times, Jane's Weekly* updates, and the *Navy Safety Bulletin.* Takes about five minutes to go through all of them and the *Navy Safety Bulletin* is the most entertaining. Read the article on motorcycle seat belts. I like the co-ed part the best."

Beau pulled the settee closer to Duncan, earning a quick

look of disapproval from Gonzales over the top of her glasses. "You going to tell me more or what?"

Duncan relayed what the admiral had said about their mission and showed Beau the tickets and orders.

Beau crossed and uncrossed his legs while his fingers drummed a tattoo on the chair arms. Eliciting no response from Duncan, he said, "I told you I can't go." He put his feet down and leaned forward.

"What do you mean, you can't go? Lieutenant commanders don't decide when they can go and when they can't, or even where," Duncan replied. Neither could Navy captains, apparently.

"Duncan, remember Alisha?" he pleaded. "It's taken us three months to arrange tonight. She traded with another stewardess for the New York to Washington run. She's staying for three days! Three days at my apartment!"

"Beau, you'll have to arrange another time with her. Tonight at six, you and I and this lieutenant are going to be at Dulles International."

Admiral Hodges opened his door and stepped into the room. Duncan and Rod stood.

The door leading from corridor H burst open and a tall female officer with dark wavy brown hair that nearly touched her shoulders strolled, possessively, into the reception area. The door clicked shut behind her. Her snub nose seemed too small for her face and her eyes too far apart, but when she spotted Captain Duncan James and Lieutenant Commander Beau Pettigrew, she smiled. The smile brightened her face, apple green eyes sparkled, and the features of her face melded together to radiate a pixy cuteness. The metamorphosis gave her the feminine look that was missing when she entered. She straightened and ran her hands lightly down her khaki blouse and skirt to smooth any wrinkles.

Duncan thought the feet seemed too big, but Navy shoes had that effect. His stomach churned, but he didn't think it was the brandy doing it. He shut his eyes for a second as a feeling that this week was going to get worse, if that were possible, rushed over him.

Hodges saw what he wanted to see and stepped back into his office, shutting the door behind him. Inside, he chuckled and did a quick two-step as he crossed to his desk to pick up the phone. He had to tell the others. Hodges had no doubt that Duncan would shitcan the female for them. And Pettigrew was his ace in the hole. The man's brains were in his pants. Even if James failed to come through, Pettigrew would do something dumb to settle the issue.

In the outer office, the woman crossed the room to where the two warriors stood.

"Captain James, Lieutenant Commander Pettigrew, Admiral Hodges called and told me I had a chance to meet you before we left tonight," she said as she shook hands with Duncan and then with Beau. "I was afraid I was going to miss you."

"And you are . . . ?" Beau asked as he shook hands with her, his voice trailing off as his eyes roved down to an ample bosom and then quickly back to her face to discover the apple green eyes had turned into apple green daggers. Thirty-eight D, he guessed, but he kept his eyes up and his guess to himself.

Duncan realized his mouth was open and shut it.

"Sorry, I thought you knew. I'm Lieutenant Heather J. McDaniels. Everyone calls me H. J., after my first two initials. I kind of prefer H. J. to Heather. Thanks for taking me along on this exercise, Captain. It'll be my first since Coronado, but I think you'll find me up to it, sir."

Duncan recalled where he had heard her name. H. J.

was the first woman to successfully complete SEAL training. *Navy Times* had a big article about her nearly a month ago. He was right, his week had just gotten worse. "You're welcome," he mumbled.

"And I'm having to give up Alisha," Beau said softly to himself as he compared the Amazon in front of him with the petite stewardess he was leaving behind.

"Sorry, Commander. What was that?" H. J. asked.

"THERE IS ONE GOOD THING, DUNCAN," BEAU SAID AS he eased his Triumph TR2 onto the George Washington Parkway.

The wind whipped through Beau's blond mane, giving it an even more windswept appearance than normal as the small convertible weaved through the traffic toward Reston.

Clouds moved across the sun.

"What's that?" Duncan asked. The problems with his wife and the Navy intermingled in his thoughts while he half-listened to Beau.

"I remember. It's Spanish women. Have you ever noticed how Spanish women can look at you with those liquid brown eyes? It's phenomenal. They can undress you, ravish you, do vile things in your fantasies, throw your clothes haphazardly back on, and by the time they've walked past, you've been mentally patted on the butt, your knees are watery, and your underwear's soaked."

"Don't you ever think about anything else?"

"Sometimes, like why are they sticking a woman on a Navy SEAL team?" Beau asked, his eyebrows raised. "I bet that's a question you're asking, right?"

"I'm not sure, Beau. It is a training exercise and Admiral Hodges wants her to get her feet wet as soon as possible. You heard him. The Navy wants a positive endorsement on her performance."

"Well, I'm kind of thick at times, so explain to me why they are sending a full Navy captain on a routine training exercise that any lieutenant could handle. Why are they sending a Navy captain who has been told to go home—no offense, Duncan—overseas when he should be preparing for civilian life? And, what is so damn important that they send me along with you—not that I mind going with you or anything, but I find it hard to add all this up."

"I don't know, Beau," Duncan replied, "but when I have the answers I'll tell you." What was the hidden agenda? Admiral Hodges had bucked the idea of a woman SEAL until Congress and the Department of Defense had steamrolled over him. Yet, he had ordered Duncan to bring back a positive endorsement on her performance. Why would he send her with an angry Navy captain who was being SERBed? Maybe Hodges had burned more bridges than Duncan knew with his strong opposition and now thought that a positive endorsement would rebuild them and further his Navy career. If that's what Hodges thought, then he was full of it. Duncan had no intention of rubber-stamping women into Naval Special Warfare. Admiral Hodges must be stupid or really have a low opinion of him. Duncan shut his eyes. Hodges's hidden agendas and political wiliness were too much right now for him to try to figure out. He'd think about it later. He ran his hand over his stomach, trying to soothe the fight going on inside it. His thoughts turned to other, more important, problems, like did he have enough clean underwear for the trip?

"Come on, don't give me that captain crap. Tell me the truth."

Duncan ignored Beau's question, reached over, and turned on the radio. He squeezed his small, but growing love handles. Maybe an inch. The news interrupted his thoughts.

". . . during the night. The American ambassador to Algeria has asked all U.S. citizens to remain calm and stay inside until events are clear. Many units of the Algerian Army, thought loyal to the government, remained in their garrisons and there are questions on whether they would respond to calls to oppose the rebels. France has issued a warning to its citizens to remain indoors and has cautioned the Algerian government and the Algerian Liberation Front—the FLA—that it would hold them responsible for the safety of its citizens. Mers El Kebir, the major Algerian Navy base west of Algiers, appears to have fallen to the rebels. Unnamed sources at the State Department speculate that Algiers may also fall sometime today. CNN will keep you up to date as events occur. This is Mortimer Shell for CNN, Algiers."

"Well," said Beau, reaching over and turning the radio down. "That takes the cake. Just when a great liberty site like Gibraltar appears to be unfolding away from the eyes of do-gooders, along comes a crisis to throw a rock into it."

Duncan tuned Beau out as the lieutenant commander commenced his familiar diatribe against liberal fifth columnists ripping the fabric of American society apart.

If Cathy returned today, would he take her back? She had hurt him, but deep inside he still loved her. You don't spend twenty years of your life sharing a house, sleeping in the same bed, and enjoying the little challenges that creep up without love growing deeper. He must have done something wrong. He didn't know what. He wished he did. He'd do anything to win her back except grovel. He wasn't going to beg. Even so, this emergent deployment to the Mediterranean sealed his hope of saving his tattered marriage.

For once, maybe Hodges was right. Maybe a few weeks in the Mediterranean, focused on operations, would take his mind off his problems and when he returned he might discover her waiting for him. Then, again, he may not.

"Damn," said Beau as he rounded a curve and hit the brakes. They had come up against the inevitable Washington bumper-to-bumper gridlock.

Duncan accepted it as another example of how things were going this week. He looked up at the darkening clouds and gliding seagulls. He knew one of those birds had his name engraved on its asshole and that was probably next on the agenda for Duncan James. He put his hat on. Instead the birds disappeared as a summer shower burst upon the two men. Duncan shut his eyes and tilted his face upward letting the rain beat on his face, baptizing away his marriage. His hat fell off into the small space behind the seats. He swallowed, but the lump in his throat remained.

"Yeah, there's something about the eyes of Spanish women, Duncan!" Beau shouted as he jumped out of the car to raise the top. "Bedroom eyes! That's what they got."

The summer shower turned into a downpour. "Damn, Duncan, the top's stuck! Give me a hand."

He ignored Beau as the rain soaked them—a perfect ending to a perfect day. Behind him the cursing of his number two, straining to raise the top, was muffled by the heavy rain pelting the hood.

TWO

"CAPTAIN, THE COOLANT PUMP ON THE STARBOARD CLOSE-in weapons system broke again, sir. The electronic technicians are running in-depth diagnostics and we should know something in a couple of hours. And, yes, sir, I have already checked and Supply has a spare pump if we need it."

Captain Heath Cafferty stretched and jumped down from his bridge chair. "Keep me informed, Ensign O'Toole. We turn east soon and that system needs to be on-line. It's on the side of the ship facing Libya."

"Aye, aye, sir," Mr. O'Toole replied. Saluting sharply, he turned to leave the bridge.

"Mr. O'Toole," Cafferty said, stopping the ensign, who was halfway through the hatch.

"Yes, sir." Ensign O'Toole stepped back onto the bridge.

"That's the CIWS you've had problems with since departing Norfolk. After you finish fixing it, I want a wrap-up of everything that has gone wrong with that lemon.

We'll send a message to SurfLant telling them to do something or I'm going to use it as a spare anchor."

"Yes, sir."

"And, Mr. O'Toole, if you're going to wear the ship's belt buckle then shine the damn thing."

"Yes, sir, Captain."

Cafferty scratched the end of his sunburned nose. Naval Surface Forces Atlantic couldn't do anything his ship's force hadn't done, but it was better to keep those no-loads at SurfLant informed in case it turned into a major casualty. Then when they swarmed on him like a bunch of pissed-off hornets, asking dumb questions—why hadn't he done this, why hadn't he done that—he could point to the messages, showing he had given heads-up on the problems.

"Mr. O'Toole, if it's still broke at noon I want a casualty report issued. Let the battle group commanders and SurfLant know that the starboard CIWS is inop. You've got two hours, no more. So, go and fix the damn thing and bring me great tidings of joy when you do."

"Aye, aye, Captain." Ensign O'Toole, the electronics maintenance officer, nearly bumped his head on the overhang as he hurried off the bridge, trying to put as much space as possible between him and the captain before the Old Man remembered some other piece of instruction to sling at him. The chief could have told the captain, but had refused. Said it was the officer's job to carry bad news to the skipper. Bad enough he had one of the most important jobs on the ship, keeping everything electronic and electric working, but he was a real officer—college degree and all that—not a mustang like his predecessor. An electrical engineering degree was a whole world away from practical application. That redheaded bastard was making life miserable for everyone. He never thought he'd miss the old captain.

Commander Cafferty smiled as he watched the gangly ensign scurry away. One thing he'd done right since his arrival was making his presence known. Relieving in the middle of a deployment was never an easy transition for a new commanding officer, especially when you inherited a lax ship. He sauntered over to the open hatch, the sound of the boatswain mate of the watch yelling "Captain off the bridge" ringing in his ears as he stepped onto the bridge wing. Raising the binoculars from around his neck he scanned the horizon to starboard before focusing ahead on the haze that masked the shore.

After a few minutes, having seen nothing, he stepped back inside, to the background of the BMOW shouting, "Captain on the bridge." He grabbed his porcelain coffee mug with the USS *Gearing*'s emblem on one side and COMMANDING OFFICER on the other and immediately stepped back outside, smiling as the BMOW shouted, "Captain off the bridge." Had a nice ring to it. Each time the BMOW announced the captain the quartermaster made an entry in the ship's logbook. Handwritten logs remained a Navy tradition even with portable computers humming in every office, nook, and cranny on the modern warship. Even the bridge had two portable computers, one for the navigator to conduct ship's business, since he was also the administrative officer, and a second for the captain, although no one had seen him use it yet.

Cafferty leaned on the railing, his cup cradled in both hands and eyes partially shut as he allowed the rays of the hot summer sun to bathe him. He pulled a small tube of cream from his pocket and rubbed some of the ointment on his nose to protect it from the sun. A soft breeze flowed across the bow created by the ship's twelve knots as it cut through the mirrorlike ocean of the Gulf of Sidra. No natural breeze stirred and no waves broke the surface and the ship-made breeze did little to cool the desert heat coming from the south. The Mediterranean lay quiet, like a mirror on its back reflecting the sky, making the ship appear to be sailing in midair. Its wake the only thing, besides an occasional flying fish, to break the illusion. A school of porpoises played, riding the pressure ridge created by the ship's bow as it knifed through the still sea. Cafferty finished his coffee and sat the cup on a shelf below the starboard railing. Pulling a handkerchief from his back pocket, he wiped the sweat from his face.

The navigator stepped onto the bridge wing and waited to be acknowledged. After a few seconds, he cleared his throat.

"Yes," Cafferty said, without turning. He raised his binoculars.

"Sir, we're five miles to track—"

The sudden turn of the captain startled the navigator, causing the junior officer to stop in midsentence and stumble backward a step.

"What are you basing our position on?" he asked gruffly. The captain's binoculars swung back and forth on the thong around his neck. Cafferty narrowed his eyes, hoping it enhanced his attempt to look stern.

"GPS, sir. We tried a running fix, but the haze over the coastline is hiding the landmarks." The navigator licked his dry lips.

Cafferty shaded his eyes and looked up. "Have you thought about taking a fix from the sun, mister, or have we forgotten how to do proper navigation?"

"No, sir, we haven't, but—"

"Don't 'but' me, Navi-guesser; either you've done it or you haven't and I can tell you haven't, so get your butt in there and break out the sextant and charts and get me a fix before we arrive on track!"

"Sir, that'll take me longer than five minutes."

"Then bring it to me when you figure out how to do a fix from the sun, Lieutenant Junior Grade. That is, if you ever hope to make lieutenant. Now get your act together! We're sailing in an area where anything can happen and you've done nothing but flip a switch and hope some satellite, sitting overhead, is right. In my eighteen years of naval service I can tell you there are multiple reasons for technological convenience to go wrong. There is no substitute for good, precise stubby-pencil work. Do you understand? If not, let me simplify it for you: GPS isn't sailing into danger, we are!"

Cafferty flicked his thumb back toward the bridge. "Now move it and I don't want to see you again until you know our exact position!" he said through clenched teeth, never thinking how that order would endanger the ship within the next twenty-four hours.

The navigator scrambled back inside, to the relative safety of the bridge. His knees wobbled slightly as he walked to the navigation table on the port side, unaware of the skipper smiling behind him. Only two more years left and his obligated service was up and the Navy could color him *gone.*

The lead quartermaster watched the entire episode on the bridge wing. She had seen enough ass-chewings to recognize one. Her officer's pale face revealed enough for her to know that whatever the ass-chewing was about it meant extra work for the navigation team. She rolled her eyes up and thought, *Lord, protect me from scared junior officers and rank-seeking commanding officers.*

"The captain wants a sun reading to complement the GPS position," the navigator said angrily.

"That's dumb and it's a waste of time, sir," she said, grabbing a nearby compass rose. "GPS is exact and even if we do celestial we're going to be a few miles off. This close to land we need a running fix. It's more accurate than a sun fix."

"Don't argue with me, First," the navigator said with a low growl. "Break out the sextant and charts and get busy."

"Yes, sir," the first class replied, whipping off a brusque salute and tossing the compass rose onto the navigation table. "I hope the *lieutenant junior grade* is aware that the sextant is packed away—God knows where—in the chart room. I'll have to find it and then it's going to take a while to unpack it and set it up . . . not to mention probably have to wash the goddamn thing to get the dust off the lens."

"We don't have a lot of time. So hurry up and do it," he whispered. "That's an order. And, we don't salute inside the skin of the ship."

"No, sir, and we don't do celestial when we got GPS either," the first class replied.

"First, not another word. Go fetch the sextant and quit wasting time arguing with me."

"Well, sir, the last thing I would want to do is waste time when I've been given a direct order."

The quartermaster sauntered off, enveloping herself with a cloud of curses about "wuss" officers and muttering about the new Navy as she slammed the hatch leading into the chart room.

Cafferty, unable to hear, had witnessed the exchange. It may have been a lax crew he inherited, but, by God, he was going to turn it into a fighting ship if it killed him. This may be a routine Freedom of Navigation operation to everyone else, but for him it was an opportunity to hone the crew. Knock out the little things that impact the fighting edge a warship needs.

A torrent of nautical terms sprinkled with a stream of colorful curses reached his ears. He leaned over the railing. Below, on the main deck, a First Division working party was sanding, scraping, and knocking away flaking paint from the motor whaleboat. A second class boatswain mate paced back and forth behind the nonrated seamen, with a steady stream of circus-quality invectives decorating his professional instructions.

"Boats!" the captain shouted down to the second class.

The second class boatswain mate stopped his dialogue abruptly. "What the fuck!" the boatswain mate yelled. Holding the ubiquitous cup of destroyer coffee in his left hand he shaded his eyes with his right to see who was shouting at him. Recognizing the captain, he turned the shading hand into a snappy salute. "Sorry, sir. Didn't see you."

"How's that job coming?" Boatswain mates were the real Navy. They were the true nautical flavor of the Navy, running through history all the way to sailing ships. A language of their own and a job that technology had yet to replace.

"Pretty good, Captain, but we won't be able to paint the goddamn thing until we turn out to fucking sea again!"

"Why's that?" Captain Cafferty asked, a puzzled look on his face.

"It's this shit-sticking sand, sir," the boatswain mate shouted. He held his hand up, rubbing his fingers together. "See! It's everywhere, Captain. Can't do a proper paint job with this shitty stuff everywhere. It's like a fine dust. It'll mix with the paint and we'll have to redo whatever we paint within two weeks. The ship will need a good washdown when we finish this shore water operation and even then, sir, I don't think it'll get rid of this shitty stuff."

"You're right, Boats. At least it'll give us a chance to exercise the seawater wash-down system and see if it really works."

"Fucking a ditty bag, sir!"

"Carry on, Boats, and let me know if you see anything else I should know about."

"Aye, aye, sir," the petty officer replied, hiking his pants up as he returned his attention to the detail. Yeah, the captain was a fucking a-okay Joe, even for an officer. He yelled at a seaman to quit goofing off. Yeah, the captain was okay.

Cafferty stepped away from the railing, leaving the imprint of his hand on the gray stanchion. He wiped his hands and then brushed his khaki shirt near the belt line where desert sand from the railing had stained it.

"Damn." The captain stepped inside.

BMOW shouted the usual, "Captain on the bridge."

"Boats," the captain said to the BMOW. "Call the executive officer and the combat systems officer to the bridge on the double!"

"Yes, sir." The BMOW grabbed the 1MC microphone and lifted the boatswain whistle to his lips to pipe the summons, but the intercom interrupted.

"Bridge, Combat; is the captain still there?"

"Combat, Bridge here; that's an affirmative." The officer of the deck glanced at the captain to ensure he heard.

Cafferty nodded and motioned to the boatswain mate of the watch to belay the announcement.

"Go ahead, Combat, the captain's listening."

"Captain, Combat Information Center watch officer here, sir. We have a helicopter off the port bow about sixteen miles."

The captain eased past the OOD, who moved quietly to one side. Cafferty pushed the reply button and said to the CICWO, "That'll put him over land. What's he doing?"

"Sir, we've been tracking him about three minutes. He came from the east and is flying due west. Not sure if he is conducting a reconnaissance, doing routine zone flying, or just transiting."

"Electronic Warfare got anything?"

"Just a sporadic radar reading that may have come from him, but it wasn't up long enough to identify. The direction he's flying his radar isn't pointed our way so doubt if we can get a valid identification."

"Combat, I would say it's Libyan since it's over the coast. Any other air activity out there?"

"Only the Harriers flying a combat air patrol about eighty miles northwest of us, sir."

"Do we have contact with the USS *Nassau*?"

"Yes, sir, we do, but we are experiencing some sporadic communication difficulties caused by the sun, but that's to be expected. So far, nothing serious enough to keep us from exchanging operational information. The Harriers are operating under the control of the *Nassau*'s ATC."

"How about Sixth Fleet?"

"Sir?"

"Comms! We got comms with Sixth Fleet?"

"Sorry, sir, yes, sir; when we conducted morning communication checks, everything was fivers with Sixth Fleet and Commander Fleet Air Mediterranean. The *Nassau* is one hundred fifty miles northwest of our current position and the op order calls for them to steam eastward to maintain a closing position so that her air arm can support our operation."

"Is the executive officer down there?"

"Yes, sir. He just came in."

"XO, this is the captain. Come up to the bridge, please. CICWO, keep tracking that helicopter and inform the *Nassau* and Sixth Fleet that our presence is probably known by the Libyans. We'll assume worst-case scenario that the helicopter is flying a coastal recce."

CICWO acknowledged the order as the hatch opened and the executive officer walked onto the bridge.

"BMOW, go ahead and call the combat systems officer."

The BMOW keyed the mike and the boatswain whistle echoed over the 1MC loudspeakers throughout the ship. "Now hear this. Combat Systems Officer, lay to the bridge on the double!"

"On the double" meant a situation existed that required the immediate attention of the person to whom it was directed. To be summoned "on the double" meant dropping whatever was being done and running to wherever the summons ordered.

Less than a minute later the hatch burst open and the combat systems officer rushed breathlessly onto the bridge, bumping the quartermaster, who had just walked out of the chart room, carrying the wooden box containing the sextant. The quartermaster lost her grip, dropping the box, but with a quick grab caught the sensitive instrument before it hit the deck. She felt the sextant move against the inside cradle that held the sensitive instrument tight to protect its calibration.

"Damn, sir," the quartermaster said.

"Sorry," the combat systems officer replied as he walked around the petty officer.

"Captain," he announced his presence.

"Lieutenant, glad you could make it."

The navigator interrupted with an announcement that the ship had reached the fifteen-mile limit with a recommendation to come to course one one zero to commence track.

"Very well. Officer of the Deck, bring us to course one one zero and maintain twelve knots."

"This is the officer of the deck. I have the conn. Helmsman, left fifteen-degree rudder."

With a smooth motion the electric drive, generated by four turbine engines, brought the ship to starboard with a minimum list. When the ship neared the track the OOD began easing the rudder, bit by bit, until the ship steadied on course one one zero.

"Steady on course one one zero. Keep us at twelve knots," Cafferty added. The Admiral Zumwalt DD-21–class land-attack destroyer was one smooth class of ships: different engineering technology; integrated power systems driven by the electric drive; and fully designed from the keel up with the concepts of Network Centric Warfare and offensive distributed firepower in mind. Of course, Network Centric Warfare assumed the ship was acting in concert with other units. For the Freedom of Navigation operation, the USS *Gearing* sailed alone. The sounds of the four turbine engines that generated the power for the electric drive vibrated the ship when increased power was required.

"Aye, sir. Course one one zero. Steering one one zero. Twelve knots."

"Steering one one zero, twelve knots," repeated the helmsman.

"Very well," replied the OOD.

At the navigation table the navigator made appropriate log entries to include the distance from the Libyan land mass, unaware that the GPS position was erroneous. The USS *Gearing* was three nautical miles inside Libyan territorial waters.

Cafferty briefed the two officers on how he wanted the guns and sensitive antennas and weapon systems covered. "Those that can be plugged, plug 'em. Those that can be tarped, tarp 'em. For those that need to be exposed to the weather, pack grease around them to keep the sand off the sensitive elements and gears." The combat systems officer took notes. The XO nodded.

On the port bridge wing, the quartermaster turned the

sextant back and forth, checking the settings. The clumsy combat systems officer had knocked it out of calibration. Even so, the navigator wanted a sun fix and that was that. The quartermaster smiled. When she finished her sun fix, they would be spot-on GPS. She left the navigator sweating at the plotting table and went to take the reading topside, above the bridge. The signalmen always had better coffee up there than this shit they kept bringing up from the mess decks for the bridge. Plus, there was always the chance Sinclair may be there. Maybe she couldn't drink on board, or smoke belowdecks, but when the sun went down . . . well, that was a different kettle of fish altogether.

THE OVERHEAD SPEAKER BLARED TO LIFE IN THE OPerations room. "Command Post, this is Flight Twelve. Intruder has arrived."

Colonel Alqahiray nodded once as he twisted the end of his mustache.

The operator picked up the microphone and in colloquial Bedouin Arabic acknowledged the transmission and asked the pilot to put the data system on-line. Sharp, crisp voice comments passed as the two exchanged equipment settings. When satisfied that the two systems were aligned properly the operator turned to the colonel. "Everything is ready, sir."

"Download, then."

The operator touched a heat-sensitive switch. A small red light on the console blinked a couple of times, then turned a steady green. At the PC, decrypted data began flowing across the CRT as it downloaded from the Puma helicopter that had been painted to resemble an oil company helicopter. The operator flipped a switch and the data on the CRT was routed simultaneously to an overhead display for everyone to see.

The colonel rose from his seat and walked down the three steps to the main operations floor, his boots clanging on the metal rungs. He stopped in front of the communications systems array. Tilting his head back he watched the decrypted data scroll rapidly across the screen. He'd have it printed later to study, but even as it scrolled up he recognized the radar signatures and the highlighted navigational fix, placing the American warship three miles inside Libyan territorial waters. Later, in the afternoon, a scheduled Mirage V reconnaissance flight would provide photographic proof of the American warship's intrusion.

"Walid, enter the time as eleven twenty-three hours for event zero zero seven. The American destroyer has entered Libyan territorial waters in clear violation of international law."

Alqahiray turned to the plotting tables, where several soldiers stood.

"Air cover?" the colonel asked.

A soldier pointed at another display screen overhead.

"Yes, sir, radar reflects two American Harrier aircraft northeast of Tripoli approximately seventy nautical miles in a racetrack orbit. Pattern suggests combat air patrol in support of the American warship."

"Keep an eye on them and tell the Air Force to put two MiG-25s on strip alert at Tripoli. The Americans will be expecting it, so let's not disappoint them."

He rubbed his chin. "Get me Colonel Alli Abu Gazellin at the airfield. Ensure it's on the red line."

The communications officer acknowledged the order. He lifted the secure phone, pressed seven digits, and waited while the airman on the other end tracked down Colonel Gazellin.

The colonel returned to his chair and hoisted himself into it. A broad smile showed the officers and troops that he was pleased with their performance and how well the plan was going. They smiled respectfully back.

Alqahiray lifted the phone on the chair arm and dialed a number committed to memory. The call went through several diversionary electronic relays until it was answered with a loud click.

"Stand by," the colonel said. He reached over and pressed the cipher button. He drummed his fingers as he waited until the digital display read "secure."

"*Salam-alay-ikum,* my brother," the colonel said. "You can lodge the complaint with the American interests section at the Swiss Embassy that an American warship is violating our territorial waters."

He listened. "Of course! You don't think we confirmed it? It is nine miles from the coast. Three miles inside internationally recognized territorial waters, ninety-one miles inside Libyan recognized territorial waters." He paused. "The Americans will deny it as they always do."

A raised voice came from the earpiece.

"Quit worrying, Ahmid Tawali Mintab! You file the diplomatic paperwork and do it today. We can't file it afterward, *ya effendi.* Just do it and then go back to writing your speech. You leave for New York when? Tomorrow?" the colonel asked curtly.

He listened for several seconds and then replied, "*Taib,* Ahmid. You have your orders and you know the importance of your role. May Allah be with you." He hung up before the person on the other end could reply.

"Allah protect me from cowards and worriers," the colonel muttered. "Walid, come here," he snapped.

The major hurried from his seat to where Alqahiray sat and saluted when he arrived.

"Walid, send the signal to our friends that event zero zero seven has occurred. Notify me immediately after they acknowledge. I don't like doing this. Too much of a chance of Jihad Wahid being detected, but it is critical that they know exactly where we are in our operation, otherwise Jihad Wahid is no more than all the other plans tried and failed."

"Yes, my colonel." Walid saluted and began to leave.

"Walid, don't be so impatient. Come back here," the colonel said, his mercurial mood swinging to one of jubilation. He leaned forward and, for a brief second, placed his hands on Walid's shoulders. "After you send the signal, bring me the documents on the electronic array system concealed along the coast. I want to review again how it's going to work."

Sharing his thoughts, the colonel added, "I never feel comfortable with things I can't touch. Though, we are tweaking the tiger and he doesn't even know it." He grinned as he reached out and patted Walid gingerly on the cheek.

Walid's face turned red. "Colonel, these are great days in our history," he stuttered.

"They are indeed great days for Barbary, Walid. You and the others here will be heroes for our children and our children's children. They will read about and glorify us in the years to come."

He gently shoved Walid. "Go ahead. Send the signal and bring the operating document on the array. Maybe then we can grab a few hours' sleep before the next event. You'd think they'd have some modern name for the system instead of 'electronic warfare array.' Something like 'electronic signals suppression' or 'radar and communications interruptions device.' " Seeing the bemused look on Walid's face, Alqahiray stopped. "Never mind, Walid. Tell our friends of event zero zero seven and then bring me the papers on the array."

Walid saluted and ran from the platform to his console. Even as he threw himself into his seat his fingers danced across the keyboard; file pages spewed to the screen immediately, to be covered by other file pages until in the upper left-hand corner the system reported the signal sent. It would be a few minutes before he received a receipt.

Satisfied the signal was transmitted, Walid departed the operations room in company with Major Samir. He returned alone fifteen minutes later with a leather satchel, which he carried directly to the colonel.

"Thanks, Walid." Alqahiray took the satchel, unbuttoned the leather straps, and pulled a heavy folder out. Opening the folder, Alqahiray began reading the documents, which were covered in Arabic script with photographs and diagrams on nearly every page. Even a country such as Libya, with a small military force, could afford to be a technological warrior.

Walid returned to his console. Seeing the colonel occupied, he reached down and, with his back to Alqahiray, picked up his secure phone.

"Ambassador Mintab, please," he said quietly when he heard the click on the other end.

MOST OF MERS EL KEBIR NAPPED THROUGH THE HOTTEST part of this June day as sailors raced up and down the length of the Algerian Navy Kilo–class diesel submarine to their "sea and anchor" detail. Dull, reddish areas dotted the thirty-year-old ship where wire brushes had won recent minor battles against the war on rust. The *Al Nasser* was built by the old Soviet Union and bought from the new Russia that sold off its armaments to any nation possessing the hard currency to purchase them. Along with the purchase of two Kilo attack submarines by Algeria came peripheral contracts for spare parts, maintenance, and operational training so the weapons could live up to the buyer's expectations. The Algerian submarines had spent a lot of time at sea in the intervening years perfecting tactics and developing professional expertise to the point where they were as good as most other Mediterranean navies.

The contract with the Russians had been limited to spare parts and overhauls for the last three years. The glazed eyes of two dead Russian tech reps stared sightless through the front window of an office that overlooked the submarine pens. Revolutionary Algeria had just terminated the contract with a bullet to the forehead of each tech rep.

Four doubled-upped lines ran from the light gray hull to the bollards on the pier. One from the port bow, two amidships, and one from the port stern. Amidships the lines crossed in an X to provide stability to the moored boat as the tides fought to shift it forward and backward. The bow and stern lines held the sub to the pier.

The four teams, of four sailors each, formed up at their stations supervised by an Algerian chief petty officer. On the pier opposite each team two dockworkers waited impatiently to assist.

From the conning tower came the word to single up all lines and in unison the pierside teams fought the tight topmost line off the bollards and, once free, the submarine crews, hand over hand, quickly pulled the lines back aboard. As the lines were hauled aboard, a sailor flemmed each back and forth in neat loops on the deck, far enough behind the teams so no one would trip over it, making it ready for storage as soon as they cast off.

The captain ordered the officer of the deck to take in

lines one, three, and four. The remaining line would be used to pivot the stern out as the captain momentarily ordered all engines ahead one-third and left full rudder.

The submarine pivoted so that the bow crept closer to the pier while the stern began to slowly angle out.

The captain ordered rudder amidships; all engines back one-third.

The submarine eased farther away from the pier as the sailors fed out line to the same number two line, being used now as insurance against a helmsman or engine room mistake. When satisfied they had sufficient clearance from the pier the captain ordered the remaining line to be cast off. They were under way. He gradually increased speed as the submarine slowly merged into the channel. He shifted the rudders to left full for ten seconds to straighten out. Visually satisfied with the position of the boat, he brought the rudders to amidships and ordered the forward speed increased to four knots. His seamanship brought the warship perfectly into the middle of the vacant channel. The captain was proud of his boat-driving skills and knew this submarine like the back of his hand. No one else could maneuver the *Al Nasser* like he could.

On deck, sailors went about the business of storing the lines and the mooring cleats so that the hull of the submarine became sleek and smooth to allow it to slide through its underwater world with minimum effort and noise. Behind the *Al Nasser* the second Kilo submarine, *Al Solomon,* moved into position three hundred yards astern. The sailor manning the stern watch on *Al Nasser* kept a continuous monologue going through his sound-powered phone as he reported the relative positions of the two submarines.

Wearing sound-powered phones, the port and starboard lookouts passed, on demand, compass bearings from the boat to various charted shore markers, to the navigation team in the control room. After plotting the results, the navigation officer made course recommendations to the captain, who corrected the heading and speed of the ship ever so slightly to keep the submarine in the center of the channel.

Two hours later the two lethal attack submarines were out of the harbor and steering the navigational channel bordered with a series of green and red buoys. *Al Nasser* was first past the outer marker where open sea began. The submarine turned to a northwest course and increased speed to a more efficient twelve knots. The *Al Solomon* followed suit and the two submarines continued in line astern formation, their surfaced tandem maneuvering hidden from overhead eyes by thick summer clouds.

The captain of the *Al Nasser* moved to the signal light. Motioning the signalman to one side the captain took control of the light and flashed a short coded message to the *Al Solomon.*

On board the *Al Solomon,* the executive officer flashed an acknowledgment and breathed a lot easier. The most dangerous part was over. They were out of port and nearly through Algerian waters. The captain of the *Al Solomon* would have been on the bridge, but he was suffering a bad case of cut throat, courtesy of the executive officer. The crew believed the story of the captain suffering a slight bout of food poisoning, a malady that everyone on board an Algerian Navy vessel endured eventually.

Thirty minutes after they exchanged signals, armed sailors boiled out of the insides. Using their rifles, the sailors prodded groups of officers and sailors to the bow of the submarine, their hands behind their heads. With a pistol to enforce their new authority, the leaders screamed at the captive officers, chiefs, and sailors until they were lined up along the seaward side of the submarine. Then, shouting, the leaders lined the armed sailors across from their former shipmates. Quick directions and a chopping arm motion and the sailors opened fire. Most of the prisoners stood shocked, unable to believe what was happening. When the first bullets ripped through the captives a few spontaneously leaped overboard.

The squads rushed to the side and fired at those in the water even as water suction, flowing along the submarine hull, pulled some through the chopping blades of the propellers. Most who jumped avoided the bullets; unfortunately the firing squads shoved the dead and dying bodies into the sea. The submarine was near the horizon when the first sharks arrived. Only five survivors would make it to shore and then only because a fishing boat happened upon them early the next morning. By then, it was too late to warn loyal Algerian military forces.

Two miles later, the executive officer of *Al Solomon* watched crewmembers bring the commanding officer's body topside and dump it overboard along with the blood-soaked mattress from the stateroom. There were plenty of empty mattresses on board to replace it.

The Algerian Kilo submarines preferred to surface when their batteries needed recharging so the internal air could be recycled quicker. The advantage of a diesel over a nuclear-powered submarine was that battery propulsion was very quiet and seldom detected by passive sonar. The batteries of the two deadly Kilos were fully charged.

The captain of the *Al Nasser* turned to course two seven zero at depth fifty meters and passed this information via underwater communications, UWC, to the *Al Solomon. Al Solomon* would follow on the same track two hours later at seventy-five meters. They would rendezvous later before starting the dangerous part of their journey. The first two warships of the revolution headed west.

The captain prayed that they would arrive at their destination before the Americans did.

THREE

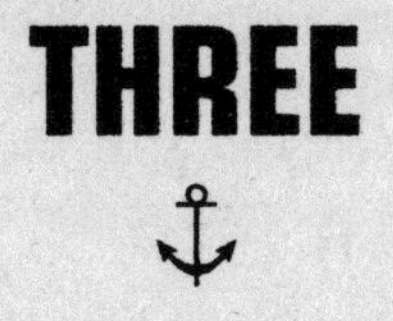

ANWAR PUT THE PHONE DOWN GENTLY. "TONIGHT WE strike a blow against the great Satan. A strike that will be heard throughout the world. *Allah Alakbar!* It is a glorious moment to be alive." He smiled.

Anwar turned to Taradin. "Give Kayal his khat," he commanded. "Tonight he greets Allah in paradise as he leads us into battle. Don't you, my drug-crazed zombie?" Anwar laughed, directing the question to Kayal. Derision dripped from every word.

Taradin, sitting on the couch beside Kayal, unscrewed the container top and pulled some of the Yemeni plant from it. "Good," he said. "I hate it here in Naples. The stink, the smog, the thieves."

"The Italians, the Americans, the traffic, the heat, the humidity," Anwar added.

Kayal reached weakly for the narcotic as his tongue pushed the chewed khat in his mouth out, letting the mixture splatter down his chin onto his shirt.

"Wait, Kayal," said Taradin, testily pulling the container

away. "You will have chewed all of this before this evening. Be patient. When this is gone there isn't any more."

"Plus, we must not forget that you don't like Naples because you got mugged last week, Taradin. You!" Anwar's laughter filled the tiny apartment. "The renowned Taradin of Beirut held at gunpoint and robbed by petty thugs who pushed and shoved you while you did nothing but beg."

Taradin controlled his anger, as he had for the past two weeks.

"We both know what is good about visiting Naples, Anwar."

"What's that?" Anwar asked, his eyebrows raised.

"That eventually we're going to leave. It is a pigsty. It stinks. The air chokes you with the captured exhausts of its cars and the smoke of its factories and then they prey on everyone including each other, robbing, mugging, and shooting. I have never figured out why the Americans, who love their own comfort, would put so many of their people in this place. My family is safer in the Bekaa Valley, with only the Israeli Air Force to worry about, than they would be here."

Anwar beamed. "Oh, Taradin, you are never going to forgive them for the mugging. Besides, we know why the Americans are here. Their admirals are here and we can thank Allah for that. If they had kept Rota, Spain, we could never have gotten this close, for it is an isolated farming area. We would have been fingered within hours of arriving. They vacated London, praise be to Allah. The British have too much experience with their own terrorists, the Irish Republican Army, for us to be able to target the Americans and avoid their MI-5 at the same time."

"No, we are lucky they chose Naples to homeport their leaders. The Americans have never allowed history to teach them lessons. They prefer to relearn them."

Anwar chuckled, then, changing the subject, continued. "Time to go. Take Kayal, Taradin, and start for Gaeta. Let us hope our practice runs have been enough. Kayal's Hizballah brother departed Rome an hour ago and will do his job about the same time as you."

"It doesn't take that long to drive to Gaeta, Anwar. Why leave now?" Taradin snapped.

"Traffic, Taradin," Anwar replied in a patronizing voice. "We've always done our practice runs at night when the natives were bunkered safely in their houses, or when those with common sense have evacuated Naples. It's"—he looked at his watch—"six forty now and the workforce of this medieval city is already clogging the roads of the autopiste for your drive north. You need to be there by ten when the sun is setting. You'll have to hurry."

Anwar walked to the couch. Drawing back, he slapped Kayal with all his might. The man's head jerked to the side as the sound of skin on skin reverberated within the small apartment. The youth never stopped chewing nor uttered a word as Anwar's handprint appeared in scarlet on Kayal's left cheek.

Anwar laughed, grabbing his stomach as his head tilted back. "Stupid people. They all are, Taradin. Khat makes them immune to pain, to the world around them, even to their own comfort. To them, khat is all that is important. The brain continues to send the word *chew*"—he waved his hands in a circle—"to the mouth regardless of what happens to the body."

Taradin pushed Kayal off him. "Fine, Anwar. For him it is his khat. For you, you have to beat someone. Now, quit hitting him. Every time you do he bounces against me and I have to push him back up. The question is how is he going to drive, drugged on the amount of khat you've been feeding him since this morning?"

"He will. Won't you, Kayal?"

"Allah Alakbar!" Kayal muttered, spitting pieces of khat into Anwar's face.

Anwar wiped the wet mixture from his face with his left hand as he drew his right back to hit the man again.

Taradin jumped up and grabbed his arm. "Stop it, my friend. We need him tonight and with you slapping and beating him every few minutes to amuse yourself he won't be in any condition to do it."

"Maybe I should beat you instead, Taradin?" Anwar asked, shaking himself free from Taradin's grip.

"Remember, Anwar, you may be the leader of this team, but even Hizballah makes mistakes. Do not make one with me. I'm not Kayal. Now, go and make some coffee for him," he said, pointing to Kayal. "Thanks to you he's had too much khat."

At the word *khat,* Kayal reached out to paw Taradin's hand. Taradin pushed the hand away. "No, Kayal. There is no more khat until we reach Gaeta."

Anwar stormed off toward the kitchen muttering Arabic oaths under his breath. Taradin caught the words *mother* and *camel dung.* Taradin swallowed his pride. Tomorrow would be soon enough to revenge the insult.

Too much depended on each of them to begin fighting each other. Besides, Anwar was not an Islamic warrior. Islam never condoned either violence or the infliction of pain on the innocent and unprotected.

It was hard to reconcile Islam with Anwar. The man was a sadist and Taradin hated as well as mistrusted him. Anwar boasted how he had been responsible for the successful interrogation of the American sailor snatched a week ago from Gaeta. It was true that without the information gained from the sailor they would never have known the schedule of the Sixth Fleet flagship, the USS *La Salle.* Neither would they have known that the commander of Sixth Fleet, Vice Admiral Gordon Cameron, was hosting a social gathering for his staff tonight at a popular bistro overlooking Gaeta.

It was true. Anwar had been successful in the interrogation, but he took too much pleasure in this unfortunate aspect of war. He continued even after he had the information they needed!

Taradin had seen the sailor's body after the interrogation and hated the man he obeyed as the leader for this raid. He spit on the rug. Respect would never be given. The sailor's mutilated body rested on the bottom of Naples Harbor, held down by concrete blocks tied to his feet. He was dead before they dumped him early this morning. If he had not been, Taradin would have killed him as an act of mercy. He wondered briefly how many dead bodies swayed in the currents of Naples Harbor.

Anwar brought a tiny cup with thick, steaming Turkish coffee from the kitchen. Taradin took it from the reluctant Anwar and held it lightly against Kayal's lips. He knew Anwar would have shoved the hot concoction into the drugged man's mouth for the pleasure of watching the skin burn. Taradin was fed up with the constant bestiality. If possible, Anwar needed to accompany Kayal to paradise. His last bullet would see to that tonight.

When Kayal finished sipping the strong coffee the two men forced the Yemeni to his feet and struggled down the stairs to the underground garage, where they wrestled him into the front passenger side of the dark blue Mercedes sedan.

"There!" huffed Anwar after he shut the door. "Damn! He's heavy."

"He's a big man."

"Yeah, he's yours now." Anwar smiled.

"And what good is he going to be in this condition?"

"Don't worry; Yemenis are resilient. Keep the khat away from him during the drive to Gaeta and by the time you arrive, he should be in that twilight zone of doing what he's told without being sober enough to question it. Talk to him on the trip there and keep repeating what he's to do so he doesn't forget what it is." Anwar reached into his pocket and gave an envelope to Taradin. "Here is an American Navy identification card with Kayal's photograph on it and this sheet of paper is what they will ask for at the gate. It authorizes the car to drive onto the pier."

"*Aiwa, ya effendi,* but what does Kayal do when they ask him a question? He doesn't speak English, you know."

"Ah, my friend. You have such little faith." Anwar handed a folded paper to Taradin. "This is a medical slip written on a prescription sheet from the United States Navy Hospital forbidding Kayal from speaking because he has laryngitis. All he has to do is point at his throat and they will wave him through. Put this sheet of paper in the window of the car. The gate guard will see it. Give these two papers, an American military ID card and a Naples Hospital medical chit, to Kayal and make sure he understands that he is to show it to the gate guard as he drives onto the pier. Understand?"

"Yes, I understand," Taradin answered curtly. "Do you think I haven't done this before?"

Anwar chuckled again, a high-pitched chuckle that grated on Taradin's nerves and patience.

"Taradin, I will see you around the corner after you turn the steering wheel over to Kayal. I will be with Qadafa, Sabiq, and Abu Tollah. Said Abu Said will join you at the corner where you get out." Anwar looked at his watch. "Said Abu Said has been there about an hour now observing the Americans. When you arrive, if you do not see Said

Abu Said, then keep driving. Don't stop. Him being there is the sign that everything is all right and nothing has changed. Him not . . . well, then something is wrong."

Anwar opened his arms, as was customary, to hug Taradin. Taradin would sooner hug a tarantula. He ignored the gesture by turning abruptly and walking around the car to the driver's side. He got in, leaving Anwar standing near the passenger door. Taradin cranked the car and backed out quickly from the parking space, coming as close as possible to Anwar, secretly hoping to see the man jump. Instead, what he got was a sneer from the cell leader, who never moved as the car narrowly missed him.

As he drove out the exit, he noticed in the rearview mirror Anwar climbing into the front seat of another Mercedes parked in the lane behind where they had been parked. That would be the second vehicle with the assault team. Anwar had not mentioned the other car being here. Probably to ensure they didn't change their mind. It never ceased to amaze him how untrusting the religious right was of its warriors. From what he had heard, it was the same in the Western world. Only minute differences separated religious zealots of all religions, politically correct do-gooders of America, and the old, decades dead, political commissars of the Soviet Union. Different ideas, skewed perspectives, same implementation methods.

It was seven thirty before he reached the autopiste, only to find himself bumper to bumper in traffic inching out of the smog-laden city northward, sometimes reaching the mind boggling speed of ten miles an hour. At this rate, it would be morning before he reached Gaeta.

An hour later Taradin remembered he should be preparing Kayal for his sacrifice.

"Ah, Kayal," Taradin said. "Tonight you join arms with Allah. How I envy you this opportunity to show your loyalty to the Islamic faith." He felt silly doing this, but it worked. At least it did the three other times he had driven a suicide driver to his destination.

The young man lay with his head against the closed window, his mouth open and sweat running down his head from the summer heat that was winning against the car's air conditioner operating on full power. One eye opened slightly and seemed to focus on Taradin.

"Then would you like to take my place?"

Taradin was startled and failed to answer the question. He'd thought Kayal was unconscious.

Kayal sighed. "Of course not. Taradin, I have been preparing to give my life for Allah since . . . since whenever. The khat was nice. I have lived with khat my entire life in Yemen. It affects me less than Anwar thinks, but our Iraqi brethren breathe easier thinking they know everything, including how corrupt and useless we Yemenis are."

"You've been faking?" Taradin asked in amazement.

"A little. Khat is doing what it is supposed to do. It calms the fear skulking within the soul and it tempers the nerves as it channels the mind to the great single purpose at hand. Everyone in life has a single great purpose for which Allah put them here. Mine is to die for Him."

Taradin reached behind him and pulled the container from the floorboard of the backseat. "Here, Kayal."

"No, Taradin. I will greet Allah without the fog of khat. Save it. You may need it or, better yet, give it to Anwar and tell him I sent it."

"I'll give it to Anwar, my friend. I chewed the stuff once and it made me sick as a dog."

Kayal laughed, his green teeth showing flakes of khat stuck to them. "Not supposed to swallow it."

"Now you tell me."

Taradin increased the car's speed to sixty kilometers an

hour as the traffic thinned out twenty kilometers north of Naples. He looked at the dashboard clock. "It's nine o'-clock. We've been on the road over an hour and a half. Hope they're still there. We were supposed to be in Gaeta by ten and we still have sixty kilometers to go."

"Don't hurry for my demise, Taradin."

"Sorry."

Kayal leaned back against the headrest and shut his eyes. "Allah will provide, Taradin. When events are organized such as this, the complexity of the events themselves produce obstacles. Obstacles that stop most. Obstacles most refuse to jump or go around or beat down. Obstacles that are greeted with thanks so they can rush back to the safety of home to tell everyone what an impossible task it was. Secretly breathing easier that they avoided danger for another day and safe in the knowledge their own cowardice can be blamed on others or 'things' for their failure. We will succeed tonight. It matters little if we succeed in one hour or two hours. The important thing is that we succeed."

"You don't sound like the young man who spent the whole morning begging for khat, Kayal," remarked Taradin.

"I know, but sometimes it is better to let others view you as they think you are rather than show your true self." He sighed. "Taradin, I am prepared for what I have to do. This has been my destiny since I was sixteen. Forty of us left Yemen to train in the hills of Lebanon under the tutelage of the Ayatollahs. We know what to expect at the moment of martyrdom. Martyrdom and I are one. We have more in common with the Japanese kamikaze pilots of World War II than we have with our fellow Arabs. We understand what drove them and why they chose the path they did."

Kayal shut his eyes and leaned back against the headrest.

After a minute, Taradin thought he had fallen asleep; then Kayal spoke. "Taradin, drive quietly and let me sleep. I have to admit, as used as I am to khat, I was ill prepared for the amount Anwar shoved into me today."

Taradin acknowledged the request. He was amazed with himself on how his perception of Kayal had changed in the past ten minutes: a disgusting drug-crazed beggar had become a religious prophet destined for greatness.

He drove the remaining sixty kilometers in silence, periodically checking the motionless figure snoring in the seat beside him. He was impressed how Kayal, a man about to die, was able to sleep. If he had known earlier what he knew now about the man, he would have killed Anwar for the disrespect shown this hero of Islam. He silently offered a prayer to Allah for the man who was to die in Allah's name.

TARADIN SLOWED THE MERCEDES AS HE TURNED THE dark blue luxury car onto the city street that circled Gaeta Harbor. Ahead, the USS *La Salle,* flagship of the Sixth Fleet, appeared gray and huge at the north end of the harbor. It was "Mediterranean moored"—stern to the pier. On the right side of the ship was the unexpected presence of the submarine tender USS *Simon Lake.* Taradin smiled. Bargain week at Gaeta, Italy. Two blocks later his smile broadened as a dark silhouette against the port side of the *La Salle* took form in the shape of an American attack submarine.

Taking his eyes from the American warships, Taradin scanned the sidewalks for Said Abu Said as he drove slowly along the harbor street. A block before the road curved to the left, toward the entrance to the port facilities, he spotted his contact, leaning against a street lamp. He nearly missed the short, dwarflike man, but the raised nod of Said's head caught his attention. Taradin jerked the steering wheel to the right, earning an angry blast from the driver behind him, and deftly pulled into a vacant parking spot twenty feet ahead of where Said stood.

Taradin sat patiently while Said Abu Said remained leaning against the pole. Both of them waited a few minutes to see if Taradin had been followed. If so, Said would have walked away, leaving Taradin and Kayal to the consequences.

Taradin reached over and woke Kayal. "We are here, brother."

The Yemeni stretched and rubbed his eyes. "A last sleep for the condemned, wouldn't you say?"

"A last sleep for the hero. Wait here. Said Abu Said is behind us. Let me talk with him and see if we are to continue. I'll be right back."

"Sure. I've noplace to go." Kayal glanced back to where Said Abu Said stood.

Taradin turned off the engine. Leaving the keys in the ignition, he shut the door behind him and walked around the car to the sidewalk. He looked in both directions. Satisfied, he nodded at Said, who returned the nod. The two men walked toward each other, meeting three cars down from where Taradin had parked.

The sound of tires screeching caused both men to turn toward the Mercedes. Said started to run toward the car, but Taradin grabbed his arm and stopped him.

"No! It's too late."

They watched as Kayal swung the car into the right lane, causing an Italian Fiat to swerve into oncoming traffic and clip the left front fender of a car in the other lane.

Said pulled away from Taradin's grip. "What's he

doing?" he said. "He's supposed to wait until we are ready. Anwar will not be happy."

"Anwar is never happy. Be quiet!" Taradin responded. "Kayal is afraid we'll ponder, discuss our plans, and find reasons to call it off. He has taken that away from us." Then he whispered respectfully, "Go with Allah, Kayal."

"Anwar and the others are around the block," Said said quickly, looking at his watch. "It's after ten o'clock. We're nearly on time. It will be dark in thirty minutes."

The two men walked at a brisk pace to the corner of the block and turned uphill away from the harbor.

KAYAL SLOWED AS HE APPROACHED THE LEFT BEND IN the road. Public attention focused on the accident behind him. The two drivers, standing nose to nose, screamed at each other, their arms waving wildly, as only Italians can do to accent their argument. He thought of the joke about the Italian who lost his power of speech because they amputated both his arms. A crowd was growing from nearby coffee shops and as pedestrians and cars stopped to enjoy the spectacle. And everyone had their own opinion.

At the port, Kayal waited patiently for two cars to pass before he turned into the narrow entrance. His eyes shifted from side to side as at any minute he expected security forces to swarm over him. He took his hands off the steering wheel and wiped his sweaty palms on his stained trousers. The American sentry motioned for Kayal. An Italian sentry stood on the right side of the gate area while on the driver's side an American Navy petty officer in uniform held his hand up for Kayal to stop.

"ID," the petty officer said.

Kayal handed the envelope with the papers to the sentry. Sweat ran down Kayal's face. The American removed the sheet authorizing access to the pier. "Hey, mate, you have to have this displayed on your window to drive on the pier." He reached inside and tossed the paper haphazardly onto the dashboard.

"Tell me, how the hell does a second class petty officer rate a Mercedes, Garcia? Ain't fair."

Kayal pointed to his throat.

"Okay, next time tell me. I want a Mercedes for a government vehicle also. Here's your ID back, Garcia. Don't give that sore throat to any of us." He waved the man through.

Kayal drove about twenty feet and stopped.

The Italian sentry, seeing him stop, shook his head and started walking toward Kayal to tell the dumb *American* that parking spots were to the right and to move the car because he was blocking the narrow entryway. As he approached the rear of the Mercedes the car gunned its engine, popped the clutch, and peeled rubber, accelerating as it began to cross the hundred yards separating it from the sterns of the two larger ships tied together. Both ships were moored within ten feet of the pier.

The Italian sentry, a sinking feeling crushed to his stomach, guessed immediately what was happening. Adrenaline and terror rushed through his body. He pulled his pistol and began firing at Kayal. The American sentry ran toward the Italian, screaming at the top of his voice for the stupid Italian to stop.

Two bullets shattered the rear window of the car. One lucky shot hit Kayal at the base of the neck, shattering the spine and sending the terrorist into Allah's arms at the same moment that the car hit the edge of the pier. The car catapulted toward the middle ship, the USS *La Salle*. Moored against the forward port side of the USS *La Salle* and barely visible from the pier floated the USS *Albany,* a nuclear attack submarine that had arrived earlier in the morning for a routine port visit.

The car hit the port stern line, flipping the Mercedes upside down in its flight, causing it to drop below the steel and cement pier before slamming into the stern gate of the USS *La Salle.* The impact crushed Kayal's head between the steering wheel and the roof as one thousand pounds of semtex packed into the backseat, the trunk, and within the panels of the car exploded.

The explosion blew off the back doors of the Mercedes, sending the right one careening back like a deadly Frisbee toward the harbor gate. The door decapitated the Italian sentry, who took two more steps toward the car before his torso collapsed. A half second later it sliced the right arm and shoulder off the American sentry. Then at the end of its trajectory, a full second later, it blasted through the front door of the module logistics office near the parking lot. The sides of the prefabricated hut blew apart as the impact killed the three inside.

On the USS *La Salle* the explosion destroyed the stern gate, breaking it loose and sending the twisted remains splashing into the harbor waters. The explosion shook *La Salle* violently, knocking those standing off their feet. The concussion blew upward, hitting a group of sailors, who had been smoking on the main flight deck above the gate, killing those nearest the stern instantly. Deadly shrapnel, of what had been an automobile, propelled outward at bullet speed a millisecond later, cutting through sailors, dismembering them like a gigantic garbage disposal. Body parts rocketed over three ships, the pier, and the crowd of Italians surrounding the two arguing drivers. Most of the American sailors died immediately—others before they hit the water and the ships. Some lived a few minutes without regaining consciousness—mercifully—before life poured out of their limbless bodies.

With no stern gate to maintain the ship's watertight integrity, seawater rushed into the well deck of the "amphibious" turned "command" ship. The USS *La Salle*'s stern section sank immediately, stopping only when it hit the shallow bottom of the port. The bow of the ship rose some twelve feet, creating a twenty-degree list to the stern. She was partially sunk, but still afloat. The ballast tanks, which the former amphib could have used to refloat, had holes blown in them from the explosion.

The USS *Simon Lake,* protected somewhat from the explosion because the command ship absorbed the bulk of it, had a hole blown inward on its port stern side the size of the Mercedes. The left back door of the Mercedes penetrated two frames below the *Simon Lake*'s waterline, bringing Mediterranean waters flooding into the compartments.

The majority of the ships' crews were on liberty. The duty watch sections of the three ships rushed to their damage control stations even before the alarms sounded. The USS *Simon Lake* sank slower than the USS *La Salle*. It began to list to the port side as its stern settled beneath the waters. Wrenching steel, crashing of gangways tearing loose, and the ripping and falling of antennas, lifeboat stanchions, and masts mixed with the screams and cries of wounded sailors as the two gray behemoths caved into each other. Their main decks entangled in a mass of aluminum, steel, and flesh.

The General Quarters alarm of three ships broke the eerie seconds of silence that followed the massive explosion. On the USS *Albany,* the duty officer pulled himself up from the deck and, doing well for such a junior officer, assessed the situation correctly. He shouted an order to a nearby sailor to cut the stern lines. The sailor grabbed a fire ax and ran to the stern of the submarine and cut the aft line attached to the USS *La Salle.*

The USS *Albany*'s 1MC blared. "Security alert, topside. Security alert. Away the security alert team." On board the lone undamaged warship, M-16s and shotguns were unlocked from storage and thrown to eager hands that snatched them in midair, grabbing a handful of ammo at the same time. Like angry ants erupting from a disturbed nest, the submariners poured out of the dark hull.

The *Albany* duty officer, holding a pistol in one hand and the topside bullhorn in the other, announced, "*La Salle* and *Simon Lake,* stand by for *Albany* security force personnel to pass through your ships to secure the pier." He repeated it several times as the submariners, anger in their faces, fear in their stomachs, and tears on some cheeks, rushed up the slanted brow to the *La Salle.* Everyone had their finger on the triggers and the guns were loaded.

They raced through the *La Salle* and across the connecting brow to the *Simon Lake.* The officer of the deck of the *Simon Lake,* cradling a broken arm and sitting with his back against a bulkhead, motioned the *Albany* crewmembers onto the ship's starboard side ladder, leading to the pier. The ladder canted to the right and swayed precariously between the ship and the pier. Within ten minutes of the incident the USS *Albany* had secured, by arms, the pier and the harbor entrance.

The *Albany*'s duty officer watched the damage control teams of *La Salle* and *Simon Lake* race about their injured ships. He took a deep breath and successfully controlled his emotions. He leaned against the conning tower and looked at his watch. "Topside watch, make the following log entries. . . ."

On board the USS *La Salle* and USS *Simon Lake* the lights flickered a couple of times and then went out as flooding belowdecks shorted the generators. The *La Salle* creaked as it hit the bottom of Gaeta Harbor. The ship rocked to starboard, bringing a new round of wrenching steel as it pushed further into the *Simon Lake* and settled lower in the mud.

"I DON'T LIKE SITTING HERE," COLONEL WALT ASHWORTH stressed in a low voice to Admiral Cameron's tall executive assistant commander, Jerry Baldston.

"Colonel, the seating arrangement was made a week ago and I passed that on the LAN," Baldston objected to the stockily built, crew cut Marine, who stood five inches shorter than his own six-foot-five frame.

"I know, I know, Jerry, but I was temporarily deployed to Kosovo last week. Remember? I didn't return until this afternoon so how in the hell could I read my e-mail and send you a reply. I couldn't, so there."

"Yes, sir. Look at it this way, Colonel: you asked to be seated near the admiral before you went on this TAD trip and you are."

"Jerry, I didn't know that I was going to be sitting with my back to the door facing the admiral!" Walt whispered emphatically.

"Colonel, I'm sorry, but you may try trading places with someone else. Besides, Diana is already deep in conversation with Elsie, the chaplain's wife. I'm not going to tell her she has to move."

Walt looked to where Jerry pointed. Diana and Elsie were head to head, exchanging the latest gossip. He sighed. Walt would never move her now. At least they had a great view of the valley out of the windows that lined the back of the bistro.

"Okay, Jerry, you damn politician," he said congenially.

"You win, but in the future don't put me where my back is to the door, okay? It makes me nervous. Never know when some bill collector is going to show up."

"Yes, sir, Colonel. I'll remember," Baldston replied, thinking that Colonel Ashworth was going shell-shocked at the old age of forty-seven.

Colonel Ashworth wandered toward his chair, exchanging greetings with other members of Admiral Cameron's Sixth Fleet staff, until he stood behind his wife.

"Honey, I told you there are some things even a Marine Corps colonel can't change," Diana whispered, her smile accented by soft blue eyes. The same eyes that first attracted him to her at college. She patted the chair beside her. "Now sit down and quit acting like a spoiled child."

He bent down and kissed her. Twenty-six years of marriage this past April and her hair was still mostly blond. A wisp or two of gray speckled the sides. "Maybe two nights in a row?" he whispered in her ear.

She playfully slapped his hand and patted his stomach. "Oh, you naughty boy, you." She laughed; her eyes sparkled. How she loved this tall, muscle-bound Marine—the man who swept her off her reluctant feet in college. Twenty-six years, two grown boys, and a life of moving every three years and they still acted as if they were new-in-love teenagers. Plus, unlike other middle-aged men, four of Walt's six-pack were still intact. Maybe when Walt retired he'd grow a small stomach, but she doubted it. She tried to imagine him with long hair, but found it impossible. He'd be a Marine until he died.

Turning to her friend, Diana said, "Can't take Walt anywhere, Elsie, unless I take him twice. Second time to apologize."

Heads turned as Admiral Cameron and his wife, Susan, worked their way along the narrow opening between the long table and the row of windows behind to their seats located in the center directly across from Walt and Diana. At the admiral's movement, those engaged in conversation over before-dinner drinks started moving to assigned seating. Everyone remained standing until the admiral and his wife took their seats.

Admiral Cameron leaned forward. "Walt, good to see you, but much better to see your better half. Diana, how do you keep track of him?"

"I don't know, Admiral. After twenty-six years I can't even keep him in bed past five in the morning."

Before Tailhook the admiral would have replied with something like, "You wouldn't have that problem with me," followed by ribald laughter around the table. He did miss the humor of the old Navy.

"You're lucky, Diana," said Susan. "Gordon sleeps until seven. Used to be, he was up and running by six."

"I'd call the doctor if Walt was in bed at seven."

"Admiral, I would like to ask you to disregard any opinions my wife may voice concerning me. The good ones I give her money to say; the negative ones she invents."

They laughed.

"Walt, you are such a twit," Diana said sweetly. "Admiral, how much would I have to give you to keep him at work longer hours?"

"I have problems now getting him to leave on time. My goal has always been to be the last off the ship in the evening and I've found that unless I leave first the rest of the staff feels it's their duty to stay. I like to think that any three-star admiral worth their salt is capable of taking care of him- or herself."

"Yes, Walt brags that you are a low-maintenance admiral."

"Diana!" Walt objected. "Admiral, like I said, I don't know where she dreams these ideas."

"She is right, Walt. I like to think of myself as a low-maintenance admiral. Don't want a large entourage milling about trying to take care of me." Admiral Cameron took a sip of his wine and squeezed Susan's hand.

"It's amazing how things you thought were resolved years ago resurrect themselves again," Admiral Cameron said, changing the subject. "Like the Greek-Turkish thing last month. The Greeks are still flying combat air patrols around the Aegean and have even started flying them during the daylight hours off eastern Crete. They buzzed Fleet Air Reconnaissance Squadron Two's EP-3E aircraft over international waters yesterday and the EP-3s fly out of Crete."

"It'll calm down, sir. I would say it's more the eastern Mediterranean macho thing that keeps stirring those two up, but they haven't had a major incident in nearly ten years; not since the SA-10 crisis in Cyprus. Just words and, of course, around election time the inevitable sword rattling to get out the votes."

"EP-3E?" Diana asked.

"The EP-3E is an electronic reconnaissance variant of the P-3 Orion patrol aircraft. Fleet Air Reconnaissance Squadron Two, we call VQ-2 when we're at work. The *Q* stands for electronic warfare. They are a descendant of the 'Old Crows' from World War II, which was the first squadron ever designed for electronic warfare."

"What do they do?"

"If I knew, Diana, they'd have to shoot me."

Everyone laughed politely at the old joke.

The Italian waiters moved along the table, setting out bottles of house wine along with olives and cheese, as the conversation continued among the group. Admiral Cameron seldom had an opportunity to socialize with his staff, what with the myriad political and military conferences and meetings he was forced to attend. He tried to rally everyone together at least once every three months. It was good for morale. It helped the spouses strengthen their ties and periodically the alcohol loosened a tongue to tell him something he needed to know. Five years ago when he became an admiral he discovered that few would risk offending him by bearing bad tidings.

The admiral looked down to the end of the table at Commander Jerry Baldston and raised his wine in a silent toast to his executive assistant. Baldston had been with him since he was a one-star at Cruiser Destroyer Group Eight in Norfolk, Virginia. While he had risen to three stars, Baldston had zoomed through the ranks from lieutenant to full commander. But Jerry stood the strong chance of stopping there. The admiral intended to correct a misjudgment that he felt the bureau had done in failing to give Baldston his own ship. Without an at-sea command, Baldston would never make captain, and Admiral Cameron knew the man was flag material, just needed the opportunity to prove it.

Baldston wiggled in his seat, trying to fit his refrigerator frame under the low Italian bistro table without falling off the small straw-seated chair. Over the years Jerry had adjusted to being a big man in a small world. Learned quickly after the academy how to duck through hatches and hunch his shoulders together when passing others in tight passageways.

The mobile phone rang. He pulled the phone out of its holster, pressed a button, and put it to his ear.

"Commander Baldston here."

On the other end the excited voice of the Sixth Fleet staff duty officer garbled something about a bombing thirty minutes ago. He shook his head because the SDO couldn't have said what Baldston thought he said.

"Slow down, Lieutenant," said Baldston quietly, trying to avoid attention from the others around the table. "Tell me slowly what you're trying to tell me."

The blood drained from his face as he listened. "Stop a moment and start over. Tell me, chronologically, what happened, the damages, and what actions have been taken." He reached in his shirt pocket and extracted one of the three-by-five cards he carried to take notes.

Mentally, he envisioned the lieutenant on the other end taking a deep breath. Then, with slow, methodical military precision, the officer relayed the events of the bombing. Forty known dead, two ships completely out of commission—their sterns mired in the bottom of Gaeta Harbor, their sides caved in upon each other.

Baldston scribbled furiously to capture the words because he knew he would never remember what was being said with the emotional surge that was racing through him.

Baldston looked toward the admiral and saw the admiral staring at him. Conversation around the table trailed off as everyone's attention focused on Baldston.

"Lieutenant, security posture?"

The SDO reported the *Albany*'s security alert force had the immediate harbor area secured while members of USS *La Salle* and USS *Simon Lake* damage control teams worked to bring the flooding under control and restore power. A damage control team from USS *Albany* was on board *La Salle*, the most seriously damaged ship. The damage control parties had shored up several weakened frames below the waterline of the *La Salle* and flooding had been contained. The commanding officer of the *La Salle*, as senior officer present, had established a joint damage control cell on the pier to direct the combined teams. Muster of personnel was being hampered because of liberty hours so the true number of missing and dead would not be known until everyone was accounted for.

"Lieutenant, cancel all liberty and recall everyone. Relay to the skipper of the *La Salle* to do the same for the three ships. I'll call back as soon as I've briefed the admiral. Unless you hear otherwise expect us back within the next thirty minutes." They were on the other side of the hills from Gaeta and the long, winding drive would take at least ten minutes.

Baldston folded the cellular phone and slipped it back into his coat pocket. Conversation ceased as everyone stared at him.

"What's going on, Jerry?" asked the admiral in a voice that carried the length of the table.

Admiral Cameron shivered as he looked at the face of his executive assistant.

Susan put her hand on his arm. "You alright, honey?"

"I just felt someone walk across my grave," he said so quietly that she nearly missed it.

She squeezed his arm and left her hand there.

Baldston stood and began to ease himself down the tight space between the back row of people where the admiral was sitting and the wall of windows behind them that looked out over the mountains and the valley to the east.

"What's happening, Walt?" asked Diana, leaning over to her husband.

Walt heard a lot of whispering around the table.

"I don't know, honey. Just wait," he replied. He took a bottle of house wine and refilled his glass, knowing Jerry was delivering bad news. From the look of the big man's face it was very bad news indeed.

Walt's mind instinctively recognized the clicking sound behind him. Chills raced up his spine.

The Hizballah terrorists burst through the front door,

their guns firing as they entered. Two Italian waiters near the door fell victim as bullets knocked them against the wall. Streaks of blood marked the wall as the elderly men slid to the floor.

The large man moving along the wall attracted the terrorists' fire; a line of red holes exploded up the center of Baldston like new buttons tacked on a white shirt. The executive aide catapulted backward, shattering the window behind him to land halfway out, his left arm and lower body draped inside.

Walt grabbed his wife's chair and pushed away from the table. As the chairs fell backward, Walt slung the wine bottle over his head in the direction of the terrorists. It was the only weapon he had.

Taradin ran down the steps from the mezzanine toward the tables directly into the lucky trajectory of the bottle. The bottle caught him in the temple, knocking him out. Taradin collapsed on the floor. The momentum sent the small submachine gun the terrorist carried sliding across the floor toward Ashworth.

Walt rolled to the left, grabbed the gun as it slid toward him, and jerked it up. He fired a sweeping burst at three terrorists who were gallery-shooting at the trapped Americans from along the railing that separated them from the raised floor above.

His first shots went wild, but it was enough to cause the three terrorists to rush toward the door. Walt pushed himself up onto one knee to steady the weapon, corrected his aim slightly, and shot a close sharpshooter pattern to kill the nearest terrorist, who was bent over and firing at people under the table.

The terrorist flew backward like a jerking doll as three bullets collected in his midsection. The dead man's gun clattered off the mezzanine and landed near the table. A hand reached out and grabbed the automatic pistol. Ashworth recognized the second armed American as the staff's meteorologist.

"Let's go!" shouted Anwar.

Anwar joined the four remaining terrorists as they ran toward the door.

Ashworth stood and charged the fleeing terrorists, screaming at the top of his voice. He was no longer at the bistro. He was back in Desert Storm, leading an attack against an entrenched Iraqi position. With two controlled bursts he shot two more terrorists in the back, grabbing one as he fell to shove him down the steps. The other flung his arms outward as the bullets ripped through him, both terrorists dead before they hit the floor.

The meteorologist fired at the two remaining Hizballah terrorists as they ran out the door. His bullets missed Said Abu Said, who disappeared into the darkness outside. The gun jerked to the right, causing the last bullet to hit Ashworth in the calf just as the colonel charged up the steps. Ashworth tumbled onto the mezzanine.

A spread of bullets ripped through the air where a split second ago Ashworth had been. The terrorist leader, Anwar, fired a couple of bursts at the prone Marine, missing, before he, too, disappeared into the darkness beyond the door.

Ashworth jerked the weapon from under him and fired a couple of random bursts into the darkness. From outside a short cry was heard, followed a couple of seconds later by a car spinning gravel as it raced away.

The meteorologist ran to the colonel. "I'm sorry, Colonel. God, I'm sorry."

"Don't worry about it. It's a nick. I've had worse. Grab those two guns and give them to someone. I'll cover you."

The meteorologist grabbed the two guns and handed one to the staff intelligence officer, Captain Kurt Lederman, and the other to a junior officer who had been sitting at the opposite end from Baldston.

Colonel Ashworth grabbed a nearby column with one hand and pulled himself up, keeping his eyes and the weapon on the entrance. He turned to the table, ignoring the pain from the bullet wound. Blood soaked his trouser leg.

Diana lay on the floor. A pool of blood was spread around her head; the wineglass was broken in her hand. Across from her the admiral was facedown across his wife. Ashworth saw the telltale signs of bullet wounds across the admiral's back.

His eyes dropped to Diana as realization crashed. "No, no," he cried and limped to her. He threw himself beside her, lifted her gently, and eased her off the chair, pulling her head onto his lap. Diana's blood mixed with his to soak his pants. The gun remained pointed at the door, his finger still on the trigger. Nestling her in his lap, tears fell on top of her head. A wail, like a solitary wolf on a moonlit night, joined other cries around the table.

The few who escaped the carnage moved to help the wounded. The dead remained as they were. In the background sirens penetrated the shock of the room.

"This one is still alive," the meteorologist said.

Ashworth gently moved his wife's body off of him. Limping over to the moaning terrorist, the colonel fired one bullet into each knee. The terrorist begged in Arabic as he waved his hands at Ashworth, who looked impassively at the enemy in front of him. In his mind he knew what he was doing. What he didn't know yet was if he would kill him. The Marine part of him said no, but the emotional part of him cried yes.

Ashworth moved the barrel of the gun to the terrorist's elbow, keeping his eyes locked on the frightened eyes of the enemy. Just as Walt began to squeeze the trigger, a hand grabbed his shoulder. Another hand grasped the hot barrel, swinging it up and away from the terrorist.

"Don't, Walt. Give me the gun."

Ashworth turned. It was the chief of staff, Captain Clive Bowen.

Walt took a couple of deep breaths and reluctantly broke eye contact with the terrorist.

"No, I'm okay. I'm not going to kill him, but he's not going to get away!" He wrenched the gun away from Bowen and hobbled back to Diana.

Clive Bowen motioned to the meteorologist and pointed at the terrorist. "Guard him, Jim. I want to find Baldston's telephone."

A minute later Clive found it, still clutched in the dead aide's hand. He pried it loose and punched the redial, knowing that the number would be the cellular telephone of the Sixth Fleet SDO.

"SDO, this is Captain Bowen. Now listen carefully. We've had a terrorist attack against Admiral Cameron at the bistro. I want a Marine security force dispatched ASAP. The fleet surgeon is here, but we need medical assistance, also. You got that?"

Unaware of what had happened at the port, Captain Bowen listened as the lieutenant briefed him on the situation at the harbor.

"My God, my God," Captain Bowen mumbled as he listened.

Through the front door rushed two Italian policemen, their guns drawn. Clicks of four weapons coming to bear stopped the policemen.

"Don't come in!" yelled Ashworth.

The policemen backed away, their hands up, but pistols

still in them. Their eyes shifted rapidly around the bistro, quickly taking in the magnitude of the situation.

The Americans lowered their weapons slightly when they recognized the intruders as Italian policemen.

One of the policemen shoved his pistol away and ran back outside to the car radio. Shouting, the policeman told headquarters to send every ambulance possible to the bistro and that they needed several squads of attack policemen to seal off the area.

The meteorologist motioned the junior officer to guard the terrorist. He hurried out the door with the other policeman. In Italian the meteorologist described the two terrorists who had escaped. An Italian woman from across the street stumbled down the rough bank in front of the bistro and ran to the policeman, waving a sheet of paper. Screaming, she shoved the paper at them. She had seen the car speeding off and written down its registration number.

Still on the radio, the Italian policeman relayed the information to Italian police headquarters, where it was put on the net. On the autostrada, Italian security forces moved rapidly to establish roadblocks in vain hopes of catching the fleeing murderers.

A white Navy van roared up the gravel road, screeching to a halt outside the bistro. Fully armed United States Marines boiled out of the van, M-16s at the ready—armed and wanting someone to fight.

The gunnery sergeant raced inside the bistro, his nine-millimeter Navy Colt drawn. Seeing Colonel Ashworth sitting on the floor cradling his wife, the gunny ran down the several steps to the Marine Corps officer.

"Colonel. I—" the gunnery sergeant started, then stopped.

Ashworth looked up. "Gunny Cohen, secure the site. Don't let any son of a bitch in until told to do so."

"Yes, sir!"

The gunnery sergeant saluted. At his command, five of the eight Marines took outside strategic positions around the bistro while the gunnery sergeant and two others established a security post at the entrance to the bistro.

Captain Bowen moved from person to wounded person, trying to memorize the number of dead and their names, and the same for the wounded. Dr. Jacobs leaned over the admiral to apply a pressure bandage, made of cloth napkins, to the wounds on the admiral's back.

"How's the admiral?" Captain Bowen asked the doctor.

"He's alive. Unconscious, but alive. Minor wounds, I think. Won't know how dangerous until we open them up. Hopefully, nowhere near the spine. Clive, we need to take him back to the ship where I can operate."

"Can't do it, Doc. A suicide bomber has hit the ship. Both it and the *Simon Lake* are stern down in Gaeta Harbor."

"Oh, my god! What is going on?"

"I don't know, but I do know that someone is going to pay for this and they're going to pay dearly," he said, his teeth clenched. Then he asked, "The admiral's wife?"

The doctor shook his head. Beneath his hand a moan escaped from the admiral. "Didn't make it, Clive." He shook his head. "Didn't make it."

Clive looked at Susan, who minutes before had clasped her husband's hand beneath the table. A neat hole drilled the side of her head. He did not want to lift it to see where it exited. The pool of blood on the table told the story.

"Colonel!" shouted Gunny Cohen. "Ambulances and police are arriving."

"We need to carry the admiral to the hospital, Clive," Dr. Jacobs said.

The chief of staff nodded. He crawled across the top

of the table to Colonel Ashworth, who was nestling Diana's head in his lap.

"Walt, we have to start moving the wounded to the hospital. Starting with the admiral," Clive said, deferring to the senior marine at the scene even though, technically, Clive was the senior officer present . . . or, at least, the senior officer conscious.

"How is Admiral Cameron?"

"He's alive, but unconscious. Wounded, but won't know how serious until Doc Jacobs can get him to the hospital."

Walt nodded and looked around the room until he spotted Gunny Sergeant Cohen coming in the door.

"Gunny Sergeant, let the Italian medical personnel inside!" barked Ashworth. Walt's eyes trailed off to the terrorist being guarded by the junior officer.

Clive saw the Marine's trigger finger tighten.

"Don't, Walt. He's our only lead on who did this."

The gunny saluted, drawing Walt's attention away from the wounded terrorist.

The Marines moved aside as Italian medical personnel and ambulance attendants scrambled inside. The Italian medical teams administered first aid, even as they marked priorities for the ambulance trips. The admiral was first out the door, accompanied by two armed Marines.

"Gunny!" shouted Colonel Ashworth. "Go with them. I'll handle the situation here. You protect the admiral!"

"Aye, aye, sir!" The gunny raced through the door and leaped toward the back of the ambulance as it gunned away from the bistro.

Bowen watched the commander of the United States Sixth Fleet disappear down the road in the ambulance with the gunnery sergeant being pulled inside by the other two Marines. He turned back to the bistro. The police came out with the terrorist Taradin strapped to a stretcher. They tossed him roughly into the back of a police van and drove off. Clive noticed that no medical personnel accompanied the wounded terrorist.

He took a deep breath, thanking God that his wife and family had chosen this month to visit her parents in Frederick, Maryland.

A Marine sergeant ran over to Captain Bowen. "Captain, there's been an attack against Admiral Phrang near Naples."

"Casualties?"

"Don't know, sir. The watch just reported that his car was bombed. There have been some deaths."

"Try to get more information. I need to know whether he was injured or not. He's the senior Navy officer in Europe, Sergeant. If he's dead, then . . . I don't need to tell you."

"Aye, aye, Captain," the Marine responded, wondering briefly what it was the Navy captain didn't need to tell him. He snapped a salute and ran outside to where a radio had been set up. Damn swabbies. Where would they be if it weren't for the Marines taking care of them?

Clive looked back through the doorway at the carnage inside. Tonight marked the beginning of a long time. He moved around the table, talking to the survivors, assuring the wounded as they waited their turn for the ambulance. Tears trickled down his cheeks. He wept unabashedly.

FOUR

"LADIES AND GENTLEMEN, THE PRESIDENT OF THE UNITED States."

The twelve men and two women seated at the long mahogany conference table in the White House briefing room stood as President Garrett Crawford entered. His long strides took him quickly to the head of the table. President Crawford was aware of his fast pace. Everywhere he went, he walked too fast. Only his wife ever asked him to slow down. When he consciously thought of his pace, a mental image of a scared rabbit looking for a hole to hide in came to mind.

"Sit down, please," he said, the familiar friendly smile embracing everyone. He tapped the side of his nose, satisfied the Band-Aid was not flapping loose. Next week, it was back to Bethesda again to look at the spots on his back.

The president's national security advisor, Franco Donelli, marched behind, in Crawford's shadow, out of breath from having run up three flights of stairs with the president, who was able to talk and breathe at the same time! Donelli checked the pocket notebook clutched in his right hand. Still there. The notorious black book, the Bible of the administration, was tucked tightly under his left arm. The president would want it later.

President Crawford sat down between the secretary of state and the secretary of defense, shaking hands and mumbling greetings to both. Franco pulled up a chair beside the secretary of state, slightly back, but between the secretary and the president. In position so he could cue the president. He arranged the pocket notebook and the black book on the table in front of him.

Bob Gilfort, the aging secretary of state, looked at Donelli and, smiling, whispered, "Franco, when you going to give up and start taking the elevator like the rest of us?"

Franco nodded and continued breathing deeply.

"Morning, Bob, morning, Roger," Crawford said to the two secretaries. "Hasn't been a good night for either of you, I bet."

"No, Mr. President," they responded.

"Where's the DCI?" asked President Crawford, craning his head slightly, searching the table.

"The director of Central Intelligence phoned this time, Mr. President. He is stuck in traffic on the beltway. Traffic accident on Sixty-six. He should be here anytime, sir," said Roger Maddock, the secretary of defense, looking at his watch.

"Well, I see you made it from Fort Meade on time, General Stanhope," the president said to the director of the National Security Agency.

"Yes, sir, Mr. President. Sometimes it's easier to make fifty miles from Fort Meade than ten from Falls Church." The DIRNSA's smile pushed his wide ears farther out. The NSA civilians joked that he looked like a taxi coming down the road with its doors open, hence the nickname "Taxi," which he had heard, though no one had been able (or willing) to explain to him how it had come about or what it meant. Nicknames to military professionals were badges given by their comrades in arms; the level of prestige to a nickname was determined by how it was earned and what it meant.

The door opened and the minuscule director of Central Intelligence burst into the room.

"Sorry, Mr. President. I got caught in the early morning beltway gridlock," he said, his alto voice rising a couple of octaves. Farbros Digby-Jones nodded to everyone around the table, a forced smile on his face. His disheveled appearance made him look as if he had slept in his suit. With papers held loosely under his left arm, he scrambled to his seat. Everyone expected the papers to fall any moment.

"Sit down, Farbros," the president said sharply. "If you're ever on time, I'll know it'll be because I'm late."

"Oh, no, sir, Mr. President. Never that, sir." He dropped the papers on the table and shoved his heavy black-rimmed glasses back onto his narrow nose as his small frame disappeared into the plush leather chair. The president thought of them as "chastity glasses." If you wore them, you didn't have to worry about getting laid.

The president recalled a discussion a year ago with the first lady about Farbros Digby-Jones, recognized budget weenie wizard and pork barrel slasher, being put in charge of this nation's intelligence apparatus. That was before she withdrew. He missed her quick, on-the-mark analyses. Nearly a year ago while lying in bed, sharing a bottle of wine, they privately decided that Farbros won the prize as the worst selection of his administration. Of course, they admitted, it was Digby-Jones who found the funds to push through Crawford's health plan. And that nationwide health plan got him elected to a second term. The graying of America voted for comfort, which was the reason he quit dying his hair and let the strands of gray slowly speckle his sandy brown stock of hair. That being said, he and his wife decided they learned one thing from hiring Farbros and that was never hire a man with a hyphenated name. God, he missed his wife beside him.

Crawford shuffled through the briefing material in front of him while everyone waited quietly for him to signal the briefing to begin. Even as he shuffled and recognized the papers as ones he had seen earlier during breakfast, his mind wandered to the two objectives for this second term. One, to mark a place in the history books for his administration, and two, to hold the spot for his party in the next election. He glanced at the black notebook in front of Franco. Last night's polls showed a high approval rating of forty-seven percent. If he could maintain that, plus or minus five percent, his party would sweep into the White House two years from now. Even if his less competent vice president followed him, Garrett Crawford would receive credit for the victory.

"I know, Farbros, I know," said the president, bringing his thoughts back to the table.

A female Air Force lieutenant colonel stood at the far end of the table beside a large screen. The military services alternated weekly the dubious honor of doing the intelligence briefings for the president. Most mornings, Crawford read the intelligence notes sent up from the basement while he sipped his two allowed cups of coffee and shoveled lightly buttered oatmeal around a bowl with his spoon. Last night's events remained unclear. He touched the Band-Aid again. Maybe not unclear, he thought. What he needed was facts. Once arranged in his mind, orderly and chronologically, things would become clearer and clues to the relationships between the events, as always, would pop up and reveal themselves. His innate ability to discover hidden agendas and see the big picture was more than acute political skill. Until he was clear about what was happening the anxiety bubbling around his emotions would never disappear. He may not be one to call an emergency session of the National Security Council lightly, but . . .

"Go ahead, Colonel," said the president.

"Good morning, Mr. President, ladies and gentlemen, General Stanhope. I am Lieutenant Colonel Frasier-Allen, your briefer for this morning."

Shit, the president thought, *another hyphenated name.*

A picture of Algeria flashed on the screen, showing Algiers and Mers El Kebir highlighted with "campfire" symbols.

"Last night rebel forces completed the capture of Algiers and demanded the few remaining loyal government units to return to their garrisons or face execution. Few have accepted the offer. Government forces still retain control of western Algeria from here to the city of Oran." Her laser pointer highlighted the largest city in the western portion of Algeria. "The rebels control all of eastern Algeria." The red laser beam moved across the map.

"Initially President Alneuf directed government forces to return to their garrisons. We think he believed this would defuse the situation. Instead, where government forces obeyed the orders and returned, Islamic fundamentalists overran them, scoring easy victories. The casualty figures are staggering. The rebels are rapidly occupying the cities and already control most of the countryside. In western Algeria, where loyal military units continue to fight, we are seeing slow retreats mixed with some units holding stubbornly to strategic defensive positions."

An overhead image of Algiers flashed onto the screen. "This is Algiers, Mr. President. The American Embassy, located here, is twelve blocks from the harbor. Early morning imagery shows armored personnel carriers and soldiers of the Algerian Liberation Front taking positions around Embassy Row. According to the DATT, the main concentration of insurgents is around the American Embassy. Initial assessment by DIA is that the Islamic rebels intend to restrict access to the embassies by Algerian citizens. The American, French, British, Italian, and Spanish Embassies are surrounded, but with the exception of sporadic gunfire in the vicinity, there have been no overt hostilities against the embassies or their personnel."

"The DATT, our defense attaché in Algiers, Colonel Markum, earlier today met with rebel leaders at the main gate to the American Embassy compound. He was told the insurgents' presence was to protect the Westerners from the ire of the Algerian people as they throw off the yoke of their oppressors. The utilities, water and—"

"Tell me more about this meeting. Did the colonel express our concerns to the Algerian rebels? Colonel, the last thing we want is another Tehran," the president interrupted. Heads nodded in agreement around the table.

"Well, sir," she said hesitantly. "Colonel Markum strongly protested their presence and expressed in the vernacular his doubts as to their intentions."

The president looked at Franco Donelli. "Franco, let's ask the embassy to give us a statement on that meeting. Let's show that we have some semblance of dialogue with the rebels."

"He said, 'Bullshit,' " Roger Maddock added, testily.

"He said what?" President Crawford asked. Large bushy

half-inch-wide eyebrows, by which the president was caricatured in political cartoons, rose upward in surprise over his wide eyes.

"Bullshit."

The president thought for a few seconds. Then his head bobbed several times. "Why couldn't he have said something such as 'Nuts,' like that general in World War II?" He tapped the Band-Aid on his nose.

"Yes, sir, he probably would have, if he had thought about it, but what he said was 'Bullshit.' "

The president grinned. "Well, Franco, can we release this to the press? What do you think they'll say when they hear that a lone United States Army colonel, standing at the door of the American Embassy, surrounded by angry rebels aiming guns at him, replied, 'Bullshit'? I think the American public will love it!"

"They'd react like you did, sir. They will love it. But, you shouldn't be the one to release it."

"Plus, Mr. President," Roger Maddock added, "he had thirty Marines, armed to the teeth, standing behind him."

"That would give me the confidence to say 'Bullshit,' " General Stanhope said, unbuttoning his Air Force dress uniform tunic.

Roger Maddock smiled. "Me, too."

"Okay, work it out with Roger and Bob, Franco."

The president turned to his secretary of state. "Bob, what does the ambassador have to say about the events in Algeria?"

"I talked with her earlier this morning. Her comments agree with the briefer's. The only addition is she believes the insurgents are preparing for a variation of the debacle we had in Tehran in 1979. She doesn't think they'll occupy the embassy, but she doesn't believe their claim of being there to protect them. She has initiated the phone tree, requesting American citizens remain in their homes until the situation clarifies itself. Other than the contact between Colonel Markum and the rebel force commanders, there has been no other communication. She says that it's a standoff between thirty Marines against several hundred rebels."

"Sounds like a mismatch to me if there's only several hundred rebels," General Stanhope said softly, drawing chuckles from the table.

Bob Gilfort, secretary of state, pushed his bifocals back on his nose and continued, "Ambassador Becroft said the embassy still has electricity and water service, but she has ordered the generator topped off in the event they have to make their own electrical power. The embassy has a well, though we don't know if the water is potable. She is having the water checked. Sewage control is her major concern if, or when, we bring our citizens to the compound. They can sterilize the water, they can make electricity, but for sanitation all they have are three portable chemical potties. The utility of the potties is directly tied to the number of people using them."

"What preparations for evacuating American citizens has she done?"

"She does have a plan," the secretary of state responded. His voice tapered off as something on the screen attracted his attention.

The president waited a few seconds for the secretary of state to continue. "Well, Bob. Would you like to tell me what it is?"

"Oh, sorry, sir. In the event that we have to do a noncombatant evacuation operation—a NEO—she intends to use the embassy grounds as a helicopter-landing zone with the evacuees rendezvousing at the embassy for processing. There are twelve hundred forty-seven American citizens in

Algeria, with most located in the major cities along the coast. Those not in Algiers are to be evacuated by sea. The oil company personnel in the south will be a problem. We may have to fly them out through a sub-Saharan route."

The president turned to the secretary of defense. "Roger, what do we have militarily in the area to go in and bring them out?"

"Sir, the *Nassau* amphibious task force is off Tunisia, providing air protection for a destroyer that is conducting a Freedom of Navigation operation along the Libyan coast. With the USS *Nassau* are the amphibious ships *Nashville* and *Trenton;* the cruiser *Yorktown;* and destroyers *Spruance, Hayler,* and *Gearing.* The arsenal ship *King* and the submarines *Albany* and *Miami* are also in the battle group. The USS *Gearing* is the one conducting the Freedom of Navigation operation off the Libyan coast. USS *Albany* is in the port of Gaeta, helping in the aftermath there."

"I want to discuss more about what happened in Italy last night, Roger."

"Sir, we can break off the Freedom of Navigation operation and have *Gearing* rendezvous with *Nassau.* We can order the *Nassau* to take position over the horizon from Algiers. Then, if we need a visible presence we can send a ship or two within sight of the shore. Doing this puts an evacuation force in place. As for the *Albany,* I recommend we leave her in Gaeta for the time being."

"Okay, do it," ordered the president.

"Yes, sir." The secretary of defense motioned to a nearby Army colonel who had been sitting quietly behind him. Roger whispered the necessary instructions to his assistant, who quickly left the room to start the redeployment of forces. His first call would be to the vice-chairman of the Joint Chiefs of Staff.

"Colonel," the president said to the briefer, "can we shift to the events in Italy?"

"Yes, sir, Mr. President. There are a few more slides showing rebel force disposition and a short naval order of battle that reports the disappearance of two Algerian Kilo submarines. We don't know exactly where the two subs have gone and low cloud cover in the area is adversely affecting overhead monitoring of the situation."

"Okay, thanks, Colonel. Let's go to Italy."

Several slides flew by on the screen as the Microsoft PowerPoint operator moved the briefing forward to the bombings in Italy.

"Mr. President, yesterday at approximately sixteen hundred hours eastern standard time a suicide bomber, driving a dark Mercedes, ran the gate at Gaeta, Italy—home port to Commander United States Sixth Fleet. Latest report indicates sixty-eight dead and two hundred sixteen wounded. We do not expect those figures to rise. USS *La Salle,* the Sixth Fleet flagship, and the USS *Simon Lake,* the submarine tender based in La Maddelena, but in Gaeta on a port visit, took the brunt of the explosion. The stern of the USS *La Salle* was blown off and the *Simon Lake* suffered major damage to her left rear side. Ships' crews were in an off-duty status at the time with only duty personnel on board. The USS *Albany* had arrived that morning and was tied up alongside the USS *La Salle*. The *La Salle*'s bulk protected the submarine, which suffered no material or personnel damages. It was her crew who stormed the pier and secured the perimeter."

"Good God," the secretary of energy gasped, looking at the photo on the screen showing two ships down by their sterns and the body bags laid in rows on the pier. She had heard CNN while driving to the summons, but had failed to grasp the full impact. "What is this world coming to?" she asked, not expecting an answer.

"Twenty minutes later, at an officers-only function hosted by Admiral Cameron, a team of five to six terrorists attacked with small arms. Five of Admiral Cameron's staff were killed along with six family members who were attending. Admiral Cameron, Colonel Ashworth, and six others were wounded. The last update, three hours ago, reported the admiral had undergone emergency surgery at the Gaeta Municipal Hospital."

"Italian authorities have one terrorist in custody," Roger Maddock added. "From what we—"

Franco Donelli interrupted. "Mr. President, this is the terrorist I briefed you about on the way up. Seems the press have obtained information that one of the Sixth Fleet officers wrestled a gun from the captured terrorist, routed the attackers, and killed two of them. He then kneecapped the captured one."

"Kneecapped?"

"Yes, sir. He put a bullet into each of the terrorist's knees. He won't ever walk again without a limp. Rumor has it that he would have put a bullet into each elbow, but the Sixth Fleet chief of staff stopped him."

"Good!" the president said. "Should have shot the bastard." His outburst startled everyone at the table. The elderly, overweight secretary of energy patted her ample bosom.

"But don't quote me on that." He nodded at the briefer. "Continue, please."

"Forty-five minutes after the attack at the bistro in Gaeta, a second suicide car bomber rammed Admiral Phrang's staff car when he departed a reception in Naples. The explosion destroyed Admiral Phrang's car along with the trailing security vehicle and the bomber's Mercedes. Admiral Phrang died instantly."

"Mr. President," said Roger, "Admiral Phrang was our senior Navy officer in Europe, and he held two important jobs. He was the commander in chief of United States Naval Forces Europe, the component arm for European Command, and he was the NATO Allied Forces Southern Command, AFSouth."

"How many killed in the Admiral Phrang bombing?" the president asked.

Everyone looked to the briefer. "Next slide, please," she said. On the screen appeared a grainy photograph of a street with smoke rising from the chassis of three vehicles.

"There were no survivors, Mr. President. Admiral Phrang, accompanied by his wife and his aide from a black-tie dinner with fellow NATO flag officers and civilian dignitaries, were killed instantly by the blast. A Navy van, following with a small personal security force of three Marines and an Italian driver, were killed also. A total of six Americans and two Italians died in the attack."

"I am angry," said the president, the blood noticeably rising in his face. "How could this have happened without us knowing?" He looked down the table to where the DCI sat across from the director of the NSA.

"Farbros, how did terrorists mount an operation like this without the intelligence community knowing? It doesn't take a rocket scientist to see that this was a coordinated attack against the top brass of our Navy in Europe. An attack against the United States of America!"

"Mr. President," the DCI stammered, leaning forward so the wings of the chair didn't hide his face. "I can't answer your question, sir. We had no indications of this. None whatsoever. If we had had anything suggesting a terrorist action we would have alerted everyone."

"That's bull, Farbros. I don't believe it. You go back and scrub everything for the past two months and then come back this afternoon and tell me what you found. Nothing like this happens without someone somewhere knowing something."

The president turned his focus to General Stanhope. "General, are you going to tell me NSA didn't have anything either?"

"Sorry, Mr. President. I have the agency scrubbing everything we've seen in the past seventy-two hours for anything that could be related to this attack. If we don't find anything in that time span we'll increase the depth of our search. But, as you know, sir, this is complicated by the fact that it took place on Italian soil." Stanhope mentally patted himself on the back. Intelligence officers learn early in their career never to say "don't know" or "no." Always tell them what you're doing and make it sound good. If you can't blind them with your brilliance, then baffle them with your bullshit.

President Crawford nodded. "Keep me informed, General."

He looked at the secretary of state and the secretary of defense. "Bob, Roger, did the French or Germans have anything? They're usually pretty much on top of the terrorist groups operating in Europe. And how about the British? MI-5?"

"The British are as much in the dark as we are, sir."

"We're having secure communications difficulties with the French and Germans and have had for about week," Bob Gilfort added. "It's on their end and both of them are working the problem. We asked if they had any data that might relate to the Gaeta bombings and both indicated they would review their intelligence sources for anything and get back to us."

The DCI raised his head. "We're having the same problems at the action officer level with the French and Germans."

"That's odd," added Roger Maddock. "Three days ago the French dropped off-line to conduct some upgrades to their communications systems. Said they can receive, but are unable to send anything classified until they finish upgrading their software and complete necessary technical and security checks. The Germans said basically the same thing yesterday."

"So, we have no action officer level contact with our French and German allies at the State, Defense, and Intelligence levels. Bob, do these communications difficulties have anything to do with the political differences we're having with them?"

"I hope not, sir. Politics have had little effect in the past on our intelligence and military relationships. But, for two key allies with a well-known history of collusion to drop all contact—which it seems they have—at the level where desk officers routinely communicate and exchange items of interest is odd," said Gilfort.

"It could be coincidental," said the DCI.

"Or maybe not," said the secretary of defense, looking at the president. "Within ten minutes of Admiral Phrang's car bombing, General Jacques LeBlanc, the new French deputy to Admiral Phrang, announced the immediate assumption of duties as Commander Allied Forces South. I was surprised on the quickness of his announcement. Almost as if the obituary had been written prior to the bombing."

"Let's don't go too far down this road. I don't want to turn this into another conspiracy theory, Roger," the president said. "We've had conspiracy theories for every assassination this century, starting with Kennedy. Let's not have this august body pointed to as the source of the next one."

"Yes, sir, Mr. President, but as you know, the appointment of a French officer as deputy AFSouth was done as a conciliatory action for the French, who had demanded that the AFSouth NATO command be a rotating European officer. General LeBlanc was the first appointee and we were surprised at the quickness of his nomination. The French had been recalcitrant on their position to accept a secondary role under an American officer. Then, with no explanation, about two months ago, the French agreed to the proposal and General LeBlanc arrived within a week."

"What is LeBlanc's background?"

"Infantry officer. Very parochial. Once commanded the famous Foreign Legion. Golden boy of someone with enough influence to move him rapidly up the promotion ladder. Not much combat or field experience, preferring the politics of Paris to the mud of Bosnia and famine of Africa. Where other senior French military officers have a sampling of foreign assignments, he had a one-year tour at Djibouti, followed a few years later with a six-month deployment to Chad. Not much military experience in comparison to other French flag officers, but a heavy background in military intelligence. Though he does have the obligatory tours in Africa, unlike a lot of his peers he did not try to make a career of Africa but actively sought out duty in Paris. Speaks fluent Arabic and English and is well known for his anti-American, pro-European convictions. Appears to have some strong political backing within the government."

The president cupped his hands under his chin. He recalled a briefing last month from the chairman of the Joint Chiefs of Staff that showed if the United States gave up leadership of NATO's AFSouth Command, the United

States Sixth Fleet would come under the control of a French general. It was the issue of Sixth Fleet that generated the rigid American position that the flag officer commanding AFSouth must always be an American.

He looked at his secretary of defense. "Roger, how long before we can replace Admiral Phrang?"

"Sir, we could do it today, but we have to vet our nominee through NATO and NATO is not known for its swiftness. By the time we finish the approval process, it'll be a month at the soonest, three months more likely. On the plus side, the chairman of NATO is British and that will help."

"Meanwhile, we're stuck with a French general who has NATO authority over our Sixth Fleet."

"Technically, when Sixth Fleet is called to service under NATO it is known as Strike Force South. Last night, European Command designated Sixth Fleet as Commander Joint Task Force in response to the worsening situation in Algeria."

"Going to be hard for Admiral Cameron to be a United States Task Force commander if he's dying," Franco Donelli added.

"He's not dying. That's just the press. The truth is, he was wounded, but the wounds are not life threatening. We can always transfer Rear Admiral Pete Devlin, who is Commander, Fleet Air Mediterranean, to Sixth Fleet if Admiral Cameron is unable to resume his duties. Admiral Devlin is in Naples. I'll be able to tell you more later today, Mr. President," Roger offered.

General Stanhope snorted, failing to realize how noise carried in the amphitheaterlike conference room.

The president looked down the table. "You've got something, General?"

"My apologizes, Mr. President," General Stanhope

replied, his face a beet red. "I know this is out of line and not within my purview, but I would recommend you start meeting with the Joint Chiefs of Staff, sir. You've got two attacks against your two most senior naval officers in Europe. Attacks that were obviously coordinated and well executed. You've got Algeria going down the drain. 'The game is afoot,' as Sherlock Holmes would say. What game? None of us know yet, but my initial evaluation, Mr. President, is that you are going to need the military for whatever happens in the Mediterranean theater and your military experts are the Joint Chiefs of Staff."

No one spoke, waiting for the president to comment. After several seconds he turned to Maddock. "Roger? General Stanhope is correct."

"Mr. President, we agreed when I took this job that the JCS would deal through me with you. So far, that has worked fine. I have already scheduled a meeting with them later this afternoon to discuss the situation," Roger said, throwing an angry look at General Stanhope, who smiled and nodded politely to his boss.

Stanhope was retiring within the year anyway. *Screw you, SecDef,* he thought. *The JCS are supposed to work directly for the president; not through a cabinet member.*

"This afternoon! Why not now? Why are we waiting so late to discuss what should be the overriding concern of Defense?" Calm down, President Crawford reminded himself. Control your temper. Remember your blood pressure.

When no answer came, the president continued. "Mr. Donelli, call General Eaglefield and tell him that I want him in the Oval Office in thirty minutes."

"Mr. President, I'll take that action, sir," interrupted the secretary of defense.

'No, Roger, I've told Franco to do this. You're going to be busy because I want you, the DCI, and General Stanhope to tell me why the greatest intelligence apparatus on the face of this earth failed to see this was going to happen." He slammed his fist down on the table. "Christ! I'm the one who has to go before the American people and explain this. I'm going to look the right fool, standing there, licking my lips with nothing to say!"

A red light blinked on the telephone beside the secretary of defense. The president barely stopped himself from answering it.

"Hello," Roger Maddock answered.

Taking his pen from his pocket he scribbled comments from the conversation on a pad of paper in front of him. "Okay. Keep me informed and have the public affairs officer develop a press release for my approval."

"What's going on?" asked the president before Roger Maddock finished hanging up the phone.

"A suicide car bomber tried to run the gate at Patch Barracks in Stuttgart, Germany, about an hour ago. He shot both MPs on the gate, but one lived long enough to give the alarm before she died. Quick reaction by base police cornered the terrorist as he was speeding toward General Sutherland's house. One police vehicle rammed the car while the police in the second leaped out and grabbed the terrorist. The car was packed with explosives. They have roped off the car and bomb experts are working to defuse it. General Sutherland, the commander of European Command and head of NATO military forces, has been relocated along with his family to a secure area."

"I think that confirms my concerns, gentlemen and ladies. The United States is under attack. From whom, it is obvious we don't have the gawldamnest idea, but we're going to find out. Franco, you call General Eaglefield and tell him I want to see him ASAP and bring the entire JCS with him. Roger, on second thought, you had better attend also."

"General Stanhope and Mr. Digby-Jones, crank up your organizations and find out what the hell is going on. I want preliminary assessments by this afternoon."

"Franco, prepare some releases expressing our condolences to the families and saying something along President Reagan's line about 'you can run, but you can't hide.' "

The president turned his attention to the lieutenant colonel at the front of the room. "Is there anything else that you have to make my day, Colonel?" Seeing her jump made Crawford realize how short he must sound. "Sorry, Colonel. I'm not snapping at you." He gave her one of his "we're in this together" smiles and was pleased when he saw it work.

"Yes, sir, Mr. President. I understand perfectly. In answer to your question, sir, I do have an item that is of concern to our Navy analysts. The Joint Chiefs of Staff can explain it better."

"Go ahead."

"We have lost the whereabouts of the Algerian Kilo submarines. They were last photographed in port at Mers El Kebir two days ago, but as of this morning they are unlocated."

"You're right. I probably need a little more explanation as to what that means. Where is Mers El whatever?"

"It is in western Algeria, Mr. President."

General Stanhope cleared his throat. "Mr. President, Admiral Dixon can give you a more in-depth explanation, but we only have two American submarines in the Med. The two Algerian Kilos are diesel, making them quieter, and, with the situation in Algeria, we don't know whether they are loyal to the government or operating for the Algerian Liberation Front. Until we know which side of the fence the two Algerian submarines have come down on, then we have to treat them as hostile threats to our ships."

"Sir," the lieutenant colonel added, "they could also be heading for sanctuary. This morning two Koni-class warships docked in Málaga, Spain, requested asylum, much like what the Albanian Navy did when it sailed to Italy during the civil unrest in 1997. But, if they are heading to sanctuary then they're doing it submerged."

The president stood. "Okay, keep me appraised. I want another meeting with the secretaries of state and defense, the DCI, and DIRNSA this afternoon. Plan a late working lunch and be flexible. I need alternatives, options, and recommendations—pros and cons on all of them. Franco, rearrange my schedule accordingly."

Everyone slid their chairs back and stood.

The president turned to the secretary of defense. "Roger, put our forces on alert against further terrorist attacks. The attacks are focused on admirals and generals, our senior officers, so put armed guards on every flag officer in Europe until we know what the hell is going on." He took several steps. "Better put them on every flag officer above the rank of two stars and every flag officer who is overseas."

He turned to Franco. "Give me the book," he said testily.

Franco handed it to him.

"Let's see what the polls say," President Crawford mumbled as he left the room.

"GENERAL," SAID MR. DIGBY-JONES, "CAN WE HAVE A short, private discussion before we head to our respective agencies?"

The nasal-drip, patronizing tone irritated the crusty general. He motioned the DCI, who also had no military experience, to an isolated area on the far side of the room. The other members of the NSC remained near their seats. Conversation erupted as soon as the door shut behind the president, further isolating the two intelligence leaders.

"General, does NSA have any information on the whereabouts of President Alneuf of Algeria?"

"No, but I can task the agency to search its data to see if we do. Any specific reason?"

"This is kind of sensitive, but we have an agreement with Alneuf that makes it to our benefit to locate him. In fact, it is critical that we locate him."

"Farbros, are you telling me that Alneuf is a CIA agent?"

"Oh, no. Nothing like that! Nothing could be further from the truth. In fact, President Alneuf is not considered friendly to the United States, but we did maneuver a private security arrangement with him. We want to locate him and, if he so desires, help him leave Algeria. I am sure you know how much we can gain by spiriting the disposed president out of Algeria."

"I understand and I'll see what I can do, but you keep NSA out of this goat rope. I've seen what happens when we try to go down that road. Does Pinochet mean anything to you?" And, no, he didn't understand how much it would benefit America to rescue the disposed president of a "gone to shit" country.

"I only want information, General. That doesn't necessarily mean the president would approve an insertion to pull him out."

"Information, Farbros. That's the name of the game—information." General Stanhope paused. "If we hear anything we'll pass it on to you. There are several other items. . . ."

FIVE

"PRESIDENT HAWALI ALNEUF," SAID COLONEL YOSEF, his voice intentionally low. He stepped out of the night shadows of the alley into the faint light so the fleeing Algerian leader could see him. Yosef's thin countenance belied the sculptured muscles beneath his gray military uniform. His gaunt face, on the other hand, betrayed his concern. His hawk nose and pencil-thin mustache were easily visible while the darkness hid his wide weathered brown eyes from view. Yosef worked hard to keep up his image of a professional soldier, though continuously worried that others saw through his disguise. It was a useless worry. As colonel of the Palace Guard he had earned Alneuf's confidence and trust during these five years on the job. His men worshipped and respected him and would gladly follow him into combat, which they were doing now. Small-arms fire echoed from several streets away. The sounds of battle were closing in on the small band. The choice was move, or wait for the inevitable discovery and death.

"The British Embassy is surrounded. We cannot go closer without risking your capture."

The Algerian president slumped back against the wall of the milk crate where Colonel Yosef had unceremoniously shoved him an hour ago. "What now?" he asked.

Shock resonated in the tone of the president's voice. There were no words of encouragement Yosef could give without lying, so he chose to just answer the question.

"Sir, we're going for the harbor. Hopefully, God willing, we'll find a boat to escape from Algiers to Tunisia." Yosef nervously scanned the surrounding buildings and the deserted street.

"Colonel Yosef, do you know anything about boats?"

"No, but the other alternative is less appealing."

"Maybe the Navy still retains possession of the harbor?"

Yosef looked at the president, shrugged. He doubted it. "We don't know, sir. We haven't heard from any of our forces in over four hours. I fear the worst for Algiers." Yosef bit his lower lip.

"What happened, Yosef?" President Alneuf looked up. Colonel Yosef's haggard face, barely visible in the gray darkness of the street, showed the fatigue from the last few days. A tall athletic soldier, his usual crisp uniform was torn and dirty. A crumpled garrison cap, pulled down tight against the forehead, covered the short-cropped hair.

President Alneuf sighed. "How could this happen in such a short time? A week ago we had the rebels on the ropes"—he squeezed his fist together—"like this, we had them in our grip. . . . And today, like criminals, we sneak out of our own country. Our own country!" Alneuf lowered his head onto his knees. "I pray that Allah will have mercy on Algeria."

Yosef gazed for a few seconds at Alneuf. He wished he knew who had ordered the troops to their garrisons. If the

Algerian Army had remained deployed, it would be the FLA running now instead of them. Alneuf seemed to have shrunk in size. "Mr. President, the last signal received reported loyal forces fighting a successful counterattack from Oran. We may still control the western half of the country. If we do retain that control, then we will join them. Your survival means hope for Algeria, Mr. President. With you and those remaining forces, we can restore democracy to our country."

President Alneuf's gray face, depression etched into each wrinkle, disappeared back into the shadows. "I am in your hands, Colonel Yosef," he mumbled.

Colonel Yosef lowered the top of the milk crate and pushed down. The nails slid easily into their original holes. The open sides permitted the warm night air to flow through the cramped crate. If the president had been a large man, he would never have fit in it. The only protection the crate offered was its ability to hide Alneuf's presence.

Yosef motioned the driver of the electric milk truck forward. The vehicle moved off, the quiet hum from the battery-powered engine lost in the sounds of nearby gunfire.

A half block in front, two Palace Guardsmen darted from doorway to doorway along the dark street, avoiding the few remaining streetlights. It amazed Yosef the electricity was still working. If he had been in charge of the revolution his first target would have been the power plant. You shut down a city's infrastructure and you own it. Even so, not a light shined from the gray windows mourning the battle-scarred street.

A mile away a series of explosions lit up the night behind them, the sound roaring by a second later.

"They've started the assault against the presidential palace," Yosef said to Sergeant Boutrous, walking beside him. "I hope they are gone." Yosef referred to the forty

Palace Guardsmen who had volunteered to remain behind and delay the FLA terrorists. Yosef had issued strict orders to the young captain to abandon the palace an hour after Yosef left with the president. He looked at his watch—sixty-eight minutes. More time than he'd expected. Hopefully, an empty palace greeted the rebels.

"I am sure they are safely away, *mon colonel,*" the squat, square-shouldered sergeant replied. "Besides, you know how the captain is. He would never disobey your orders."

Yosef turned his attention forward as he walked alongside the milk truck. Another hour, he estimated, before the search of the palace revealed that President Alneuf had escaped. By then, they should be at the harbor before rebels swarmed through the city, searching for the first and last freely elected leader of Algeria. The capture of President Alneuf would mark the end of the battle for Algeria. The country would descend into the same religious nightmare running rampant in Iran and Egypt.

The Guardsman at the point of the column waved his hand, pointing emphatically to the left.

"Quick, turn the truck in here!" Yosef ordered, pointing to a narrow dead-end alley to the right.

He motioned the Guardsmen to take cover. Once everyone was out of sight, Yosef took position near the milk truck.

Ahead, two armored personnel carriers, with rebels on top, sped across the road to disappear in the direction of the embassies.

The point man ran out and peered around the corner of the building. A couple of minutes passed before he pumped a raised fist several times, signaling all clear.

"Let's go," Yosef said, glancing up and down the street to make sure it was empty.

The vehicle backed quietly into the road and the column continued its march toward the harbor. Yosef tapped his chin. About three more miles to the warehouses that lined the west side of the port area. Months ago, when the government renewed its offensive against growing terrorism, Yosef had developed several scenarios around sprinting the president to safety. They were just planning exercises in the privacy of his room. More to ensure his survival and escape, as he had been ordered to do when he accepted this mission, than for the president. Good thing he never submitted them. They would have found their way into rebel hands and, by now, they would either be dead or prisoners. The milk truck had been a pleasant discovery after exiting their underground escape route from the palace. Yosef didn't know how long the batteries would last, but it wasn't much further to the harbor. It was just dangerous.

Yosef knew his life was worthless if caught. They would shoot him and the Guardsmen. Him, for being an officer, and them, for being members of the infamous Palace Guards.

President Hawali Alneuf, if captured, would remain alive only long enough to quell fighting by government forces; then, once the country was firmly in the hands of the rebels, his life would be forfeited also. Quietly, to disappear in some far region of Algeria—the Sahara was a big wasteland that had swallowed thousands without trace. He touched the pistol strapped to his side. No, Alneuf would not fall into FLA hands.

Ten minutes later the point guard raised his hand again. "Stop the vehicle, Omar," said Yosef to the corporal driving.

The Guardsman motioned Colonel Yosef forward. Yosef ran down the street, where the man crouched at a corner behind a telephone junction box installed flush against the side of the building.

"What is it?" he whispered.

The Guardsman pointed up the connecting street to where a large opened-back military truck was parked. Surrounding the truck were rebels, herding civilians into the back of it. Arguing and crying could be heard coming from the captives.

"What are they doing?"

"I heard English and French from the civilians, *mon colonel,*" the Guardsman replied.

A rebel shouted, "Search the buildings and see if there are more Westerners hiding there. I count twenty-eight and there are supposed to be thirty-two. Twenty Americans, ten French, and two British. Come here," the voice demanded.

The rebel leader walked over to a male captive. "Where are the others?" he screamed.

"Bloody hell! I don't know," a posh English voice replied.

The rebel leader jammed the barrel of his gun hard against the forehead of the man. "This is the last time I ask. Where are they? There are twenty-eight others here I can ask, so unless you answer, your life is as useless as the two over there." He moved the gun long enough to point to where two bodies lay on top of each other.

A woman in the back of the truck spoke up, her voice shaken. "I'll tell you. Don't kill him, he doesn't know, he's English and the missing are Americans."

"Veronica, don't," the Brit said.

Two rebels leaped onto the truck bed, pulled the American woman to the tailgate, and shoved her off. She threw her hands out as she landed hard on her knees in front of the rebel leader. A cry escaped as she toppled sideways, her knees and hands torn and bleeding.

The leader, lips curled, moved the barrel of his pistol to the Englishman's chest and pushed him roughly away. The British captive stumbled and fell, whereupon the rebels began kicking the older man as he struggled to his feet. Like a ball tossed between a circle of players, they herded him toward the tailgate where eager hands of the captives in the bed of the truck pulled the old man on board. The Englishman's eyes searched for the American woman.

"Oh, Veronica," he said, tears leaking from the corners of his eyes.

She looked up from where she crouched on all fours. Their eyes met and she mouthed, "Michael, I—" A nearby rebel kicked her hard in the stomach and her breath whooshed out; he continued to kick her, but less violently, giving the American time to regain her breath.

Yosef pulled his pistol. He tapped the Guardsman twice on the shoulder and put his mouth near the man's ear. "Go bring up everyone but Corporal Omar and two others. Tell the corporal to stay with the president."

The Guardsman nodded and took off running.

Yosef motioned to the point man on the right side of the road.

"Where are they, woman?" the rebel shouted.

Veronica tried to stand, but a rebel behind her put his foot on her back and shoved her roughly back down onto the cobblestones.

"The Americans left here over an hour ago," she said, her voice wavering in fright. Looking up, expecting to be hit again, she eased off her knees. "They got restless and struck out on their own. They were oil riggers, drunks, and we were glad to see them go." She reached up and wiped the blood from her lips.

The sound of flesh on flesh reached Yosef as the rebel leader leaned over and slapped her. The slap knocked the woman flat onto the street. "Don't lie to me, infidel! No one has left the premises since this afternoon. You don't think we have been watching? You think that the Algerian people are your friends? You are a stupid bitch."

"Don't hit me," she screamed. "I'm an American!"

"I'm not going to hit you, you American bitch," he snarled. He grabbed her hair, pulling her head up off the street.

Unexpectedly, she reached up and, with a wild scream, pulled her sharp fingernails down both his cheeks, ripping the skin down both sides, drawing blood.

The rebel leader punched her, knocking her head down against the road. With a quick motion he rammed his pistol against her head, drawing a groan from his hostage, and pulled the trigger. "You Americans disgust me." The shot echoed off the silent buildings, mingling with the cascade of distant gunshots and explosions. The civilians in the truck began a renewed round of screaming and crying. The rebel leader pulled his scarf out and wiped his cheeks. "Damn, bitch!" he said, seeing blood on the cloth. He fired two more shots into her back.

He swung the gun toward the captives. "Shut up! Or I will personally kill every one of you!" he screamed, his face contorted in anger. Two of the hostages held the British gentleman by the arms as he fought to go to the side of his dead American lover.

The Guardsmen from the milk truck ran silently up to Colonel Yosef. Counting the colonel, there were ten of them. Omar and the two staying behind made thirteen—not much for an offensive operation.

"We need to get across the intersection without them seeing us," Yosef said to Sergeant Boutrous.

Another shot came from the direction of the truck. The

screaming of the captives took on a new intensity. The berserk FLA commander had killed again.

"Sir, they are killing the hostages," the point man said, pointing toward the truck.

"I know, but if we stop to help, then we compromise our position."

"Yes, sir, but if we don't, then the FLA will massacre those people. People we could save."

Yosef looked toward the scene again. The FLA commander continued to scream and while Yosef watched, he pointed his pistol into the crowded bed and fired again. Yosef took a deep breath.

"Okay. For all the wrong reasons we are going to engage this force. I counted twelve rebels. The Westerners are on the truck. We are going to go in, do the job, and get the hell out of here as soon as we can."

"They'll kill us before we're halfway to them," a Guardsman standing beside the point man added.

"No, they won't. They'll think we're fellow revolutionaries. Just follow me and act like you're FLA."

"What about President Alneuf?"

Yosef looked back at the milk truck. "I know. I thought about it, but Corporal Ghatan is right. If we do nothing, they'll kill the hostages. President Alneuf will be okay for the few minutes we need." He started to move forward, then turned and spoke. "If something goes wrong, all of you get back here and get him away. Sergeant Boutrous, take four and flank me."

Yosef straightened and began marching confidently up the left side of the street, his head held high. His men glanced at each other, shrugged their shoulders, and then spread out on both sides as they nervously followed the colonel. Sergeant Boutrous paralleled Yosef on the other side. When they were fifty yards away, the rebels saw them and raised their weapons.

"My brothers," Yosef shouted, "to whom am I speaking?" He hoped his voice sounded stronger than he felt.

"Who are you?" the rebel leader shouted, moving cautiously to the front of the vehicle.

"I am Colonel Safir. What is going on here and who are you?" Colonel Safir was a senior officer in the Algerian Liberation Front.

Hearing the name, the FLA commander stepped in front of the truck and saluted. "I am Kafid. Kafid of Altamira," the rebel leader replied, identifying himself with a small farming village southwest of Algiers where two years ago the FLA killed and dismembered every one of the three hundred inhabitants—women, children, and babies included.

One of the worse acts of terrorism that Yosef had ever witnessed. His hand unbuttoned the holster as he remembered walking between two rows of heads impaled on stakes, lining the one dirt street that ran through the middle of the village.

"We are rounding up infidels—the Westerners." Kafid patted his bleeding cheeks again with the scarf. "Damn bitch," he mumbled, glancing at the blood on the scarf. Kafid noticed the Algerian Army uniforms, but many of the rebels were members of the Algerian Army.

The Guardsmen closed the gap. Yosef hoped his men could control their anxiety until he gave the signal.

"I had not heard that we were going to round up the Westerners. What are you going to do? Shoot them like you did this woman and those two? And how many have you killed in the back of the truck?" Control your anger, Yosef said to himself.

"She was an infidel, and a woman," Kafid said. He spit

on the street. "She interrupted men talking, she was too old to bear children." He laughed. "She was too ugly to copulate with and she was an American." He held the bloodied scarf for Yosef to see. "What more excuse do I need? See what she did! She attacked me. Yes, Colonel, I am going to kill them—every one of them. Kill them all as a warning to the West."

Behind Kafid the rebels bunched together, shouting chaotically in agreement. Their weapons were held at their sides.

"Kafid, you hear the sound of fighting coming from over there? That's our force capturing the Algerian traitor Alneuf. By tomorrow, Algeria will be ours. *Allah Alakbar!*"

Kafid and the rebels raised their guns above their heads and fired into the air as they shouted, *"Allah Alakbar!"*

Yosef pulled his pistol and fired. The shot blew a quarter-inch hole in Kafid's forehead and took the back of the head off as it exited, spraying red and gray matter over the rebels around him. The bullet knocked the dead terrorist backward into two rebels standing behind him, knocking them down. A dying twitch caused Kafid's gun to go off. The bullet nearly hit Yosef; he felt the wind and the heat as it passed by his left ear. Gunfire erupted as Guardsmen fired into the packed group of rebels while on the truck the captives' screams and cries grew in intensity. Yosef calmly stepped forward and shot the two rebels wriggling free from beneath Kafid's body. He leaped over the dead and dying to reach the back of the truck. A rebel appeared around the tail at the same time as Yosef. Yosef ducked back and shot him. On the other side of the truck, Sergeant Boutrous stepped around the edge of the tail and shot another rebel. The shooting stopped. The entire action took less than twelve seconds.

Yosef peeped around the tail edge and looked up at the

packed truck. The burly Bedouin sergeant did the same from his side. Seeing the two faces, the captives shoved and pushed each other as they fought to get as far into the military vehicle as possible.

"You're safe!" Yosef shouted in English and then in French. He stepped around the edge and faced the Westerners.

"We are Algerian soldiers. Who is in charge here?" When no one answered, he continued. "Okay, if no one is in charge, who knows how to drive this vehicle?"

Michael, the British man beaten a few minutes ago, edged forward, dabbing blood from the top of his head, the red easily discernible in the white hair. "At the risk of volunteering again, I do. I was in the Sixteenth Lancers years ago, before the bloody Tories did away with the regiment. I suspect I can acquaint myself quickly, considering the alternatives," he said in a shaken voice. Tears made his eyes shiny.

"Then I guess you are in charge. Please listen, everyone. Algiers is gone. I cannot tell you what to do, but we are unable to stay and provide protection. Unfortunately, you are on your own. The embassies are surrounded and there is fighting to the west. Eastern Algeria has already fallen." Yosef shook his head. A fat lot of good that did! He had rescued them; they were alive; but he could offer no hope. Still, they had a better opportunity to survive than they had two minutes ago. He had his own concern and that concern was hiding in a milk crate on a damn slow milk truck and he still had three miles to go. Yosef motioned to his men and turned to leave.

The British gentleman eased himself down from the back of the truck and took several steps to where the body of the American woman named Veronica rested. He lifted her body gently, getting blood on his suit coat, and kissed her cheek before carrying her to the back of the truck. Two of the men in back helped lay her body in the center of the truck bed.

"You can't leave us!" cried one of the women.

She moved forward, clutching a baby to her breast while her other hand gripped tightly the small hand of a young child. In the dark, Yosef could not tell if the toddler was a boy or girl. They reminded him of his wife and children killed in a market bombing nearly ten years ago. He'd never forget. That bombing shattered his life, leading him to where he was tonight. When this was over, if he escaped, he would return to their graves and sit among the rocks and olive trees. . . .

Yosef realized he was staring at the woman.

"I'm sorry," Yosef stammered, followed with a cough to clear the lump in his throat. "Leaving you is not something we want to do, but what you see here is all that remains of free government forces in Algiers. We can't help you. I'm sorry."

"What are we to do?"

"You could try to get through the lines to one of the Western embassies. I don't think the rebels will bother you if you can get in sight of them. It's one thing to kill with no witnesses. The last thing they'll want is to give your countries a reason to intervene. No, you'll be safe if you reach Embassy Row."

"Come on, sir," Yosef said. Two Palace Guards gently turned the British veteran toward the cab of the truck.

"Are you okay, sir?" Yosef asked softly.

"Yes, quite okay, now." He looked at Yosef. "She was a good woman, you know."

Yosef nodded. He took the gentleman by the elbow and handed him off to a nearby Guardsman, who escorted the Englishman to the driver's door. The keys were in the ignition. Yosef's small force spread out. Yosef raised his hand and made a circling motion with his finger. Other Guardsmen hurried back to the intersection where they could guard the milk truck and watch the Westerners at the same time.

The truck roared to life.

The driver saluted Yosef. "Good luck, Colonel."

"Good luck to you, also."

The truck lurched forward, gears grinding to the driver's unfamiliarity with the Russian vehicle's loose clutch and tight transmission. Yosef and the remaining Guardsmen walked behind the truck until it picked up speed and passed through the intersection. The two point Guardsmen turned toward the harbor while the others took up positions around the milk truck.

MOHAMMED STEPPED FROM THE DOORWAY. HE HAD been inside the building, searching for Westerners when the shooting started. By the time he raced down three flights of stairs the fighting was over. Mohammed watched from this vantage point until the Palace Guard and the milk truck passed through the intersection. He gave them several minutes before he eased out of his hiding place.

He walked among the dead, checking to see if any were still alive. He prodded each comrade's body with his combat boot. Finally, he came to Kafid. Kafid had a nice hole through the forehead. No major loss to the revolution, Mohammed thought. Better that Kafid died at the hands of the enemy than having a comrade like him kill him. Mohammed spit on Kafid's body and then kicked it hard several times.

"See the dead, Kafid. If you had not been blinded by your own evil they would be alive." He kicked the body again and then turned, leaving the carnage behind him.

Mohammed walked quickly and carefully to the intersection and peered around the corner. He caught a glimpse of the milk truck vanishing into the darkness. It was headed toward the harbor. That was where this street ended. Mohammed ran across the intersection in the same direction of the truck full of Westerners.

AN HOUR LATER THE MILK TRUCK STOPPED. IT COULD go no farther. A chain-link fence topped with rolls of razor-sharp barbwire ran along the perimeter of the harbor. Two Guardsmen finished cutting a hole in the fence.

"Ah, that feels good," said Alneuf as Yosef helped him out of the milk crate. Alneuf stretched. He lifted first one leg and then the other. "Can you hear the bones creak?"

Yosef shook his head.

"No, you're right. Only the owner of old bones hears their complaints."

The Guardsmen forced their way through the opening. Yosef ripped his shirtsleeve on a sharp edge of the cut fence as he maneuvered himself through the opening. The diminutive Alneuf stepped through easily. The armed group walked between two towering warehouses. Yosef felt hemmed and urged them through the alley quickly until they saw the piers.

Several large merchant ships and a couple of tankers rocked slightly against their lines. Yosef ignored the huge ships. He pointed to the right, toward the private piers two wharves away. If they stood any chance of escaping Algiers, it'd have to be on a yacht or fishing boat or something a bunch of land-weary soldiers could manage. If they turned to him to show them how to run a boat, then they'd be paddling their way out of Algiers. But, first find a boat and then worry about how to operate it. They were soldiers, not sailors, but Yosef knew they were going to have to learn seamanship the hard way.

Two point men raced ahead, leap-frogging from box to crate to crane as they sanitized the area ahead. A hundred yards behind walked Yosef with President Alneuf. The remaining Guardsmen flanked the two men, with two other Guardsmen bringing up the rear.

Ahead, a hand came up. They stopped and quickly took cover behind harbor fixtures and abandoned pallets of crated goods. The go-ahead signal came several seconds later. The group rose and commenced its silent progress once again.

Sergeant Boutrous hurried back to Yosef. "*Mon colonel,* there is a fishing trawler down the next pier with a light on. A very faint light, but I saw someone walking in front of it. They may be preparing the ship to leave."

"Very well, Sergeant Boutrous, take two men and seize the boat." Yosef motioned to the corporal on the left flank even as he gave directions to the sergeant. "Try not to use your weapons, if possible."

The corporal ran across, crouched, and saluted. "Corporal Ghatan, take two of your men and go with Sergeant Boutrous."

Boutrous saluted and ran to the right. Tapping two on the shoulders the three raced ahead, followed by Ghatan and the two other Guardsmen.

"Mr. President," Yosef walked back to the president and said, "I have dispatched a squad to seize a fishing boat that may be preparing for sea. If so, we will board and depart Algiers."

President Alneuf sighed. "Colonel Yosef, maybe my place is here, leading the fight for my country. What will the people think of their president sneaking out of the country, hiding in a milk crate, and now fleeing in a fishing boat? Someone must stay to give them encouragement."

"Mr. President, I understand how you feel. But Algiers is lost and the best place for you to lead the fight is elsewhere and, if you stay here, you will be killed. You can't lead it dead. It is a sad day whenever a patriot runs, but sometimes it is true what they say about retreating so you can fight another day."

"Colonel? You should have been the politician. I don't think the cliché is how you phrased it. I think it is more about running away so you can fight another day."

"I, too, wish we could have fought better. To see our country fall in two days . . ."

"Don't blame yourself, Colonel Yosef. No one saw this coming, nor did we suspect that the FLA was so well organized. We will return. That I promise you. We will regain our country, restore peace, and when we do, we will make sure this doesn't happen again."

They stopped at the end of the cement pier leading to where the fishing boat was tied. The squad leaped aboard the vessel. Two minutes later a Guardsman jumped from the boat to the pier and waved for them to hurry.

"Come on, sir. The boat is ours." Yosef placed a hand under the arm of the aged president, noticing for the first time the long wisps of hair, which Alneuf meticulously combed every day over his bald spot, matted to the side of his head, exposing the man's dark dome.

"Yosef," said President Alneuf, pulling his arm away, "I'm not that old."

"Sorry, sir."

"That's alright. I know you're concerned for my safety—my health. And I am grateful, you know? Without this dash to safety, we would both be greeting Allah at this time. I am thankful my wife did not live to see this."

The fishing nets were grouped along both arms of the trawling equipment. The vessel's square portholes, painted a dark, unrecognizable color in the faint light, stood out against the fading white wooden hull. A small, faint bulb burned near the ship's controls. This was the light that had attracted Sergeant Boutrous's attention.

Belowdecks Yosef heard men talking and was surprised when a woman's soothing voice joined the chatter, trying to quiet the sudden squalling of a baby. He turned to the Guardsman on the pier with a questioning look.

The Guardsman smiled and shrugged.

A chubby middle-aged fisherman, wearing a tattered shirt, crawled up on deck accompanied by two Guardsmen.

Bowing continuously, the fisherman begged, his hands clasped together in front of him. "Please, do not kill me and my family. We are just a poor fisherman's family, trying to stay here in safety until morning."

"This your boat?" Yosef asked.

"No, ya effendi. I work on the boat. I am but a fisherman. . . . And not too good of one, if you listen to my captain." He grinned, showing his teeth as he swabbed the sweat from his brow.

"Then what are you doing here?"

"When . . ." he stuttered, then stopped and tilted his head slightly to the side. "Excuse me, sir, are you Algerian Liberation Front freedom fighters or are you renowned members of loyal government forces?"

"We are soldiers of the Palace Guards."

"Oh, praise be to Allah!" the fisherman cried, beating his chest. "I am a loyal follower of Alneuf and the People's Democratic Party. I have voted for the government in every election since 1997—*sometimes twice.*" He held up two fingers. "I apologize, *mon colonel.* When the fighting started I was afraid for my family and came here to hide until the shooting stopped."

"You mean until the winner was determined," Yosef mumbled. "Stay here!" Turning to President Alneuf, he said, "Sir, we need to get you below."

Alneuf nodded and failed to object this time when two Guardsmen helped him down the ladder to a small table crammed into the center of what passed for a dining space. The fisherman showed no recognition of the Algerian president as the trio passed; his concern focused on Yosef, his own well-being, and his wife and child below.

"Do you know how to drive this thing?" Yosef asked the fisherman.

"Of course," the man replied, acting shocked that anyone would think otherwise. "I am the helmsman whenever we are fishing."

"Can you start her and take us out of here?"

The fisherman looked puzzled. "Why would we want to do that? You are here, in control of the harbor, so we must be winning the battle for Algiers."

"Fisherman, I asked, can you start the engines and take us out of the harbor?"

"But, of course. . . ."

"Then, do it!"

"Yes, sir. Yes, sir," the fisherman replied, hurrying aft. There, he opened the hatch above the engine and crawled down. A minute later, after several outbursts of cursing, followed with intense hammering sounds, the diesel motor coughed twice and then chugged to life. The fisherman climbed out, wiped a greasy hand across his sweating forehead, then tugged the cover over the hatch.

"There! We are cranked." He smiled at Yosef. What he didn't say was that this was the first time he had ever cranked the engine and it was only luck that he stumbled across the on-off switch.

An explosion to the left caused everyone to reflexively take cover and raise their weapons in that direction. Grenades blasted the locked gates of the harbor's main entrance. The smell of cordite rode the summer night winds to whiff across the boat. Two armored personnel carriers burst through the smoldering ruins of the gates. Automatic weapons fire from armed rebels, riding on top, hit the pier in front of the boat.

The two Guardsmen at the top of the pier came running out of the darkness.

"Get this thing underway!" Yosef yelled, shoving the fisherman toward the helm.

Yosef jumped onto the dock and, with two Guardsmen helping, disconnected the four lines keeping the boat tied to the pier. Throwing the lines onto the fishing trawler, they leaped on board.

The two APCs roared onto the top end of the pier. The first turned so fast the left wheels came off the road, tossing a rebel off the top.

Yosef brought his gun up, led the APC slightly, and fired a ground-level burst. The front right tire on the APC blew. The vehicle veered right and crashed through a stack of wooden loading crates, knocking those on top off, before hitting a concrete bullock, driving the engine of the APC into the chest of the driver. Smoke poured from the wreckage. The second APC swerved left to avoid the crash. It squealed to a stop, running over and killing a rebel, who had crawled from the burning APC. Rebels leaped off and started running down the long pier toward the boat, their weapons raking the fishing trawler as they charged.

The fisherman shoved the throttle forward. Hand over hand he whipped the wheel to the left until it locked. The low-power engine didn't do much for Yosef's confidence. Hiding behind barrels and fishing nets on the stern, the outnumbered Guardsmen returned fire against the attacking force. A rebel bullet caught a Guardsman, who clutched his stomach and tumbled into the filthy harbor waters.

Shots peppered the fishing boat, lodging in the wooden hull. A stitch of bullets sped up the bridge, narrowly missing the frightened fisherman, who repeatedly pushed the throttle harder, even though it was as far forward as it would go. He reached over and flipped on the running lights.

"Turn off those lights!" shouted Yosef.

It took two tries for the fisherman's shaking hands to flip the lights off.

The Algerian rebels reached the mooring as the fishing trawler disappeared into the night. Standing on the pier, looking out at the dark silhouette heading out to sea, Mohammed cursed. Five minutes earlier and he'd have caught them.

The rebel leadership believed that President Alneuf was on that boat, escaping out to sea from the capital of the new Algeria. He picked up his mobile phone and dialed Colonel Safir. He cursed. Someone else would have the glory of capturing Alneuf.

SIX

DUNCAN PLACED HIS HAND OVER THE KHAKI UNIFORM cap, tucked under his belt, to keep the helicopter's prop wash from sucking it into the engine intake or blowing it overboard. His seabag bounced off his left leg.

Beau and H. J. trailed as the three ran from under the props of the helicopter. An officer, wearing the hat with the scrambled eggs of a captain, waved them toward the entrance of the forecastle on the amphibious carrier USS *Nassau*. The oily aviation fuel and hot exhausts filled the air.

The captain's lips moved, but noise from the flight deck drowned his words. Duncan pointed to his ears and shook his head. The captain nodded, shook hands briefly with Duncan, and pointed to the nearby hatch. The four ducked as they entered. Inside, the officer pushed the lever down, closing the watertight door, muffling the flight deck noise outside. A master-at-arms, the ship's sheriff, stood nearby with two sailors sporting shaved heads and standing at attention. Brig rats.

"Welcome aboard, Captain James. I'm Dan Carter, the *Nassau*'s executive officer."

"I thought XOs of amphibs were commanders," Duncan replied congenially as they shook hands again.

"They are. I just put it on the first of the month," Carter replied, smiling.

"Congratulations."

"Thanks. The commodore will meet you in the operations conference room. I know you must be tired from your trip over, but the current operations brief starts in a few minutes. The commodore specifically asked that you attend."

Captain Carter looked at H. J. "I'm sorry, I didn't know that a woman was coming. I was told to expect three SEAL officers so I arranged for two of you to share a stateroom and you to have one to yourself, Captain."

"She's a SEAL," interrupted Duncan.

"A SEAL? I didn't know that they had women in the SEALs."

"They've been discussing it for years. Even tried it once before with mixed success, but she's the first one to make the grade. Lieutenant McDaniels will be going on our exercise with the Spanish. Are they on board?"

"Right now they are, but not for much longer. They are being airlifted off this afternoon to Sigonella for further transfer to Spain."

"Why? We're supposed to conduct a joint exercise."

"Events of the past few days have changed that. Spain is very concerned over the Algerian crisis and . . ." he paused, glancing at the brig rats. "Why don't we wait until we're at Operations and then answer any questions you have, Captain."

"Okay, I'll hold them until then. Meanwhile, put Commander Pettigrew and me together in the stateroom, Captain Carter. Lieutenant McDaniels can have the single. That should solve your berthing problem."

"It would make it easier."

Carter turned to the MAA. "Sheriff, have your brig party take their bags to staterooms thirty-six and thirty-seven."

H. J. leaned over Beau's shoulder as they fell in line behind Duncan and the executive officer. "We could have bunked together. It's not like we're children or something," she whispered, miffed over being singled out.

"Let's not suggest it, H. J. Surface Warfare officers seldom have the humor we SEALs do. They don't call them the conservative arm of the Navy for nothing." But, Beau thought, the idea was appealing.

"Come on, Beau. Would I embarrass you?" she smiled, arching her eyebrows.

Beau's face flushed red. He hurried to close the gap between him and Duncan. H. J. shook her head and followed. Men! He was cute . . . in a juvenile way.

Single file they followed the ship's executive officer down a deck to a hatch marked OPS CONFERENCE ROOM. A revolving red light warned everyone that a classified briefing was in progress.

Carter opened the thin aluminum door and led the way into the conference room. A long rectangular table surrounded by green-cushioned government-issue metal chairs filled the small space. Along the starboard bulkhead a small green-topped metal table held the inevitable coffee mess. The glass vial on the forty-cup percolator showed a half-full pot.

Duncan ran his hand over his head. No telling how long since it had been perked. A skinny white-aproned mess man—an eagle with a banner reading *United States Navy* clutched in its beak tattooed on his left forearm—entered through a side door, carrying a large tray of fresh donuts and raisin bread. Hot aromatic clouds rose from the pastries to surround his shaven head before spreading their sweet aroma to offset the metallic scent of the compartment. It was a bleak, no-frills ship's compartment that reflected the harsh reality of the sea. "Make a hole," the mess man broadcasted as he weaved his way to the table near the coffeepot. Hands reached over and around him to grab the fresh pastries even as he raised his elbows in a vain attempt to keep their hands out of the tray.

"Officers," Carter announced, grabbing the attention of those in the room. "This is Captain James, Lieutenant Commander Pettigrew, and Lieutenant McDaniels. They've just arrived on the Sigonella shuttle and will be joining the SpecWar teams on board."

The few nearby shook hands. A lieutenant wearing desert cammies began working his way through the tight room toward them. The mess man exchanged the now half-full tray for the empty one and, shaking his head, griped about ungrateful people of doubtful parentage as he left the crowded compartment.

"Captain James, there's coffee on the cupboard," Carter said. "And donuts for dunking. Help yourself and, with this bunch, if you want donuts you'd better grab them fast. I'll be right back. Oh, nearly forgot, the captain sends his respects and the commodore looks forward to meeting you." Then in a low voice he added, "You won't have to worry about talking too much with the commodore. He'll take care of the conversation."

Grinning at his private joke, Carter left the wardroom. The three weaved their way to where the condiments of the uniform professions—coffee and donuts—waited. From a nearby chair a tall, dark-skinned, mustached man stood and began to work his way toward them as they poured their coffee. He arrived slightly behind the lieutenant in cammies.

"Captain James, I'm Mike Sunney, the OIC of SEAL Team Four. Welcome aboard."

"Mike, I'm glad you're here. Can you maybe tell us what is going on?" Duncan asked. "Seems our exercise has gone tits up and the Spanish are heading home."

"Where's the sugar?" asked Beau to no one in particular.

"Yes, sir. It's 'Tango Uniform,' " he replied, then, noticing the dark-haired mustached officer, introduced him. "Captain, this is Major Jesus Alcontira."

"Captain James?"

"Yes, I am," Duncan replied, eyeing the tabs on the collar of the uniform identifying the officer as a major in the Spanish Army. The uniforms had changed little since Franco's era.

Beau squatted as he riffled through the table drawers. "There has to be sugar here someplace. What kind of coffee mess doesn't have sugar?"

"Sir, I am sorry we will be unable to conduct a joint exercise."

"What going on, Major? I was whisked out of Washington two days ago for this to find out when we landed that it's been called off. Are you the senior officer?"

"Where's the sugar, dammit?"

Major Alcontira pulled a cup from the stack and poured some coffee as he talked. He reached in his shirt pocket and pulled out a pack of sugar and emptied it into his cup. "I am the senior officer. We were looking forward to this chance to work with the U.S. Navy SEALs. I understood we would participate with Lieutenant Sunney and his teams when we were told three specialists were coming to do the exercise with us. I apologize that I was unable to arrange an officer from my country of equivalent rank. Unfortunately, by the time I found out, the exercise had been canceled."

"No problem, Major. I am a little confused. I was led to believe that the reason I was sent was that you had sent a colonel. It's not a big problem, it's just a typical Washington screwup. This is Lieutenant Commander Beau Pettigrew," Duncan said, pointing down at Beau, who was searching the bottom shelf. "Who is slightly taller than he seems."

Beau reached up and shook hands with the major before returning to his sugar search.

"And Lieutenant McDaniels," Duncan continued.

The major's eyes widened. Alcontira pitched the empty sugar pack toward the trashcan; it missed and fluttered down in front of Beau. "A woman?"

"I was the last time I looked, Major." H. J. smiled, sticking her hand out. Their eyes locked for several seconds until the major blinked and looked away. H. J.'s smile grew wider.

"And a very *bonita mujer* at that, Lieutenant," Major Alcontira replied as he grasped H. J.'s outstretched hand with both of his and held it.

"Hey, *por favor,* Jesus, where did you find the sugar?" Beau asked, standing up and waving the empty packet.

"From a European I accept the compliment, Major," H. J. responded in fluent Spanish.

"Ah, you speak Andalucian," he answered, also switching to Spanish, referring to the dialect prominent in southern Spain. He reached in his shirt pocket, and, without taking his eyes off H. J., extracted another sugar packet and handed it to Beau.

"Yes. My father was a career sailor who spent two tours of duty in Rota, Spain. I graduated from the Department of Defense high school there—Admiral Farragut High School—more famous for its parties than its sports programs."

Beau turned the packet over, examining it.

H. J. reluctantly pulled her hand back. Alcontira grinned and bowed his head as he released it.

"Ah, yes, Rota. It is too bad your navy decided it was not worth the small amount it cost. Rota was good for both of us. Before the new millennium we had such a good, strong relationship that centered on your presence in Rota. Our people worked closely with your SEAL team there, the Naval Security Group Activity, and those fearless individuals who flew the four-engine aircraft . . . what did they call them?" He snapped his fingers. "Oh, yes, Orions. They used the Sandeman emblem for their squadron." He smiled, revealing a bright set of teeth. "Oh, well, *mariposita,* we can never go back to the past. It's never the same. You can never go back. One must always move on."

"Jesus, you have any white sugar?" Beau interrupted, holding the unopened packet toward Alcontira.

"Oh, shut up, Beau," said Duncan, pouring himself a second cup of hot, black coffee. "Sugar's bad for your teeth."

"Your father? He is still in the Navy?" Alcontira asked.

"No, he died two years ago in the States."

"I am so sorry." He reached in his other pocket, extracted a packet of white sugar granules, and exchanged them with Beau. He regained eye contact with H. J.

Duncan wondered if the mess specialist had a bucket of cold water in the galley. He guessed he should say something in Spanish so the two would know he spoke the language and was following their conversation. But then, he thought, what the hell!

"I know what it means to lose a father. Mine, too, died

last year. It remains in here," he said, touching his chest. "One never forgets; one learns to live with it."

"Don't be sorry. He enjoyed and had a full life. Took sick one afternoon and was dead by nightfall. He went the way he would have wanted to go. Quick and without a lot of fuss."

"I apologize, Lieutenant, if I seem mesmerized. It is just that in Spain we do not have women in our military and to find one in the United States Navy SEALs is quite . . . how do you say, a shock?" Jesus replied, switching to English.

"It's still a shock to Captain James and Commander Pettigrew," H. J. responded, also in English.

"It is not," said Beau, glancing over his shoulder as he played with his coffee.

"She was going to participate in the exercise," Duncan said.

"I think Captain James believes he's in the hot seat for this one," H. J. said. "In fact, Major, it is I who have to prove myself, as every person who becomes a SEAL must do."

"I understand that you and your team are being airlifted off the *Nassau* this afternoon to return to Spain?" Duncan asked.

"Yes, Captain James," Alcontira replied, reluctantly taking his eyes off H. J. He picked up his coffee and took a small sip. "Unfortunately, with the events in Algeria, my government has asked that we return immediately. The antigovernment riots in Morocco and the unrest in Algeria affect Spain's interests very much."

"I understand, Major. I wish my bosses had told me." Duncan paused a moment. "Major, how long have you known that you were to return to Spain?"

"Two days ago they canceled the exercise and asked for us to return."

"Damn. Sorry, Major. It's just that I was ordered out here two days ago."

"Perhaps they did not know the exercise was canceled."

Duncan took a sip. "Oh, knowing Admiral Hodges, I doubt it."

Captain Carter entered and held the door to the briefing room open for two other captains. "Attention on deck!"

Everyone in the room snapped to attention.

The commodore walked to the head of the table before he responded, "As you were, please. Sit down."

The other captain took the seat to the left as the commodore wiggled his ample bottom into the green armchair at the head of the table.

"That's Captain Ellison, the commodore, at the head of the table. The captain to the left is Captain Farnfield, commanding officer of the *Nassau*. Hope you went to the head before you came in," Mike Sunney whispered.

Everyone sat down to the rustle of shifting chairs, with the exception of several junior officers, who leaned against the bulkhead because of the lack of seats.

"Welcome aboard, Captain James," the commodore said after the noise of seating faded. "I'm Commodore Frank Ellison of Amphibious Squadron Two. Glad to have you aboard." Ellison pulled a decanter over and poured himself a glass of water. "There, that should do it," he said to no one in particular.

Then returning his attention to Duncan, he said, "Captain James, I don't need to tell you that things are a bit hairy in Algiers. I'm glad you're here as there is a significant possibility that we will need you SEALs. When I told Bill Hodges the other day how things were heating up over here he promised us a hotshot captain with evacuation and hostage rescue experience. That's not to say that Mike Sunney is doing a bad job. Far from it. Fine man. Fine young officer, I must say. But, we both know there's no substitute for experience."

Duncan leaned forward. "Commodore, how long ago did you talk with Admiral Hodges?"

"Let me think, Captain. Yes, it would have been Sunday. About four days ago."

"Thank you, Commodore," Duncan replied, leaning back. The next time he saw Bill Hodges he was going to rip the admiral's lips off. "We've been in transit since day before yesterday. Other than CNN Headline News and a day-old copy of a *USA Today* newspaper, that's all we've heard or seen concerning events in Algeria. I'm afraid that Admiral Hodges lacked the time to brief me on everything before we left. Probably because of the short notice." It was going to be a short, dynamic conversation when he returned.

"Yeah, and he forgot to brief me, too," whispered Beau, stirring his coffee a little too fast, causing it to spill over the rim onto the top of the table, earning him a cut-eyed stare from a beefy supply corps commander seated across from him, to whom Beau smiled, threw a kiss, and stirred harder.

"Well, we'll bring you up to date," said the commodore, peering over his bifocals at everyone.

"Officers, we have turned the *Nassau* battle group westward and are steaming toward the Strait of Sicily at a *mind-boggling* speed of six knots. I would prefer to be doing twenty, but European Command has yet to give us permission to pull USS *Gearing* off its Freedom of Navigation ops. Until we receive permission to stop the FONOPs, we have to remain within fighter coverage of the destroyer while it skirts the Libyan coast. The eight Marine Corps

Harriers we have on board the *Nassau* are the only fighters we have in the Med until the aircraft carrier *Roosevelt* returns from the Persian Gulf. I have asked Sixth Fleet to intercede for permission to terminate *Gearing*'s mission. We need the *Gearing* with us. The DD-21 class is a battle group by itself. Though I have great confidence in the older Aegis cruiser *Yorktown* and the destroyers *Spruance* and *Hayler* accompanying *Nassau*, *Trenton*, and *Nashville*, I want the modern punch the *Gearing* brings as a DD-21 and its Network Centric Warfare capability to control the arsenal ship USS *King*."

Colonel "Bulldog" Stewart, the senior Marine Corps officer, raised his hand. "Commodore, have we received any messages other than the one from JCS ordering us to prepare for a noncombatant evacuation operation for our citizens in Algeria?"

"Colonel Stewart, that's the only one. As you know, Vice Admiral Gordon Cameron was shot during the terrorist attack at Gaeta two days ago. What you may not know is that the wound is not as serious as the press reported. Over secure voice communications this morning, Captain Clive Bowen, Sixth Fleet chief of staff, said they were expecting the admiral back aboard the USS *La Salle* today. The admiral was shot three times, but the bullets hit him at an oblique angle that resulted in little internal damage. He was one lucky bastard. We should have some direction from Sixth Fleet by this afternoon."

The commodore paused, took a sip of water, and continued. "Sadly, a lot of the dead from the attack on the bistro where he was hosting a wardroom social were family members, including the admiral's and the chaplain's wife. The Marine who disrupted the attack, stopping the massacre and saving the lives of the survivors, was Colonel Walt Ashworth. I think most of you know him?"

"I know the colonel very well," Bulldog added, clearing his throat. "We were stationed together at CMC headquarters. My wife and I spent a lot of time with them during that tour. Walt Ashworth is a damn fine Marine."

Captain Ellison pulled his handkerchief and blew his nose. "And a damn fine hero, too. Unfortunately, the colonel's wife was one of those murdered by those sons of bitches. Later today, Intell will brief what we know on that attack and the car bombing that killed Admiral Phrang, his wife, and his EA. He will also brief on the other attacks that have occurred in the past seventy-two hours.

"We believe these to be state-sponsored attacks. Everyone in the intelligence community is working hard to identify who is behind them. Admiral Phrang's death and the attack on Sixth Fleet . . . you'd have to be stupid not to see that those two attacks—the car bomb attack on the USS *La Salle* and the USS *Simon Lake,* moored together in Gaeta, and the attempt late yesterday against EUCOM—are coordinated actions." A sigh escaped. "Damn cold." His double chin bounced as he blew his nose.

"Here is what I expect to come our way, once the powers that be start reacting, and each of you needs to plan accordingly. First, we will be told to cease the FONOPs. Second, *Gearing* will be ordered off station. When those two events happen, we will recover the Harriers conducting the combat air patrol and steam at full speed to take station over the horizon from Algiers. Once at MODLOC, we must be prepared to conduct an evacuation of American citizens, who are gathering in the American Embassy compound even as we speak. I want to emphasize our role in this internal conflict going on in Algeria. We are going *in and out.* Do it quick. Avoid any entanglement in this civil war. I don't want us involved other than to evacuate our citizens. If they want to kill each other, let them, but we're going to stay out of their war. We do not want to be lulled into doing something stupid that will cost unnecessary lives. We saw what happened in the Balkans when we got entangled in someone else's war."

Duncan rubbed his eyes. What the commodore may fail to realize was that staying out of wars was harder than getting into them. America had been a player in every modern war in the past hundred years. That didn't mean Duncan didn't agree with what the commodore was saying. Most military officers agreed that it was best to avoid combat whenever possible; unfortunately, they also knew, with the demise of the draft years ago, the military experience in government had declined to where using the military as a foreign policy instrument came easier—and, often, it became the first choice. Wholeheartedly, he agreed with the commodore. In and out. Do it quick and don't get involved. But he knew from his own combat experience that events had a way of reeling you into them regardless of how hard you fought to avoid them and stay out.

Duncan shifted his weight in the chair. He may as well be comfortable. His left butt cheek needed some fresh circulation. Rank did make for a captive audience, and the commodore obviously enjoyed that perk of rank. He tuned his ears back to the commodore.

"Yesterday, as most of you know," the commodore continued, "we airlifted, via two helicopters, a company of Marines into the American Embassy—thankfully, before the Algerian insurgents gained complete control of the area. That gives the thirty Marines at the embassy an additional thirty with our two fire teams. Tunisia has been a great help, allowing our helicopters to refuel at their air bases. One of the helicopters returned late last night. The other chopper took small-arms fire, somewhere along the way, and is sitting disabled at the Tunisian Western Area Air Base. We're flying a repair crew off later today."

Beau leaned over to Duncan. "I'd also ask Admiral Hodges, before you kill him, if he lost those golf games."

"Colonel Stewart," the commodore said. He pointed his finger at the lean Marine. "You, as the commander of the amphibious landing force, are to be ready to conduct the evacuation immediately upon our arrival at the operating area off Algiers. While we hope that the Algerians will give permission to bring our people out, we must be prepared to conduct the evacuation in a hostile environment. Please ensure everyone understands the 'Rules of Engagement' issued by Sixth Fleet when we inchopped the Med. I do not want us initiating combat, but if we're fired upon we will return it. That being said, I would like a quick rundown on where we stand right now."

"Aye, Commodore. My staff and I worked through yesterday and the night brushing off the contingency plan for an Algerian evacuation. My intentions are to send a full combat-ready company with the first two CH-53s. They'll augment the embassy security force and the Marine fire teams inserted yesterday. They will reinforce embassy perimeters and engage any element perceived to be a threat to the evacuation. Accompanying the 53s will be four Cobra attack helicopters. Two flying ahead, to sanitize the corridor, and two flanking, to protect from small-arms fire and manpack surface-to-air missiles.

"According to Commander Mulligan"—Bulldog continued, nodding toward the pudgy intelligence officer sitting beside Captain Farnfield—"Algiers has fallen. Complicating this operation is the lack of a proper government to arrange peaceful flight operations."

"Okay, Colonel. I would like you to get together with

Captain Farnfield," the commodore said, "so the USS *Nassau* fully understands your requirements.

"Captain Farnfield, the professionalism of your ship and crew in the next few days will determine the success of our mission. Please pass to your officers, chiefs, and sailors that I expect each to do their duty, as the lives of American citizens depend on them as well as us."

The commodore took another sip of the water. He swished it around his mouth before swallowing.

Then, before independent conversations erupted, Ellison continued, "Captain James, it will be your job to organize the SpecWar teams needed to support the Marines and, if necessary, conduct rescue of any hostages. Admiral Hodges told me that you wrote the book on hostage rescues; here's a chance to add another chapter. Bulldog, I'm adding a third helicopter for the SEALs, so incorporate a third 53 in your CONOP."

"Sir," interrupted a lieutenant commander, straightening from where he had been leaning against the bulkhead, "we only have two CH-53s available. The third is damaged and sitting at the Tunisian base. The one that returned from the embassy run has to go through a maintenance check; two are down hard, awaiting parts, and the other has a chip light that we are still trouble-shooting."

"Is it a valid chip light?"

"Appears to be, Commodore. Most likely shavings from a bent piston rod. If so, then we'll have to break down the engine to replace it and—"

"Okay, Commander," Ellison interrupted. "How long do you estimate until the helo is up?"

"If we have the parts on board we can have it operational in two days. Otherwise, we'll have to fly them in from Sigonella."

"Okay, Colonel, substitute the third 53 with a 46 from

the USS *Nashville.* Captain James, welcome to my staff as the senior Navy Special Warfare representative. I want a CONOP on my desk by eighteen hundred hours, showing me two plans. One to support embassy security and a second for hostage rescue. You'll need to coordinate your communication requirements with the staff's COMMO."

Two hours later, the briefing finished, bladders bursting, the commodore departed. Duncan hated conferences, meetings, briefings—anything that rooted him to one place for more than thirty minutes. He wished he hadn't drunk the coffee. The Navy was probably right in SERBing him and sending him home to his farm in Georgia. He slid his chair under the table. Where is the nearest head? Then, intuitively, he followed the mumbling crowd.

Ten minutes later the three regrouped, said good-bye to Major Alcontira, and then followed Lieutenant Mike Sunney to a small office in the bowels of the ship.

"This is it, Captain. Sorry about the cramped space. XO said it's where they always put the SEAL officer in charge."

"They must really like you, Mike," Beau snorted, reaching up and peeling a small chip of paint off the flaking bulkhead.

"Mike, what resources do we have on board?" Duncan asked.

"Three full combat teams, Captain. All attached to Commander Task Force Sixty-one. With you three we can build four full teams."

"Okay, here is what I want. I am assuming command of the detachment. Lieutenant Commander Pettigrew will be my second and you will continue with your duties as the OIC of the teams. How many officers are there, other than yourself?"

"We have one more, sir. Ensign John Helliwell—we call him 'Bud.' Mr. Helliwell is a limited duty officer, a former senior chief gunner's mate who was commissioned in January. Has a Purple Heart from action in Liberia when he was a second class and another during that Iraqi episode a couple years ago."

"Good. A mustang with combat experience is always handy. Lieutenant McDaniels will serve as your assistant officer in charge," Duncan said.

Mike Sunney's forehead wrinkled as his eyes narrowed. "Aye, aye, sir."

The door opened and a stocky ensign, wearing camouflage utilities, entered. Duncan could see where the high and tight haircut would make it easy to mistake the combat veteran as a Marine.

"Captain, this is Ensign Bud Helliwell."

Following introductions the ensign leaned against the bulkhead, the room being too small for another chair. Duncan noticed flakes of paint falling on the deck from where Bud's shoulder rubbed the bulkhead. It was not like a United States Navy ship to tolerate a poor paint job.

"Let's review our tasking. I want to ensure we understand our mission. When we finish, Beau, I want you and Bud to work up the kits for the teams. Mike, you work on a strawman concept of operations with H. J.

"H. J.," he continued, "hand me the chart you nicked from the ops table." Duncan held his hand out.

"How did you . . ." she started to ask.

"I've been doing this too long to start letting little things escape my attention. In this case, we needed a chart and you procured one for us. If I presume correctly, it is of Algiers and, hopefully, not some MWR holiday map of Italian beaches."

"Yes, sir," she said. H. J. unbuttoned the bottom button of her khaki shirt, revealing a glimpse of a pink silk T-shirt. She pulled out the folded chart.

"That's another thing, Mike. We'll need desert cammies. H. J., ditch that silk and put on cotton. This isn't a dance we're going to. Silk will rub when you start running and sweating. Cotton soaks it up."

Beau winked at H. J. and, seeing no one looking, unbuttoned his shirt to reveal a red silk undershirt.

H. J. rolled her eyes and smiled slightly.

Duncan unfolded the city map of Algiers and spread it on the metal table. The small-scale map covered the table with the top and bottom hanging off the edges.

"Okay, perimeter support is the easier of our tasks. Boring most of the time. Let's hope it's boring this time. If a NEO is executed we will go on the third helo, a CH-46. Marine fire teams will be on the two 53s. I want two teams, eight of us, prepared for insertion. I want a third team on board *Nassau* on thirty-minute alert. Our primary mission will be to back up the Marines. That means we'll need at least one communicator and one sniper in each team. Beau, have our guys alternate choice of close-in weapons. Our strategy is to pin down any attacking force sufficiently so that no hand-to-hand combat situation occurs. That'll be the snipers' primary duties. The rest of us will maintain and reinforce perimeter security where needed. If necessary, we must be prepared to fight; otherwise, a nice, boring mission is the goal. Understood?"

They agreed.

"Beau, you, Mike, and H. J. work out a backup plan for moving the evacuees to the port area. I know it wasn't a subject during the operations brief, but with anarchy comes chaos and to rely only on a helo-borne evacuation invites catastrophe. So, work out a backup plan. Meanwhile, I'm going to hunt down Colonel Stewart so we can coordinate our actions. He'll be Commander Amphibious Landing Force, the CALF, if we have to go in force."

"You mean an amphibious assault?" Beau asked.

"Let's hope not; just a boring, simple NEO of American citizens."

"Well, that should be something new and different."

"Let's keep our minds on the mission," Duncan said. "Beau, get rid of your silk, too."

"Aye, Captain," Beau responded with a mock salute.

"Sir, how soon until we're in position to conduct the NEO?" Bud asked, raising his hand.

Mike Sunney answered. "We're waiting word from Sixth Fleet and EUCOM. Meanwhile, the ship is slowly steaming westward, but it is also tasked with air support for the USS *Gearing,* operating in the Gulf of Sidra. Until they cancel the FONOPs and divert her, the *Nassau* is limited as to how far west she can sail. We have to keep a continuous combat air patrol of two Harriers while the *Gearing* skirts the territorial waters of Libya."

"Libya been giving us any problems since Qaddafi's death ten months ago?" Duncan asked.

"Not really. No one seems to know who is running the country since he died. Navy Intelligence believes that a junta has taken over the government, but Libya is Libya and it's still hard to figure out what it'll do. I think with Qaddafi dead, there'll be a lot of cowboys loose in that country."

"I have never trusted the Libyans. Only the North Koreans are more unpredictable," Duncan added.

Bud stood up. "Lieutenant Sunney, with your permission, sir, I'll go break out the weapons and start outfitting the men. Who's going?"

"The four of us will be," Duncan answered. "Bud, I'll want a weapons outfit list from you as well as a quick skills breakdown on the teams. I want at least one MG-60 in each team."

"Aye, sir. I'll have that for you in an hour. As for the teams, you three"—Ensign Helliwell pointed at Duncan, Beau, and Mike Sunney—"and me?"

"No, you and the three of us," Duncan corrected, pointing to himself, Beau, and H. J. "Lieutenant Sunney will command the reserve team."

Duncan caught the quick glance between Mike Sunney and Bud Helliwell. Enough to understand their unspoken disagreement with his order.

"No offense, Captain, but it is my understanding that this is Lieutenant McDaniels's first SEAL operation. Are we sure we want to endanger our teams—or *her*—on her first time out of the chute?" Bud asked, ignoring H. J., who visibly straightened.

"News travels fast, I see," Duncan said, directing the comment to Mike Sunney.

"Ensign, this may be a surprise," Beau interjected. "In the Navy are many surprises. Some pleasant. Some not so pleasant. In this case, Lieutenant Heather J. McDaniels is the surprise and we're still debating if it is a pleasant one or not. But, she is a member of our team—"

"She is a Navy SEAL and *will* be going as a member of my team," Duncan said sharply. "Any problems with that, Ensign?" His head snapped to the right. "Lieutenant?"

"No, sir," the two answered together. Bud Helliwell's expression did little to mask his disagreement. Duncan bit his lip to keep from saying more. The two would have to get used to H. J. being a woman just as he and Beau did.

"With your permission, Captain," Bud Helliwell said and opened the door. "I'm going to get started on organizing the teams' kits."

Duncan nodded. As the compartment door closed behind the mustang, he spoke. "Okay, at the minimum we have a day and a half before the *Nassau* battle group becomes the *Nassau* amphibious group and comes within range of Algiers. Let's get busy. I want to see a double-spaced rough draft plan by fourteen hundred. I'll work the hostage rescue portion. You two, Beau and Mike, will chop it before we submit it to the commodore. I'll be back as soon as I finish speaking with the colonel. Plus, I have to send a short message to my very dear friend Admiral Hodges." Duncan slammed the door behind him as he walked out.

"I don't think I'd want to be Admiral Hodges right now," Beau said. "Of course, he is in Washington and I am out here. . . . H. J., you have anything to add?"

Yeah, she thought as she shook her head no. *Have you ever noticed what Spanish men can do with their eyes?*

SEVEN

COLONEL ALQAHIRAY'S HIDDEN EYES JERKED FROM ONE screen to another. The detection lights running along the top of the intelligence screens glowed red, revealing four of the enemy's overhead surveillance systems had moved out of coverage range. He ran his hand through his hair and then wiped it on the pants leg of his uniform. According to the intelligence profiles, provided by their friends, the absence of these four meant Benghazi was uncovered. Amazing how simple math, geometry, modern technology, and balls allowed a simple Bedouin like himself to twist the tiger's tail. He chuckled softly. Bedouin! The only time he spent in the desert was in the army. He turned and paced to the right.

Another light turned red. Timing was everything. He wiped his chin and nearly knocked his cigarette out of his mouth. Something could go wrong. Something usually did. The Americans were unpredictable. Just when you thought you had them figured out, they up and surprised you. Even old Saddam jerked them one time too many and look at divided Iraq today. He had this one chance. If, as planned, his comrades in Algeria did their job right, the Mediterranean would be sealed off to the American Navy. If he could keep them out for two weeks—that was all he needed. He sighed. War was not for the fainthearted. He rubbed his stomach.

"Colonel," Major Walid said, interrupting Alqahiray's thoughts. "The American battle group is moving northwest away from the American destroyer that remains in our waters. It is as you predicted."

Predicted! Allah's will and luck, but never let your subordinates know you had any doubts.

"Of course, Walid. Let's hope everything continues as expected. Americans are like the democracies and empires that have disappeared throughout history—complacent in peace and clouded by prosperity. Too wrapped up in their own overcalculated importance to recognize their own decline."

Alqahiray took a deep drag of the Greek cigarette, smiled, and continued, letting the harsh bluish smoke filter out his nostrils. "Look at the virtual location display." He pointed to an intelligence screen overhead. "See where the American warship USS *Gearing* is located, its southwesterly course and twelve-knot speed. Now look at the *Nassau* and her group. In four hours, even at five or six knots, they will be so far apart that the low-performance aircraft protecting this intruding warship will be useless, unless they are prepared to sacrifice themselves." His smile broadened and he laughed. "I don't think they are! Besides, a Harrier against a MiG-25? Even the modern vertical-launched jets are unable to offer a dogfight worthy of a true warplane. Even one of the age of a Foxbat."

He stubbed out the cigarette and tossed the butt at the

nearby ashtray. Like most of the others, it missed. The ashtray was the cleanest item around him.

"What does radar show and coastal surveillance report?" the colonel asked an operator to the right. He rubbed his day-old stubble, reminding himself he needed a shave. A military man must look military, but the past three days had required continuous attention.

"Sir," the operator replied, "the American warship remains within our territorial waters. It is keeping a constant nine miles off the coast. Army electronic warfare units have identified the radar emitters and communications on the ship. We have downloaded the parameters into the electronic warfare system. The computers are revisiting their electromagnetic calculations for the third time." He turned in the seat so he could look directly toward the colonel. "Sir, we are ready whenever you are."

The colonel nodded at the young soldier. He took a deep draw on a new cigarette, held the breath, and let the smoke slowly ease out. Even as a few whiffs of the strong Greek fag drifted out his nostrils, the colonel lifted the cup of tea beside his chair and sipped. It had gone cold. A few drops of tea fell from his mustache. When the mustache drops tea it's time for a trim. He smiled at Walid. With the back of his hand he wiped his mustache.

"Have our friends said anything yet?"

"No, sir, not since they acknowledged event zero zero seven. We did receive an algorithm modification for the electronic jamming parameters and have already corrected the program accordingly. The weather forecast shows no expected changes for the next seventy-two hours. This algorithm should be good for that period."

"What were the corrections?" the colonel asked.

Walid opened his mouth to reply.

"No, no, no," Colonel Alqahiray interrupted, waving

his hand and shaking his head. "Don't explain, Walid. I wouldn't understand it anyway." Sometimes, he thought, Walid was a little too smart.

Colonel Alqahiray looked up at the event log just as it changed to reflect event zero one zero completed. Event zero zero nine remained "in progress." Well, they had their problems and he had his. The next three events were his, and *then* he'd worry if event zero zero nine wasn't complete. He noticed two other events in the chain were due to commence soon, both crucial to the success of event zero one five. It had taken a lot of work to reach today. If Jihad Wahid continued as it was going, the American navy would be driven from and denied access to the Mediterranean. History showed that the nation that controlled the Med controlled the world and he was going to lead the new nation that stole control of the gold ring known as the Mediterranean Sea. He looked around, checking to see if anyone was watching, paranoid that someone may suspect his ultimate purpose.

Alqahiray tweaked his nose. He'd like to sleep. He was so tired after three days of dozing in his chair and not leaving this room. Soon, he promised himself. He had managed a morning shower and to change uniform in the latrine connected to the room.

Jihad Wahid had taken so much energy and so much time to arrange. The talking, the planning, the juggling of egos to balance the varied agendas, the different political perspectives, and the myriad tribal animosities they'd had to get around to work together for this one purpose. It had been tedious and hard. Only he could have done it and it was a fragile coalition at best. The agreement centered on this grand scheme to return Arab greatness to the level it was nine hundred years ago when Bedouin warriors galloped across North Africa and into Europe to spread the one true religion to the infidels. With Jihad Wahid surging forward the forges of war would soon overcome the differences of the Arab world in peace. If they could stand together for a few more days, they would achieve their grand objective and then appear before the world as one. He grinned. How shocked and surprised the world powers would be when Mintab announced their success.

"Samir, come here," the colonel shouted into the speaker box beside the chair. "I want to know the current situation in Algeria. Let's see how our brothers in Islam are doing."

"Yes, Colonel. I will be right there. We are processing the daily situational message and CNN is showing some interesting stuff, such as—"

"Samir, if I had wanted you to tell me this over the squawk box I would have said, 'Samir, tell me over this squawk box.' Right?"

"Yes, sir."

"So, come tell me the good news."

"May I have five minutes?"

"Of course you may have five minutes. Would you like an hour? Maybe two hours? Or, maybe you would like to take a nap before you get your butt off that chair and get your ass in here!"

"I'm on my way, Colonel."

Alqahiray flipped the mute button on the console speaker.

"Walid, remind me in the new government to shoot all firstborn who show a propensity for being intelligence officers."

Ashes from the ever-present cigarette fell on the arm of the chair. Walid reached up and brushed them off onto the floor, where they joined the ever-growing circle of cigarette butts and crushed packs surrounding the colonel's chair. The colonel meticulously completed each cigarette to where only a small millimeter of cigarette paper around the edges of a yellow-lipped butt remained. Walid reminded himself to have someone clean up this mess.

"Walid, it is time. Contact Benghazi Navy Base and tell them to execute event zero one one immediately. I want the Nanuchka missile patrol boat and the Foxtrot submarine underway and out of the harbor within the hour. After you have passed the order, ask Admiral Asif Abu Yimin to come to the phone, so I may discuss this operation one more time with him." Yimin was old Navy and Alqahiray wanted reassurance the admiral hadn't decided at the last minute to "improve" the plan. Innovation was not needed. There would be time later for that.

Walid saluted and hurried to his console. Ten minutes later he was back at the colonel's side as Alqahiray stubbed a cigarette out and ripped open another pack.

"Our warships are under way, Colonel."

"Good, let's blind the American intruder. Captain!" Alqahiray shouted to the officer who was standing near the three electronic warfare console operators. "You may activate the system and keep me informed on what you're doing. I want to follow what is happening."

The colonel leaned forward, put his hand on Walid's shoulder, and gave it a friendly shake. "Walid, relax. Have a cup of tea." He leaned back and pressed a button on his chair arm. A few seconds later a steward wearing a starched white apron elbowed his way through a door in the rear carrying tea, dates, and biscuits. *Walid is too nervous,* Alqahiray thought. *He must be doing something he shouldn't be doing.*

"Bring another cup for Colonel Walid."

"Colonel?"

"Yes, Walid. It is the time to recognize the heroes of the revolution. You've been a major long enough." *It is time to seal loyalties, my fine ass-kissing friend.*

"Six months, Colonel," Walid said, incredulously.

"For some, six months is a lifetime." *Without me, you would be a permanent major,* Alqahiray said to himself. And he'd ensure that Walid didn't forget that.

The steward had an extra cup on the tray and handed it to Colonel Walid.

"Thank you, Colonel. Thank you. I don't know what to say." Walid focused his attention on the tea, hoping his guilt was not apparent. The deep-seated eyes of Alqahiray created a nightmarish, unnerving appearance in the blue light of the operations room—like a talking skull transfixing everyone with fascinated horror.

"You don't have to say anything, Colonel Walid," Alqahiray replied. He leaned forward, put his hand under Walid's chin and lifted the new colonel's head, and stared into Walid's eyes. "Remember, Walid, that when I need you, I want you there. Together we will accomplish what no one in the Arab world has been able, or willing, to do since the eleventh century. Remember that in the next few days. Bills are sent, debts collected, and those who fight today will rise as leaders of the revolution! Those who place their own welfare before the good of the nation will perish." *As will those who place their welfare before mine,* he added mentally as he released Walid's chin.

Walid shuddered, frightened for a moment, until he realized it went unnoticed by Alqahiray. His face twitched involuntarily. "Yes, Colonel. Our loyalty is to the cause—to the greatness that has lain dormant upon our shores. We are proud to be beside you at this momentous occasion—to serve with you. No other could ask for more," he said, his voice nearly breaking because of the constriction of his throat.

"I know," the colonel replied, studying Walid intensely, his eyes narrowing.

Walid turned away to avoid the stare, pretending to watch the electronic warfare operators. He licked his dry lips and hoped his voice did not betray his nervousness. "But, it is more than Libya that rests in the balance here."

Ah, Walid, Colonel Alqahiray thought, *What is it you hide?*

After several seconds of silence Alqahiray's attention moved to the activity around the EW module where the electronic warriors of the twentieth-first century prepared for battle. A low, confident murmur reached his ears. The young Army captain read each item on the checklist line by line. The operators acknowledged each command as, one switch after another, they worked through the complex procedure to activate the electronic warfare system that would cause an umbrella of electromagnetic silence to descend over the Gulf of Sidra.

"Captain," Colonel Alqahiray asked, "how much longer?"

"Five minutes, Colonel."

"Keep me apprised. I can't understand what you're doing from where I am up here." He leaned back against the headrest.

The captain saluted and returned to the process of reading instructions to the operators. There was a spot on his back where the skin began to itch. The exact spot where the piercing eyes of Colonel Alqahiray burned into him. His attention slipped, causing him to have to redo several checklist items before he was ready. He did not want to disappoint the Maadi.

"Switch on, Colonel!" the captain shouted, his voice filled with pride, as the electronic warfare operator gave a thumbs-up. "System activated." He crossed his fingers and prayed it worked. If it didn't . . . well, he didn't want to think about it.

Miles away along the hazy Libyan coast a series of LANs, local area networks, connected via coaxial landlines, began receiving and exchanging, via their various programs, technical data collected on the radar and communications signals emanating from the USS *Gearing*. Several minutes passed before the operators along the coast reported their component activated. Then, as Colonel Alqahiray watched, the operators rapidly assimilated and confirmed the computer program parameters via data streams with those at the coastal observation posts.

"Captain, what is happening? How will I know this is working? Will I see something when we are successful?" The colonel pushed himself out of his chair and strolled to the metal stanchion that surrounded his raised observation area.

"Colonel, I cannot answer," the captain replied honestly. "The program the Chinese provided should simulate large-scale erratic sunspot activity. It will disrupt the communications signals and affect most of the radars on the ship thereby limiting their effective range. The ship should see a myriad of unrelated problems within their electronic systems. Communications should be impossible, but their Aegis radar system may be able to burn through the interference."

"Wait a minute, Captain. I have flown Mirages and whenever we were jammed or someone tried to spoof us we could tell by how the radar scope responded."

"Yes, sir, but in this instance there are no telltale signals to reveal the presence of an external source. Our electronic attack targets no specific system. It disturbs the electromagnetic waves in the targeted area. You might say we are jamming the atmosphere, not the ship. The ship personnel will believe either their systems are experiencing atmospheric difficulties or they are having a system malfunction. They may suspect an electronic attack after they have exhausted all other avenues to correct the problems."

"Are you telling me this will not fool them indefinitely?"

"I would say we have twenty-four hours before someone figures out that it is an external force disrupting their electronic picture and capabilities," the captain said firmly, his confidence growing with the conversation.

"Can they sail out of range?"

"Of course, sir. The electronic warfare network is disguised as coastal surveillance platforms located at equal distances along the coast. As long as they are within twenty to thirty miles of the coast their sensors are useless."

"Will it affect their fire control radars the same way?"

"No, sir. Fire control radars have limited range, but they have the power to burn through the electromagnetic disturbance, much like their Aegis radar. It's easier to jam them directly, but American fire control radars are very complex with multiple jumping frequencies. Most fire control radars can avoid electronic warfare jamming techniques and some, like their HARM missiles, can use them to their targeting advantage. And, of course, their sonar will be unaffected."

"And, their communications?"

"They will lose all their communications, including satellite."

Alqahiray nodded and strolled back to his seat. Good, they can have their radars. Radars were limited in range. As long as they could not communicate, they were his. The DD-21 class depended on computer and communications links with other ships to fight effectively. Everyone waited until he sat down. "Okay, Captain. You may continue."

He saluted. "Thank you, Colonel."

Along the coast hidden antennas inside mock coastal surveillance platforms transmitted a coordinated broad band of oscillating radio wave frequencies of multimodulated energy. The signals rose in intensity as the artificial phenomenon disrupted the surrounding electromagnetic environment. The captain nodded at the operator, who punched in a series of computer commands. Additional instructions implemented certain subprograms within the operating system. The covert Libyan electronic warfare attack subtly distorted the USS *Gearing*'s communications. The American warship lost contact with the rest of the world one minute after the system activated.

Fifteen minutes passed before the captain turned to Colonel Alqahiray and Walid. "Sir, it is done. Electronic communications are impossible in the Gulf of Sidra. No changes have been reflected in their electronic parameters. Any orders we wish to give must be via landline as long as we are transmitting. Aircraft above one thousand meters will still be able to communicate."

"What do you mean no change?"

"Well, sir, if they suspected they were being jammed, they would have changed their electronic settings in search for a clear frequency. I don't think they'd be successful, but if they were successful, then we'd have to revisit their electronic profile and that means bringing ours down while we are doing it."

"Wait a minute, Captain. I was led to understand that when this electronic blanket descends over an adversary it's like an impregnable glass bowl. It captures and makes their electronic eyes blind!" He swished his hand in front of his eyes.

"Yes, sir," the Captain replied, looking around at the technicians who were monitoring the EW array. "And it does, Colonel. Plus, the system changes automatically when they change their parameters. So we should be undetectable. But if they successfully change to a technical setting that our system fails to respond to correctly, then we may have to bring it down to revisit their electronic profile. You change the eyes, then you have to change the glass bowl."

The colonel leaned back. "Walid, include electronic warfare officers with the proclamation on intelligence officers for a better world." He leaned down and whispered to Walid, "Never keep anyone around who knows more than you do."

At Benghazi, the Nanuchka patrol boat, loaded with four surface-to-surface missiles, and the Libyan Foxtrot submarine, outfitted with sixteen torpedoes, sailed slowly out of port. Their movement was undetected by overhead Western satellites.

"Colonel, Colonel Gazzelin is on the line."

"Walid, log events zero one two and zero one three as executed. Zero one four is starting. Ask the admiral to wait while I finish with this phone call."

Colonel Alqahiray kept Colonel Gazzelin on the phone for twenty minutes going over tomorrow's fighter plans for Tripoli and Benghazi airfield. When he finally hung up and took the admiral's line, he received a full blast from the older, more senior ranking officer, who was unaccustomed to waiting. Alqahiray held his temper until the admiral finished his barrage, then apologized and explained the delay, which seemed to appease the admiral.

They talked for ten minutes with Alqahiray inviting the admiral to share the podium with the ruling junta at the celebrations following this momentous occasion. The admiral wanted to know if Alqahiray had heard anything about something called Jihad Wahid. Alqahiray pleaded innocent, promised to investigate, and would phone the admiral if he found out anything. The admiral shared with Alqahiray his own plans to remain on the base. Tomorrow, the admiral would be at his own operations center during the planned actions. As one military professional to another the admiral confided about some Western wine and British port he had cached to share with his wardroom following their success. He invited the colonel to participate.

"I wish I could be there, Admiral; unfortunately, the junta demands my presence here."

"I understand, Colonel. I will save a bottle of the best for you."

"Thank you, Admiral. I will pray for your success."

"And, I too for you, Colonel."

THEY HUNG UP. THE ADMIRAL TURNED TO HIS AIDE. "What do we know of the colonel? He's not one of those hard-core Islamic fundamentalists who wants to turn Libya into another Egypt or Iran, is he?"

"I don't know, sir," his aide lied. He took the bottle of port from the admiral.

The aide's eyes narrowed as he bit his lower lip in a successful effort to keep his mouth shut and his thoughts to himself. Every time he touched the bottle of alcohol he sinned against Allah, but in the spread of the true religion it was necessary for warriors to make sacrifice. *And, soon, Admiral,* the aide thought, *you will enjoy that sacrifice yourself.*

"Did you say something, Ahmad?"

"Oh, no, sir. I was just saying that I didn't know anything about the colonel's background." He'd have to be more careful. He had been unaware that he had mumbled aloud his thoughts.

FOUR HOURS LATER THE OLD NANUCHKA MISSILE patrol boat, trailed by a Libyan Foxtrot submarine, passed the six-mile channel marker due west of Benghazi Navy Base. The Nanuchka activated a Don Kay surface search radar. Russian merchant ships used Don Kay radars. This one had been removed from a dilapidated vessel found rusting pierside in a small port north of Benghazi. Rewired and restored, the radar gave the Nanuchka an electronic signature of a merchant vessel.

"WHAT DO YOU MEAN WE HAVE NO COMMUNICA-tions?" the USS *Gearing*'s COMMO asked the radioman chief.

"Just what I said, sir. We lost synch with Sixth Fleet, Commander Task Force Sixty-seven in Naples, and Commander Task Force Sixty-one on the *Nassau* about an hour ago. I thought it was just something in the patching or a simple software glitch. But, regardless of how we've tweaked the systems, we have been unable to reestablish contact."

"Have you changed the circuits? Checked the fuses? Rebooted the software?"

"Sir, it's not the circuits or the fuses or the software and it's not double-A batteries. We've checked every item and run a series of diagnostics. I sent a low-power test message from the transmit antenna to our receive antenna and we got it okay. Well, not exactly okay. There were a lot of garbles in the text. The only thing I can think, Lieutenant, is that we are in the middle of some gosh-awful sunspot activity or we have a problem—a short—between our receive antenna and the receivers. I called Chief Brown in the EMO shop and he is sending a couple of electronic technicians as soon as he can. Right now, the only two sailors with training on this system and the antennas are also the only ones who know how to repair the CIWS system. Chief Brown says the Old Man is griping and bitching about CIWS and he can't leave it without having the Old Man demanding to know 'what the hell.' "

"Okay, Chief. So what you're saying is that we don't have comms with anyone right now and it's not our equipment?"

"No, sir. What I'm saying is that we don't have comms with anyone and I don't know if it's our equipment or what."

The chief leaned over and lightly slapped the back of the head of a young sailor who had his hands on a knob of one of the receivers.

"What'd I tell you, Seaman Jones, about touching anything in here until you make petty officer?"

"Sorry, Chief, I just thought—"

"Not supposed to think. You're a seaman. Seamen don't think, they do what they're told. Kind of like ensigns."

Lieutenant Junior Grade Tauten ran his sleeve across his mouth. "Chief, can I talk with you over here, please?"

They moved near the hatch away from the rest of the sailors in the "Radio Shack."

"Chief, how much longer until we know what's wrong?"

"Give me another couple of hours of darkness, sir. The heat from the day will be down and the sun will be far enough on the other side that, if it is sunspot activity, we should be able to make contact on the night frequencies." The chief paused and then added, "Mr. Tauten, you need to tell the captain."

"Not hardly," Lieutenant Junior Grade Tauten snapped, shaking his head back and forth. "No way! The last time I told him we were having problems he chewed my butt up one side and down the other. Then he kept me up all night, along with you, until we fixed the cipher gear. No, Chief, before we excite Captain Cafferty, I want to make sure we know what's wrong."

"Aye, aye, sir. I understand, but if you don't tell him and he finds out from someone else that we've got problems in Radio . . . Or at least tell the operations officer."

"Okay, Chief. You've told me. You don't have to lecture me. I'm not an ensign anymore! Let's find out what's wrong before we stir up a hornet's nest by telling the Old Man. The ETs will be here soon. Then, between our information systems technicians and them, they should be able to troubleshoot the problem."

"Okay, Lieutenant; it's your butt, but I recommend you pass it up the chain of command if you want to keep your butt in one piece."

The communications officer, turning to leave, paused and said in a soft voice, "Chief, one other thing: Quit hitting the sailors. You're going to get us in trouble."

"I ain't hitting them, sir. I'm educating them. This is a warship, not a fucking social barge." He raised his hands as the lieutenant opened his mouth to say something. "I remember, sir, what you told me about raising children. You said those social welfare types believe that correcting a long-term whatever was best done by slow, proper attention and support. But, you know something, sir, problems sometimes need a short-term attention-getter so they'll still be alive for the long-term solution."

"Well, for our sakes don't touch them. All we need is a hot line phone call and there goes our careers."

"Well, right now, sir, there ain't no danger of anyone

making any hot line phone calls, until we figure out what's wrong with our comms," the chief said, his lips tight.

Lieutenant Junior Grade Tauten pulled the door shut behind him as he departed.

Careers, the chief thought. *You ain't been in the Navy long enough to worry about a career.* "And junior officers shouldn't be touching things or speaking out until they're full commanders—unless they're Naval Academy graduates and then they should wait until they're captains," the chief mumbled to himself. He tugged his pants up and ran his hand around the inside of the waistband. At least two inches he'd lost. May even pass the body fat standards this test cycle.

He walked to where the seaman stood and slapped him lightly on the back of the head.

The seaman rubbed his head. "What was that for, Chief? I ain't touched nothing."

"No, but you were thinking about it." He tousled the sailor's hair. Training sailors was a hell of a lot easier than training junior officers. He straightened up as a touch of pride shot through his ego over the young sailors that made up his radio. Damn fine bunch. Navy should never have changed the name of the radioman rating to information systems technician. He still considered himself a radioman regardless of what rating badge he wore on his left arm.

"Hey, Chief!" a petty officer near the transmitter shouted. "Can you come here? I need some help."

"Come on, Seaman Jones. Let's see what teeny-weeny problem Petty Officer Potts has. I'll watch; you answer. They probably taught you the solutions in school and I am just dying to see what new and bright things those pencil pushers have dreamed up to help us poor, stupid sailors at sea."

Within seconds the group was deep in animated conversation, discussing ways to approach the problem. From seaman to petty officer they tossed out ideas. The chief stood quietly in the background listening to the exchange. The captain needed to know about this, but he had told the officer. With the old captain he would have made sure the Old Man knew, but with Cafferty, the chief shook his head. The new captain shot messengers, so reluctantly he understood the COMMO's position. That didn't make it right, but he understood. He looked at his watch. It'd be breakfast before he could voice this concern with his fellow chiefs in the goat locker. He could sneak down to chiefs berthing and wake the command master chief, but the CMC had not had a full night's sleep since Cafferty assumed command. A chief's responsibility was to the ship and its sailors, but sometimes it was a "Christly" hard job to do.

EIGHT

COLONEL YOSEF DOZED UNDER THE SHADOW OF THE bridge, out of the hot morning sun. He drifted within that gray area of fatigued consciousness so familiar to veteran soldiers awaiting the next battle. The shout brought him fully alert, his weapon coming up.

"Colonel, aircraft approaching!" Sergeant Boutrous pointed north out to sea.

Yosef pulled himself off the deck of the fishing trawler and climbed to the bridge. The fisherman was still at the helm. A night without sleep mixed with a day-old beard and sweat-matted hair accented by red-rimmed eyes gave the fisherman the look of a wild man. Yosef knew he looked as bad. He shoved his shirttail into his pants and ran his hand over his inch-long desert brown hair, blinking his eyes several times to clear them.

"No sleep?" Yosef asked. He rubbed his nose where the day's heat had burned it while he slept.

"No, sir. But I am fine. I can continue," the fisherman

responded, unconvincingly. "See, I told you I was the helmsman."

Yosef pushed the fisherman aside gently to look at the compass. They were still heading east. Good, after last night's disappointment of discovering that the combined knowledge of maritime navigation between him, his men, and the fisherman hovered between being able to read a compass and being able to spell it. Two kilometers to the south, a morning haze clouded the coastline of Algeria. They were following it to keep from getting lost.

The fisherman had not lied about manning the helm. Unfortunately, he failed to mention that it was always under the close eye of the boat's captain.

"I see it, Sergeant." Yosef grabbed a pair of binoculars from a nearby shelf and scanned the air until he focused on the aircraft.

"MiG-29," he said as he lowered the binoculars. "Tell everyone to go below and keep out of sight until we know what he is doing."

"Corporal Omar, get the men below," Sergeant Boutrous relayed.

Corporal Omar slid down the railings on the narrow ladder to the main deck. He roused the morning sleepers and with shouts and foot shoves hurried them down the ladder. About half were through the hatch when the MiG-29 roared past directly overhead. The gigantic engines of the warplane shook the small vessel as it passed low overhead, the heat from the afterburners taking the breath away from those topside. The deadly fighter turned upward, gaining altitude.

"Damn!" Yosef shouted.

"Seems they have found us, or it could be one of our loyal pilots from the west," President Alneuf said from behind.

"Mr. President, what are you doing up here? You must stay below, sir. The pilot may be Air Force, but even Air Force officers can recognize that men in suits are not normally crewmembers of a fishing trawler."

Alneuf smiled. "I am sorry, *mon colonel.* It is just that neither do fishing crews wear desert utility uniforms like you and your men."

Yosef nodded in agreement. "You are correct, President Alneuf, but it is you who will stand out. Please go below until the aircraft leaves."

The MiG-29 turned left as the pilot circled for another pass. Yosef, the president, the fisherman at the helm, and five Guardsmen remained topside on the wooden trawler.

"He's coming back, Mr. President. Would you please go below, sir," Yosef pleaded urgently.

"I'll go, Colonel Yosef. I think we are too late. Don't you think the pilot has already reported our presence? I do. So the question is not so much what the fighter will do, but how long before the first helicopters with rebel commandos come rumbling over the horizon, heading for our floating sanctuary?"

The president disappeared slowly down the ladder, his head disappearing as the fighter straightened for its approach.

The MiG-29 descended to about fifty meters.

"Wave at him!" shouted Yosef. "And keep your weapons out of sight!"

They waved at the pilot, whose black helmet was clearly visible as the aircraft approached the boat. The noise of the fighter blasted the boat again. The trailing exhaust fumes burned the eyes and raised the ambient temperature across the trawler until the faint sea breeze cleared the air. Yosef noted the pilot failed to wiggle his wings; not a good sign. The MiG-29 climbed and turned left for another circuit.

Yosef leaned over the bridge railing. "Okay, this is it. Be alert. This is his third pass. He's not sure who we are or what he's seeing. So wave, grin, and think the friendliest thoughts you know!"

The aircraft completed its circuit, dove back to sea level, and, with afterburners blazing, bore straight for the trawler. Five hundred meters out, the fighter triggered its nose cannon and a series of five sprays erupted about fifty meters in front of the fishing vessel as thirty-millimeter cannon shells hit the water.

A Guardsman standing on the bow whipped his AK-47 from under a towel and fired a long burst at the aircraft as it zoomed, untouched, past the boat. The fighter flipped its starboard aileron and flaps as it zigzagged into a left roll and climbed. Increased power applied to the MiG's afterburner sent the decibel level climbing, causing the men to cover their ears.

"What are you doing!" screamed Yosef as he ran at the Guardsman, his shout lost in the noise of the jet fighter.

"He fired at us, Colonel!"

"No, he didn't!" Yosef shouted, slapping the young private. "He fired in front of us. If he wasn't sure before who we were, he definitely knows now. Fishermen don't carry automatic weapons! You fool! You bloody fool!"

"I'm sorry, Colonel," the man said, his head lowered.

The fighter started a fourth circuit.

Yosef turned to the helmsman. "When I give the word, you turn this boat toward the aircraft. Give him as small a target as possible."

Sweat poured down the fisherman's pudgy face, joining the yellow stains on the front of what used to be a white shirt and increasing the stale ammonia smell of days-old sweat. Yosef knew he smelled little better than the fisherman did.

The fighter completed its circuit and descended for another run against the slow fishing vessel.

"Now! Turn this boat toward the aircraft! Turn it now!"

But the boat remained steady on course.

Yosef took two steps, jumped for the ladder, and with one leap was on the bridge. "Turn the boat!" he yelled, shaking the fisherman.

The fisherman stared ahead, eyes wide and knuckles pale white. He held the helm in a fear-frozen grip.

Yosef knocked the fisherman out of the way and spun the helm as fast as he could, but all his verbal urgings failed to swing the trawler faster than six knots allowed. As the boat crept toward the direction of the fighter, Yosef pulled the fisherman off the deck and onto his feet.

"Keep this boat pointed at the aircraft, fisherman!"

"Yes, sir. Yes, sir," the man said as he hurriedly replaced Yosef at the helm.

White flames flashed from the plane's thirty-millimeter cannon, creating a geyser path of death, tearing up the sea as the shells headed toward the boat.

"Take cover!" Yosef shouted, diving down the ladder. He rolled across the deck.

Seconds later bullets tore a path across the boat, ripping up deck and tearing through the sides before the fighter roared by again.

The boat continued its turn. Yosef leaped up the ladder to the helm. The fisherman lay across the wheel. A thirty-millimeter shell had made a large entry hole, but it made a larger exit, taking the fisherman's entire back with it before blasting through the other side of the boat. Involuntary muscle spasms caused the dead man's mouth to move as if trying to speak. Yosef rolled the twitching body to one side and spun the helm in the opposite direction. Sergeant Boutrous bounded up the small ladder.

"Here, take the wheel and head for shore."

"We'll run aground, Colonel."

"That's the point. If we don't run aground, we'll be sunk out here."

From the deck below came a shout. "Here he comes again!"

Yosef raised his gun. "Well, shoot the son of a bitch!"

The ocean erupted as the path of death raced again toward the boat. Gunfire from the Guardsmen reached for the aircraft. Bullets hit the aircraft nose area. Yosef doubted they affected the heavily armed fighter. Shooting down a fighter aircraft with small arms was nearly impossible. The aircraft's cannon shells ripped through the trawler again. The pilot climbed, flipped to the right instead of the left, and began another circuit, positioning the aircraft for a stern-to-bow attack. The cannon shells, this time, would pass straight down the middle of the trawler.

"Yosef, what is going on? The woman has been wounded by splintered wood!" shouted President Alneuf, who poked his head up the ladder from below.

"Stay down, Mr. President! We are heading for the beach. Pack up any food and water you can find. We are going to need it!"

The head disappeared.

"Here he comes again!"

Cannon shells ripped into the engine compartment. The private who had fired the first rounds at the aircraft dove to the right directly into the path of the thirty-millimeter shells, which cut him in half. His top torso fell overboard. The legs collapsed slowly. What remained of his body tumbled forward, sending blood and a wad of intestines flooding onto the deck.

The bridge looked as if it had been through a frenzied chain saw attack. The small half-roof was gone. Tattered bits of smoking wood swung from the sides. No windows remained. Sergeant Boutrous stood miraculously unscratched as he spun the helm, lining the bow dead-on to the beach about five hundred meters ahead. No dirty windows obscured his vision. Yosef shook his head, amazed the sergeant was alive with so much damage around him. Sergeant Boutros pushed the throttle forward as far as it would go. From the engine compartment the diesel noise increased as the motor strained to provide more speed. Yosef gripped a nearby railing as the fishing trawler picked up a couple more knots.

"Corporal Ghatan, Corporal Omar!" Yosef shouted, releasing the railing and waving his arms at the Palace Guardsmen. "Prepare to abandon ship or whatever it is that sailors do when they run like hell!"

The fighter jet turned right again.

White smoke trickled out of the boat's engine compartment.

By the time the aircraft finished its circuit for another attack, dark billowing smoke poured from the engine room.

"Colonel, we're slowing down!" yelled Boutrous, shifting the throttle back and forth, trying to keep the engine going.

The wind blew the smoke to the left, obstructing Yosef's vision.

"Swing that wheel as far to the right as it will go!"

The boat started a slow turn to starboard into its smoke. The cannon shells whistled through the smoke. Two shattered the bow. The others missed the boat entirely.

"Keep it pointed toward the beach!" The beach was about two hundred meters away.

Sergeant Boutrous whirled the helm, hand over hand, to offset the strong riptide. A sharp current pulled the boat south, helping them close another hundred yards. Yosef hoped the fading momentum of the boat would carry them to the beach. Less than a hundred meters from the beach, the engine sputtered, coughed, and died.

"He's leaving! Praise be to Allah!"

Yosef shielded his eyes as he scanned the sky for the MiG-29. The contrail caught his attention. The aircraft was heading west toward Algiers. Fighter aircraft used a lot of gas in combat. Yosef suspected his party's luck was due more to lack of petrol than to Allah.

The boat lurched, nearly throwing Yosef off his feet, as it crunched onto the sand beneath the outgoing tide. They would have to wade the remaining twenty meters to shore. Perfect targets if the aircraft returned.

"Come on, everyone. Overboard."

Sergeant Boutrous jumped down from the bridge area.

"Sergeant, take three men up there above the beach and see where we are."

Boutrous pointed to Corporal Ghatan and two other Guardsmen. "Come on!" One after the other they jumped overboard into knee-high waves. Seeing their weapons would be in no danger from the water, they lowered them from over their heads and slugged through the sucking tide to the beach.

President Alneuf emerged, leading the woman; a blood-soaked bandage hastily wrapped around her head covered her left eye. The president carried the wailing child.

"Amir, Amir," she said when she saw the body of her husband, then she began the oddle-ooping titter common of grieving Bedouin women. She hiked up her dress and started to the bridge, but Yosef grabbed her arm.

"No, he is dead. Remember him as he was. You do not want to see what he looks like now."

"But he was my husband. What will I do without a husband?"

"You are young. But you won't grow older if you stay here." He tugged her to the side of the boat. Corporal Omar, his weapon slung across his back, stood in the water helping everyone down from the wallowing craft. Yosef helped the wounded woman over the side to the waiting corporal. Yosef took the baby from the president and passed the boy to the woman.

"Mr. President, it is your turn."

"Why did the aircraft leave, Colonel?" Alneuf asked, lifting his leg and straddling the low railing.

"Don't know. Probably running low on gas, Mr. President. What we can be sure is that he reported our location to his headquarters. I think your earlier prediction may come true. Helicopters or troops or both are probably heading our way. We have to move. You'd think they'd still be sleeping this early in the morning."

Corporal Omar reached up and helped President Alneuf down into the water.

President Alneuf looked up at Yosef. "Seems to be a new era, Colonel. Maybe we should have spent more time awake. If we had, maybe Algeria would still be Algeria."

Yosef turned away and crossed the deck. Now was not the time to argue politics. He glanced back to see Corporal Omar lift the president between the linked arms of two Guardsmen. The two carried Alneuf to the beach and stood him up on moist sand.

Yosef ran below and grabbed the two bags President Alneuf had stocked from the limited larder on board. He looked at the doorway leading to the deck. Where to now, was the question.

He rushed up the ladder and tossed the bags to Corporal Omar below, who immediately headed toward the beach. Yosef looked around the boat one last time before he, too, jumped. He was the last to reach the beach. Ahead, several Guardsmen surrounded President Alneuf, helping him over the dunes. A shout from the top of the crest caught Yosef's attention. He shielded his eyes from the sun. Sergeant Boutrous waved, urging him to hurry. Yosef jogged to catch up with the president and the other Palace Guards.

"What now, Colonel Yosef?" asked the president, his question coming between short, rapid breaths.

"Mr. President, we have to keep moving. We can expect company soon and we need to get as far away from here as we can."

President Alneuf stumbled, but was caught by Yosef on his left and Corporal Omar on the right.

They climbed the short, winding trail to the top of the hill, taking it slow because of the president, though their lives depended on speed.

"Colonel, I feel I am an encumbrance. Unlike the Palace Guards, I am an old man. I am beginning to realize how old I am. I think, without me, you may make Tunisia or some other safe abode. With me, I am afraid it will only be a matter of time before they catch us."

"Mr. President, soldiers are paid to risk their lives in defense of their country. You are our country and our responsibility."

President Alneuf shook his head. "No, Colonel, countries always survive. It is the people in them who change. The rebels would voice the same opinion that you do. They love our country as much as we do. It is just that they have such a rigid opinion on what is right and what is wrong that they lack the humanity to accept others' rights to their differences—the freedom to express yourself, even when it differs from the government." He stumbled again. Alneuf put his hand on Yosef's sleeve. "Can I just take a moment to catch my breath?"

"Sorry, Mr. President." Yosef and Corporal Omar placed a hand under each arm. President Alneuf did not ask him this time to unhand him. "Forgive me, sir, but we must hurry."

President Alneuf nodded as he held on to the arms of the Guardsmen carrying him.

Five minutes later they reached the top of the low crest and released President Alneuf.

The boat, below and behind them, swung back and forth to the motion of the outgoing tide. It pivoted as the waves burrowed its keel deeper in the soft sand. The smoke from the engine room appeared to be lessening. It surprised Yosef that it hadn't blown up.

Fifty meters inland, surrounded by Guardsmen, an old Volvo two and a half–ton lorry waited on the coast road. The rust on the hood and doors gave the once green cab an Army jungle camouflage look. Wooden railings encompassed a thirty-foot flatbed crammed with sheep, baaing their discontent, unable to move from being so tightly packed.

"Come on, Mr. President. It looks as if your presidential car has been traded in for a more useful vehicle."

"Who are you?" Yosef asked the driver as they approached the truck. He reached out and pushed down the barrel of a gun that a Guardsman had trained on the driver.

The man had the dark skin and eyes of the Bedouin. The stained tail of what could have been a white headdress trailed a couple of feet down the back of the large man, who was easily three inches taller than Yosef and many inches wider. The traditional aba hung from the driver's shoulder to the ankle, swishing an inch above a pair of sun-cracked leather sandals. Farm stains, perspiration, and days of wear had turned the white Arab garb to a dingy, dirty yellow.

The driver raised his chin, revealing a couple more hiding under it, to stare, eye to eye, at Alneuf. "Mr. President, I am honored," the man said in a deep bass voice that echoed like gigantic loudspeakers. He bowed his head. "Allow me to introduce myself. I am Bashir Ibn Howadi Al Sannusi of the Sannusi tribe. It is an honor to be at your service." He touched his head and brushed several of his chins and his chest as a gesture of servitude and respect.

"Thank you, Said Bashir. It is fortunate that we meet, even if it is because my soldiers stopped you."

Sergeant Boutrous, standing beside Said Bashir, interrupted. "No, sir. We didn't stop him. He was waiting when we came up. He whistled to catch our attention. We thought it might be an ambush, but found only him and his sheep."

"That is true, Your Excellency. I watched the lopsided battle along the beach." He laughed, placing his hands over an ample, bouncing stomach. "It was quite a sight. I have never witnessed such a David and Goliath. Of course, you lacked the stones and the slingshot that David possessed and thirty-millimeter shells do make a mean Goliath."

"Thanks for stopping, Said Bashir. We need your truck," said Yosef.

"Of course, Major."

"Colonel," Sergeant Boutrous corrected.

"Of course, Colonel," Bashir continued unabashed. "I knew when I saw you deserting the boat that you were in need of assistance. I am but a poor farmer, but even a poor farmer can figure out who must be on the beach when he sees soldiers surrounding a man in a suit. Even if that man lacks the Western tie that is considered essential for the apparel that he wears."

"You don't speak like a poor farmer," said Alneuf. "You

say you are of the Sannusi tribe? Would you be a descendent of Abdallah?"

"Abdallah bin Abid Al Sannusi," Bashir finished for the president, spreading his arms wide. "The exiled king of Libya who was disposed from his throne in the 1960s. Yes, Your Most Excellent Excellency, I am the first grandson of the first grandson of him who would be my great-great-grandfather!"

"Mr. President," Yosef interrupted, "we have to go." He turned to Bashir. "Said Bashir, can you take us to the Tunisian border?"

"I could, but it would not be good going that way. I have spent the last twelve hours traveling from the east. Every few miles are roadblocks. Three hours ago I passed four tanks heading east accompanied with truckload after truckload of 'new Algerian' soldiers. All of them heading to the border and most looking as scared as a boy who knows he is about to lose his virginity."

"Colonel, it looks as if we are slowly being trapped," Alneuf offered.

"Mr. President, we have to keep trying until—"

"Oh, no, you're not trapped," laughed Bashir. "Help me with the tailgate and we shall let some of my babies loose to fend for themselves. That way we can get all of you into the truck." He whistled and clapped his hands three times.

On the bed of the truck four men, previously hidden among the sheep, stood up. Each held an ancient Kalashnikov rifle, the stocks individually decorated in Arabic script and strips of hand-patterned tin as a sign of pride and ownership.

"My nephews," said Bashir, grinning as he tilted his head and spread his thick hands. "There was always that chance that you weren't who I thought you were—and on whom can anyone ever depend if not on their kinsmen?"

A minute later the wounded woman and her child, along with the remainder of Yosef's force, were on the bed of the truck. The Guardsmen took defensive positions around the bed to give them compass coverage.

"Leave the tail section down," Bashir said. "But for heaven's sake don't let the remaining sheep fall out. They make such a mess when they hit the road and cry so pitifully when you scoop them up and throw them back on the truck."

To move the wooden tail section out of the way a couple of Guardsmen slid it against a side railing. Then three of them sat down with their feet hanging off the back.

"Hold on if you're going to sit there," Bashir warned. In reply to their questioning looks he added, "No shocks. That, plus those, makes the truck bounce very rough." He pointed to several potholes nearby.

As the Guardsmen slid further inside and away from the open tail, Bashir, Yosef, and President Alneuf walked to the cab.

"Come on, Mr. President," said Bashir. He and Yosef helped the president into the front of the old vehicle.

Yosef crowded in afterward, placing the president in the middle. Bashir hoisted his heavy frame into the driver's seat.

Their rescuer reached under the steering column and touched two wires together. The engine misfired. He tried again; the engine caught. Laughing, Bashir pulled the truck off the shoulder, back onto the road, and headed west.

"We are heading back toward Algiers," said Yosef. "We need to be heading east, my friend."

"I have told you, Colonel, we would not travel ten kilometers before running into the new Algerian Army."

"Well, we can't go back to Algiers. The city has fallen," Yosef said, almost apologetically.

"Oh, everyone knows that Algiers has fallen. The only fighting is around Oran near our western borders and they won't last much longer." Bashir punctuated his comments with quick laughter, shaking his head, as if the situation in Algeria struck him as ironic or comical. Yosef couldn't tell which.

"How do you know the fighting is about to stop around Oran?" Yosef asked.

"Oh, *mon colonel,* did not your little fight tell you? This morning the Air Force has come out in support of the new government."

"And the Navy?"

Bashir shrugged his shoulders. "I don't know, but the Algerian Navy has never been a major player in our politics like our Army and our Air Force." Using the tail of his headpiece he blew his nose and then wiped the sweat from his forehead before tossing it back over his shoulder. "Or should we call it their Air Force and their Army? Besides, navies never determine the outcome of revolutions. They only influence the outcome."

Yosef turned to Alneuf. "Mr. President, we have little choice. We must try for Tunisia."

Bashir interrupted. "Tunisia is impossible, Colonel. We fool them? No?" Without waiting for an answer he continued. "Let me take you to a small village I know west of Algiers where I have many relatives and—you will be pleased to be thanking me—they are all loyal to you, President Alneuf. They will be pleased to receive you, for your government has been nice for our enterprises and, without doubt, the new government will not be as understanding of the rights and freedoms of those who scratch out a life in the soil."

The truck hit a series of small potholes, throwing everyone around the cab and tossing those in back off their haunches. A renewed vigor of baaing came from the sheep. Bashir glanced in his rearview mirror to see if anyone had fallen off.

"Of course, I know you are President Alneuf, but I wonder who the rebels think they have. . . ." Bashir drummed the heavy fingers of his right hand on his chin while steering with the left. He glanced sideways at Yosef and Alneuf and laughed. Suddenly, he grabbed the steering wheel with both hands and jerked it to the left in an attempt to avoid a large pothole. The back right wheel hit it, bouncing Yosef into the roof.

"What do you mean?" Alneuf asked.

"While you were fighting with the warplane the radio reported that President Alneuf had surrendered the country to the new 'people's government of Algeria' and had ordered all government forces still resisting to put down their weapons and return to their garrisons."

"But I haven't said that."

"Of course you haven't, Mr. President. Only the radio has said that." Bashir let out an audible sigh. "Pity those troops who do return to their garrisons. My first nephew by my second sister, who is riding in back, watched from a hidden spot above the small garrison in Bukra Al Buriha. The rebels relieved the soldiers of their weapons as they returned to the garrison in response to the radio. This morning they called them out to stand in the morning sun. My nephew by my second sister is a fine lad with impressive hearing"—Bashir flicked his right ear—"but he was unable to hear what they said. But we discussed it and decided that the rebels offered the soldiers a chance to fight for the new government. Many came forward. Some more quickly than others, I hesitate to add. Officers were crowded off to another side and it appeared they were not invited to join the new Army, I think, for none came forward. When they finished, those who volunteered, which were most, crawled into trucks that quickly departed the garrison and turned east to join the border troops."

Bashir downshifted as the truck reached a slight hill. The front left wheel crashed into another pothole, throwing the speeding truck to the left and Yosef into the roof again. Bashir pulled the truck back onto the right side of the road.

"What happened to the others?" Yosef asked, rubbing his head.

"They were lined up and shot," Bashir replied in a matter-of-fact tone. "Let's face it, Colonel, in the new Algeria only the quiet, docile members of our society will live peacefully in their ignorance and then only if their neighbor lacks envy."

At the crest of a hill they passed two cars, traveling in convoy. Personal effects were tied loosely to the roofs. With the exception of the two men driving, crouched protectively over the steering wheels, all the three in the cab saw were women and children crammed inside both vehicles. Fearful glances came from the people inside the vehicles, but no acknowledgment; no casual wave came as they passed.

"They won't go much farther," Bashir commented.

"Why is that?"

"The rebel roadblock will stop them and turn them back. This is the new Algeria, Mr. President. That is, until you return to power."

"And you think I'll return?"

"No, I don't, Mr. President," replied Bashir after a few seconds. "Please accept my most humble apologies. But, you will be the catalyst; the figurehead to those who will slip into the underworld of Algeria to fight. Now the colonel, he is young. He could return to free Algeria from these new tyrants, who will jerk freedom away in the name of religion or in the name of social equality. They will find reasons to stop those freedoms we had begun to enjoy; just as communists did during the days of the Soviet Union in the name of socialism or as the Americans do in the name of political correctness. Hold on!"

The bright sun blinded the three as they swerved around a bend in the road. The truck bounced through another series of potholes before straightening out. Bashir pulled the sun visor down, reached above it, and extracted a pair of gold aviator sunglasses. He put them on. They looked out of place; too small for his broad face, large jowls, and multiple chins.

"Do you have sunglasses, Mr. President, Colonel?"

"I am afraid, Said Bashir, that when we left the palace last night we hardly had time to pack. What you see is what we have," Alneuf answered, holding his coat open slightly.

"Open the dashboard, Colonel. I think I have some spare sunglasses in there."

Yosef opened the dashboard. Dozens of aviator sunglasses tumbled out, with several pairs landing on the floor. Some were in carrying cases, most were not, and all had the manufacturer's tag still on them.

"A lot of sunglasses for a simple truck farmer, Mr. Bashir," said Yosef.

Bashir's laughter rocked the cab. "Even a truck farmer must supplement the meager earnings made from the sale of vegetables and sheep."

"You're a smuggler?" Alneuf asked, amazed.

Bashir's laughter rocked the cab. "No, Mr. President.

Let's say that until this new change of government I was active in tax-free marketing."

"Okay, hold on, here is where we turn." Without slowing, Bashir whipped the truck to the left, bouncing off the road. The wheels dropped six inches from pavement to sand, tossing everyone in the back into the air. Bashir continued down a rough incline before, with brakes squealing, abruptly stoping amidst a cloud of dust.

Bashir shoved the door open and leaned out of the cab. "Shove those sheep out!" he shouted. He reached back inside and put the gears in neutral and pulled the emergency brakes. Moving fast for a large, overweight man, he jumped out, leaving the driver's door open.

"Wait here, Mr. President," Yosef said cautiously.

Yosef opened his door and hurried back to where his men and Bashir's cousins were pulling and pushing the sheep off the truck.

"What is this for?" he asked.

"The sheep will tear up the dirt and erase our tracks," Bashir said. Then seeing the men herding more sheep to the edge of the truck bed, he shouted, "No, not all of them. Keep ten. We may need them for food and drink."

"Drink?" Corporal Ghatan asked.

"Yes, drink. You see, Corporal," said Bashir, reaching down and grabbing one of the sheep by its scuff, "if you make a small cut here, you can drain some of the blood. Warm blood satisfies both hunger and thirst." He released the sheep.

Ghatan's lips curled in disgust. "Well, you've just satisfied mine."

Bashir turned to a nephew and whispered something to him. The man ran to the road. Bashir's nephew ripped a bush from the ground and began erasing signs of where the truck had turned off the road.

Yosef motioned to a nearby Guardsman to go help Bashir's nephew. He was still deciding whether to trust Bashir, but knew they had little choice at this time. They outnumbered the smuggler cum farmer if he decided the man was untrustworthy. They could always take the truck and abandon Bashir and his nephews. He turned to discover Bashir staring at him. The smuggler smiled, winked, and broke eye contact. Yosef would have been correct if he had surmised that Bashir knew what he was thinking.

Bashir pulled himself up into the bed of the truck. The huge Arab waded through the remaining sheep to the back of the cab. There, he grabbed a dirty canvas sheet off the floor, sheep droppings rolling off as he unfolded it. Then, Bashir rigged the canvas so it ran from the top of the cab to halfway across the bed. He anchored it to the side rails. The smell of unwashed sheep overode the smell of Yosef's unwashed Guardsmen.

"That will give some shade as well as something to hide under if we are spotted," he said to Yosef. He looked at the woman and her child. "Saida, you should place yourself and your child here in the corner. The road ahead is very rough and the corner will help balance you."

Bashir helped her move. "When we arrive at my relatives, I have a cousin who nearly completed a year of medical school. He will attend to your wounds." He patted her head and turned to Yosef, who watched through the rails and whispered, "He also treats the sheep."

The nephews helped Bashir down.

"Where are we going?" Yosef asked. He shaded his eyes and looked south. Miles and miles of waist-high thorny bushes and rough arid land stretched from the road to the horizon. Beyond the horizon lay the Sahara Desert. No one would ever find them there, but who would care because few went in and even fewer came out.

"Colonel, there is a small trail that only I and my friends know. We should be safe, Allah willing. By tonight, we should be at the village of my relatives."

"I seem to remember that there are minefields out here."

"Of course. Old World War II minefields, first laid by the Germans and then by the French and then later by the Americans and then later, after the war, the French again. By the time they finished, we had minefields on top of minefields, a polyglot arrangement of international death."

"I am assuming you know your way through them."

Bashir patted his ample stomach and laughed.

"Oh, Colonel, you bring such mirth with you. I will tell you this. I have yet to be killed by any of the mines and if I am, then you are welcome to blame me on our way to paradise. Back on board, my friends! We have miles to go!" Bashir shouted, clapping his hands twice.

The Guardsmen and Bashir's nephews climbed onto the bed of the truck. Two of the nephews slipped the tail section in place as Bashir and Yosef hurried to the cab.

The truck hit a bump as soon as Bashir drove off. "Try to make yourselves as comfortable as possible, Mr. President." He reached up and took the sunglasses off of Alneuf. "Here, let me remove the tags, Mr. President." Finished, he handed them back.

"We have five kilometers to go before we turn into a small wadi that runs nearly the entire way from here to the other side of Algiers," Bashir said, then mumbled audibly, "if we make the five kilometers without someone seeing us."

"Mr. Bashir," Alneuf said. "We owe you a great debt for this."

"Mr. President, you owe me nothing, but if you want to pay me, let's talk about that farm bill you sponsored last year."

NINE

DUNCAN PAUSED INSIDE THE ENTRANCE TO COMBAT IN-formation Center, allowing his eyes to adjust to the blue lighting. He stifled a yawn. The commodore, Captain Farnfield, and Colonel Stewart were huddled over the plotting table in the center of the large compartment.

Highly qualified petty officers were hunched over each console. Scattered, seemingly haphazardly, young seamen shuffled restlessly at assigned displays. Long black cords led from bulkhead sockets to sound-powered phone sets wedged tightly on their heads like fierce mandibles of warrior ants—fingers constantly on the mouthpiece as they "rogered" and relayed information throughout the ship to other background peers on the sound-powered phone web of the USS *Nassau*. Like an uncoordinated Mexican wave, hands shot out as petty officers pressed buttons on consoles while others triggered radio circuits to relay information. All across Combat cool professionals manipulated sensors and weapon systems as the sailor warriors of the twenty-first century shared and coordinated elements of the task force, keeping the ships and aircraft in proper formation as, like a hurricane, the amphibious armada moved relentlessly toward its objective.

Duncan weaved his way around the manned consoles—the low murmur of operations, a constant buzz in the background—until he reached the plotting table. The smell of sweat, old coffee, and fresh morning pastries filled the air. Duncan glanced at the clock: about an hour before reveille sounded. The last watch before reveille was an hour into its four-hour duty cycle.

". . . and how long has it been?" Duncan heard Commodore Ellison finish. "Hello, Duncan. Sorry to jerk you out of the rack, but thought you needed to be here."

"Commodore," the Combat Information Center watch officer answered, "we last had contact with USS *Gearing* at nineteen hundred hours during routine comms check. Since then we haven't had a reason to contact her. It was only when Radio tried to raise her a couple of hours ago for daily cipher change that we realized we had lost contact with her. I checked the logs on the other circuits and discovered she had failed to acknowledge any group calls during the night."

"What else, Lieutenant?"

"We tried calling on secure voice, the electronic warfare net, the aircraft control circuits, and even the antisubmarine warfare net—no reply. I have the operators calling every minute on the minute in an attempt to reestablish contact."

"The Network Centric Warfare grid?" the commodore asked, referring to the tactical satellite warfare system connecting warships together digitally to share national and joint force intelligence, sensor, and surveillance information.

The CICWO shook his head. "Checked, sir. She is no

longer anywhere on the NCW, or even the global information grid. I have the information technicians checking to see when she dropped."

The commodore stroked his chin, then added, "Okay, inform me when we reestablish contact. Let's give her twelve hours, but if we haven't established comms by zero seven hundred hours, I want an aircraft to check on her."

The CICWO glanced at the twenty-four–hour digital clock above the plotting table. "Aye, aye, sir." He had nearly two hours. He turned and made his way to the air search console.

The commodore pushed his bifocals back on his nose. "Gentlemen, European Command has finally gotten off its ass and given Sixth Fleet permission to break the *Gearing* off track. Of course, to break off, we got to contact them. Sixth Fleet has ordered us to sortie at flank speed to take station just over the horizon from Algiers. Since yesterday things have been going from bad to worse. Intell reports an American killed last night—executed by Algerian insurgents, who are going ape-shit and killing everybody and everything in sight! Ironically, remnants of the Algerian Army engaged the insurgents. They saved the remainder of the hostages from the same fate only to abandon them to their fate in an old Russian truck. They must have had God with them, for they made it to the American Embassy."

Ellison paused, then continued. "It don't look good, men. The new Algerian revolutionary government, which no one knows who the hell they are or even where the shit they're located, is rounding up foreigners—the ones they don't shoot—and forcing them into the American Embassy compound. As of two hours ago the American Embassy had over two hundred refugees, of various nationalities, jammed into its small courtyard—a virtual United Nations of citizens from the sane world."

"They have electricity and water?" Duncan asked.

Commander Mulligan, the staff intelligence officer, stepped out of the shadows into the faint light. Duncan wished he'd quit doing that.

"Yes, sir, Captain," Commander Mulligan answered. "They have the basic sanitary facilities, but trucks filled with non-Algerian citizens are continuing to arrive. They started arriving around midnight and continued nonstop until about three o'clock. It's tapered off some, but has not stopped. The embassy began redistributing the refugees to their respective embassies. This should reduce the impact on the limited American facilities. They started"—he looked at his Rolex watch—"about thirty minutes ago, around first light."

"Thank you, Commander Mulligan," the commodore said, shoving his bifocals back on his nose. Every time he wrinkled his forehead or squinted his eyes they slid down. Ellison coughed and then pointed to the chart in front of them.

"Gentlemen, this is where we are and this is where we are going," the commodore emphasized, using his pencil to mark the two locations. "As soon as we reestablish comms with the *Gearing*," he added, his voice rising. Then he shouted across Combat, "Lieutenant, you got comms with the *Gearing* yet?"

"No, sir. We're still trying," the CICWO replied, rolling his eyes at the nearby junior CICWO.

She rolled her eyes in reply. "As much as he likes to talk and buttonhole people, you'd think he'd be more patient," she said softly to the lieutenant.

"Damn. As soon as we contact her I want those Harriers recovered. You hear? I want them recovered!" Ellison yelled, and then turned to the three men around the table. "Then we'll turn our noses toward Algeria and, our butts to Libya, sail through the Strait of Sicily. With luck, sometime late tomorrow night we'll be on station just over the horizon from Algiers. Bulldog, how are you doing with your portion of the operations plan?"

Colonel Stewart's thin, razor-sharp frame made him look as if he were perpetually at attention. "Sir, my concept of operation is completed. When directed, the United States Marines will board two CH-53 helicopters while Captain James, with his SEALs, will follow on the CH-46. We're going to have four Cobra attack helicopters with us. We will low-level into Algiers via the harbor route, thereby avoiding major municipal areas. The troop helicopters will loiter at the harbor to effect a four-minute insertion separation. Two Cobras will remain with them while the other two escort the troop helos to the embassy. I estimate four minutes from the harbor to the American Embassy. Marines inside the compound have cleared a landing site. The first CH-53 will land, disembark its company, rapidly load a contingent of evacuees, and depart. Time on ground will be four minutes. Commodore, four minutes will be the standard time for every operation in this evolution. Using the same time element helps reduce confusion and makes it easier for pilots and ground personnel to synchronize their actions."

The commodore nodded. "I'm impressed, Colonel."

"By the time the first CH-53 is airborne out of the embassy, the second 53 will be in the landing pattern. Same evolution for it; third helo will be Captain James and his SEALs on the CH-46. We'll take evacuees out on it also. If the plan goes smoothly we'll have three choppers full of evacuees airborne and heading out of Algiers in twelve minutes."

"Thanks, Colonel. I would like to see the written version on my desk following breakup of this meeting."

"Duncan, your guys ready?"

"Yes, sir, Commodore. We have two teams; four SEALs to a team. Each team will be equipped with one sniper, one MG-60 per team, and one communicator. Every SEAL will also be outfitted for close-in combat support. I will command one team and Lieutenant Commander Pettigrew the other. Lieutenant Sunney will remain on board with the backup team on thirty-minute alert. Colonel Stewart and I have discussed our role. We will support the Marines where perimeter integrity appears vulnerable and take on any Lone Rangers. The snipers are available if we need them."

The hatch to CIC opened and a sandy-haired sailor in sharp-creased dungarees entered, his eyes searching the operations space. "Shut the door!" a voice shouted at him. He did.

Seeing Commander Mulligan, the sailor walked directly to him. The intelligence officer took several steps away to meet the sailor, whereupon the two held a close, whispered conversation inaudible to the three men at the table. Duncan and the colonel tried to eavesdrop with no success as the commodore continued his diatribe.

Commander Mulligan dismissed the sailor and rejoined the three captains.

"Commodore," Commander Mulligan interrupted, "things have really deteriorated in Algiers."

"What do you mean?"

"The American Embassy tried to move the citizens to their respective embassies, as I briefed earlier. The truck traveled about fifty yards outside the compound before the Algerians stopped it. They ordered it back, at gunpoint, to the embassy. When the truck started to turn around, an Italian citizen jumped off and started running. Don't know why, but the Italian Embassy is in sight of the American Embassy so he may have been trying to make it there. Instead they shot him before he ran twenty feet."

"They shot him?"

"Yes, sir, but it gets worse."

"Not for the Italian it doesn't."

"At that time he was still alive, sir."

"At that time?"

"Yes, sir. Three Marines at the gate ran to the truck, believing it was under attack, and, needless to say, a small firefight broke out, with two of the Marines being wounded and several of the insurgents being killed. One of the insurgents, as he ran for cover, put a bullet into the head of the Italian when he passed him. A Marine shot and killed the Algerian who killed the Italian. Marine security force personnel poured out and surrounded the truck and escorted it back inside the compound. No more shooting has occurred. It appears we are at a standoff right now. The embassy reports more Algerian troops arriving and taking position around the American Embassy. The ambassador says she believes they are preparing to attack the embassy."

The commodore spun on the CICWO. "Shit! Lieutenant, have you gotten the *Gearing* yet?"

"No, sir. Still no joy."

"I don't have to tell you that if they attack our embassy, it's a whole new ballgame. President Crawford ain't Carter," Ellison said, then yelled at the CICWO, "Have you tried INMARSAT?"

"No, sir, Commodore. You said we were never to use it."

"Well, I think you can use it for this, don't you!" He lowered his voice and looked at Duncan. "I hate using INMARSAT. It costs an arm and a leg from our OPTAR to pay for it and it's insecure as hell. Except for the security aspects I wish military comms were as effective as their commercial counterparts."

The CICWO reached for the INMARSAT handset located beside the captain's chair.

At that moment a secure voice speaker above the plot table interrupted the commodore.

"Sixty-one, this is Air Force Romeo Charlie One Three Five on track western Mediterranean. Interrogative my comms."

The CICWO replaced the INMARSAT handset and picked up a nearby microphone.

"Air Force Romeo Charlie One Three Five, this is Sixty-one. I read you fivers, go ahead."

"Well, that's good news," the commodore said. "The EP-3E went off station nearly an hour ago. The Rivet Joint is here. The RC-135 is the best reconnaissance platform around. But, whatever you do, don't tell the Air Force. Their heads are big enough as it is. If they knew the Navy thought that, they'd being doing the Mexican wave at their base in Mildenhall. CICWO, did they bring protective air cover and tanker support?"

"Rivet Joint, interrogative your air cover and fuel support?"

"Sixty-one, I've got an F-16 Fighting Falcon, armed to the teeth, under each wing. Sigonella air station KC-135 scheduled for top-off at ten hundred hours. Wait one, Sixty-one."

A few seconds later the RC-135 returned on the circuit. "Sixty-one, Fighting Falcons prepared to escort Rivet Joint over Algeria if so desired."

"Right!" said the commodore, sarcastically, to the three officers. "I'm going to give permission for an unarmed RC-135 with only two fighters to overfly Algeria?"

"Sixty-one, stand by for Rivet Joint Sitrep One. We are showing large-scale military movements in Algeria toward the eastern and western border areas. Additionally, a massive search is under way approximately forty-five kilometers east of Algiers with helicopters and ground troops. We are still evaluating the raw data, but onboard analysts' opinion is that they may be searching for President Alneuf, who dropped out of sight two days ago. We are seeing a lot of isolated fighting around the country, much more activity than we have the resources to cover. Therefore, a lot of the minor stuff is being tossed into the bit bucket for later processing."

The communications circuit dropped for about fifteen seconds before resynching with the aircraft.

". . . aircraft shooting up a fishing boat that subsequently beached itself. The search is centered on that area. Over."

Commander Mulligan motioned for the microphone from the CICWO.

"Romeo Charlie One Three Five, Sixty-one here. We copy your last. Hold one, I have our India Oscar here who has some questions."

The CICWO handed the microphone to Commander Mulligan.

"This is the intelligence officer for Sixty-one. Do you have any indications as to why forces are moving toward the border areas? And what is the situation around Oran?"

"Sixty-one, don't know, they may be sealing their borders. We are showing sporadic fighting around Oran. It looks as if government forces are being pushed back. At this time, Oran remains in government hands, but I wouldn't give it much longer. Our premission briefer said she heard before our briefing that national intelligence has linked the antigovernment riots in Morocco and the Algerian revolution to the anti-West government in Egypt and whoever is running Libya now. Seems Tunisia is the only remaining stable country on the North African coast."

"What is the situation at the Algerian Mers El Kebir Naval Base east of Oran?"

"Wait one." Several seconds passed before the Rivet Joint responded. "Negative indications on Mers El Kebir, India Oscar. We don't know who controls it right now, but give us ten hours on station and we should be able to downlink a complete profile to your C4I console."

"Roger your last, One Three Five, Sixty-one standing by on this circuit. Out."

Commander Mulligan looked at the C4I console operator. "Do you have a link with the Rivet Joint?"

"That's an affirmative, sir. We have a good connection at this time and they have already begun downloading their intelligence picture."

"Good, I want to be kept up to date on their reports."

"Yes, sir. You should be receiving them in the Intell spaces, since this console's data is being piped from there."

Commander Mulligan nodded and glanced at the commodore, who was bent over the plotting table trying to locate Mers El Kebir.

The intelligence officer handed the microphone back to the CICWO.

"Well, Lieutenant," the commodore said, looking up and peering over his bifocals at the young officer.

The lieutenant looked puzzled.

"The INMARSAT phone call to *Gearing*? If you please!"

The CICWO grabbed the INMARSAT phone, punched in the number for the *Gearing,* and waited for an answer. It continued to ring. The commodore watched the CICWO shrug his shoulders. The lieutenant put his hand over the mouthpiece to tell the commodore there was no answer, when he heard the familiar click of someone picking up the other end.

"*Gearing,*" the voice answered.

"*Gearing,* this is Lieutenant Stumple on board *Nassau.*"

"Go ahead, *Nassau,* this is the CIC watch officer, Lieutenant Smith, on *Gearing.*"

"Wait one, *Gearing.*" He lowered the phone.

"Commodore, we have *Gearing* on the line."

"Give me the phone." He jerked the handset out of the lieutenant's hand.

"This is the commodore, CTF Sixty-one. Let me speak to your Charlie Oscar."

"Sorry, sir, the commanding officer is in Radio. We had a small fire earlier and he is assessing the damage. Do you wish to wait while I send for him, sir?"

"No, that's okay. Who am I talking to?"

"Sir, this is Lieutenant Smith. I am the duty watch officer here in Combat Information Center."

"Okay, Lieutenant Smith, relay to your skipper that the FONOP is curtailed. You've been on track long enough to log this as a completed mission. Use this time"—he looked at the twenty-four–hour clock—"zero five thirty hours as the time for completion. You are to immediately break off and at flank speed rejoin the battle group. Do you understand?"

"Yes, sir. Present mission curtailed. We are to rejoin *Nashville* battle group."

"*Nassau* battle group," the commodore corrected testily. "*Nashville* is in company with us. I'm on *Nassau*!"

The commodore cupped his hand over the mouthpiece. "What is this? Am I surrounded by imbeciles this morning?" he asked Duncan, Bulldog, and the skipper of the *Nassau,* Captain Farnfield.

"Sorry, sir. *Nassau* battle group," the voice of Lieutenant Smith responded.

"Now, repeat what I just told you." He looked at the

others and with a finger made a circling motion around his left temple.

Looking at the commodore, the words *pompous ass* sprang to Duncan's mind.

"Commodore, we are to break off, break off."

"FONOPs, Lieutenant. FONOPs is what you're to break off. Are you sure you understand my directions?" He held the phone out and looked at it in disbelief before placing it back to his ear.

"Yes, sir. Sorry, sir. It is just that we are still at General Quarters because of the fire. We are to stop present operations and at fastest speed rejoin the battle group."

"That's right, son. Now, I want your Charlie Oscar to give me a call when you are off track and heading our way. I want to hear from him ASAP. That's A-S-A-P! Got it?"

"Yes, sir, Ass A-P."

"Don't get smart, Lieutenant. You tell him I expect to hear from him within the next ten minutes."

"Yes, sir."

"Son, how bad was the fire?"

"Not too bad, sir, but Radio is inoperable for the time being."

"Okay, you tell Captain Cafferty I'm waiting for his call."

The commodore hung up the phone.

"Trying to joke on the circuit. Never would have done stuff like that when I was a junior officer. The caliber of JOs keeps going down as the years go by," he said to no one in particular. "Different Navy, gentlemen. Most of the good ones leave after their obligated four years are up or when . . ." He noticed nearby junior officers and sailors listening and smoothly changed the subject. "Fire must have been worse than Lieutenant Smith said. I mean, why else would they still be at General Quarters?

"Duncan," the commodore said as he remembered something. "This message came for you from Washington." He handed Duncan a sealed envelope. " 'Personal for' delivered from Radio. They didn't know where you were hanging your hat so they sent it to me."

Duncan took the envelope and ripped the top to extract the single-page message. He read it, folded it, and put it into his top pocket.

"Nothing important, I hope?" the commodore asked.

"No, sir," Duncan replied sharply. "A personal matter that Admiral Hodges offered to sort."

"Lieutenant," the commodore said to the CICWO, his interest in the message gone when Duncan failed to elaborate. "Recall the Harriers. Clear the deck for their landing. Time to change this group of warships from a blue-water battle group to what it was designed to be: a brown-water amphibious task force. Ain't versatility great? Reminds me of the seventies, when *Jane's Fighting Ships* revealed that the Soviets had more cruisers than us. Did we build more cruisers? You bet your sweet ass we didn't. We just went and redesignated all of our destroyer leaders, like the USS *Bainbridge,* from DLGs to cruisers. *Bainbridge* went from DLGN-25 to CGN-25."

The lieutenant rushed to recall the Marine Corps Harriers.

"Overnight, the United States Navy had more cruisers than the Soviets. Same thing now. Congress says we only need eight aircraft carriers while the Navy says we need twelve, so they went and redesignated these amphibious ships to light carriers. Lots of difference between the eight Harriers I can carry and the one hundred fighter aircraft that a real carrier can launch."

The commodore turned to Captain Farnfield. "Skipper, as soon as *Gearing* is off station, I want those Harriers on deck. Until then, put them in the pattern. Once recovered, I want *Nassau* turned toward our MODLOC. You have the message I drafted earlier with the sailing directions?"

"Yes, sir."

"Release it as soon as those two events are completed. I want max speed and I want us through the Strait of Sicily by this afternoon."

"We can do that, sir, but the USS *Nashville* is an older ship and her max speed is twelve knots. They are still running with a warped port shaft. It'll take divers to correct it and with the damage to the USS *Simon Lake* we may have to send her to a civilian port for repairs."

"Okay, detach *Hayler* to stay with *Nashville* once we increase speed. Give me an estimate by noon how long we'll be on station before *Nashville* shows up. I knew when SurfLant canceled her overhaul last year that we'd have trouble with that ship," Ellison confided.

"Why did Naval Surface Forces Atlantic cancel it?" Duncan asked, more as a courtesy than a curiosity. His mind churned over the message in his pocket.

"Funding was cut—again."

The INMARSAT phone rang. Lieutenant Stumple answered it. Placing a hand over the mouthpiece, he said, "Commodore, it's the *Gearing*'s skipper on the phone."

The commodore took the phone. "Heath, this is Frank Ellison here. I take it you got my orders."

"Yes, sir, Commodore. We are twenty-five miles off track on a course of three three zero at twenty-five knots. What is your position? We are experiencing heavy electromagnetic interference in the area."

"I heard you had a fire in Radio?"

"Yes, sir. No one injured, but we have a lot of electronics to repair and parts to replace."

"Heath, you alright? You sound like you've got a cold or something." He held the phone away momentarily and looked at the handset.

"Yes, Commodore. It is this blasted sand off the desert, covering my ship. We breathe it in and it seems to stay in our chests."

Commander Mulligan leaned toward the commodore and whispered, "Sir, you may want to go secure and engage the STU-III." He pointed to the enciphered voice button on the INMARSAT set.

The commodore waved him away, his eyes narrowing over the interruption. He pushed his bifocals back up on his nose.

"Blasted? Heath, you're mellowing in your old age," the commodore chuckled. "Look, when we finish I will put the lieutenant on who will pass our coordinates. We are recovering the fighters and will be heading to an operating area off Algiers. Anything we can do about your equipment casualty?"

"No, sir. My technicians are working very hard to repair the blasted malfunctioning things."

"Okay, Heath, I'll let you return to your repair work. Don't lollygag about down there. I need your ship with us as soon as possible. Okay?"

"Yes, sir. We are hurrying to join you now."

"Heath, if you have not repaired Radio by sunset, I want you to initiate periodic checks via INMARSAT so we can plot your position until you come into our radar picture. Okay?"

"Yes, sir. I understand, Commodore. This is *Gearing* signing out."

The commodore handed the phone to the CICWO, who

moved to one side to pass the battle group coordinates before hanging up.

"Strange," Ellison said, "I've known Heath Cafferty since he was a spry lieutenant. He sounded almost formal on the phone. Not himself." He shook his head. "Didn't hear one curse word."

"Must have been the enlisted and junior officers manning Combat, sir. Probably wanted to show proper respect," Commander Mulligan offered.

He shrugged his shoulders. "You may be right. First time I've known Heath to temper his speech when things weren't going right. Said *blasted* instead of using the *F* word like he normally does. He's one of the few ring knockers I've known who can outcurse a boatswain mate."

Duncan patted the folded message in his pocket. He needed some time to himself to digest the news from Admiral Hodges.

"Captain Farnfield, I'm going down for a late breakfast, and then I'll be in my stateroom," the commodore said. "Let me know once the Harriers are on board and we are heading north."

Captain Farnfield acknowledged the order as the commodore departed CIC.

"That's the lecture for the morning, gentlemen. See you later," Captain Farnfield said good-naturedly. He patted Lieutenant Stumple on the shoulder. "Lieutenant, let me know when the Harriers are on board. If anything comes up, give me a call"—he nodded his head emphatically. "After breakfast I'll be on the bridge, watching the rest of sunrise."

"Good CONOP, Colonel. Think everything will go according to plan?" Duncan asked after Captain Farnfield and Commander Mulligan departed.

"No, I don't," Bulldog replied. "Nothing ever goes according to plan, but it makes Ellison happy to have something in writing. Between you and me, I have a bad feeling about this so-called noncombatant evacuation. I think we're going to have to fight our way into and out of Algiers and it's going to be bloody, Duncan. I just hope we don't get sucked into their little rebellion."

"I hope you're wrong, Bulldog, but plan for the best, expect the worse. You won't be disappointed." Duncan shook hands with the Marine Corps colonel as the two made their way toward the exit. It was going to be a long day. He patted his pocket.

THE COMMODORE'S EYES FLEW OPEN AS HE DOZED AT the desk in his stateroom. Something was nagging at the back of his mind, and had been ever since the short INMARSAT conversation with Heath Cafferty. He leaned back in the chair, his hand over his mouth, and picked up the Baby Ben clock from his desk. It showed eight o'clock. Realization slammed into him like a freight train. His head shot up as chill bumps raced up his spine and adrenaline surged through his body. He was still tucking in his shirttail as he rushed out of the stateroom, his bifocals nearly falling off.

The person on the other end of the INMARSAT conversation had not been Heath Cafferty. How he knew, he couldn't say, but he knew.

Something was wrong.

"Damn wrong," he mumbled as he shoved a sailor aside to hurry up the ladder toward Combat.

TEN

CAPTAIN IBN AL JAMAL BENT SLIGHTLY TO AVOID THE steel overhead of the small hatch as he entered the control room of the *Al Nasser*. Revolutions were never pleasant. It seemed he had been fighting his entire life for some cause or other. The war-fighting camaraderie of the crew had dissipated with the executions necessary to gain control of the submarine. Unlike on board *Al Solomon,* he refused to establish a revolutionary Islamic court to conduct "thumbs-up, thumbs-down" kangaroo trials. Islam was a great religion, not a vindictive one.

"Allah Alakbar," he whispered softly. Truly, God was great. He had no intention of doing anything further to exacerbate the distrust and fear among the crew.

The *Al Solomon*'s former XO, now its skipper, had bragged to him less than an hour ago during a short underwater communication exchange, that his Islamic court had already executed six heretics. Boasted! Six heretics! Captain Ibn Al Jamal had tried tactfully to suggest that it would be better to temper the revolutionary fever until back in port. He had pointed out that it was better to sail with a crew trusting each other, than have it torn apart by paranoid witch-hunts. His younger, zealous counterpart vehemently argued that the revolutionary courts enhanced solidarity. Ibn Al Jamal knew that zealotry enhanced solidarity only when one individual remained.

Even without asking, the younger man enthusiastically volunteered how effective the garrote had proved in executing those who opposed the revolution. It had been all that Ibn Al Jamal could do to keep his recent lunch down. He recalled how his lips had curled in revulsion over his counterpart's pleasure in the trials and the executions. The only thing those executed were guilty of was an inability to express their faith in such a way as to convince the zealots of their religious beliefs. Individualism in revolutions and religions is never tolerated. It is mistrusted. One can never be a pacifist during a revolution or a benign agnostic when religion leads it.

The initial executions that had been necessary in order to seize control of the *Al Nasser* had damaged crew confidence and sown huge seeds of fear and distrust. The past two days had witnessed some easing of tension, but he knew only time would restore confidence and camaraderie and he had doubts that he had time to do it. The Americans would be coming. They never missed a conflict or a war.

He returned to the problem of the *Al Solomon.* He imagined how the trials on the other Algerian Kilo submarine sowed fear, rising in each officer and sailor as they anxiously waited to see if they were next.

He shook his head. No. Revolutionary courts were not an instrument of Islam. They were vindictive instruments that allowed the dormant sadism in man's heart to burst forth and run unchecked—much like the French Revolution over two hundred years ago. Ibn Al Jamal's disappointment in the revolution was beginning to fester and the revolution was only two days old. He prayed he had not made a mistake. A mistake that was uncorrectable, he knew.

What he was witnessing in the other submarine and had heard before they submerged and started on these missions had nothing to do with the benevolence that Islam preached—his Islam. The Islam he practiced daily and Allah who he worshipped without reservation. Such zealotry as on the *Al Solomon* tore apart the very fabric of the Koran subscribed to by him and the majority of devout Moslems. Tolerance and understanding paved the true path for a proper Moslem. He leaned his head against the bulkhead and uttered a short prayer, starting it with the familiar *"Allah Alakbar wa Allah Alzim."*

A few seconds later Ibn Al Jamal raised his head, blinked his eyes, and moved to the sonar console to watch the soothing pattern as the sounds in the water wove its magic on the screen.

Al Nasser had its challenges—like the attempted mutiny yesterday by the engineers. Revolutions were never without their "challenges." In the freezer two bodies lay stacked on top of each other. It had been a nasty affair, with bullets flying inside the submarine. The submerged boat had been lucky—the shots fired hit the bodies of the mutineers. A bullet underwater could be more dangerous than a bullet fired inside an aircraft. An aircraft could always recover, or have survivors once it crashed, but a submarine hit the bottom and stayed there . . . a living tomb or water-imploded shell.

The freezer on the *Al Solomon* held six victims of revolutionary zeal. Killed not in self-defense or survival, but in religious zealotry. Ibn Al Jamal prayed his counterpart on the *Al Solomon* kept enough crew alive to complete the mission.

Revolution was like a game of poker. No one knew the true winner until the game finished. Losers fell even as cards were shuffled, but the ultimate winner always boiled down to two players. He shut his eyes and wondered whether he would be a winner and live, or a loser and die, as he rode the erratic ebb and flow in the sea of revolutionary chaos. Nothing challenged a sailor's loyalty more than a change in leadership. A leadership that failed to provide clear-cut objectives or goals. He knew this. He had spent the past two days trying to reassure the crew of their roles. He needed their loyalty. The new government needed their patriotism. Loyalty, like respect, had to be earned. He sighed. How could he recover that loyalty when even his loyalty was being peppered with doubts? It was hard for Ibn Al Jamal to reconcile Islam with the actions of a man like the new captain of the *Al Solomon.* He was glad both his parents were dead and did not have to see what Algeria was becoming.

He patted the sonar technician on the shoulder before moving to the helmsman. The escape of the two submarines out of Mers El Kebir had been with Allah's grace. He smoothed the chart on the plotting table. They would avoid the naval base at Mers El Kebir on their return. The last report showed the base at Oran still remained in loyalist hands.

Ibn Al Jamal reviewed the orders issued, including the instructions to the *Al Solomon* skipper to return to Algiers in thirty days unless otherwise directed. But, the *Al Solomon* had to remain outside the Strait of Gibraltar for thirty days. Al Jamal hoped the young man listened to orders.

He had this uncomfortable feeling, like an angry itch in the middle of his back that couldn't be quite reached no matter how you twisted and turned. He knew the inexperienced captain of the *Al Solomon* endangered their mission—of that he was sure. The young man was lost in the passions of inquisitions and seemed more interested in executing his people than his mission.

They were now in the Atlantic Ocean. A quick peep through the periscope showed the sun below the horizon and summer night slowly descending. At 2210 hours, *Al Nasser* and *Al Solomon* exchanged a single sonar ping to locate each other. Twenty minutes later they rendezvoused south of Tarifa, Spain—the windsurfing capital of Europe. He was surprised the *Al Solomon* made it safely through the crowded Strait of Gibraltar, such was his lack of confidence in its skipper.

He clicked the UWC twice. A return click acknowledged his underwater communication signal. Al Jamal ordered the *Al Nasser* to descend to fifty-five fathoms and slowed his speed to underway, barely making way, just enough to keep the bow pointed toward the wide Atlantic.

Behind, the *Al Solomon* maintained course at thirty fathoms. A single ping fifteen minutes later by the *Al Nasser* verified that its sister submarine had passed and was in front of them. Captain Ibn Al Jamal waited another half hour and when five single sonar pings failed to detect the *Al Solomon* he uttered a blessing for the crew of the other submarine. Now, he had his own mission to do. He should have reminded the young captain about the thirty days. To return sooner would endanger the submarine.

ALONE, THE ZEALOT ABOARD THE *AL SOLOMON* WAS truly now in charge of his own destiny. Without the micromanaging, conservative, disapproving leadership of the *Al Nasser*'s older, if more experienced, captain, the rogue skipper intended to show the revolution a true Islamic warrior. One hour later the *Al Solomon* changed course to approach the Spanish coast. It penetrated Spanish territorial waters off the Bay of Cadiz a few minutes after midnight. Here, *Al Solomon* raised its periscope and did a quick navigational fix, using the lights of the oldest continuously inhabited city in Europe and other isolated lights blinking along the coast. Then *Al Solomon* commenced a quiet five-knot racetrack circuit as it monitored the Spanish fleet at the naval base at Rota and commenced a watch for any approaching American naval force. As far as he knew, there wasn't an approaching American naval force, but there would be, and when it arrived it would find the brave revolutionary warriors of *Al Solomon* blocking its path. He looked at his watch—the one taken off a patriot executed yesterday. He smiled, tapped the watch crystal a couple of times, and headed toward the mess decks. He had another court to attend. When his ship returned to the new Algeria, not only would they be heroes of the revolution, but there would only be Islamic warriors on board.

CAPTAIN IBN AL JAMAL OF THE FORMER REPUBLIC OF Algeria Navy waited patiently to see if the *Al Solomon* was detected. Soon an American battle force would come this way. He nodded as he gave silent thanks to Allah for the decision by the Americans to leave Rota Naval Base ten years ago. Only Spanish antisubmarine forces remained to endanger the Algerian submarines. The Americans had given up their only logistic hub at the entrance to the Mediterranean. The Americans would have to come through the strait without the benefit of a forward-deployed force to sanitize their path into the Med. Of even more importance was the fact that without Rota Naval Base, the survival of Israel was threatened. America could never remount the air resupply line it did in 1973 to save that terrorist country without somewhere to refuel.

The only concern to him was the Spanish Armada, led by its Harrier aircraft carrier the *Principe de Asturias,* four F-100–class frigates, and several auxiliary ships. The frigates were the biggest danger to the submarine. The F-100s were variants of the United States Navy's old single-screw FFG-7 ASW frigate. They were Spain's premier antisubmarine forces. Each frigate could carry two Sikorsky S-70L ASW helicopters; though Algerian Navy Intelligence reported that normally only one was embarked on the two-hanger ships. The *Al Solomon* could maneuver unmolested, awaiting the imminent American carrier force, as long as the Spanish kept their Navy in port. From his own experience, he hoped the captain on the *Al Solomon* did not underestimate the Spanish. Spain was a maritime nation with a long naval history—a proud history. Its Navy would not hesitate to attack a submarine violating its territorial waters and though Spain's naval force was small, it had the tenacity of a barracuda on the seas.

He watched the compass needle move as *Al Nasser* turned slowly toward the strait.

Five minutes later, Ibn Al Jamal secured General Quarters to allow the crew to eat, use the toilet, and, for those capable, grab a few minutes' sleep. There were two American submarines in the Mediterranean and, while Algerian Navy Intelligence had located one in Gaeta, the other remained missing. His ASW crew searched with passive sonar, looking for the telltale noise that nuclear submarines made. He was proud of his skilled plotting team. He looked over their shoulders as they monitored, plotted, and tracked every contact in an effort to maintain a surface picture of the ships above.

At midnight, satisfied they had completed the first part of their mission without being detected, Ibn Al Jamal gave the orders for the *Al Nasser* to commence its lone transit back through the Strait of Gibraltar and into the Mediterranean. It was now time for the second part. He brought the submarine to periscope depth to take a navigation fix against the evening lights at Algeciras and Gibraltar. Satisfied, Ibn Al Jamal calculated they would be through the strait and near Málaga by dawn. He looked at the air monitor. They could stay submerged another week without surfacing. He tapped the battery meter. Battery was fine, but it never hurt to keep the submarine's battery power topped off. He wanted to be in a position by tomorrow night to either surface or snorkel to recharge the batteries and exchange the air. Plus, his plans called for them to be off Algeria in safer waters by tomorrow night. He would prefer to surface to recharge.

An hour later, the submarine passed abreast of Algeciras, the large Spanish port near the entrance to the Strait of Gibraltar. Ibn Al Jamal quietly urged the crew back to their battle stations. When every station was manned, he called the stern torpedo crew and gave them what he sometimes thought of as his "patriotic talk number two" about Allah, Algeria, and the revolutionary brotherhood, encouraging them to do their job quietly, thoroughly, and professionally.

He nodded to the plotting team watching him. He saw the questions in their eyes. When informed by the watch officer that the stern torpedo crew was ready, and he was satisfied the plotting team knew the importance of their role, he gave the order to launch.

From the stern tubes, in controlled sequence, magnetic-acoustic influence mines, designed by the long-dead Soviet Union and propelled by compressed air, shot out. They traveled nearly twenty meters before inertia took over and gravity pulled the rusty weapons to the bottom. In the control room, the plotting team marked on the chart each mine's location.

It would be three hours before internal programs activated the mines. A magnetic detection of a target would turn on a sound analysis system where preset decibel levels would determine if the mines would attack. Modern mines were nothing like the floating balls dotted with sensitive pins used during World War II. Modern mines were computerized, capable of determining when, and if, to explode. They could count the number of ships passing overhead or the number of blades on a propeller. They could be programmed to attack on any combination of aural and magnetic factors. They were truly the weapons of choice for a secret war at sea. Even if one of them were recovered, they could not be traced to Algeria—only to the Soviet Union . . . and the Soviet Union was dead.

These were the only mines of this sophistication in the Algerian inventory. When the sensors of the mines agreed, and the computer program directed, they would separate from their weights and, like small torpedoes, home toward the propellers of their target. Mines, unlike torpedoes, attacked from below and the chance of detecting them prior to impact was minute. Even if an astute surface ASW operator serendipitously detected the ascent, a surface ship would have little opportunity to avoid the initial hit.

He changed the course of *Al Nasser* slightly and commenced a zigzag transit through the Strait of Gibraltar. The Kilo submarine carried eighteen mines and nine torpedoes, unlike the *Al Solomon,* which waited for the Americans with a full complement of eighteen torpedoes.

He envied *Al Solomon,* in a professional way. When the American carrier task force arrived, and he knew it would,

Al Solomon would be the sword of the revolution, protecting the Barbary Coast against America's might. The *Al Solomon* would be the first obstacle to stop America from returning in strength to the Mediterranean. When Ibn Al Jamal finished here, tonight, the Mediterranean would be sealed to the American Navy and the success of the "plan" would be assured. Only the small American amphibious task force would stand between them and ultimate victory. The Mediterranean would truly be theirs.

Ibn Al Jamal stopped his train of thought. His stomach churned slightly as he realized he sounded like the fanatics that made up such a large portion of the Algerian Liberation Front.

The Americans would respond. Too many through history underestimated the resolve of the North American power. Slow to anger, but once angered, capable of unleashing a frightening show of force. So, the question was not if the Americans would respond—the question was when. America lacked the military power it had during Desert Storm, so how long would it take a declining power to respond? He believed America was a declining world power. Most of the world agreed, too. Only America refused to accept the inevitable. Twenty years from now America would be a has-been. Another in a long line of world powers, like England, that had its moment in history and watched its glory ebb away.

Al Nasser was outfitted for a forty-five–day on-station time, though plans called for everything to be resolved within a week. If they could stop the West from intervening in Algeria during the next week, then everything would be settled—it would be too late for intervention. If he returned to port three weeks before the *Al Solomon,* Ibn Al Jamal intended to ensure that his fellow Kilo revolutionary did not continue his rampant zealotry.

The stern torpedo crew reported ready. He looked at the chart and ordered dispersal of another mine. For the next three hours he maneuvered the Kilo-class submarine back and forth across the narrow strait, depositing the deadly cargo, until the *Al Nasser* emerged from the choke point at four in the morning. The mines were essentially harmless, as long as no supertanker, American aircraft carrier, or submerged submarine entered or departed the Mediterranean. In thirty days they would deactivate. Saltwater would flood their cavities and those floating above the ocean floor would join those already on it, where they would eventually be buried for eternity by the shifting sands of the sea bottom. Captain Ibn Al Jamal picked up the microphone and congratulated the crew. The Mediterranean was now sealed off to the Americans. He smiled. The Mediterranean had become an Islamic lake. He forgot the French, Italian, and Greek navies in his exuberance. The Europeans would take strong exception to the idea of the Mediterranean being an Islamic lake.

The plotting crew pulled another chart out and taped it to the plotting table. The navigator made several quick calculations before he gave his course and speed recommendations to Ibn Al Jamal, who nodded in agreement. *Al Nasser*'s next destination was off the coast of Algiers, where it was to patrol the waters and protect the new capital. Western ships would appear eventually to evacuate their citizens—most likely French and Italian. His job was to keep them away.

The new executive officer ran into the control room. Ibn Al Jamal cringed as the man's head barely missed the top of the steel door. Breathless, the XO saluted before reporting that two sailors had been caught sabotaging the propeller shaft on the *Al Nasser.*

Again? He asked where they were and was told they were under heavy guard in serious condition in sick bay.

He nodded and told the executive officer he'd look into the charges later, after a quiet rest.

Ibn Al Jamal ordered the crew secured from General Quarters and, with a fresh cup of tea in his right hand, he left the control room at the same time as the ship's mullah chanted the crew to morning prayers.

Discipline was everything to a warship. Mutineers and saboteurs were different breeds from those who lacked an ability to articulate their faith to an overeager executioner gripping a raised scimitar above their necks.

Being captain of a warship was not a business for the squeamish.

ELEVEN

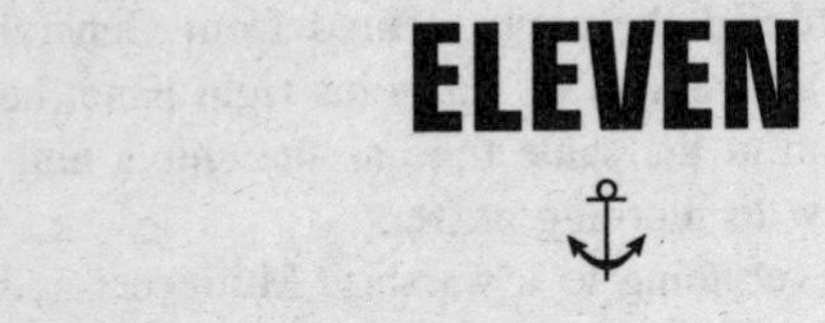

CAPTAIN CAFFERTY WAS STEAMING ANGRY WHEN HE marched into Combat. He'd have him some officer's ass about this. No comms with anyone for over twelve fucking hours and he had to discover it during breakfast by overhearing the supply officer bitching about having to issue spare parts during the night.

"Captain in Combat," a shout announced from somewhere inside the darkened compartment. A moan escaped from elsewhere in the shadows.

"Lieutenant," the captain said sharply to the CIC watch officer. "What does the tactical picture look like?"

"Sir, we had problems earlier with the radars, but we shifted the parameters and cleared up the scopes. The Harriers remain orbiting northwest of us. We have a slow-moving contact to our east that, on its current course and speed, will pass within sight of us in about two hours. We have had no communications with the *Nassau* battle group since Radio went down last night."

"Lieutenant, why the hell didn't you notify me or the

executive officer about the radar problems and the lack of communications?" Cafferty asked. It was exasperating training this crew to function as he wanted them to.

"I did, Captain. I came on watch at zero seven forty-five, for the eight-to-twelve, sir. After I relieved, I failed to find a log entry that this information had been passed so I called the XO and briefed him. He said to keep him notified. I briefed the operations officer when he made his morning rounds a few minutes ago. Ops said that he would brief you."

"I haven't seen Ops," the captain said.

"He was heading aft to the torpedo room to check on what the torpedomen were doing. Preventive maintenance check or something, Captain."

"Call back there and have him come see me. Have you tried INMARSAT telephone to contact the *Nassau*?"

The lieutenant picked up the handset from the INMARSAT system located beside the captain's chair. "Yes, sir, I tried it with no joy. Radio called on your way down to give us a heads-up that they're going to transmit at max power. We've put our comms in standby, but it shouldn't affect our surface search or air search radars."

"Fire control radars?"

"They've been in ready standby since we began the Freedom of Navigation op, Captain. Even if they were on and emanating, Radio's power is in the high-frequency bands so it shouldn't affect them."

"Alright," Cafferty acknowledged. He climbed up into the barber's chair. He had to admit that the antique replacement for the normal captain's combat chair was comfortable. But that didn't make it right. He was still going to replace it. His predecessor had been much too lax.

The supervisor of the watch brought him a cup of coffee. Black and fresh, the aroma gave Cafferty the first comfortable feeling he'd had this morning. Leaders have such a lonely job, he thought. Give him another three months, on top of the three he had been CO, and he'd have this crew whipped into fighting shape.

"Thanks, OS One," he said to the first class operations specialist as he took the cup.

Cafferty spun the chair so he could see the polar display on the electronic warfare console. "EW," he said, "what are you showing out there?"

"Sir, we're getting sporadic hits from that ship approaching us. Looks like a Russian merchant, Captain. The computer identifies the contact's navigational radar as a Don Kay. That radar has been around since the 1960s, but a lot of ships still use them."

Cafferty took a sip of coffee. "Let me know when it pops up again." *The radar has been around longer than that, young lady,* thought Cafferty.

"Captain, he's popped up again! Either he's increased his power or we are sailing into a ducting zone."

Cafferty spun around to the surface search radar operator. "What do you show on the contact?" he asked, half-listening to the reply as he seethed over the comms snafu. God! With the exception of him, did imbeciles man this ship?

"Captain, he's about thirty miles from us. Still constant bearing, decreasing range—CBDR. When we altered course slightly about an hour ago seems he did too."

"Why would he do that, I wonder?" the captain asked aloud. This was the second time he'd had problems with the COMMO. He may have to relieve him.

"Don't know, sir, but we have a solid ping on him." The operator stopped. "Damn!"

"What?" the captain asked.

Lieutenant Howard moved to the console and leaned

over the operator's shoulder. "What is it?" the CICWO asked.

"There must be two of them. I don't know why . . . No! It's not two. I have video separation," he said, his voice trembling. He shook his head. "Captain, I don't know if I'm right. I've only seen this during exercises, but it looks like a possible missile separation from the contact!"

Cafferty's attention was contracting to Combat as he shoved the comms issue to the back burner.

"Inbound missile!" shouted the EW from her console. "Styx, surface-to-surface missile class two Charlie!"

"Can't be. Check your systems!" ordered Lieutenant Howard.

"Stay calm, everyone," Cafferty said. "Check your data again."

The captain set his cup in the holder on the arm of the chair. A cold chill flew up Cafferty's back and down his arms. He tried to swallow and found his mouth dry. He took a deep gulp of hot coffee, burning his lips as the scalding liquid brought tears to his eyes. He cleared his throat.

"Combat, this is the captain. I have command." He surprised himself with how calm his voice sounded. Cafferty licked his lips, soothing the burn.

"Lieutenant, sound General Quarters! EW, activate automatic electronic countermeasures system. Surface search, time to impact?" A bogus call, most likely. God! He hoped so. No comms and him with a lax ship. Damn good thing he knew what he was doing! If it was bogus, at least today's GQ drill would be done and out of the way. He reached up and stroked the back of his neck. But what if it wasn't? Unconsciously, Cafferty crossed his fingers.

"Sir, missile inbound thirteen miles separation from contact. Two point seven minutes to *Gearing*, sir."

Bogus radar video was common at sea. Cafferty ran his hand through his shaggy red hair. The Gulf of Sidra was notorious for ducting and radar ghosts. That's probably all this was. Cafferty leaned toward the surface search operator, waiting for him to report the video fading . . . disappearing. Tears ran down the young man's pale cheeks. "Stop that."

The hot, windless weather of the past two days, and the early morning changes daybreak brought, lent itself to electromagnetic phenomena.

"Lock-on! Captain! The missile has locked on us!" yelled the EW.

A fresh wave of chill bumps raced up his body.

"Radar!" Cafferty yelled.

"Video remains inbound, Captain. Speed four hundred knots."

The radar return wasn't fading. A deep sigh escaped Cafferty, like the last breath of a dying man, as he realized this was no drill and no bogus signal. The bongs sounding General Quarters brought home the solitude of command. This was not a war game in Newport, Rhode Island. It wasn't the Fleet Trainer at Dam Neck, Virginia. It was not even an exercise—the few the Navy could afford—off the Virginia Capes area near Norfolk. It was the real thing. He wanted to disbelieve what the information in Combat showed. Years of training rose easily from the recesses of his mind, surprising Cafferty that he was able to recall it so easily, considering the fear that threatened to break out and disrupt his countenance. He took a couple of deep breaths and felt a strange calm descend over him. No second chances. Only a few hundred miles from where America had fought the Barbary wars. His decisions would determine whether the ship lived or died. He uncrossed his fingers.

"Fire Control, I want a solution on the ship. Lieutenant Howard, man your weapons systems."

Sailors piled into Combat, some half dressed, others carrying their shoes in their hands. All bitching about being roused from their beds for a drill.

"It's not a drill!" Lieutenant Howard shouted.

Sailors momentarily stopped. Then, with a burst of adrenaline-fed energy, dove for their General Quarters stations. Two minutes since GQ sounded and the USS *Gearing* was manned and bristling for war.

Cafferty pressed the intercom. "Bridge, Captain; we have an inbound missile; I want flank speed, hard to port, steady on three one zero. Keep us heading north, away from the Libyan coast and further into international waters."

"Captain, this is the XO, I have the conn. Hard to port, we are coming to flank speed, course three one zero," the XO repeated.

"XO, get us out of here. We want to close the Harriers."

"Aye, sir."

The USS *Gearing* shook, vibrating as the noise of an explosion shook the ship. Cafferty grabbed the arm of the chair to keep from being thrown onto the deck. Others picked themselves up. Frightened glances were exchanged among those in Combat. The lack of comms meant they were no longer in the Network Centric Warfare grid. The DD-21 was designed to fight with multiple ships, not alone.

"I thought you said three minutes!" he shouted at the surface search operator. "That's one more minute!" But it could fight alone if it had to.

"Captain, it's still inbound! That wasn't the missile."

"Combat, Damage Control; torpedo hit starboard side!"

A speaker overhead interrupted. "Combat, this is ASW,

we have a second high-speed prop, probably torpedo, bearing one niner zero."

"Combat, Damage Control; we have taken a torpedo hit aft, starboard side. Main engine room number one flooding. Securing engines in MER number one! Fire in compartment two dash two six one dash two. Damage control teams responding."

"Do we have a firing solution on that ship?" Cafferty felt the ship slowing as MER number one wound down.

"Yes, sir, coming through . . . now! Got it, Captain! I have two Harpoons targeted on the attacking vessel."

"Fire, goddamn it, fire!"

The USS *Gearing* shook again as the antiship cruise missiles blasted upward from the vertical launch systems on the bow. The noise vibrated the forward half-inch aluminum bulkhead as the Harpoon missiles on the other side of it sped off toward the attacking surface vessel.

"Combat, this is ASW; we have another pair of fast props in the water, bearing one niner two degrees—probable torpedoes. Signal-to-noise ratio increasing in intensity. Total torpedoes in the water three. I repeat, three torpedoes in the water!" The voice cracked slightly. "Torpedo noise fading into our baffles, sir!"

"Launch decoys, ASW!" Cafferty ordered. Then, he turned quickly to the CICWO. "Lieutenant, fire two over-the-side torpedoes down the line of bearing of those inbound torpedoes!"

"Sir, I don't have a target!"

"I don't give a shit! Enable the torpedoes as they're fired. Let them search in auto. I want two away ASAP! If they don't do anything else but scare the shit out of that submarine, at least they'll be doing something!"

The ship lurched to port as the two remaining turbine engines in MER number two fought to give the DD-21 electric drive the extra power needed to bring *Gearing* around in time to free the starboard CIWS—the last-ditch weapon to stop the inbound missile.

"This is the starboard bridge watch, I see it! I see it! It's coming over the horizon now! Gawldamn! Ain't never seen a black contrail! That missile is coming right at us!"

The sound of Super RBOC, launching its canisters of chaff clouds, echoed through the ship as millions of pieces of small aluminum strips seeded the air to cloud the targeting electronics of the inbound missile.

The loud automatic rapid fire of the CIWS echoed through the ship.

"CIWS is hitting the missile!" the lookout shouted through her sound-powered phone. "It ain't working!"

"I have another video separation. Second missile launched. Time to impact estimated at three minutes forty-five seconds. Threat has increased speed to twenty-five knots!"

The loud roar of a rocket engine penetrated the darkened compartment. The impact knocked everyone to the deck as the missile tore into the USS *Gearing.*

"Combat, Bridge; missile hit starboard side aft at the waterline. Directly under the five-inch sixty-two gun mount. Heavy smoke coming from . . . from where it hit."

A flashing red light on the naval gunfire system console confirmed the report from the bridge. The aft five-inch gun was out of action. "Aft gun out!"

"Combat, ASW; torpedo impact in thirty seconds! Decoys in the water."

"LAMPs, this is Combat. Are you ready to launch?" Cafferty shouted into the intercom.

No answer came.

"Combat, this is ASW. First torpedo decoyed. Prop noise fading. Decoy two in the water, NIXIE streamed." NIXIE was a small noise-making device, towed behind the destroyer, that emitted sounds into the water designed to confuse and decoy a torpedo.

"Captain!" Lieutenant Howard shouted. "Two torpedoes away. We're reloading torps for another shot!"

"Give me another firing solution on that ship."

"Captain, two Harriers heading our way! Goddamn, get your asses down here, Marines!" shouted the air search operator. A flurry of activity followed, with the operator flipping switches and turning knobs. The air search operator leaned back, looked at the radar console, and shook his head as he pulled himself forward before shouting, "Captain, something's not right about those Harriers! They're at Mach one point two according to the computer! Harriers can't go that fast!'

The ship shook as the port engine went full astern. The USS *Gearing* twisted to port. The sea behind the ship churned like boiling water, creating a hard knuckle to decoy the torpedoes. Cafferty mentally congratulated the XO—smart thinking. He felt the port engine switching back to all ahead flank. Without engines number one and three from main engine room number one, the USS *Gearing* had only its port turbines to provide the power to fight the ship.

"Passing course zero two zero!" announced the bridge.

Cafferty glanced at the surface radar. They were twenty-five miles north of the Libyan coast and still headed north.

"I show High Lark radar bearing three three zero!" shouted the EW operator.

"High Lark?"

"MiG-23 Floggers, sir."

"Can't be!" Cafferty yelled in disbelief. "They're Harriers!"

"Combat, Bridge; coming to course zero double zero."

"System may be lying, Captain, but it's been right so

far!" the EW operator shouted, her voice sounding almost apologetic.

"Combat, this is Damage Control. Fire from the torpedo hit contained. Flooding continues. Missile penetrated frames two three zero at the waterline." A momentary pause occurred. "Captain, the missile hit women's berthing. There are casualties."

Every berthing area had a damage control watch assigned during General Quarters, plus there would always be one or two who were slower than the rest to respond to General Quarters. He looked at the clock: three minutes since GQ was sounded.

"Combat, Bridge; Captain, recommend base course zero zero zero!"

"Lieutenant, I want firing solution on those inbound aircraft. Automate CIWS." Cafferty hit the button on the speaker. "XO, Captain; base course zero zero zero."

"Steadying course zero zero zero. Commencing evasive maneuvers."

"CIWS *is* automated, sir. Been automated since we turned on track."

"EW, are you sure they're MiGs?"

"Captain, I'm as positive as the tits on my chest!"

"You're flat-chested, Murphy!" someone shouted from the shadows.

"Shut up!" the CICWO yelled.

"They are definitely not ours," Murphy said. She reached up and patted the AN/SLQ-32 console. "We are definitely right!"

"XO, commence zigzag maneuvers. Make those fucking pilots earn their flight pay!"

"Commencing zigzag; base course zero zero zero."

The USS *Gearing* lurched to port, causing the surface

plotter to lose his balance and fall, as the ship zigzagged at nineteen knots.

"Radio, Combat! Have you got the Navy Blue out yet?"

"No, sir, Captain. We still don't have comms!"

He flipped off Radio.

"Aircraft inbound three minutes, Captain."

"Missile impact in one minute!"

"Bridge, Combat; we have another inbound missile starboard side. I want max speed. Bring her up to twenty-nine knots and hold her there."

"Bridge, Chief Engineer; Captain, we have lost main engines one and three to torpedo damage! I only have two and four. I can't give you more than the twenty knots you've got without damaging the shaft or seizing the engines."

"Chief Engineer, if we don't get out of this, your engines will be the least of our worries! Now give me all you got. Put her in the red if you have to, but give me speed until she seizes or blows up, and if she does, get your crew out there with paddles. But give me speed!"

"Bridge, this is the aft lookout; I have two aircraft approaching relative two niner zero. Large contrails. Looks like afterburners on. They're leaving a gray trail behind them! Look like MiG-23s."

The ship shuddered as it heeled full left to uncover the CIWS and bring both it and the forward five-inch sixty-two gun to bear against the attacking aircraft.

"Lieutenant, fire the five-inch. I want proximity rounds, seeding the flight path at hundred-feet intervals. Cloud that area with shrapnel!"

THE STYX MISSILE PENETRATED THE ONE-INCH-THIN aluminum frame before exploding inside women's berthing. The unused liquid fuel splattered, flooding the compartment. Two milliseconds later, the exhaust ignited the remainder of the liquid fuel, turning it into a napalmlike inferno, sticking to the skin, baking two sailors scrambling from the compartment for their General Quarters stations and who were a minute slower than their shipmates. The explosion, ten milliseconds later, killed them before nerves could register the pain of their skin burning away. Oxygen was sucked from both compartments to feed the furnace. The ocean rushed in, right behind the missile; then, blown back by the explosion, it pored in with a vengeance through a larger hole, pushing burning fuel against the bulkhead and deeper into the ship.

Women's berthing was divided into port and starboard compartments. The two slow ones died in the starboard compartment from the impact and explosion. Three seconds later, burning fuel rolled on top of the water through the connecting hatch into the port compartment, catching the GQ berthing watch as she ran, turning her dungarees into a funeral pyre, her sound-powered phones ripped from her ears. Her screams were cut short as burning fuel filled her lungs, evaporating them. She fell, eyes wide with terror and still alive, unable to scream, as the sea rushed over her, extinguishing the fire. Two seconds later she mercifully died.

Twenty seconds later, diminished oxygen and rushing waters smothered the fire. The flames sputtered out, leaving hot black smoke rolling within the compartment like an angry Tennessee storm, blinding two survivors who were in the head when the missile struck. The blast slammed the door shut, sealing the bathroom from the inferno outside and saving their lives.

On the level above, a third class petty officer pulled himself to his feet and rushed to close the watertight door. The wire trailing from his sound-powered phone jerked him up short as he reached the door, nearly knocking him off his feet. He jerked them off and tossed them aside before throwing himself to the deck and sticking his head inside the compartment. Smoke poured out, sending him into a spasm of choking and coughing as he pulled back. Rubbing his eyes, he shouted for anyone in there to come out. A quick flash of flame erupted through the hatch, singeing off hair on his head and hands. His long dungaree shirtsleeves protected his arms and the top button—buttoned—kept the heat away from his chest. His face and hands looked as if he had suffered bad sunburn. He'd live. The smoke began to taper off as the fire burned itself out. He continued calling and refused to shut the watertight door.

The warrant officer slid down the ladder, saw the damage below, and shouted, "Shut this damn hatch! You want to sink the ship? And put that fucking phone back on and tell Damage Control what's happened." Then the warrant jumped through the smoke-filled hatch, feet first, into the water below. Shaking the water from her head, the warrant looked up, smoke obscuring her face; the water was waist high and rising. "I said shut the hatch, sailor!"

"But, Warrant!" he protested, as he fumbled with the headset.

"Dammit, sailor. I'll be all right if you'll just shut the hatch! Now, tell Damage Control what's going on. You can do it." Without waiting for a reply the *Gearing*'s only warrant officer grabbed a nearby bunk and pulled herself forward into the smoke and waded out of sight.

The third class petty officer gripped the handle on the watertight hatch. His hands shook as he dropped it.

"Damn you, Warrant!" he repeatedly cried as he spun the wheel, sealing the compartment below from the rest of the ship. "Damn you!"

The sailor pushed the speaker on his sound-powered phone set and shoved the earpiece against his ears to seal out imagined cries from below. Then in a weak voice he reported to Damage Control Central. Afterward, he stood alone in the emergency-lighted compartment and several times successfully fought the urge to throw off his headset, open the overhead hatch, and flee topside to the perceived safety of the open air. Everything would be alright, he kept telling himself.

"FIRE CONTROL, DO WE HAVE SOLUTION ON THE AIRcraft?"

"Nearly there, Captain!" A couple of seconds passed. "There! We have a firing solution!"

"Then blow them out of the air! Fire, fire, fire!"

Cafferty pressed the intercom. "Helo Deck, Combat; do you read?" Once again, no answer. Cafferty had no way of knowing the helicopter props were turning as it prepared to take off or that the helo deck sound-powered phone operator had plugged into the wrong circuit.

The sounds of Super RBOC, reseeding the air with chaff, echoed through Combat.

"I have video separation again! Video separation!" cried the air search operator as he announced the enemy ship's launch of another surface-to-surface missile.

"How long to Harpoon impact?" Focused. Stay focused. One battle at a time. Can't lose it. Keep it together for them and the ship. What the hell is happening on the helo deck?

"Thirty and thirty-two seconds!"

The roar of the Styx antimissile shook the *Gearing*. What was this antique weapon doing here in modern warfare, Cafferty wondered.

"Combat, Bridge; missile passed astern of *Gearing* about one hundred yards. Missile miss! I repeat, missile miss. It's heading for the horizon!" A cheer went up inside Combat.

"Quiet! Focus, Combat! Stay focused!" shouted Cafferty. God must have been watching; now fight the ship. Concentrate. What next? What next?

The ship executed a series of zigzag movements as the enemy aircraft approached. Lieutenant Commander Leroy Nash, XO, was doing a great job maneuvering the ship. Cafferty made a mental note to recommend the XO for a medal when this was over—if they survived.

"I have inbound air-to-surface missile," said the EW, interrupting Cafferty's thought.

Ten seconds later the first air-to-surface missile hit the helicopter as it rotated on the flight deck. The explosion rattled the USS *Gearing*. Streams of metal and smoke rocketed a hundred feet into the air. When the smoke cleared two sailors on the helo deck were gone. The second missile exploded harmlessly off the port bow, sending a wash of water over the front of the ship. The third passed directly over the ship, between the two masts, barely missing the signal bridge, to hit the bullnose on the bow, blowing off the flagpole, but doing little damage otherwise. A fourth air-to-surface missile misfired and exploded in the air off the starboard beam, sending bridge personnel diving to the deck. The lead Libyan pilot misinterpreted the fiery damage to the helicopter as a mortal blow to the ship. Smoke from the burning helicopter obscured the enemy pilots' view of everything aft of USS *Gearing*'s amidships quarterdeck.

The two MiG-23s followed their missiles, raking the ship with twenty-three–millimeter cannon shells from stern to bow as they roared past. They executed a quick split as they climbed upward, one breaking to the left and the other rolling to the right.

The one breaking left came within radar contact of the ship's port Vulcan Phalanx—the good one. The CIWS locked on and immediately fired a tattoo of two hundred shells racing toward the MiG-23. As the aircraft, nose up, gained altitude the depleted uranium bullets stitched a fine weave up it. The radar-guided stream of bullets tore the fighter-bomber's jet engines apart, laddered up its fuselage, and turned the inside of the cockpit a splattered red as it chewed through it and everything within it before blowing off the MiG-23 High Lark radar in the nose cone. Blazing pieces of what had been a MiG-23 rained from the sky.

"Scratch one MiG!" came an exhilarated shout from the bridge. "All the King's horses and all the King's men won't put that MiG-23 together again!"

A loud chorus of hurrahs echoed through Combat.

"Quiet! We're not done yet!" shouted the captain.

THE NUMBER TWO DAMAGE CONTROL PARTY RUSHED to the helo hangar from where they had just finished containing the flooding in main engine room number one. A minimum manned ship lacked the personnel needed for multiple damage control parties. Fire was the more dangerous element to a ship. Sailors could always pump out a flooded compartment and refloat a ship, but they could not rebuild what fire destroyed. So, when faced with the two choices, putting out a fire came first. The radioman chief led the team.

"We've got to shove that helo off the ship! Smitty, rig the hose while I try to shove it overboard."

The chief jumped into the parked yellow forklift and turned the electric engine on. He pushed the pedal to the floor. The small one-man forklift moved forward and rammed the burning helicopter. The back wheels of the forklift spun as it fought the inertia to shift the helicopter. A tilt by the ship aided the effort as the burning wreckage moved slightly toward the edge of the deck about ten yards away. The chief hunched over the steering wheel to avoid the heat. Glancing at the cockpit, he saw the outlines of the bodies of the pilots dancing within the flames.

The fire blazed up, burning his eyebrows away. Blisters began to rise across the top of his hands and his exposed neck. He turned his hands over and gripped the wheel from beneath, but this did little to protect his exposed fingers and nothing for the back of his neck.

"Can't do it!" he shouted and took a step to abandon the aviation truck.

He had one foot off when water cascaded around him like a fine-mist umbrella. It soaked him and drove the heat away. He immediately sat back down and rammed the truck against the helicopter, shoving it toward the edge of the deck. The DC team walked behind the chief and kept the fine, heavy mist sprayed over him. The water cooled his exposed, blistered skin. A second hose team washed burning fuel over the side, keeping it away from the insides of the USS *Gearing*.

Suddenly, the helicopter lurched to a stop, jerking the chief forward.

"Tie-downs!" the chief shouted, pointing to the tail where a chain ran to the deck to secure the helicopter to the ship.

"Chief, no torpedoes on her!" shouted the number two team leader. "No danger there."

Two members of the team ran to the two remaining tie-downs, glowing from the heat. Despite the heavy gloves, the tie-downs burned through the fire-retardant cloth, blistering their hands. Ignoring the pain, they twisted the locks loose and disconnected them. Two other team members pulled a body found near the tail of the helo, previously hidden by the smoke, to the rear of the hanger. Nothing held the helicopter on board now except its own inertia.

The chief pushed the pedal to the floor and the forklift, once again, shoved against the helicopter. The starboard strut of the helo shifted, trapping the left arm of the forklift. The chief, unaware, inched the SH-60 toward the edge. He continued the slow push of the burning wreckage until it reached the port side. As it began to ease over the side, the ship took a hard left turn.

A sharp tilt of the deck sent the helicopter tumbling overboard. The entangled forklift followed. The chief leaped, making a wild grab for the deck edge.

Seaman Jones grabbed for the chief's outstretched hands, barely touched the fingertips, missed, and nearly went overboard himself. The chief's head caught the edge of the deck, knocking him unconscious and leaving a smear of red along the edge. The radioman chief followed the helicopter and forklift into the sea. Someone grabbed a life ring off the hangar bulkhead and tossed it after him. The burning helicopter's tail disappeared beneath the sea as the damage control members raced to the side.

They saw no sign of the chief.

"NUMBER ONE HARPOON ON TARGET!" ANNOUNCED THE surface search operator. A couple of seconds passed. "Number two Harpoon on target!" He turned to the captain.

"Captain, they've hit. I show one video!"

"Combat, ASW; I have two explosions underwater. I think we've hit the mofo! No torpedoes in the water at this time!"

"Inbound missile. Time to impact twenty-five seconds!"

"ECM not effective!" yelled the electronic warfare technician. "Missile is locked on!"

"SAM away!" shouted Lieutenant Howard.

The remaining Libyan fighter twisted to the right. Flares erupted from its ECM pods, successfully decoying the USS *Gearing*'s surface-to-air missile. The starboard CIWS fired for a full five seconds before the coolant pump burned out and the weapon system locked up.

"What happened?" Cafferty demanded.

"Starboard CIWS is out of commission, Captain. She's froze up again!"

The fifty bullets spent before the CIWS ceased firing hit the MiG-23's left wing, damaging the aileron and severing a hydraulic line. The Libyan pilot manually fought the controls, keeping the aircraft airborne. His fuel transfer light started blinking, forcing him to break off. The MiG-23 banked right and headed for the coast and safety.

"We have a miss. Enemy aircraft is in a starboard turn for another attack!"

"The surface video has disappeared, Captain. We've sunk her! Whoever fired those Styx missiles is a dead son of a bitch!"

"Ten seconds to impact!"

"Combat, Chief Engineer! Sir, I am losing another engine. All gauges in the red. Max speed I can give you is twelve knots!"

Even as the chief engineer spoke, Cafferty felt the ship slowing. The rudders of the USS *Gearing* were pegged as far right as they would go as the ship turned hard to starboard in an attempt to uncover the vertical launch system in front of the bridge and hopefully bring the port CIWS into play against the inbound antiship cruise missile. He looked at the display showing the location of the *Gearing:* about twenty-five miles north of the Libyan coast.

"Second SAM away. Third away."

On board the fleeing MiG-23, the internal warning system began beeping incessantly in the pilot's ears. Flares and chaff exploded from the Flogger as the Libyan fighter ran for the coast. The loss of hydraulic fluid made the aircraft barely maneuverable.

Two seconds later. "Both misses."

"Captain, enemy aircraft departing area," added the air search operator.

"Signal bridge reports a smoke trail coming from the aircraft," repeated a sound-powered phone talker in Combat.

"Styx missile impact five seconds. Five, four, three, two . . ."

"Missile starboard side!" XO yelled from the bridge.

Like slow motion, the sound of impact rippled through the forward bulkhead. The missile hit the USS *Gearing* where the forward five-inch sixty-two mount stood firing ineffective rounds at it. The blast shattered the frame integrity to the bow, causing the front of the USS *Gearing* to shear away at the waterline. The explosion ripped upward, tearing the gun from its mount and sending the barrel through the front of the bridge. Combat had the misfortune of being on the same level as the bow. The forward bulkhead to Combat imploded from the shock wave of the hit. Pieces of missile and shrapnel sawed through to ricochet within Combat. The electronic warfare technician died first. Murderous pieces of metal tore apart the AN/SLQ-32 EW console before decapitating her. Fires broke out at numerous locations as electrical surges and broken wires burned out and flamed up the very positions needed to fight a modern warship.

Cafferty woke on the deck with the barber chair on top of him. Blood flowed from a wound on his forehead. Dazed, he pushed the chair off and pulled himself up. Pulling a handkerchief from his pocket he pressed it against the gash across his forehead.

"Bridge, Combat!" he shouted into the intercom. He wiped more blood from around his eyes. No reply. He then saw that the intercom was no longer connected to anything. He pushed his way toward the ladder leading up to the bridge. Around him, survivors discharged CO_2 bottles on the small fires while others began to search for the living and injured buried under the debris. Captain Heath Cafferty dragged himself up the ladder to the bridge. The ship seemed to be tilting forward.

ON THE BRIDGE, BODIES LAY HELTER SKELTER WHERE they had fallen. Lieutenant Commander Nash was on his knees, dazed. Blood covered his face. A shard of glass in the broken bridge windows cut his hands as he leaned forward, blinking his eyes to clear his vision. Where a bow used to slice through the mirror-smooth seas, nothing remained from the waterline up. The twelve-knot speed was pushing her under. The executive officer, a mustang with twenty-six years of naval service, reached for the annunciator and pulled it down to the reverse setting to slow the ship's forward motion and, hopefully, keep her afloat a little longer. *Keep her afloat a little longer . . .* the thought made him reluctantly admit the *Gearing* was sinking. His hand smeared the throttle with blood. Anything he did would only delay the inevitable. Shocked, he sat down on the deck beside the helm and shut his eyes for a moment as he concentrated on slowing his breathing.

The door from Combat banged opened and Cafferty stumbled onto the bridge. Nash opened his eyes

"Oh, my God!" Cafferty mumbled as he surveyed the

damage. He moved to where the XO sat, his hand on the annunciator, and helped his number two to stand.

"You okay?"

The XO nodded. "I think I'm alright," he mumbled.

Water washed over where the bow of the ship used to be. The ship was slipping beneath the sea. The forward tilt had already increased a couple of degrees since the captain had left Combat.

The XO moved to the front of the bridge and leaned against the remnants of the bulkhead.

"Captain, we are going to have to abandon ship. She's sinking." He walked over to where the navigation table used to be. He touched the two bodies there on the neck to see if by some miracle they were alive. Both were dead. Nash shoved a few items around on the floor until he found the logbook. He tucked it under his arm, leaving a bloody hand imprint on the cover.

"I'd give her ten minutes at the most. Captain," the XO said with a tremble in his voice. "You fought the good battle, sir. No one else could have done it as well." He looked at the sinking bow area. "We have to leave before she goes down. If we go now, we can probably save those still alive before she does a belly-up."

Cafferty surveyed the damage for a few seconds. Then reluctantly he said, "You're right, XO." He looked at his watch. "Time is zero eight nineteen. Hard to believe. Nineteen minutes of battle. Nineteen minutes from a normal, routine operation to the loss of the ship."

The XO opened the logbook and with a pen from his pocket made a quick notation. His hands shook and he managed to write the time before shutting the book. He'd fill in the details later.

A moan drew the captain's attention. The boatswain mate of the watch was trying to stand. His left hand held a stump where his right arm used to be. The captain rushed over, pulled his belt out, and made a tourniquet out of it. "XO, help Boats to the life raft."

Cafferty reached over and moved the annunciator again to the stop position. The whine of the engines decreased, bringing after it an eerie silence to a devastating scene.

Cafferty lifted the 1MC and checked the switches to ensure the sound-powered system carried his voice topside. The XO, with the wounded boatswain mate leaning on his shoulder, departed the bridge through the port hatch.

Cafferty clicked on the 1MC. "This is the captain. Abandon ship. Now hear this. Abandon ship." He paused and then clicked the microphone on again. "Listen to me, sailors. We have about ten minutes, I figure. No more than that. Plenty of time to search around the immediate area for shipmates and make sure they make it with you. That's not enough time to go to your quarters for any personal gear. I am proud of each and every one of you. The USS *Gearing* fought the good battle as we were trained to do. We don't go down without taking the enemy with us. Good luck and may God be with you."

As he hung up, the power went out. The electric engines wound down internally as the engineers secured them prior to rushing to their own abandon ship stations. Cafferty moved in a daze across the bridge, checking each body for signs of life. He picked up the sextant lying against the forward bulkhead deck and tucked it under his arm. They would need this.

Finding no one alive, he worked his way down to Combat.

The USS *Gearing* had given a good account of herself. Cafferty was right. The first American warship sunk in a sea battle since World War II, but she took a Libyan surface ship, a submarine, and at least one fighter aircraft with her. Had the cost of ensuring international freedom of the seas been worth it? Cafferty didn't know and now was not the time to think about it.

ON BOARD THE FLEET AIR RECONNAISSANCE SQUADRON

Two EP-3E Orion aircraft, flying the central Mediterranean track, one hundred fifty miles north of the action, the mission commander turned to the cryptologic officer.

"Are we sure?" he asked, disbelieving. "Lord, you've got to be wrong. Maybe it's a Libyan exercise?"

"No, it's not an exercise and yes, I am sure. Your front-end crew verified the presence of Harpoon emitters. The *Gearing* is the only ship in this vicinity that has Harpoons. The lab op detected missile seekers of the old Soviet Styx missile. The Libyans still have Osa and Nanuchka warships that carry those antiques," she said. She pulled a handkerchief from her flight suit, wiped her eyes, and blew her nose.

"The *Gearing* was called off station last night by Sixth Fleet and, according to this morning's premission brief, she should have been about a hundred and fifty miles from where you're saying this took place. Because of that, we weren't briefed to keep track of her," Lieutenant Commander Andrews argued.

Without replying Lieutenant Garner handed the mission commander a message with four short lines on it and knew, even as she handed it, that the message was going to stir the United States as nothing had since Pearl Harbor. Even men cried in battle, so she felt no timidity that a few tears dotted her cheeks. "We only have ELINT, but a quick triangulation against the *Gearing* Aegis radar shows her over thirty miles off the Libyan coast. I would say that's a great difference from the hundred fifty she is supposed to be."

"Why?" he asked, trying to comprehend the enormity of what Garner was saying.

"I don't understand the why of it," Lieutenant Sue Garner, the cryptologic officer, replied.

"Neither do I," Lieutenant Commander Andrews, the mission commander, answered. "Neither do I."

Andrews folded the message and walked toward the cockpit. Every eye in the aircraft watched his progress as he hurried through. Every member of the crew had a piece of the puzzle, knowing the whole picture rested on the piece of paper in Lieutenant Commander Andrews's hand.

The last reflection was the MiG-23 pilot declaring an in-flight emergency and reporting the American warship sinking. Onboard electronic warfare suites had pinpointed the location of the action.

At the cockpit the mission commander handed the message to the pilot. "So, we're sure this is true?" the senior pilot, Commander Stillwell, asked.

"Yes, sir. We can't be completely sure without actually seeing it. But our sensors show, and every one of the analysts believes, it is a valid event. That at approximately zero seven twenty Zulu, zero eight twenty hours our time, forces of Libya attacked and sank the USS *Gearing* while she was operating in international waters."

The pilot initialed the message, adding his own line. "Go ahead and send it. I wrote that we are remaining on station, awaiting further instructions." He looked at the gauges. "We've only been airborne a couple of hours; we can stay up another eight if we have to. I hope you're wrong."

"I hope so, too. This is one time it wouldn't bother me to be told how I screwed up."

"We'll wait here," said the pilot. He put the EP-3E into

a racetrack orbit. Here, they'd wait for further instructions, which he knew would come.

Within four minutes of the time that Lieutenant Garner recognized what was happening, the message landed on the desks of Commander Sixth Fleet, Commander in Chief U.S. Naval Forces Europe, Commander in Chief Europe, and other battle force commanders throughout the world. Six minutes after the message left the aircraft the duty watch officer in the basement of the White House ran up the stairs to wake the president. Within three hours, CNN would interrupt normal broadcasting to spread the news that would send angry Americans into the streets, demanding revenge.

The curtains to the cockpit opened.

"Message, sir," said the radioman who handed the slip of paper to the pilot.

"What's it say?" the copilot asked impatiently.

"Descend to sea level, approach the action area, and verify."

"Who's it from?"

"CTF Sixty-seven—Fleet Air Mediterranean. Admiral Devlin says that if we encounter any reaction to our presence we are to depart the area immediately and bingo to Sigonella."

The mission commander walked into the cockpit.

"Well, here it is," said the pilot to Andrews as he passed the message to him. "Uncover those lenses from that video camera we carry and take pictures. I'll not want to stay all night in debriefing. Take the Intell bubbas some photos and they'll leave us alone."

Andrews quickly read the message. "Okay. Says here we're directly under Sixth Fleet direction."

The pilot nodded as he took the intercom. "Crew, this is Commander Stillwell. You all know what we think has happened. We've been ordered to visually verify it. We are descending to sea level, probably around a hundred feet. Then, we're going to approach the action location. Once there, we'll commence a broadening circle search."

"We are going to be within easy reach of Libyan fighter aircraft, so I want all of you on your toes. If you see even the tiniest indication they know we are there, I want to know about it. Meanwhile, everyone put on your SV-2s and parachutes. Just a precaution in the event we have to run for it."

Activity erupted as twenty-four crew members jostled and bumped each other as they put on their survival vests, followed by bulky parachutes pulled from overhead storage racks. The SV-2s and parachutes restricted movement somewhat, but if they had to, they could evacuate the EP-3E in a minute.

"I am sending the flight engineer back and I want number three life raft and provisions ready to drop. Put our main radio in with number three. Officers, throw your survival radios in the plastic bag. If the worst has happened, they'll have more need of them than we will."

The EP-3E continued west as it descended to an altitude of one hundred feet and then, when onboard sensors showed no radar painting the aircraft, it turned south. The noise increased from the four turboprops as Commander Stillwell applied more power. The turbulence caused by the low altitude and max speed bounced the aging aircraft as it hurried south. Aircrew fastened their seat belts and secured their coffee cups without being told. Stillwell bowed his head slightly. He was not a religious man by nature, but he asked God to make their analysis wrong.

Ten minutes later Stillwell announced, "We are five minutes, fifteen miles from the datum. There is dark smoke on the horizon and we're steering toward it. Lieutenant Commander Andrews, have your camera ready. I want an aircrewman at each of the windows, searching for anything that looks like surface debris, a ship, life rafts, anything."

Andrews moved to the large window near the aft exit and set up the video camera. In the cockpit, Commander Stillwell continued relaying information to Commander United States Sixth Fleet.

Three minutes passed.

The plane started down as the pilot spoke. "We are descending to fifty feet altitude. It's going to be a rough ride, so stay buckled in your seats if you don't have a reason to be up. Ahead of us is the stern of what looks like a ship, sticking out of the sea. I see several life rafts near it."

The EP-3E veered right slightly to broaden its turn as it started a left circle over the protruding stern of the ship. In large black letters the word *Gearing* stood out. From the front of the aircraft a short cry of anguish broke the silence.

Below them, waving from life rafts, were the survivors of the USS *Gearing*. The presence of the United States Navy aircraft gave hope. The survivors knew their battle had not gone unnoticed and a sense of relief, that only mariners can understand, spread through the survivors. The presence of the aircraft told them rescue was on its way. Little did they know, nor would they have believed, that rescue would take four days.

Lieutenant Sue Garner shoved two aircrewmen aside as she ran up the aisle to where Lieutenant Commander John Andrews filmed the scene. She grabbed his flight suit. "Gotta go! Gotta go, John! Multiple bogies airborne out of Benghazi and Tripoli. We gotta go! They'll be feet wet in thirty seconds!"

Andrews tossed his camera to the chief beside him and ran to the cockpit.

"Break off, Commander. Fighters on their way!"

"Screw them!" the pilot answered angrily. He then reached in his pocket and pulled out a pack of cigarettes. "I've just finished talking to Sixth Fleet. Admiral Cameron has given me charge to decide what we do."

"Not supposed to smoke," the copilot said calmly, handing his lighter to the pilot.

"Screw you, too. I'm not smoking; I'm just holding it in my mouth," Stillwell replied, flicking the lighter until a flame appeared. "John, we're gonna dump the life raft and provisions before we leave. I'm not going to abandon our shipmates yet. We can't outrun those fighters anyway, so we'll dump the stuff and then lead them away from here."

As Garner and Andrews departed the cockpit, they heard the pilot say, "Mr. Copilot, no smoking is fine for peacetime, but I would submit to you, that now with a state of war existing, we can smoke. May even mean we can have sex again?"

CAPTAIN HEATH CAFFERTY WAVED. HE GAVE A THUMBS-up to Lieutenant Commander Nash, fifty yards away, in another life raft, helping survivors crawl into it from the water. Every raft had an officer or chief. Like the others, Cafferty and his fellow passengers continued to pull survivors from the water. The EP-3E finished its turn and headed toward them.

The door to the aircraft opened and a bright orange package tumbled out, inflating into a life raft as it hit the water. Several sailors, still in the water, swam to it. The aircraft wiggled its wings before applying power to the engines. He watched as it turned north, leaving them to the waters.

How long would it be before rescue arrived? They were closer to Libya than to allied forces, and Cafferty was damned if he intended to be a prisoner of war to be paraded through the streets like in scenes from Vietnam.

He was about two hundred yards from the stern of the USS *Gearing.* The valiant warship was slowly sinking, almost as if fighting to remain afloat. The life rafts, the waveless mirror ocean, the haze along the horizon, the stern of the ship with its rising thick column of smoke gave the scene an eerie Salvador Dali quality.

Near the stern of the *Gearing* a head popped up. It was the warrant officer. Under each of her arms was a sailor.

"I dogged the warrant into women's berthing," a smoke-faced young man said to no one in particular. "The missile hit. I wanted to leave the hatch opened so they could escape, but the warrant ordered it shut after she jumped into the compartment."

"Paddle over," Cafferty ordered, ignoring the sailor. "We're the closest."

Using their hands to augment the two paddles, they moved along the smooth surface toward the warrant officer. Minutes later they reached out and pulled the two women from the warrant's grip.

Cafferty reached down and held the exhausted warrant officer up as she rested her head against the side of the raft. Her breath came in short, rapid gulps.

"Good work, Warrant," he said, when she looked up.

She threw up over his hands, too tired to wipe the vomit from her mouth.

Cafferty and another sailor pulled her into the orange vinyl craft.

"Warrant, I'm sorry. I thought you were dead," the young sailor on the other side said. He lowered his head onto his arms and cried silently.

"Don't worry about it. You did what I told you to. You saved the ship long enough for it to whip ass and take names," she gasped in short whispered words. "Besides, you don't think I'd risk my life if I thought I was going to die, do you? Naw, ain't gonna happen—too many boy toys I ain't met for me to die yet."

Several minutes later, the warrant slid over beside the captain.

"Captain!" a sailor shouted, pointing south. "It's a helicopter!"

Cafferty knew it wasn't American. The helo flew within a mile of their position and hovered for about ten minutes. Sunlight reflected off the camera lens from the interior of the helicopter.

"Assholes," said Cafferty. They were filming the disaster. What he wouldn't give right now for a handheld surface-to-air missile. "I guess tonight we'll be featured on Libyan television."

"Let's not disappoint them, Captain. Come on, everyone, give them the Hawaiian good luck sign," said the warrant, holding up the middle finger of her left hand.

Cafferty joined the others in greeting the Libyan helicopter. Two sailors in another life raft stood and dropped their trousers, turning their naked cheeks to the Libyans. He grinned for the first time today.

TWELVE

"ADMIRAL, EVERYTHING ORDERED HAS BEEN IN AC-cordance with your standing op order. I talked with Commodore Ellison a few minutes ago, directly after the EP-3E report. Seems he was trying to contact us at the same time to report that someone, masquerading as the commanding officer of the USS *Gearing,* spoofed CTF Sixty-one earlier this morning. Captain Ellison has launched four Harriers back along the battle group's course to see if they can locate the destroyer, but the Marine Corps aircraft do not have the legs to reach the attack area. Ellison originally believed *Gearing* was heading his way at flank speed, before he realized he was being spoofed. By then, he had already recalled the combat air patrol, turned toward the Strait of Sicily, jacked the speed up, and started focusing the battle group transition from FONOP to a noncombatant evacuation op—a NEO. Sixty-one has now slowed their progress to await your directions."

"Clive, I don't like the sound of this. Where are they now?" Admiral Cameron asked his chief of staff. He ran his hand through his brown mane of thick hair. His graying eyebrows bunched as he blinked the sleep from his eyes. The dull ache from the wounds on his back reminded him to be careful in his movements.

"The battle group is in the Strait of Sicily," Captain Clive Bowen replied.

The admiral bent down to slip on his shoes.

"Clive, I'm sorry to ask this, but can you give me a hand tying these damn things?"

The chief of staff bent down and tied the admiral's shoes and then grabbed the khaki shirt draped over the back of a nearby chair and helped the admiral pull his shirt over the thick bandages. Two three-star rank devices held the collars down.

"Thanks, Clive." He stuck his hand out and Clive helped the man to his feet. Admiral Cameron walked to the chest of drawers near the door to his private head.

Looking in the mirror, the admiral commented, "Damn, Clive, I look like a lopsided Hunchback of Notre Dame who's gotten the shit beaten out of him."

Changing the subject, he asked, "What is VQ-2 doing?" referring to the parent squadron of the EP-3E. "Is CTF Sixty-seven aware?" The sound of urine hitting the metal side of the commode accompanied his voice. The strong smell of ammonia reached Clive a few seconds later through the open door.

"Yes, sir. I talked with Rear Admiral Devlin and, with our concurrence, he has directed the EP-3E into the action area to visually verify the report."

"Okay, Clive, but a four-engine turboprop Orion is no match for fighter aircraft. I want them out of there at the first sign of any reaction. I mean any. It could be a trap to bag one of our aircraft. Just because Qaddafi's dead and gone doesn't mean whoever's controlling Libya is any less radical and anti-U.S."

He started toward the door. "Let's go to Combat. I want to be there when the aircraft arrives on the scene. Your job, Clive, is to run interference with the doc and that attractive nurse out there." He opened the door.

The admiral and Captain Clive Bowen walked into the outer room.

"Doc, don't say a word," the admiral said, smiling and waving his hand at Captain Jacobs, the Sixth Fleet surgeon snoring on the couch, and, without breaking stride, continued to the stateroom door. The nurse rose from the nearby table. "I have to go to Combat," Admiral Cameron muttered.

"Admiral . . ." Lieutenant Commander Kathleen Gray, of the nurse corps, started to argue. She took two steps toward Admiral Cameron, afraid he was going to fall.

"Stay here with the doc, Nurse. If I need you, I'll call."

"What's going on?" Doctor Jacobs asked, half-asleep.

Clive winked at the nurse as he shut the door behind them. So much for him running interference.

Outside, the two Marine sentries saluted the admiral and fell in step behind the two men. Since the attack the lone Marine orderly had been replaced by two. The two Marines had shifted from their casual uniform into combat cammies, their M-16s a sharp contrast from the usual Colt-45s they wore holstered around their waists.

One ladder, six frames, and two knee knockers later they were inside the Sixth Fleet Combat Information Center. One Marine took position outside of CIC while the other followed the admiral inside.

"Sixth Fleet in Combat," said a voice as they entered.

The staff duty officer rushed over. "Admiral, the EP-3E is entering the area now, sir, if you would like to listen."

"Yes, I would, Commander. Lead the way." A wave of dizziness swept over Admiral Cameron. He reached out and braced himself as fresh beads of sweat broke out on his forehead. Clive Bowen's hand surreptitiously took the admiral by the arm.

"This way, Admiral," Captain Bowen said and removed his hand as Cameron straightened.

Initially, the damage to the USS *La Salle* and USS *Simon Lake* was thought to be so severe that they would have to abandon the ships, but the quick damage control by the ships' companies had mitigated the damage. It took divers a whole day to cut away the sharp metal edges protruding around the damaged sterns and another day to rig a temporary seal to restore watertight integrity. By the time the USS *La Salle* and the USS *Simon Lake* had been refloated, Admiral Cameron had been released from the Italian hospital and given a quick physical at the U.S. Naval Hospital in Naples. He walked aboard with a little help from Clive and Doc Jacobs the same day the ships were refloated. There was still a lot of damage to be repaired and neither ship could get under way on its own steam, but for the time being the *La Salle* had been restored to duty as a command ship and the *Simon Lake*—a submarine tender—had its repair facilities working round the clock.

Everyone followed the progress of the wounded leader. Admiral Cameron's presence restored the shattered confidence that resulted from the terrorist attack. Spontaneous applause started with a couple of claps and then broke throughout the staff Combat Information Center into a cacophony of cheers.

Admiral Cameron had returned to the damaged flagship the previous night from two days in the hospital, recovering from the wounds he'd sustained during the coordinated terrorist attack. He ran his hand through his hair. Memories of the attack at the bistro exploded across his mind. That attack had followed the one on the ships by minutes, leaving eleven dead and eight wounded. One of the dead had been his wife, Susan.

The applause as Cameron walked through the Sixth Fleet Combat Information Center did as much for the troops as it did for the admiral. Admiral Cameron waved and smiled as he moved to the center of Combat. He tried to stand as erect as the bandages allowed as he walked. If Cameron was back on the job, things were all right. Rumors of his death—wildly exaggerated—the death of Admiral Phrang, and evolving events in the Mediterranean had created an apprehensive atmosphere of uncertainty among the officers and sailors. Seeing the "Iron Leader" in Combat, alive and moving purposely, was the medicine needed to start morale climbing back up the ladder. Word began immediately to spread through the fleet that the Old Man was back at the helm.

Admiral Cameron and Captain Bowen stopped near the surface plotting table as the applause died and the sailors returned their attention to their consoles.

"We'll be able to hear them through this speaker, Admiral."

"If I want to talk to them, can I do that from here?"

Clive brought up a high-back stool and pushed it up behind the admiral, who nodded and sat down.

The door to Combat opened and Clive saw the fleet surgeon enter and move quietly, out of the way, to a nearby bulkhead. He nodded and hoped Dr. Jacobs wouldn't be needed, but the admiral had scared him a little when he swayed as they entered. The man had only been out of surgery a couple of days and here he was thrust into a wartime situation. If he passed out, Clive had no idea how it would affect the exuberance they'd seen when they first entered. Sailors, at heart, were a superstitious lot.

"Yes, sir, you can talk to them, or anyone else you want to, Admiral, right from here. This microphone has been connected to the secure voice circuit. CTF Sixty-seven released the EP-3E to our control a few minutes ago."

The admiral nodded.

From the speaker crackled the voice of the EP-3E pilot. "Sixth Fleet, this is Ranger Two Niner, there is a column of dark smoke rising on the horizon. Am altering course to one six zero and descending to fifty feet."

"Roger, Ranger Two Niner. Report when you are five miles from scene," the voice of the ATC crackled from the speaker.

"Roger, Sixth Fleet; I am approximately fifteen miles out now."

A chief petty officer walked up to the staff duty officer, waited a few seconds, and when an opportunity presented itself passed a note.

The SDO looked at it and turned to the admiral. "Admiral, General Jacques LeBlanc's office is on the phone and asking to speak with you."

Admiral Cameron looked at his watch. "It's going on nine in the morning. Who is he?"

"He was Admiral Phrang's deputy, Admiral—the new French general who arrived two months ago. You haven't met him yet. We had you on his calendar for next week, but his plans conflicted so we were rescheduling for later in the month. When that car bomb killed Admiral Phrang two days ago, General LeBlanc assumed command of Allied Forces Southern Command. He is now in charge of all NATO forces in the Mediterranean."

"What does he want?" the admiral asked the staff duty officer.

Commander Balley looked at the note, then at the chief, who raised his eyebrows and shrugged his shoulders. Admiral Cameron looked at the chief.

"He doesn't say, Admiral. Just that it is important that he talks to you," the chief answered.

"Tell him that I can't come to the phone at this moment, Chief. Don't tell him why. Take a number and tell him I'll return his call as soon as I can." The admiral looked at the chart and then, thinking of something else, said to the departing chief, "Give him my regrets, Chief, and tell him that it is impossible for me to talk at this moment. He should understand, considering everything." Cameron reached in his back pocket and pulled out his handkerchief and wiped the sweat from his forehead. *God, don't let me pass out.*

The staff intelligence officer walked up beside the admiral.

"Morning, Kurt. How you doing?"

"Very good, Admiral. The important question is how are you? You look like shit."

"It hasn't been a good week, Kurt."

The staff duty officer nodded at the chief, who hurried away to pass the message to General LeBlanc's office.

"Sixth Fleet, Ranger Two Niner; I am five miles and approaching the area. I count eight life rafts. We are taking count of souls on board the rafts. There are people in the water. I am approaching . . ." The voice stopped for several seconds.

"Sixth Fleet, Ranger Two Niner; I am overflying the stern of a sinking ship. The stern is approximately forty feet above the water. Two propellers exposed. Ship is Navy gray. There are letters on the stern. . . ." Commander Stillwell, the EP-3E pilot, paused.

"Sixth Fleet," then his voice rose in pitch, "*Gearing.* I

say again, the words read *Gearing*. Do you copy? The motherf— The sinking ship is the United States destroyer USS *Gearing*." The Sixth Fleet staff heard the tremor in the voice of the unseen pilot.

"Ranger Two Niner, request you verify. Can you see any other part of the ship other than the stern?"

"Look, asshole. I've got American sailors in the water and an American warship down by the bow! I count two goddamn holes in her starboard aft side. I see one that would have been below the waterline, probable torpedo hit. Another hole is at the waterline that could have been either a torpedo or a missile. If I got any closer I'd be inside it. I don't like telling it any more than you enjoy hearing it, but we have American sailors, in dungarees and khakis, in the water and in life rafts. We've got a major problem here!"

No one spoke in Combat. Everyone looked at the admiral. He picked up the microphone.

"Ranger Two Niner, this is Admiral Cameron. What are your intentions?"

"What the hell . . . Sorry, Admiral, standing by for further instructions."

"You are the on-scene commander, Ranger Two Niner. You tell us what your assessment is, your recommendations, and then we'll decide." He paused and before the EP-3E could respond, Admiral Cameron added, "We'll take care of the assholes who did this. I know how you feel, but right now we need accurate information to save those sailors. Okay?"

"Aye, aye, sir." An audible sigh came over the speaker before Stillwell continued. "My intentions are to circle over this group as long as possible. There are still sailors treading water. Those in the life rafts are pulling them in. No waves or wind at sea level, making the rescue by those in the rafts fairly easy. I have my aft door opened and my intentions, Admiral, are to drop the number three life raft, along with provisions, PRC radios, and bottled water on my next pass. My recommendation is to do something ASAP to rescue our shipmates and then I recommend bombing Libya back into the Ice Age!"

"Roger," Admiral Cameron acknowledged. He turned to his intelligence officer.

"Kurt, what is the situation in Algeria?"

"Sir, we need to keep the *Nassau* headed toward Algiers. As of yesterday, one American was dead and they had an incident near our embassy, resulting in a small firefight between our Marines and the rebels. The ambassador said the Algerians are laying siege to the embassy."

"Clive, what do we have available to pick up the *Gearing* survivors?"

"Sir, there is the USS *Miami,* SSN-755, in company with the *Nassau.*"

"Too bad we don't have our Sigonella squadron," Captain Kurt Lederman added. "If DoD hadn't overridden our recommendation and relocated HC-4 back to the States we'd have long-range helicopters to—"

"Clive, how about the Air Force?" Admiral Cameron interrupted. This was not the time to be bashing an administration, even one out of power.

"If they do have any, they'd be in Germany somewhere. We'll call and start them on their way."

The admiral nodded. "Do it." Meanwhile, detach USS *Miami* from *Nassau* battle group and tell her to make best speed toward *Gearing* datum. If nothing else, it puts her and her Tomahawks within striking range.

The speaker burst to life. "Sixth Fleet, I count minimum of sixty-two souls in the life rafts and the water. Am making another pass to drop." The voice paused. "Wait one, Sixth Fleet."

A moment later Stillwell said excitedly, "Sixth Fleet, we have multiple bogeys airborne out of Tripoli and Benghazi. Minimum nine fighters and a possible TU-20 Blinder. I have no idea why a Blinder would react against us. I find it hard to believe a bomber that old can fly."

Admiral Cameron grabbed the microphone. "Ranger, get out of there. Hit the deck for home, now!"

"Admiral, if I hit the deck any lower I'm going to be submerged. As you said, sir, I am the on-scene commander and, unless otherwise directed, this on-scene commander is going to complete this run and drop the number three life raft and provisions. Then, we'll outmaneuver the entire Libyan Air Force." The number three life raft was the largest one of the three aboard the EP-3E.

The admiral keyed the mike a couple of times, fighting the urge to order the pilot to obey his command. Then, he caught himself and released the key. Most times the best one to determine the threat is the one in contact with it. He recalled his own experiences in Desert Storm and remembered his father's tales about Vietnam and rear-echelon quarterbacks . . . though quarterbacks wasn't the term he used. He'd be damned if he was going to be a REMF. He handed the microphone back to the duty officer.

The chief petty officer returned, walking briskly to where the admiral stood. The admiral looked at him. "Well, Chief?"

"Sir, General LeBlanc *himself* is on the phone and demands that you talk with him now."

"Demands?"

"Yes, sir. *Demands* is what he said, though he is French so he may not understand what he's saying. I told him you were busy, but he ordered me to tell you that he did not care what you were doing, you worked for him and he wanted to talk with you and he wanted to talk now."

"He did, did he?" the admiral asked, amazed.

"Yes, sir. He said it was very important."

"Then leave the bastard on the phone. I'm busy. Tell him he can wait, but it'll be at least an hour before I answer."

The chief left, hurrying through Combat and carrying with him a perverse sense of pleasure at being able to tell a flag officer, even if he was French—in a tactful manner, of course—to go to hell. He waited until he left Combat before he smiled. Only the British would enjoy better what he had been "directly" ordered to do.

Three tense minutes passed before the unarmed reconnaissance aircraft called again.

"Sixth Fleet, we have dropped provisions, wiggled our wings, and are turning north. The Libyan aircraft are feet wet twenty miles off their coast and about twenty-five miles from us and closing. Estimate intercept in five minutes. Commencing evasive maneuvers at this time. Have opened our side windows so we can at least shoot forty-fives at them."

"Spirited pilot," commented the admiral. He wiped the sweat from his forehead. Around him, the command team wore coats and sweaters in the fifty-degree air-conditioned space, but it seemed hot to him.

"Twenty miles from us. Have lost the Tripoli aircraft, Admiral. Their last course was zero zero seven at twelve thousand feet and we counted the Tripoli formation as one TU-20 and three MiG-25 fighters; could be four fighters. Don't know what in the hell they're going to do with the TU-20, guess we could fly side by side and fire our pistols at each other."

"What is the Libyan Blinder doing over the ocean, Kurt?" the admiral asked his intelligence officer.

"Admiral, the last thing we had on Libyan Blinders was that they were inoperative from lack of proper maintenance and spare parts. They used to do free fall bombing runs on their ranges east of Tripoli. But that was over a decade ago. Of course, they could have converted them into maritime reconnaissance aircraft."

"Sixth Fleet, Ranger Two Niner; intercept time is two minutes. We are reflecting six MiG-23 Floggers out of Benghazi. Bandits are beginning to descend from twelve thousand feet altitude."

The admiral turned to his staff duty officer. "Where are those Harriers?" His handkerchief fell out of his hand and landed on the tips of Bowen's shoes.

"Wait one, Admiral," he replied as he ran to the air plot table.

Clive bent down, picked up the handkerchief, and placed it in the admiral's hand, who nodded weakly, took it, and wiped the sweat from his face. Clive noticed the fleet surgeon, Captain Jacobs, move from his place along the bulkhead and cross Combat to stand directly behind the admiral. Their eyes met briefly before Clive turned back to the displays. He was glad Doc had disobeyed the admiral and followed them to Combat.

Admiral Cameron leaned back against the back of the stool and quietly watched the exchange between the staff duty officer and the Sixth Fleet Combat team.

The staff duty officer shouted across Combat. "Admiral, they're too far out, sir. They're one hundred miles southeast of the Strait of Sicily. *Nassau* will have to recall them in fifteen minutes due to fuel state."

"Can they reach the EP-3E?" the admiral asked.

"Sir, they can try, but then it's going to be a race to

bingo to Sigonella. They won't have the gas to return to *Nassau.*"

Clive interrupted. "They've got Air Force KC-130 tankers at Sigonella. Call air traffic control at Sigonella and tell them to launch the alert tanker." He pointed at the air traffic control operator. "Identify the nearest refueling orbit point and issue a verbal air traffic movement to Sigonella. Tell them we'll worry about hard copy later."

"SDO, I want a launch estimate on that tanker from Sigonella ASAP!"

"Roger, Admiral."

"Clive, get Commodore Ellison on the phone and tell him to turn the *Nassau* around and close his aircraft. Tell him to launch the other four Harriers also. Further, order Sixty-one to vector his aircraft to intercept the EP-3E."

Clive rushed over to the console.

"SDO," said the admiral, "sound General Quarters. I want this space brought up to combat standards now. And I mean now."

The SDO reached behind him and flipped the lever on the red sound box. Throughout the USS *La Salle* the ear-shattering bongs announcing General Quarters caught a much fatigued crew unprepared, but by the third bong, adrenaline surged through their arteries and startled-awake sailors raced to battle stations. Fear lurked in the back of each mind that once again the USS *La Salle* was under attack. On board the USS *Simon Lake* and the USS *Albany,* tied alongside, similar General Quarters bongs broke the summer morning stillness of the surrounding village of Gaeta.

One hundred and twenty-five Italian military Special Forces, who had arrived within hours of the terrorist attack two days ago against the ships, unslung their weapons. The Italians raced for their assigned defensive positions, unaware of what danger caused the Americans to go to full security, but no more attacks on Italian soil were going to occur without the attackers facing Italy's best.

Male sailors raced through the hatch of Combat pulling on their shirts, while female sailors crammed their hair under ball caps as they ran to their stations.

"Sixth Fleet, this is Ranger Two Niner. I have Libyan fighters all around me, according to our sensors, but I can't see any. We show them on the same course at six thousand feet altitude. We are under a cloudbank that bends to my ten o'clock. I intend to remain under it. My altitude is fifty feet and this aircraft is shaking like a banshee!"

"Why haven't the Libyans intercepted them?" Clive asked.

"They may not be able to see the EP-3E," Kurt answered. "That close to the water the surface of the ocean is probably obscuring the fighters' radar picture. It's not like our Aegis or the F-14 Tomcat's radar."

"Admiral," the lieutenant supervising the crew manning the strike consoles interrupted, "Sixty-one says its Harriers are reporting multiple air bogeys at their two o'clock on a course of zero one two at altitude eight thousand."

"Ask them what the location is!" ordered Admiral Cameron. "That doesn't tell me much."

"Sixty-one, this is Sixth Fleet," broadcast over a different set of speakers from the ones that connected Sixth Fleet to the EP-3E. "What is the location of the bogeys and total number being reflected?"

"Sixth Fleet, pilots are reporting minimum of eight bogeys located approximately one hundred miles north of Tripoli and one hundred miles south-southeast of their position."

The admiral interrupted. "What is the weapons load-out on those Harriers?"

"Four AIM-9 Sidewinders and two Sparrows, sir. Plus, an internal twenty-five–millimeter cannon."

"Good. Tell Sixty-one that he has authority to release the Harriers to intercept bogeys on their own radar guidance. Weapons tight at this time. If the Libyan aircraft pass the thirty-fifth parallel they are to shoot them down."

"Aye, aye, sir." The lieutenant passed the orders.

"Admiral, I am patching the circuit controlling the Harriers to the number three speaker. We can hear CTF Sixty-one's side of the conversation, but the Harriers are out of range."

"Very well, carry on."

The EP-3E speaker blared. "Sixth Fleet, Ranger Two Niner; they have passed us. I repeat, they have passed us. We are passing the thirty-fifth parallel southeast of Malta. We're one hundred thirty miles from Catania and Sigonella."

"What do you mean, they have passed you?" asked the Admiral. He wiped his forehead again.

"They are already past the thirty-fifth parallel," Clive added.

The duty officer relayed the admiral's question to the EP-3E.

"We see contrails between breaks in the cloud cover and those contrails are ahead of us. I estimate their course as three three zero. Sensors show they have descended to four thousand feet."

The admiral's eyebrows bunched together as he thought about it. Several seconds passed. This didn't make sense. Why would Libyan fighters be this far north? At this rate they were going to fly right into—

He turned to the staff duty officer. "Chart! Where's the chart?" He tried to rise, but sat back down, his breath coming rapidly. Cameron pointed to the surface plotting table in front of him. Dr. Jacobs took a step toward the admiral. Cameron waved him away.

"Put it here," Clive ordered.

The chart of the central Mediterranean was quickly taped down across the Plexiglas-covered metal table.

"Quick, Commander Balley, draw a line from Benghazi on a bearing of three three zero."

"Yes, sir," the SDO responded. He grabbed a compass ruler. He overlaid the Libyan city of Benghazi and drew a pencil along the edge of the ruler on three three zero degrees. The line ran through the central Mediterranean and through the Sicilian city of Catania.

"Jesus Christ," the admiral mumbled. "Now do one from Tripoli on a bearing of zero one zero."

He did. The line ran east of Malta and slightly north of Catania—directly through the United States Naval Air Station at Sigonella.

The chief returned. "Admiral, General LeBlanc—"

Admiral Cameron held his hand up. "Not now," he said.

Clive waved the chief away.

"Clive, call CTF Sixty-seven and tell them to prepare Sigonella Air Station for possible Libyan air attack. Tell Commodore Ellison the Harriers have weapons free authority and they are to engage the Libyans. Splash the bandits. Commander, contact Italian Air Defense and warn them."

Cameron slumped slightly on the stool. Clive reached out and took the admiral's elbow as Cameron pushed himself back up. Cameron looked up at his chief of staff and nodded. Then, the two waited while the staff duty officer relayed the orders.

"We need a quick calculation, Commander Balley. How long at five hundred knots from Benghazi to Sigonella?" His voice was so low that Clive barely heard it.

"This is Ranger Two Niner calling. The Benghazi formations have rendezvoused with the Tripoli bunch! They are on course three five five, altitude four zero. They ain't turning back, Admiral! They ain't turning back and if they keep going like they are, they are going to be feet dry over Sicily in minutes."

The commander grabbed a calculator and did a quick series of computations. "One hour fifteen minutes, Admiral."

"Thirty minutes until they cross the shoreline," the admiral commented dryly.

"Admiral, I have the Italian duty officer at Pratica di Mari Air Base on the line. What do you want to tell him?" Pratica di Mari was the air operations center for the Italian Air Force located south of Rome.

In the background continuous intelligence reports flowed from the EP-3E as the reconnaissance aircraft tracked the enemy formations.

"Tell them, we believe Sigonella will be attacked within the next thirty minutes by Libyan aircraft. Then, as soon as possible, I want to know their intentions."

He turned to his chief of staff. "Clive, what do we have at Sigonella that we can respond with?"

"Nothing, Admiral. Not a goddamn thing! It's a logistics hub. The Air Force's Air Mobility Command has at least two KC-135s and a KC-130 down there fully loaded with aviation fuel for today's refueling missions. ASCOMED, the Navy's transportation and passenger service, has two cargo C-130s on the apron, VQ-2 has two EP-3E reconnaissance aircraft, and there are four PatRon P-3C maritime patrol planes. There are also several smaller aircraft, ranging from a couple of C-12 VIP transports to a couple of short-range helicopters for local operations. Plus, other aircraft are always transiting, so there could be more.

We ordered the alert KC-130 aloft five minutes ago, so if the crew can be airborne within the next few minutes maybe . . ." Clive's voice faded, leaving his thought unsaid.

"That's eleven big boys," the admiral said. "A lot of fuel-laden aircraft sitting on that small apron . . . like Mitchell Field when the Japanese hit it." He merely mumbled the last thought aloud.

"Can only be one EP-3E and one KC-135 there," Commander Balley added. "Ranger Two Niner staged out of Sigonella and the KC-135 for the Rivet Joint mission is on station in the West Med." Rivet Joint was the Air Force RC-135 reconnaissance aircraft. The big difference between Rivet Joint and the EP-3E was that Rivet Joint had better sensors and was capable of air-to-air refueling.

Admiral Gordon Cameron spun around to the duty officer and pointed. "Commander Balley, call Sigonella and tell them to launch every aircraft they can and tell them that a Libyan air attack is inbound!"

"The *Nassau* is on the other side of the Strait of Sicily. She has launched the remainder of her Marine Corps Harriers," Clive added.

Admiral Cameron looked hard at Clive, weighing the next course of action. A curt nod of the admiral's head showed he had reached a decision. "Okay, tell Sixty-one to divert the second formation of Harriers toward Sigonella and tell him that I believe Libyan fighters are on their way to attack the base." Then, calmer, he added, "And tell him what happened to the *Gearing*. I want those Marines more pissed off than Marines normally are. Then call Italian Air Defense and tell them that four United States Marine Corps Harriers are inbound from the west and not to mistake them for Libyan fighters!"

Admiral Cameron shut his eyes. Dr. Jacobs moved forward and lightly pushed the admiral, who opened his eyes.

"Couldn't miss the excitement, Doc?"

"Can't have you flags having all the fun."

"This is Ranger Two Niner. Four of the MiG-23s have broken off and are heading west to engage our Harriers! We do not have comms with the Marines!"

"That would be the first formation Ellison launched," Clive clarified.

Admiral Cameron looked around the Combat Information Center and, like everyone else, he waited. Something he did not do well. He tried to focus his attention on the JOTS display, watching the friendly and hostile symbols close, and discovered everything appeared to be going round and round like a multilighted Ferris wheel. Clive moved silently up from behind the admiral and, with the smooth transition that chiefs of staff learn only from experience, he assumed command. Sailors stared at their officers. Chiefs waited, ready to respond to orders.

Experienced officers knew the look. It showed in their eyes and their body language when things became confused or anxiety increased.

"They're scared, but ready," Cameron said softly to the doctor. "Even the strongest look to their leaders in times of crisis, but even leaders sometimes lack the words to ease warriors' concern."

"Rest, Admiral. Even you can't order your body to heal faster."

"Got to stay awake, Doc. If you have something, give it to me. If I pass out here . . . well, you know what it would do to morale. Get me through this for the good of the men and the fleet."

Jacobs nodded, reached in his pocket, and extracted a small bottle. "Swallow these," he said, handing two white tablets to the admiral.

"These will work?"

"For a short while, Admiral, and then, I shall have the medical pleasure of watching you moan and complain about how medical science gave you the worse headache you've ever had."

"Admiral, the duty officer at Pratica di Mari says they have four Italian F-16 Fighting Falcon interceptors airborne out of Groseta Airfield near Palermo, Sicily, conducting routine training. They're not fully loaded. They only have two Sidewinder missiles each. Groseta has been patched through from Pratica di Mari. The aircraft are over the sea north of Palermo. They estimate a thirty-five–minute flight to Sigonella. Groseta has already redirected the aircraft."

"Good!" The admiral looked around him. So young, most of them. He recognized the look. These past two days had aged them as only combat veterans can age. He placed his hand over his heart. Damn thing was sprinting.

"Pratica di Mari reports the Italian fighters have been given 'weapons free.' They may fire at their discretion."

"Are they aware of the Harriers headed their way?" Clive asked.

"Yes, sir. Pratica di Mari says that Groseta has the Harriers on their air defense radar and has established voice contact with them. *Nassau* has released the Harriers to the Italians."

The NATO speakers on the starboard side of the Sixth Fleet Combat Information Center roared to life.

"Any station this net, and I mean any station, this is Souda Bay Naval Support Activity. Souda Bay Airfield, Crete, is under attack. We are under attack. I repeat, we are under attack!" shouted a voice, the slow southern drawl drawing out the transmission.

The admiral looked at Clive Bowen. "Who'd be attacking Souda Bay, Crete?" He pushed himself up on the stool.

Clive grabbed the microphone. "Souda Bay, this is Sixth Fleet. Explain attack. Who is attacking you?" He looked at the intelligence officer and the cryptologic officer, Captain Paul Brooks, who had earlier entered CIC. "Who's attacking Souda Bay?"

"Sixth Fleet, this is the air tower. We have multiple aircraft bombing the airstrip. I don't know who they are, but they ain't American and they ain't Greek. Shit! Take cover!"

The sounds of cannon fire, breaking glass, and the familiar roar of high-powered jet engines blasted from the speakers.

"Sixth Fleet, if you heard that, you just heard our last transmission. We are abandoning the tower. Jets look Russian to me, but the writing on the side is Arabic. Go figure. This is Air Traffic Control Souda Bay signing off."

"Don't go!" shouted Clive.

"Screw you, Sixth Fleet. I'm a civilian. I ain't one of yore sailors and I'll tell ya right now, you've lost an EP-3E and two C-130 transports. Every aircraft on the apron is in flames. Including that KC-135 tanker that landed earlier. That shooting you're hearing isn't at the tower, though we have taken some hits, I don't mind telling ya; it's at the aircraft parked on the apron. Shit! Here they come again." The line went quiet.

"They're gone," Clive said.

Several seconds passed.

"Sixth Fleet, I'm back. Y'all ain't gonna believe this. The Greek Air Force just showed up and they're kicking ass and taking names! You can scratch at least two of those Russian aircraft. They're in flames south of the runway and the others are running." Laughter followed. "They better run fast, I think there are some pissed-off Greeks chasing them. Earl, hand me that video camera and that pack of cigarettes. Shit! Earl, hurry yer butt up and take a picture of that. Whoosh! There's goes another Greek missile and there explodes another asshole! Damn! This is just like a John Wayne movie, Sixth Fleet! CNN will pay a fortune for this. Earl, break out that Amstel beer and pass me that fucking camera. We gonna be rich, boy."

THE GREEK NATIONAL AIR DEFENSE COMMAND TRACKED the Libyan fighter aircraft from the time they departed the coastline north of Tobruk. The attacking force, in tight formation, presented a radar profile of a passenger aircraft. The lone Greek supervisor consulted his flight plans for the day and found nothing scheduled. He scratched his head and looked at the radar contact. It showed the aircraft in the international flight corridor for commercial airliners. He hoped it wasn't another defection. He put his pen down and walked to the radio just as the speaker blared.

"Air Defense, this is Rhodes Leader. We are four Mirage F-1s airborne for sector operations east of Crete," said the lead Greek pilot, Major Demetri Andrecopouliou, into his helmet mike piece. "We will be airborne three hours thirty minutes, conducting routine patrol. Single wing tank."

"Roger, Rhodes Leader, this is Air Defense Command. You are cleared to transit to op area at altitude one two five. Report when on station."

"Roger, sir. Will do." Demetri glanced at his altimeter, confirming their metric altitude equated to twelve thousand five hundred feet.

Since the flare-up with Turkey three months ago, the Greek armed forces had flexed its military muscle by keeping round-the-clock air patrols between its eastern borders and the Turkish mainland. The east of Crete patrol was boring. No Turkish aircraft would dare penetrate this far west. The Greek patrol varied the time by doing formation aerobatics, buzzing merchant vessels, and conducting ground control intercept exercises against each other. Today started like every other patrol day.

"Rhodes Leader, this is Rhodes Two. Let's buzz some merchants."

"Let's don't and say we did." Rhodes Two was going to be a good fighter jock, if Demetri could curb his wingman's recklessness.

Demetri visually checked his formation. "Rhodes Three and Four, close up. Diamond formation, maintain fifty meters separation. Divide radar coverage, as briefed, for three hundred sixty degrees and remain in tight formation."

"Rhodes Leader!" shouted Rhodes Two. "Aren't we relieving Kostas Kelipolas and his band of renegades?"

"Rhodes Two, no names. We will relieve Corfu Formation in fifteen minutes. We're going to hit the deck, come up under them, do a visual pass, a quick wiggle, and then they're off for a well-earned rest."

"Rhodes Leader, this is Corfu Leader. The day you and your boofus bunch sneak up on us is the day I buy Metaxa brandy for all!"

"Hey, Kostas, if we lose, it's retsina we'll buy!"

"*Skita, posti!* You're a cheap bastard, Ioannis," Corfu Leader teased Rhodes Two.

"No names, I said," Rhodes Leader repeated.

"Rhodes Leader, this is Air Defense Control. Report your position."

"Air Defense, Rhodes Leader; we are passing south of Khora Station. Maintaining one two five altitude at four hundred knots."

"Roger, Rhodes Leader, do you have bogeys southwest of you? We showed what I thought was an airliner outbound Tripoli Flight Information Region, but radar is now reflecting six to seven bogeys northbound."

"Negative, Air Defense Control. If you want, we can depart track and take a closer look for you."

"Roger, Rhodes Leader; come to course two two zero to free radars."

"Rhodes Formation," Demetri broadcast, "come right to course two two zero." The four Mirage F-1s turned as one, the sun highlighting the two French Matra Mica air-to-air missiles under each wing.

The formation leveled off. The four pilots continued in a diamond formation as each watched their assigned radar sector for the unidentified aircraft.

"Rhodes Leader, Rhodes Three; I have multiple bogeys bearing two eight zero, crossing feet dry Palaiokori."

"Impossible! There are no other aircraft scheduled for this morning." Palaiokori was a small coastal village south of the air base at Chania, Crete, where the Greek Air Force shared the runway with the United States Navy's Souda Bay base.

"Air Defense, this is Rhodes Leader. Do we have other Hellinikon Air Force aircraft airborne in the vicinity of Rhodes Formation?"

"That is a negative, Rhodes Leader. Our schedule shows only you and Corfu Formation airborne at this time. Next flight not for two hours, though Chania has a 'takeoff and landing' evolution scheduled in thirty minutes."

Rhodes Leader passed the radar sighting information to Air Defense and waited for further instructions.

The controller at the Greek National Air Defense headquarters, located across the runway from the United States Naval Support Activity Souda Bay, strolled over to the window. He put his small cup of strong Greek coffee on the window ledge before lifting his binoculars to scan the skies for the aircraft that Rhodes Formation reported and his radar reflected.

A summer haze shimmered over the runway. Already going on nine thirty and the summer sun promised another record-breaking day. Good for tourism and hell on those who kept their clothes on. He'd drive down later after work, drink a cold Amstel beer at the beach bar, and watch those white tourist titties bounce across the beach—good for a man his age. Not bad for his wife either when he arrived home with that twinkle in his eye. He smiled. His wife would smile. Life would be pleasant in the Nicholas Skournopolis household.

Skournopolis was born in Thessaloníki. He was six foot even and weighed two hundred fifty pounds. When the Greek Army had drafted him forty years ago at the age of seventeen, freeing him from a life of schoolwork, he had been the same height, but a hundred pounds lighter. He had no idea what army life was going to be like, but he quickly found it a welcome change after years of Father slapping his ears to study and Mother pushing his head into schoolbooks. Every male did two years' mandatory conscription in the service of his country. His father tried everything to get the authorities to defer the draft, including bribing the local draft board chairman, but Nicholas breathed a hidden sigh of relief when Athens eventually refused the request. He discovered to his surprise that he loved the Army and made up his mind to break the news to his parents, thereby shattering their dreams, that he intended to become a career noncom. That was, until four months before the end of his two years of government service, when the small night patrol Nicholas was with stumbled across a group of armed Albanians with automatic rifles on the Greek side of the border. In the fire fight that followed, Nicholas's company pushed the armed gang back across the border into the chaotic environment of Albania, killing four and wounding no one knew how many. For

Nicholas, his Army dreams ended with a bullet through the left side, which miraculously missed his stomach, intestines, other vital organs, and blood vessels, but destroyed one kidney. His fellow soldiers had backtracked after the fight to find him bleeding and unconscious. A month later he was discharged with a small disabled veteran pension. He returned to the polytechnic to finish his degree and then worked his way slowly up nondescript technical jobs as a civilian, to where he was now one of three senior Air Defense controllers in Chania, Crete. Along the way he married a Cretan girl, who gave him three boys to brag about and challenged him in pounds. Through his own efforts in the bars, Nicholas Skournopolis the wounded soldier became Nicholas Skournopolis wounded, disabled war hero.

Nicholas pushed the window in front of him farther out and flipped the fan on high, then tilted his cup and drained it in one gulp. He wiped his lips to shake the coffee drops off his thick mustache. His thoughts partially on the beach life in nearby Chania, he lifted the binoculars and returned to scanning the skies to the south. Almost immediately, Nicholas saw seven aircraft in tight formation headed toward the runway.

Damn, he was going to have someone's ass for this. Fighters! Americans most likely. They never remembered to file a country clearance before entering Greek air space. Damn them! They think they own this country. If they thought he was going to give them permission to land they had better think again—short of fuel or not. They'd better have a better reason than "We forgot to file."

He hurried to the radio and jerked up the microphone. "Unidentified aircraft approaching Chania Airfield, this is Greek National Air Defense Control. Identify yourself."

He received no reply. He repeated himself. By the third repeat, he was screaming at the pilots, who refused to acknowledge his demand. South through the open window, Nicholas watched the warplanes break off into a spread pattern as if positioning themselves to land. Not at his damn airfield!

"Unidentified aircraft, this is Greek National Air Defense Control. You are not cleared to land and you are interfering with the air traffic pattern. Break off and call Air Defense Control immediately!"

Rhodes Formation listened to the controller. Rhodes Two shrugged his shoulders at Demetri, flying about fifty meters away and able to see Ioannis clearly.

"Rhodes Formation, this is Corfu Formation. What's the holdup? We want to go home and we need you here to turn over. Or are you trying to sneak attack us?"

"Corfu Leader, we have unidentified aircraft approaching Chania and Air Defense has asked us to make an identity pass. They're over the airfield now, so as soon as he tells us who they are we'll turn back to your area."

"Roger, we'll stay on this frequency and monitor."

Rhodes Leader clicked his mike two times in acknowledgment.

The Air Defense controller slammed the microphone down on the table and with binoculars in hand walked to the front of the tower, mumbling obscenities at the strangers. When alone he seemed to walk without any signs of the wound affecting his left side. He twisted the focus as he visually tracked the unidentified aircraft approaching the runway. The sun blinded him momentarily. He moved his glasses and waited for their flight path to clear the morning sun. When he made out their side numbers Nicholas was going to file violation reports. What the hell did they think they were doing? He reached in a nearby drawer and pulled out the short one-page forms. The Greek government would give it to the American Embassy in

Athens and then they could work it out. If they were going to land they'd better lower their landing gear. It would be amusing to see the Americans land with wheels up, even if it closed the runway, like in 1996, when an Orion had used the entire runway—a runway long enough for it to take off and land three times without going around—and still kept going off the end for another hundred yards to crash. He grinned at the thought even as his mind began to register the fact that the aircraft in his binoculars were Libyan MiG-23 fighter-bombers.

The lead aircraft dove from the east, flying parallel to the German built World War II airfield. An air-to-ground missile blasted away from the left pylon, destroying the concrete radar shack at the end of the runway. Thundering by overhead, a series of free-fall iron bombs cascaded from the MiG-23's wings to explode, cratering the runway.

"Skita!" Nicholas cursed as he dove under the nearby table. The concussion of the bombs blew out the front windows, rattling the half-raised blinds and sending deadly glass shards and metal fragments exploding through the tower. He reached above and pulled the microphone underneath the table with him. Some glass had cut his hand and blood flowed down his fingertips.

"Rhodes Leader, this is Air Defense Control!" he screamed, his voice quaking. "We are under attack! We are under attack! Minimum seven MiG-23 aircraft attacking the runway!"

"Rhodes Formation, bank right. Afterburners on. Max speed. Line abreast formation. Tallyho!" The four Mirage F-1s banked hard to the right, afterburners firing simultaneously. "Air Defense Control, we are on our way!"

"Armament switches on, Rhodes Formation. Air Defense, Rhodes Formation ten minutes to Chania. Keep talking!"

"Air Defense, this is Corfu Formation. We're coming too. Inbound at max speed. Twenty minutes until overhead. Afterburners on, Corfu Formation, right turn, staggered line formation. Rhodes Leader, hold them till we get there! Armament switches on! Tallyho!"

"Rhodes Two!" shouted Corfu Leader, anger in his voice. "This had better not be one of your jokes!"

"I wish it were, I wish it were," Rhodes Two answered softly, reaching up beneath his helmet to wipe the sweat from his forehead. Libyans! *Skita!* Next best thing to them being Turkish.

Rhodes Formation screamed down to eight thousand feet, their contrails marking the path. They listened to the monologue from Air Defense Control as two armed and angry Greek Air Force Mirage F-1 formations scrambled to where Libyan MiG-23s were bombing the airfield the Greeks shared with the Americans.

The Floggers continued the attack, unaware of the inbound Greek fighters.

Rhodes Formation, descending past three thousand feet, roared over the Greek Air Force base east of the airport, five miles from the airfield, shattering the windows in the commanding general's office and several other command buildings. Small figures of military personnel running across the base flashed through Demetri's vision. The rising sun, behind them, obscured their arrival from the Libyan bomber pilots, who were executing a turn for another attack run; this time from the west. Smoke rose from the American side of the airfield, where one Air Force tanker, an American Orion aircraft, and two C-130 transports burned.

The four MiG-23 ground-attack Floggers steadied right as they aligned themselves for another attack against the American Souda Bay Naval Support Activity. The sun reflected off their fuselages. Rhodes Leader caught the reflection and saw the telltale bursts as the Floggers' twenty-three–millimeter cannons opened up.

He searched the area, surveying the combat scene, mentally plotting the enemy positions. Demetri looked up and immediately spotted two MiG-23 fighters overhead in tight combat air cover for the bombers. As he watched, the two MiGs overhead rolled right and began descending toward them. On the international airport side of the runway a commercial airliner burned, its remains scattered on the tarmac. The humans, running for cover, looked so vulnerable and tiny from his vantage point. The Americans had no air defense capability at Souda Bay. It was just a transportation and reconnaissance hub—nothing else. Their protection was the responsibility of the Greek Air Force.

"Rhodes Two and Three; two bandits overhead, inbound. Take them out. Rhodes Four, follow me. We're going for head-on intercept. Weapons free. Tallyho!"

"We're coming, Rhodes Leader!" shouted Corfu Leader. "Hold out until we're there! And don't kill them all; save some for us!"

"Corfu, hurry!" Demetri shouted. "There's seven bandits! We're outnumbered." He looked down at his weapon systems. Satisfied, he picked out his first target.

Rhodes Two acknowledged as he and Rhodes Three accelerated and pulled back on the throttle. Iaonnis felt his lips pull tight as the G's pushed his body deeper into the seat. The Mirages climbed near vertical toward the MiG-23 fighters diving to meet them.

Good luck, thought Demetri as he and Rhodes Four lined up for their run. If Rhodes Two and Three missed their targets, he and Rhodes Four would be easy prey for the MiGs headed down. This was going to be low-level combat with little room to maneuver.

Rhodes Leader and Rhodes Four flipped to the right. Then, with a coordinated zigzag into a hard left turn, their left wings pointing straight down at the ground, they came out of the heavy "G" maneuver directly over the east end of the main runway.

From the other direction, four MiG-23s became aware of the better-trained Greeks ahead, hurrying toward them.

"I have lock-on! One away!" screamed Rhodes Two over the circuit.

Rhodes Leader glanced up just as Rhodes Two's Matra Mica missile meshed with a Libyan MiG-23, turning the older Russian fighter into a cloud of burning metal and smoke. Pieces of the enemy aircraft cascaded out and rained down. Demetri looked forward at the enemy. The MiG-23 fighter-bombers broke to the right, aborting their attack run.

"Let's take them out, Rhodes Four!"

"I have lock-on, Rhodes Leader!"

"Fire!"

"Fox one!"

Rhodes Four's missile dipped below Demetri's vision before immediately reappearing ahead of him. It weaved through the air at supersonic speed toward the target. Flames from the missile's rocket engine left a thick thread of curling white smoke behind it. He knew that on the enemy aircraft a series of beeps, increasing in intensity, rang in the enemy pilot's helmet as the missile closed. From the tail of the MiG-23 a series of flares, followed by chaff clouds, shot out in an attempt to decoy the air-to-air missile. The MiG pulled up and rolled left in an evasive maneuver against the Matra Mica missile.

On his console, Rhodes Leader lined up the second fighter, achieved lock-on with his fire control radar. "Fox one!" Demetri shouted into the helmet microphone jammed against his lips by the tightened oxygen mask.

"Rhodes Three, swing right. Swing right!" shouted Rhodes Two.

"Flares! Drop flares!"

The Libyan fighters were fighting back.

Rhodes Leader and Rhodes Four passed the end of the runway. The asphalt flashed by, giving way to thick scrub and long-deserted German World War II pillboxes. Rhodes Four's missile missed the lead aircraft before it gained a lucky lock on the second aircraft that was trying to form up on another Libyan MiG-23. It scored a direct hit. The exploding MiG curved up in a nice arch before it lost momentum and tumbled into the sea. A parachute opened above.

"Break left, Rhodes Four. Rhodes Two, Rhodes Three, this is Rhodes Leader. Scratch one MiG!"

"Roger, Rhodes Leader, scratch one here! Remaining bandit is breaking south, rejoining your three!"

"Air Defense said there were seven!"

"I've only counted six, Rhodes Leader." Iaonnis's head searched frantically from side to side for the missing Libyan. "Maybe one fled when we showed up? You got one and we got one and now there are four heading south."

"Still one unaccounted for. Rhodes Two, Three; rejoin Rhodes Leader in pursuit! Tallyho!"

"I have lock-on! Fox two!" yelled Rhodes Four as he launched his second missile. The missile drove right up the tail of the trailing MiG-23. The aircraft exploded into a massive fireball. Rhodes Leader and Rhodes Four pulled up on their controls and rode over the conflagration, avoiding the falling debris that filled the sky ahead of them. No parachute came from the MiG.

"Yasoo, Ya Guppy Moo!" shouted Rhodes Two. "This is better than sex, Demetri. You should see what I have between my legs now!" Iaonnis reached down and tugged his crotch.

Rhodes Two and Rhodes Three pulled up alongside Rhodes Leader and Rhodes Four. Rhodes Two executed a victory roll. "Steady, Ioannis," Rhodes Leader ordered.

"No names, please. You may call me 'Ace,' " Ioannis answered. "Now, let's add to our scorecard and tonight, Demetri, you may buy the Metaxa as the women caress and smother me with kisses as they congratulate me on my victories."

The four Greek Mirage F-1 aircraft tore off in angry pursuit of the fleeing Libyan MiG-23 aircraft. Thirty miles south of Crete Corfu Formation joined Rhodes for a few minutes before low fuel forced the second Mirage formation to break off. Chania Airfield was untenable when Corfu Formation soared overhead. With crossed fingers and red-flashing low fuel lights, Corfu Formation continued to Heraklion and landed safely.

Fifty miles south of the airfield, Rhodes Leader ordered break-off when the MiGs disappeared into the haze surrounding the North African landmass. Thirty minutes later, during their return to Crete, his formation was intercepted by eight fully armed Greek Mirage F-1s. Two escorted the first air heroes of the twenty-first century back to the mainland. The other six established a combat air patrol between Greece and Libya like angry hornets searching for something to sting.

In the deep-water port of Souda Bay, Greek sailors rushed to their ships as the Greek destroyers and frigates began casting off lines. Gun crews scurried to unlimber their weapons. New white surface-to-air missiles slid out onto the rails of the ships' SAM batteries. By the time Rhodes Formation landed in Heraklion thirty-three minutes later, two gas turbine–powered Greek Navy frigates, which had arrived the day before for a port visit, were knifing through the water at twenty knots as they departed the deep-water bay.

THE AGED SWEPT-WING TUPELOV-20 JET BOMBER FLEW low over the coast, startling the midmorning beachcombers, some walking their dogs, others searching the sands with metal detectors, and the few early morning sun worshippers who had already staked out their part of the beach. The flight path circumvented the port city of Catania in favor of the direct route to NATO's Sigonella Air Base.

"Salim," the copilot said, "look in the harbor. An American warship."

Salim leaned forward to peer out the copilot's window. "It is not a warship, Aboul. It is what the Americans call an auxiliary. It's an oiler. Or, one of their prepositioning ships."

"I think we should bomb it."

"We shall see, we shall see," Salim, the older pilot at thirty-three, replied. Salim was a Taureq Bedouin; a member of a hidden tribe of Saharan warrior-herders who had kept the French from conquering the interior for over one hundred years. He was only six years older than Aboul. He also knew he was the only Taureq to ever become a pilot, even if the plane he flew was an aged, cantankerous bomber. Salim had joined the Libyan Air Force fifteen years ago after spending a lifetime of moving with the tribe between Tripoli and the interior, trading and racing camels and selling sheep to the city dwellers and stealing the few odds and ends that drifted their way. During his last visit with the tribe to Tripoli, Qaddafi's draft board—a patrol of five soldiers—grabbed him and he disappeared directly into the military amidst the screams and oddle-opping of his mother and sisters. Although determined to run away, each day brought Salim new curiosities of the modern world. Within weeks he discovered military life to be easier than plodding the desert, food more plentiful and sleeping on a cot much more comfortable than the desert floor. Also, by five months he had decided he was going to fly the aircraft that daily passed over the armed camp. By then, his tribe would have had to kidnap him to rescue him. Salim was hooked. A year later, he finished technician school and three years later the Libyan military, in a gracious and short moment of equal opportunity, decided to give the ignorant Taureq a chance in flight school. Salim was not surprised to discover his superiors never expected him to graduate.

The three Tripoli MiG-25s and four Benghazi MiG-23s, flying above the Tupelov, broke off and ascended to four thousand feet. The TU-20 and MiG-23 formation quickly covered the final ten miles to the defenseless NATO base. Above them, the MiG-25 Foxbat fighter aircraft began a defensive fighter patrol to protect them during their mission.

"I see the base, Salim," Aboul said. He thought Salim had a lot of common sense, for a Taureq. But Taureqs were known to die for nothing, his father had warned when Aboul told him who his pilot commander was. They would charge over a dune, with their ancient rifles misfiring, into the face of modern weapons and never understand why they died, when they outnumbered the victims they sought to massacre. His father had cautioned him to be careful. Death was a one-time event to be put off as long as possible. Aboul would feel better if Salim's face ever showed any emotion.

The starboard two MiG-23s broke right toward United States Naval Air Facility One, where the base hospital, the headquarters building, the high school, the kindergarten, and base housing were located. The base exchange and commissary were just opening and the American children had started their second-period class for the day.

The TU-20 and remaining two MiG-23 bombers continued toward NAF Two.

"Open bomb bay doors!" Salim ordered.

The other two Floggers broke left and right.

The squealing of rusty gears and hydraulics announced the opening of the double bomb bay doors. Five racks, each with four five-hundred–pound bombs, filled the interior of the TU-20. Each aligned so that when the active rack dropped its load of five-hundred–pounders a full one rolled forward to replace it as the empty bomb rack moved aft. The Yugoslavian technicians had done an excellent job restoring this old 1970s bomber.

"Aboul, our first run will be against the apron. How stupid! The aircraft are packed side by side. Why is that, you think, my friend?" Salim asked.

"That's what happens when you station more aircraft than the airfield will handle tactically, Salim."

"Red Formation," Salim called to the two MiG-23s with him, "Blinder One on final with bomb bay doors open. First run on aircraft, second along runway, and third against the hangars."

"Roger, Blinder One. Good shooting! I'm straight in to outer taxiway. Making my run," said Red Leader.

"Blinder, I am taking the buildings to the right of the road," Red Two reported. To the right of the road, four four-story buildings dominated the ball fields, small exchange, and mess hall. The four-story brick buildings housed the bachelor officer and enlisted personnel.

Salim clicked his microphone twice to acknowledge the reports from the two ground attack–configured MiG-23s.

The Blinder descended another five hundred feet, leveling off at two hundred feet. The two Floggers followed suit. Ahead a small passenger jet taxied to the runway. Salim keyed his mike and pointed the taxiing target out to the Flogger on his right.

Red Two fired his cannon at it. The shells laced the top of the VIP aircraft. The aircraft exploded. A dark cloud of debris and burning fuel rocketed into the air behind the Flogger as it overflew the destroyed aircraft.

"Five, four, three, two, one. Bombs away!" Salim yelled over the intercom while simultaneously pressing the red button on his armament control stick.

The bombs caused the aircraft to jerk sharply as each fell away. Salim and Aboul bit their lips as they fought the controls to trim the aircraft. Moments later the concussion from the massive explosions rocked the aircraft as the four five-hundred–pound bombs hit the apron. Seconds later, other explosions echoed behind them. Aboul reached over and slapped Salim on the shoulder.

"Salim, we have just erased American Navy's air force." He chuckled.

"Not hardly, Aboul. Is the sergeant photographing this as he's supposed to?"

Aboul leaned back and looked around the flight engineer, who sat on a raised platform above the pilots monitoring the fuel, oil, and hydraulic gauges of the old bomber.

"Yes, my friend. They are photographing."

"Red Formation," Salim called, "first run complete. Am turning for second."

Salim turned the steering control as his feet pushed the left pedal to shift the tail flap. He pulled the left throttle back slightly. The TU-20 banked left at a thirty-degree angle. The two MiG-23 Floggers dove beneath the Libyan bomber and began a strafing run on a row of transport aircraft parked near the ASCOMED hangar. They executed a victory roll as the transports disappeared in a blaze of fire and metal. Human stick figures ran from the scene in all directions of the compass. Two had flames rising from the back of their shirts where burning fuel had splattered and stuck.

"Blinder One, you will have to hurry," warned Aswad Leader, flying fighter protection overhead. "Our radars reflect bandits approaching from the west. Four slow movers coming from two seven zero true and definite high-performance fighters inbound from the northwest. ETA is twelve minutes. Estimate your time to complete mission?"

"Aswad Leader, I need another fifteen minutes to fully unload my cargo."

"I am sending two to intercept the slow movers. You have ten minutes, Blinder One. We are going to have company sooner than we expected."

Salim clicked his microphone twice. Damn! That left only Aswad Leader overhead to provide air protection. He needed more time to drop his load and Salim had no intention of leaving before he finished his mission. He glanced at Aboul, not surprised to see sweat running down the copilot's face.

"You heard, Aboul. We have time for one more run. What do you recommend?"

"Let's go for the towers and the hangars, Salim. Runway repair is easy. Constructing a building is another thing." Aboul licked his dry lips.

"Okay, we will switch runs two and three," Salim told Aboul. Then he reported to Aswad Leader, the MiG-25 pilot in charge of the operation. "I am turning for run number three and, if we have time, we will go for the runway."

"Roger, Blinder One," Aswad Leader replied. "Just hurry. The four aircraft coming from the northwest will arrive first and our warning devices identify them as F-16

Falcons. We should have interception in five minutes with the slow movers."

The TU-20 finished its turn to the northwest, lined up for the attack run along the flight line, and ascended to one hundred feet to avoid some of the concussion.

"Bomb crew, as soon as this run is completed, line up the number three rack for immediate drop," ordered Salim. There was still the gray American ship in the harbor, if he failed to drop all of his bombs.

Salim throttled back. The cumbersome bomber slowed to two hundred fifty knots. The wings swept out to compensate for the reduced air speed.

"Okay, five, four, three, two, one. Bombs away!"

The first five-hundred–pound bomb hit one hundred feet from the main terminal. The second pierced the roof to explode inside, killing over a hundred Americans and Italians seeking shelter there. The third penetrated the larger hangar near the terminal and the fourth exploded on the perimeter road that ran along the security fence. The aircraft veered slightly to line up the next target.

The MiG-23 to Salim's left commenced a strafing dive toward a group of buildings. As it pulled up, free fall iron bombs fell, exploding as they hit the ground and the buildings. The cannon fire from the second MiG-23 started a series of explosions in the ammo dumps north of the airfield.

"Ready!" came the call from the TU-20 crew chief standing over the open bomb bay doors with his hand on the bomb release lever, his eyes watching for the green light that would come on when Salim pressed the red button.

"Bombs away!" Salim shouted, pressing the red button again. His thumb felt numb from the pressure exerted on the button even though he knew all it did was turn on the green light and release the safety mechanism to permit the bombs to fall.

The crew chief saw the green light and pulled the lever. Four bombs cascaded out. The first hit the apron in front of the largest hangar on the airfield, destroying two small C-12 prop passenger aircraft parked side by side. The second pierced the roof of another hangar, exploded, and sent a large burst of flame and boiling smoke rolling out the opened entrances. The EP-3E and a P-3C, parked inside for routine maintenance, followed the initial explosion with their own, sending the remnants of the roof and sides hurling upward and outward. The third bomb hit an abandoned building surrounded by double rows of barbwire fence. The fourth bomb exploded on the taxiway, obliterating a hundred-foot section of heavy asphalt in a shower of concrete and dirt.

"Look at them run, Salim! Like ants and we are the exterminators, no?"

The glee in Aboul's voice irritated Salim.

Behind them, deadly infernos filled the bright daylight with dirty, tumbling clouds of smoke obscuring the parking apron and rolling across the road to join the dark smoke pouring from the burning buildings.

"Blinder, let's go. The slow movers are American Harriers. Let's go! The Harrier fighters have shot down Aswad Two. Aswad Three is headed south and will rendezvous with us. The four are inbound; ETA eight minutes! The F-16s will be here in five. We are going!"

Salim banked the aircraft hard to the right. The hydraulic sounds of the bomb racks moving into proper position, and the coppery smell of the red fluid, intermeshed with the sounds of increased power as the jet bomber turned.

"Last run, Aswad Leader. Give me time for this last run!"

Salim heard two clicks in his headset.

A flash flew by the TU-20 pilot's right window.

"Missile!" screamed Aboul. "They're firing missiles at us. The warning beeper didn't work!" A dark stain spread in the crotch of the copilot's flight suit.

"Handheld heat seekers, Aboul. Release flares now!"

From the tail of the Tupelov a line of four flares shot out. A second missile decoyed into the second flare.

"Aswad Formation, we are taking missile fire!"

"Blinder, we see it. Red Leader, take out the position. Blinder, you have two minutes."

Near a burning building, a group of Italian airmen aimed another shoulder-launched SAM at the Tupelov. The MiG-23 rolled left in a tight turn and headed for them. Red Leader fired his cannon, sending all but two of the Italian airmen scrambling for cover.

The Italian Air Force officer and the SAM operator crouched, but stood their position. Their heads followed the approach and the departure of the MiG. Red Leader shoved his power controls all the way forward and pulled back on the throttle, sending the MiG into a near vertical climb.

The Italian officer slapped the noncom's shoulder. The surface-to-air missile blasted out of the army green tube. Flares rocketed down from the MiG, but the missile traveled up, nicking each flare like checkpoints on a road map, before disappearing into the white-hot afterburner. The MiG-23 blew apart. Its burning fuselage sailed another fifty feet before it tumbled down to explode on the runway.

"Salim! They got him!"

"Shut up, Aboul. We've one more run to do."

"No, Salim, we must go, now!" He reached over and shook Salim's shoulder. "We need to go!" he cried, terror showing on his face. Wide-eyed, fear drained his face.

Aboul's head twitched back and forth as he reached forward.

Salim reached over and slapped Aboul's hands away from the controls. "No! Don't touch anything! We have one more run and we will do it!" Aboul grabbed him. Salim pushed Aboul's hand off him. "Stay calm!"

He saw where Aboul had wet himself and Salim's lips curled in disgust.

From the other side of the runway Red Two roared toward the Italian SAM team, his cannon shells tearing up the pavement and soil as he bore in to avenge Red Leader.

On the ground, the Italian officer drew his pistol and fired at the attacking MiG, methodically pulling the trigger, one bullet after another. A third noncom ran out of the nearby building with another handheld SAM canister bouncing on his shoulder. He kneeled and fired. Red Two discharged a series of flares and rocked the Flogger to the left. The missile locked on the heat of the magnesium flares and passed harmlessly behind the Libyan fighter. The ground in front of the SAM team erupted into small geysers of dirt and asphalt as the twenty-three–millimeter shells raced toward the Italians.

The officer touched the SAM operator, held up one finger, and shook his head. The kneeling airman nodded, licked his dry lips, and forced himself to ease the pressure off his trigger finger. He knew, as well as the officer, that they needed a rear-hemispheric shot for the infrared homer to work.

The sergeant who had fired the missile that missed tossed the empty canister to the ground, stood to attention, and stuck his left arm into the crook of his raised right arm as he faced the approaching MiG. The MiG veered slightly to align the bullets with the stationary men. The sergeant dove to the side. Cannon shells tore up the ground where a moment before he had flicked off the Libyan.

The officer and airman never moved. As the Libyan fighter passed overhead, the airman whirled the SAM canister around. The Italian officer slapped him on the back. The airman fired their last missile. The missile, trailing a corkscrew contrail, veered slightly right and struck the rear exhaust of the Flogger, blowing its tail off. The aircraft, already vertical in its climb, whirled over with its nose pointing down to a field on the other side of the perimeter road. The nose cone hit first. The MiG crumbled in upon itself before a massive explosion from the remaining fuel and bombs knocked the Italian heroes off their feet as a rolling black cloud of flame and shrapnel rose over one hundred feet into the air.

The Blinder bomb crew reported over the intercom to Salim that the last rack was in place.

"Hold tight. Last run and we'll head for home," Salim said calmly. He glanced at his copilot, who lay quietly with his head resting on the cockpit window, his eyes shut and moaning. Salim thought that if he had his gun, the least he would do would be to pistol-whip the coward.

He twisted the wheel hard to the right, causing the old bird to groan in protest as it banked into a hard right turn. The plane came out of the turn perfectly in line with the runway. Salim nosed the aircraft slightly up and when the runway disappeared beneath the bomber he shouted, "Bombs away!" and hit the red button. He always wanted to say that.

The first three bombs hit the grassy area between the damaged taxiway and the main runway. The fourth five-hundred–pounder carved a hundred-foot-wide, twenty-foot-deep crater in the middle of the runway, completing the shutdown of Sigonella Airfield.

"Red Formation, Blinder One; we are done," Salim called, knowing that only the two MiG-23s attacking the other base were all that remained of Red Formation. He pushed the throttles forward and pulled back on the steering column. The large bomber began to climb.

There was no answer.

"This is Aswad Leader, Blinder. Forget Red Leader and Red Two. Take evasive action and return to home plate. We will re-form on you as you head out."

Two minutes later the Libyan attack formation of one MiG-25 Foxbat and two Benghazi MiG-23s formed around the antiquated TU-20 Blinder as it crossed the Italian coast of Sicily at eight thousand feet heading south at Mach one. The second MiG-25 joined them twenty miles further south.

"Where are the other aircraft?" Salim asked Aswad Leader.

"I have ordered the Benghazi aircraft to return to their base."

"How many did we lose?"

"Blinder One, maintain radio silence," Aswad Leader replied curtly.

Salim saw Aboul reach forward and take the steering controls. "We have done good, Aboul," he said, as if nothing had happened.

Four minutes later the Italian F-16 fighters reached Sigonella.

"*Pronto,* Sigonella Control, this is Etna Formation," said Etna Leader. Colonel Antonio Lopez was a tall, dark-haired "Valentino" who was fifth-generation Italian. His ancestors originally migrated from Spain in the mid eighteenth century as military officers and palace retainers for the king and queen of Naples, who were Spanish. He was the fifth generation of Lopezes who had made the military their career. His great-grandfather fought in World War I and his grandfather fought in Libya and Ethiopia during World War II. His father led the transfer of allegiance from the Army to the Air Force, to much derision from his grandfather. Antonio had eight years of Air Force service under his belt, but other than defensive fighter patrols over the Balkans, this was his first combat action. He wondered what his father would do and, at the same time, swore that as a Lopez, he would live up to the family name and honor. He glanced up as if suspecting his grandfathers of watching him—God rest their souls. He quickly crossed himself.

"Etna Leader, we are under attack! Large swept-wing bomber with Libyan colors escorted by minimum of two MiG-23 aircraft," shouted the Italian Sigonella air terminal controller to the arriving fighter formation. "There are fighters overhead. Two enemy aircraft destroyed. Blinder heading south from airfield."

"Where are they now?"

"They are fifty miles south on a course of one eight zero at approximate altitude seven thousand five hundred meters."

"Roger, this is Etna Formation. We are engaging. Talk us to them, Sigonella Control."

"Sorry, Etna Formation. My radar is damaged. I am transferring everything to Italian Air Defense Control at Groseta. Be advised that to your west are four American Marine Corps Harriers approaching Sigonella. We watched them engage the Libyan fighters before our radar was destroyed. They reported shoot-down of one Foxbat."

The F-16 Fighting Falcons turned noses up, afterburners blazing, and wasted two minutes overhead searching for the Libyan fighter formation.

"Sigonella Control, there is nothing here!" Antonio Lopez snapped.

"Then they departed with the bomber."

"Etna Formation, form on me!" Antonio yelled. He twisted the aircraft to the left and came out of the dive at eight thousand meters, his F-16 screaming southward.

A minute later the loose diamond F-16 formation broke the sound barrier as it passed the coast of Sicily. Windows shattered as the sonic boom rode its crest through the port city of Catania. The front window of one insurance company burst. The owner-agent brushed the bits of glass off his suit, saw the damage along the street, reached down, unplugged his phone, stepped through the broken window, and walked across the street to the nearby bistro. It was time for a holiday.

Fifteen minutes later the escaping Libyans with the pursuing Italian fighter aircraft were forty miles apart when the Libyans passed the thirty-sixth parallel west of Malta.

"Etna Leader, this is Groseta Air Defense Control. We have lost contact with the Libyan formation. Last course plots them inbound to Tripoli." The Italian Air Defense controller paused.

Etna Leader heard the controller arguing with someone in the background. Finally the controller came back on the radio. "Etna, return to base. What is your fuel state?"

"No, we have sufficient fuel to continue pursuit. We have the enemy on our radars and can do local intercept." His grandfathers would never forgive him for turning back. A Lopez never ran . . . God, country. And, of course—he smiled—there was that buxom blond at Gabriella's, who he had been cultivating for weeks, who would probably rip off her knickers and screw his brains out when he returned as an air hero. Maybe he would be the one to play hard to get . . . for about a minute, he thought.

"Yes, Etna Leader. Understand, but your fuel state, please?" the controller asked, bringing Antonio's thoughts back from the blond at Gabriella's where his mind was already tracing his fingers up the inside of her thighs.

Antonio glanced down at the gauges.

"We have sufficient fuel and do not intend to return yet. Request a tanker." He reached between his legs and pushed his rigid dick to a more comfortable angle.

"Etna, we cannot provide a tanker. The tankers were destroyed during the attack."

Etna Leader clicked twice and switched channels on his radio to the formation frequency.

"Etna Formation, we are going to intercept and destroy the Libyan scum even if it means following them to Tripoli. Unfortunately, we don't have enough fuel to make it back to Sicily and, as you heard, there is no tanker support. For those who want to turn back, now is the time to do it. For me, I am going to pursue those who have attacked our country and avenge Italy!" *And get that blond at Gabriella's.*

"What is it in the films that the American Indian says on a sunny day before a battle? 'It is a good day to die.' I think I will stay along for the ride, Etna Leader. Besides, I have an uncle who is a mafioso and he would not be a happy capo if I came back from a vendetta without a kill," said Etna Two.

"We are not going to be the ones who die, Etna Two. Besides, I know your uncle. He's not a mafioso. He runs a bakery."

"Well, he would still be unhappy."

Etna Three and Etna Four also refused to turn back. "Besides, Etna Two owes me two hundred euros," said Etna Four. "It'd be just like him to get shot down to avoid paying me."

Etna Leader switched back to the main control channel.

"Air Defense, Etna Formation will continue pursuit. Try

to arrange a tanker for us. If not, then send a ship to pick us up. We will let you know where to send rescue." He flipped off Groseta Control as the officer on the other end began to shout.

Thirty minutes later, Etna Formation passed the Libyan coastline. Ahead lay Tripoli Military Airfield, the old Wheelus Air Force Base of the United States Air Force in the 1960s.

"Groseta, I have a Blinder taxiing off the runway and two MiG-25s landing. We have enough fuel and weapons for one pass. Etna Two, take the Blinder; Etna Three, the lead MiG; Etna Four, take out the parked fighters and I will take the second MiG. After attack, break left and head north. One pass only. After missiles, use cannons. Good luck and God's grace, my friends. For Italy and family!" *And good loving.*

The Italian fighter aircraft dove at the airfield. The first missile fired by Etna Two tore through the antiquated bomber, killing the bomb crew in the rear. The Blinder split in half, the rear portion and wings burning. As Etna Two neared the missile hit, three crewmembers evacuated the cockpit. Etna Two fired his six-barrel cannon, blasting the cockpit and sending three bodies flying into the air. He increased power and sent deadly twenty-millimeter cannon shells into a tower that unexpectedly appeared in front of him. Etna Two banked left, avoiding the tower, and headed north—his internal warning system going wild from the Libyan surface-to-air missile radar system's attempting to lock on. He hit the deck at fifty meters and dodged for the coast.

Etna Three opened fire with his cannon at the six MiG-25s and four Mirages parked in a line along the edge of the apron. One of the Foxbats rolled out and began a high-speed taxi toward the runway. Etna Three fired two missiles; both of them bracketed the MiG-25. He squeezed the cannon trigger. Two twenty-millimeter cannon shells hit the cockpit, blowing apart the pilot's head and upper torso. The MiG's ejection seat activated, rocketing the headless body into the air. The burning MiG veered left into a parked Mirage V aircraft. The nose gear collapsed, causing both aircraft to collapse onto the apron. The MiG engines continued to work as the fire worked its way toward the rear, causing the unmanned fighter to spin slowly around the pivot of the buried nose gear, pulling the Mirage with it. Two other MiG-25 aircraft burned along with these two. The other aircraft parked along the apron miraculously survived undamaged from the one firing pass of Etna Three.

Etna Four's first missile hit the first MiG, landing dead center. Flames shot up fifty meters, followed by a gigantic explosion that covered the Foxbat aircraft with roiling black smoke as it fell the remaining thirty meters to explode on the edge of the runway. The second missile hit the center of the runway, blowing a small crater in the asphalt.

The second MiG-25 pilot hit his afterburner and ascended in a combat roll to the right. Etna Leader's missile missed the escaping Foxbat and exploded harmlessly on the taxiway apron. The MiG-25 looped up and over, as Etna Leader banked left. Aswad Leader came out of the loop behind Etna Leader. The Libyan veteran had Antonio's F-16 bracketed with his fire control radar.

Etna Leader ignored his wingmen calling "Mission complete." They were headed for the coast, leaving him behind. He rolled the F-16 to the right, pulled a nearly two-G climb for a couple of seconds, and then throttled back, causing the aircraft to stall. The Libyan fighter flashed past, its cannons blazing. The two adversaries were too close for missiles. Antonio knew he had to make the only remaining missile count. He needed separation.

Antonio pushed the throttle forward as he rolled the aircraft to the left on a powerless race toward the earth. He flicked the power switches. The engines caught; he twisted the steering column to the right and brought the nose up in a power climb. The thrust of the Falcon shoved him back against his seat. Antonio shoved the steering column forward, coming out of the climbing turn heading west and finding himself five hundred meters behind the Foxbat. He pressed the cannon button and a neat stitch of holes crossed the tail section of the MiG.

Aswad Leader broke right and up, taking the MiG-25 through a 360-degree roll as he took his aircraft through a series of roller-coaster maneuvers in an attempt to lose the angry Italian. Unable to shake Etna Leader, Aswad Leader hit his afterburner, went vertical, and left the slower F-16 behind.

"Thank you," said Antonio. At two kilometers, Aswad Leader opened up the distance needed for the Sidewinder missile.

Ahead, the city of Tripoli filled Antonio's window as the fight moved farther west of the airfield. Crowded slum suburbs passed rapidly beneath the Italian fighter.

The steady tone in his headset announced lock-on. Etna Leader fired his remaining Sidewinder and watched it weave through the air.

Aswad Leader dove for the ground in an attempt to use ground clutter to detract the missile. Flares erupted from the Foxbat, but the Sidewinder missile was already past the flares when they came out.

The missile hit the tail, blowing off the rudder and fins. A second explosion separated the left wing from the fuselage.

Antonio smiled and the buxom blond returned to his thoughts as he rolled the Falcon to the right and hit the deck at sixty meters as he tried to ignore the internal warnings caused by the Libyan Air Defense fire control radar's attempts to lock on. A ground flash from the left caught his attention. He watched the Libyan SAM rise from its launching pad and harmlessly pass two miles from him.

"Etna Leader, where are you?" yelled Etna Two.

"I am crossing the coast. You?"

"We have re-formed. No combat casualties and no aircraft damage."

"Roger, Etna Two, I have you on radar. So where shall we ditch, my fine fellow Italian air heroes? I have twenty-five minutes of fuel remaining, so we can try for Lampedusa or Malta."

"I vote for Lampedusa. It's Italian, and even if it's small, the beaches are covered with some of the finest women of Italy."

"And of Scandinavia and Germany, too," Etna Four added. "And, of course, who could turn down a chance to be with Italy's finest air heroes?"

"Then it's Lampedusa. But I want a promise from everyone that we will return to Groseta as soon as possible. I am sure that Gabriella will miss our business otherwise."

"Gabriella! Hell, Antonio, you mean Maria with the big bazoobas."

"I am sure that Maria will want to grace me with her presence," Antonio joked.

"Presence, hell! Her knickers will be so wet when Italy's aces march through the door that you'll be able to toss them against the wall and they'll stick!"

"Etna Three, I will request that you do not talk like that about the woman I love. Show some respect."

"Antonio, you love all women until you get into their pants, and then it's off to another conquest."

Antonio clicked his radio twice.

"Okay, my fellow air warriors. It is time to grace Air Defense with our position and status so they may celebrate our survival.

"Etna Two, would you do the honors? I am seventy-five kilometers from you and out of UHF range."

"It shall be my pleasure, Etna Leader."

FOR FIFTEEN MINUTES SIXTH FLEET OPERATORS' ATtempts to contact Sigonella held the quiet attention of Admiral Cameron, Clive Bowen, and the others waiting impatiently in Sixth Fleet Combat Information Center. With Sigonella communications gone they waited for the Harriers to arrive. Clive ordered the radiomen to turn the volume up on the Harrier frequency. They wouldn't be able to talk with the Marine fighters, but should be able to hear them.

The euphoria when the Harriers shot down the MiG-23 had dissipated as concerns of what might be happening at Sigonella filled their thoughts.

"Clive, what's the status of getting an aircraft carrier into the Mediterranean?"

"As of this morning, Admiral, the USS *Stennis* is off the coast of Norfolk, conducting routine sea trials and carrier qualifications for a bunch of F-14s and F-18s out of Oceana. Atlantic Fleet has ordered her back to Norfolk to outfit for an immediate deployment to our theater. After she turns around, two F-14 fighter squadrons from Oceana will bingo aboard as soon as she clears the Norfolk channel. Two F-18 squadrons—one of them the Marine Moonlighters from Cherry Point, couple of S-3A antisubmarine birds from Jacksonville, and an E-2C early warning aircraft out of Norfolk. We are estimating *Stennis* battle group's earliest deployment time to be three to four days after it returns to Norfolk."

Admiral Cameron paused to take a sip of water. "I'd estimate nearer five days for the carrier battle group to get organized, outfitted, and turned around. At max speed, she can be at the Strait of Gibraltar eight days later. Escorts?"

"Yes, sir. The cruisers, destroyers, and auxiliary ships needed to round out protection for the carrier and provide the logistic support to keep the group steaming are being identified."

"So, we are going to have to wait nearly two weeks before a carrier battle group arrives to help us?" Cameron asked, leaning forward, his hands spread on the table to brace himself.

"Yes, sir. It looks that way. COMUSNAVCENT is fighting the idea of releasing the *Roosevelt* from the Persian Gulf to come here. They're saying without the carrier presence, there is nothing to counter the Iranians."

Five stressful minutes later the Harriers flew over the destroyed airfield and began passing damage reports.

"Sixty-one, this is Bulldog Leader. We have taken up combat positions around the airfield. It's terrible. I've never seen anything like it. I count eight aircraft burning on the apron. At least one is a KC-135, some are C-130s and P-3s. The runway is cratered as well as the near taxiway, where another aircraft is burning. Fire engines are arriving and I count two ambulances. We have no comms with the airfield. Both hangars are destroyed, burning . . . and there's another aircraft I didn't see also burning at the end of the runway. I intend to land two at a time to refuel, if we can find the capability to do that. Sixty-one, they need help here. The scene reminds me of the old pictures of Pearl Harbor after the Japanese attack."

The staff duty officer approached Admiral Cameron. "Sorry, sir, General LeBlanc is ordering you to take his call now."

"Ordering me? What the hell does he want and who the hell does he think he is to order me?" He leaned forward. Clive put his hand lightly on the admiral's shoulder. Sweat broke out on the injured admiral's forehead as a wave of pain shot through him.

Commander Balley looked uncomfortable. "Sir, you're not going to believe this, but he wants—no, *demands* is the better word—for you to transfer your flag under his command."

"Under his command?"

"Yes, sir. As Strike Force South, your NATO hat."

"Under his command!" shouted Admiral Cameron, refusing to believe what he was hearing. He fell back, resting against the back of the chair, his breath short, rapid.

"Why would he want that?" Clive asked angrily.

"He also wants all our forces to withdraw at least one hundred miles north of Algeria and above the thirty-eighth parallel until the situation clears. He says our unilateral actions are not in line with his strategy for the North African region and endangers European security."

"Who the hell does he think he is?"

"He thinks, sir, that he is Allied Forces South and that Sixth Fleet belongs to him," Clive answered.

"Clive, call that presumptuous son of a bitch and tell him that as far as I am concerned the United States Sixth Fleet just went to war. If he wants a piece of the action then he had better get his puckered French ass up and get busy. Then, after you've called him, transfer my flag to the *Albany*. Tell Captain Ellison to stand by to embark Sixth

Fleet. The place for an admiral at war is at sea, not shuffling papers ashore."

"Aye, aye, sir," Clive replied, giving the admiral a salute. "Nothing will give me greater pleasure, sir."

"Commander," the admiral said to the staff duty officer, "contact European Command and tell them I want to talk to General Sutherland immediately. And I don't care where he is or what he's doing; get him on the phone."

The admiral stood, forcing himself to stand erect. Energy apparently blazed in his posture, but Dr. Jacobs knew the man was in great pain. Cameron turned and walked out of Combat, his Marine Corps guard and Captain Jacobs close behind him. Clive caught a glimpse of the doctor and the Marine taking Admiral Cameron's arms as soon as they were through the door. The admiral's last few seconds had exhausted the wounded leader, but his walking out unaided and his comments boosted the morale of a navy going to war. A navy that had just suffered its second Pearl Harbor.

Clive started the actions rolling to transfer the Sixth Fleet battle staff to the *Albany.* Later he would call and pass along Admiral Cameron's regrets to the French general who now controlled the southern NATO forces.

Clive hoped they were on the submarine and out to sea before Washington started bombarding them with questions. Information technology was great, but it allowed too many armchair quarterbacks an opportunity to direct the plays.

THIRTEEN

⚓

THE FIRST TOMAHAWK MISSILE BROKE THE SURFACE AS the setting sun touched the edge of the horizon. The noise of the rocket engine blasted across this Mediterranean Sea area south of the Italian island of Lampedusa, startling the crews of three merchant vessels and a small coastal freighter west of the missile. The missile quickly sped straight up and as the crewmembers' eyes tracked the contrail of the deadly weapon other Tomahawk missiles began to break the surface, one after the other, until a total of six contrails marked their path into the low cloud cover.

The two nearest merchant vessels turned hard to port to open up the distance from where the missiles had been launched—the nearest ship being only eight miles away. Little did they know that the skipper of the submarine USS *Miami* had deliberately maneuvered his boat so witnesses to the initial American response to the Libyan attack could broadcast what they had seen. American forces may have drawn down to a point where a third world nation like

Libya felt it could attack with impunity, but it was sadly mistaken.

"Okay, XO, take her to the surface," the *Miami*'s skipper said. Then, turning to the chief of the watch he asked, "You got the battle flag?"

"Better than that, Skipper. I broke out the holiday ensign we purchased for your change of command last year. It's twice the size."

"Skipper, XO," the sonar operator said, holding one earpiece away from his ear as he spoke, "two of the ships are turning west."

"One hundred feet!" announced a nearby chief petty officer who was monitoring the depth gauges.

The skipper grabbed the microphone. "Attention, all hands. Grab hold—we're going skyward!" He slapped the microphone back in its rack. "Blow all ballasts and trim nose up," he ordered.

The old Los Angeles–class submarine was at a forty-five–degree angle when she broke surface. Her nose traveled into the air nearly one-third the length of the boat before the submarine splashed back down onto the Mediterranean. Sea spray rose fifty feet into the air along the length of the *Miami*. Admiral Cameron wanted witnesses and he wanted the Libyans to know he was coming after them. Well, he got it, the skipper said to himself. No one knew how impressive a submarine looked when it surfaced like this except those who had actually seen one do it.

The sterns of the two merchant vessels were crowded with crewmembers who pointed with awe at the submarine that had fired the missiles and leaped from beneath the sea. Several cameras with telephoto lenses were busy snapping photographs. Two on the nearest merchant vessel managed to take photographs of the last missile fired. That photograph and the ones being taken now would earn them a nice chunk of change when they pulled into Marseilles in two days.

The hatch opened and sailors spilled out of the black hull. From beneath the conning tower, they hastily unfolded the collapsible flagpole reserved for special occasions such as the Fourth of July. Within minutes, a huge American flag fluttered in the wind. The skipper ordered a slight course change to increase the wind across the bow. The flag rose as the wind increased. A couple of minutes later the Stars and Stripes was plainly visible to those merchant sailors.

He stood on the deck of the conning tower and watched the spectators through his binoculars. Satisfied he had accomplished both parts of this mission, he ordered increased speed. The USS *Miami* stayed on the surface until the merchant ships disappeared over the horizon. Then he submerged and increased speed as much as possible without creating cavitation that would alert any antisubmarine forces they might encounter. His next mission was to rescue the sailors of the USS *Gearing*. It would take three days for him to reach the area at this speed.

CLIVE POKED HIS HEAD THROUGH THE CURTAIN THAT separated the cramped quarters of the small stateroom from the USS *Albany*'s single passageway that ran the length of the attack submarine. Admiral Cameron lay on the bed, his eyes open. Dr. Jacobs sat in the lone metal desk chair beside him, his head bobbing slightly as he dozed.

"Come on in, Clive," Admiral Cameron said. His voice woke Dr. Jacobs.

Clive nodded. "Birds away, sir. USS *Miami* reports six missiles fired and plenty of witnesses. He observed several with cameras."

"Good," Cameron responded, then sighed. "How long until impact?"

"The five headed toward Benghazi Naval Base should hit at twenty-three seventeen hours, sir. If they are true to target, four will take out the remaining submarines and missile boats. The fifth one will pop up and penetrate the main headquarters building. Intelligence believes the command posts inside the building will be fully manned. They will be updating their situation reports from today's events when your gift arrives over the horizon, penetrates the building, and explodes inside."

The sound of footsteps passing along the passageway caused Clive to stop momentarily to allow the sailor to get out of hearing range. "The remaining one will hit the general staff headquarters in Tripoli five minutes later. It, too, will pop up and penetrate through the top of the old building to explode inside."

Clive thought he saw moisture in the Iron Leader's eyes. His eyes locked for a few seconds with Dr. Jacobs until the medical officer reached down and began to straighten the crease on his trousers.

"That's it for now, Clive," Admiral Cameron said, leaning his head back on the pillow. "Nothing more we can do until we get a carrier into the Med."

"Sir," Clive said, "since we have launched a retaliatory attack as European Command authorized, maybe you could reconsider and let us helo you into Naples or Sardinia so you can fly back with your . . ."

Cameron shut his eyes and nodded. "I know, Clive. I should. My kids are not going to accept that I put duty above accompanying Susan's body back—" He stopped, his voice catching. After a few deep breaths he continued, "You are probably right, Clive. The only thing left to do is bring out the Americans at the embassy and that will be the usual noncombatant evacuation. The Algerian rebels are going to want them out of there as much as we want to bring them out. Commodore Ellison can handle it and Pete Devlin is arranging transportation out to the *Nassau* in a few days to meet me. He can handle the NEO until I return."

"Yes, sir. I will make the necessary arrangements, Admiral."

DUNCAN CALLED BEAU AND H. J. OFF TO ONE SIDE. The other members of the two SEAL teams were either sitting on the deck or crouched over, packing their kits. Everyone was in camouflage utilities with the trouser legs wrapped around the ankles and laced inside the combat boots. They'd be ready soon in the event the NEO timetable was moved up.

"Yes, boss," Beau said.

"Just talked with Commodore Ellison. Seems he is not as convinced now as he was earlier today that this evacuation is going to be an opposed one. It would not surprise me if we were held in reserve rather than sent in with the Marines. Either way, the commodore has agreed that as soon as the evacuation is over he will offload us at either Gibraltar or Sigonella—if it is capable of handling air traffic by then. He will be done with us after the evacuation, so by this time next week we should be back sweating in the gridlock of Washington. Meanwhile, we have this mission to do. Intelligence is arguing that there is a possibility the Algerian president escaped from Algiers. If they are right, then this evacuation operation could turn nasty. But, on the other hand, our fine friends at CNN and MSNBC are reporting the capture of President Alneuf. They listened to a broadcast by Alneuf ordering the remaining Algerian forces to return to their barracks. Looks to me as if this will turn into a nonevent."

"Alisha?" Beau said wistfully.

"Who?" H. J. asked.

"Yeah, Alisha," Duncan said. "And I can hardly wait to meet her once we get back to your place."

"My place?"

"Well, Beau, you are my best friend, and my wife has taken possession of our house. You wouldn't want your boss homeless and sleeping on the streets."

H. J. grinned. "Of course he does, Captain."

"Well, no, I don't, but . . . you are going to have to make yourself scarce when she does fly back in."

"Now I understand," H. J. said. "She's an angel."

"Can't be," Duncan said, "she sees something in Beau."

"Maybe she wants to convert him," H. J. offered.

"And I intend to let her convert me as many times as she wants and I am capable."

H. J. playfully tossed her cap at the laughing lieutenant commander.

COLONEL WALID SALUTED ALQAHIRAY. "COLONEL, WE have just received word that American missiles have hit Benghazi and the headquarters of the general staff. There have been massive deaths at both locations, sir, including members of the general staff who were weighing today's events at the headquarters building."

Alqahiray's eyebrows rose for a second, and then he smiled. "What a shame," he said, his face brightening. "All those senior officers, who doubted Jihad Wahid, dying by the hand of the great Satan." He shook his head several times and began to laugh. "What a shame. It is so unfortunate that I must be the one to tell the junta about this.

Don't you think they were smart to ride out Jihad Wahid here"—he pointed to the floor—"with us in this isolated area of the desert? Otherwise, Walid, they, too, could have been casualties—and I have bigger plans for them."

Walid looked confused, but said nothing. He knew the mercurial nature of this man and he, too, had his plans. And to ensure those plans would reach fruition, he had to remain alive. This was once a great country and he was a member of a great people. It was important that true believers guide their return to greatness.

THE COMMO SAW CAPTAIN CLIVE BOWEN TALKING quietly to the skipper, Commander Pete Jewell, near the wardroom coffeepot. He approached and waited quietly a few feet away from the two men, not wanting to disturb their quiet conversation. After a few minutes, when it appeared they were going to continue even when they knew he was there, he coughed, drawing their attention.

"Yes, John?" Jewell asked.

"Sir, I have a special category message that just arrived for Admiral Cameron. I saw Captain Bowen and thought . . ."

"Here, I'll take it," Clive said, reaching forward and taking the folder marked with bright orange stripes and the words TOP SECRET printed at the top and bottom.

He opened the folder, scanned the contents, and shut it.

"Anything I can do?" Jewell asked.

"Yes," Clive said as he sat down on the edge of a nearby seat. Fatigue washed across him. "Forget everything I said about the admiral's departure. When he reads this, he won't go. I know him too well. He'll want to continue to the USS *Nassau*."

Pete Jewell had been in the Navy long enough to know

you didn't ask why. If the senior officer wanted you to know or if you had the need to know, then you would. Otherwise, you kept quiet and followed orders.

"Aye, aye, sir. That's easily done. We have only been heading north toward Sardinia for an hour." He paused for a moment before asking, "Just to be sure, Captain. We are returning to our original destination of the USS *Nassau* battle group?"

"Yes, but it is no longer to be considered a battle group. It has now been re-formed as an amphibious task force and"—he waved the folder—"judging from this, they will get to use it."

Clive stood up and left the skipper and the COMMO alone in the wardroom. Jewell looked at his communications officer, who shrugged and mouthed the word *sorry*, for they both knew he couldn't tell the captain of the USS *Albany* what the message said.